PRAISE FOR NOVELS OF AWARD-WINNING AUTHOR

Kimberly Cates

LILY FAIR

"Once again Kimberly Cates triumphs! This book has it all—romance, adventure, treachery, revenge, and betrayal. The writing is powerful and emotional. Readers will be enthralled."

—*Romantic Times*

"Romantic and wonderful.... A classic fairy tale with a fresh twist."

—Jill Barnett, author of *Wicked*

"A wholly entertaining story of lovers who were not to be denied. A heart-touching novel filled with adventure, this is a treasure."

—*Rendezvous*

"Kimberly Cates' talent shines through with *Lily Fair*—a lush, passionate adventure."

—Jill Marie Landis, author of *Blue Moon*

"*Lily Fair* is an enchanting love story, and Ms. Cates is simply poetic as she weaves a magical spell in this extraordinary tale of love and loyalty."

—*Old Book Barn Gazette*

BRIAR ROSE

"*Briar Rose* is wonderful and enchanting....Kimberly Cates demonstrates why fans find her beloved novels so entertaining."

—*Affair de Coeur*

"Lush and lyrical....Kimberly Cates creates enchantment on every page."

—Betina Krahn, author of *The Soft Touch*

"This beautiful romance leaves an indelible mark on the soul. *Briar Rose* will lift your spirit and make you believe that fairy tales can come true."

—*Romantic Times*

"Cates' writing is luxurious and introspective, the kind of writing that one can curl up with and get lost in."

—*Booklist*

MAGIC

"Cates used Celtic lore and Irish tradition laced with humor and shimmering sensuality to produce an engaging, well-written story."

—*Library Journal*

"Fun to imagine....Cates' books always have an enchanting quality."

—*The Pilot* (Southern Pines, NC)

"The joy of fairy tales and the everlasting beauty of true love make *Magic* wonderful. It's a tale full of belief in everything good, heroic, chivalrous, and mystical."

—*Romantic Times*

MORNING SONG

"A splendid and uplifting read.... Kimberly Cates has brought her storytelling skills to a new level as she explores the dark recesses of the human heart. She weaves a beautiful story of love, redemption, forgiveness, and passion."

—*Romantic Times*

"Cates writes eloquently and emotionally. Her complex, riveting plot makes this a one-sitting novel, impossible to put down!"

—*BookPage*

"The perfect entertainment for a stormy summer night."

—Minneapolis *Star Tribune*

STEALING HEAVEN

"Kimbery Cates has the talent to pull you into a story on the first page and keep you there.... *Stealing Heaven* is a finely crafted tale...a tale you won't soon forget. It can stand proud beside Ms. Cates' other excellent romances."

—*Rendezvous*

"Stunning in its emotional impact, glowing with the luminous beauty of the love between a man and a woman...*Stealing Heaven* is another dazzling masterpiece from a truly gifted author."

—*Romantic Times*

Books by Kimberly Cates

Angel's Fall
Crown of Dreams
Gather the Stars
To Catch a Flame
Only Forever
Morning Song
The Raider's Bride
The Raider's Daughter
Restless Is the Wind
Stealing Heaven
Magic
Briar Rose
Lily Fair
Fly Away Home

Published by POCKET BOOKS

Kimberly Cates

Fly Away Home

POCKET BOOKS

New York   London   Toronto   Sydney   Singapore

An *Original* Publication of POCKET BOOKS

 POCKET BOOKS, a division of Simon & Schuster Inc.
1230 Avenue of the Americas, New York, NY 10020

Copyright © 2000 by Kim Ostrom Bush

ISBN: 0-671-02823-5

First Pocket Books printing July 2000

10 9 8 7 6 5 4 3 2 1

POCKET and colophon are registered trademarks of Simon & Schuster Inc.

Front cover photo by Pat Powers/Index Stock Imagery

Printed in the U.S.A.

To M. J. Ostrom Horstmeyer with love.
Friend, teacher, angel—
Thank you for encouraging me to fly.

Fly Away Home

1

*W*here had her little girl gone? Eve Danaher pressed her face to the chapel window, her gaze straining through the cloudy surface of centuries-old glass to see the slender young woman mounting the stairs to the pulpit. Fourteen years had passed since Eve had last seen her daughter's face, but she still knew the lift of that rounded chin, the flush on cheekbones that had once been apple-bright, the fierce earnestness that glowed in eyes so like Eve's own. Victoria was still shy. Even as she prepared to begin her speech, the valedictorian of this select school for young women still held echoes of the four-year-old moppet Eve had cradled in her arms.

How many times had Eve watched her baby girl march into situations that unnerved her, chin high, resolute, determined not to let anyone suspect she was afraid? She had faced down Santa Claus, a red giant on his throne in the mall, and the huge chicken offering samples outside a fast-food restaurant. More heartbreaking still, Victoria had braved the angry voices that had drifted all too often up the stairs of their apartment to her closet-sized bedroom years ago.

Eve's eyes burned. Chad Tolliver had taken so much from her and Victoria the day his parents' bank account won him sole custody of their child. Chad and his powerful family had robbed them of fourteen Christmas mornings and hundreds of bedtime stories shared beneath the rosebud afghan Eve had crocheted.

He'd stolen bath time when they'd painted beards and mustaches on their cheeks with handfuls of soapsuds. He'd taken away the future that was Eve's right as Victoria's mother, *time* with her daughter, the most precious thing Eve had ever possessed. But it seemed there was one thing neither Chad nor his dictator of a mother had managed to steal. They hadn't taken Victoria's courage.

Eve swallowed hard, her heart jumping in her chest as Victoria leaned toward the microphone and spoke. The chirping voice that once reminded Eve of a little bird was gone, polished by the Susan B. Anthony Academy into cultured tones that might have been dull if they hadn't sparkled with passion and sensitivity. It was a beautiful voice. Eve knew if she lived to be a hundred she would never get her fill of hearing it.

"They say our generation is lost," Victoria began. "Musicians tell us to rage at the machine, to care about no one but ourselves. There are no heroes anymore. We, the graduating class of the Susan B. Anthony Academy, know better. We've worked with heroes every day, teachers who taught us to strive for excellence, parents who sacrificed to give us the finest education possible. They want so much more for us than what the world seems to offer. Now it is up to us to show them whether or not their efforts were in vain. Every speech in every graduating class that ever was has probably ended with some promise to change the world. I don't deny that the world could use changing, but I challenge you to make your goal simpler. Make those who love you proud of you, those real heroes no one ever thinks of."

Victoria paused, peered down into the front row, and for the first time, her voice quavered. "Whatever good I do, whatever I achieve, is because of you, Daddy. I love you."

Eve's hands clenched.

Victoria tossed back her gleaming bangs, the light striking her forehead, the golden tan marred by a pale, jagged line. Eve's chest tightened, her memory far too vivid, painting pictures of the bright red gash, the blood running down her baby girl's cheeks, Victoria's pitiful sobs. *Hurts, Mama. Hurts! Make it better.*

If only Victoria knew Eve carried a far deeper scar because of that old wound. If only her little girl could know that Eve would never forgive herself for what had happened on that terrible night that had changed their lives so long ago.

Eve's vision blurred. She barely saw the parade of young women march up to claim their diplomas to the sound of applause and the blinding explosions of camera flashes. Of course Victoria loved her father, Eve scolded herself. Chad was the only parent Victoria had known for fourteen years. Eve should be grateful for the love so evident in her daughter's face. Had she wanted Victoria to be neglected by Chad? Ignored? Disillusioned with him the way Eve had been so many years ago? Or had some secret, selfish part of her hoped Victoria would blame him for exiling her mother from her life? Wasn't it only justice that Chad should somehow pay for what he had done?

Organ music swelled, thick and ostentatious, a girl with round glasses pounding out "Pomp and Circumstance" as if she were trying to make certain an aunt three states away could hear her. Eve's heart pounded even louder in her ears as the graduates began to file out of the chapel.

It was time.

Not yet! A voice cried in Eve's head. *Let me just look at her a little while longer! Think what I should say to her.*

The plea was absurd even to Eve's own ears. Hadn't she been rehearsing speech after speech in her head for two weeks now? Searching for just the right words to say to Victoria? Hadn't she been so desperate for the moment to come when she could finally speak to her daughter that every hour standing between them had seemed torture? She just hadn't guessed she would suddenly be so afraid.

Tori, I'm your mama. Remember peek-a-boo, and stargazing and Fly, the little stuffed horse I made you? Remember how I blew on your forehead at night to sweep the bad dreams away and how I promised I would never, ever go away? But they made me go away—your grandmother, your daddy and the judge. Even then, I never left you. I thought about you every day. Could you feel it, baby, even though I was far away? Do you know how much I love you?

No. She couldn't charge at Victoria like that. It would be shock enough for Victoria to see her. There would be time later to explain more gently, make certain not to hurt her.

The heavy double doors swung open, the precise lines of girls breaking into squealing clusters on the chapel lawn as they dashed over to hug each other and the throng of loved ones who poured out behind them.

For an instant, Eve panicked. How would she even find Victoria in all this confusion? But then she glimpsed a banner of bright gold hair at the edge of the crowd, gray-green eyes searching the jumble of faces. She was searching for her father, Eve knew instinctively.

Hands shaking, Eve hurried toward her daughter. At the moment when Eve would have spoken Victoria turned, flashing an expectant smile. She was too well bred to show her disappointment that the person approaching wasn't her father.

"Y–Your speech. It was wonderful." Eve was babbling. She couldn't help it. She was close enough to touch Victoria's hand if she only dared, could smell her little girl's hair—that subtle fragrance all Victoria's own. How many nights after the custody battle had Eve clutched the child's abandoned pillow to her face, breathing in that scent until at last it was washed away by time and tears?

"Thank you." Victoria gave a preoccupied smile, her gaze slipping past Eve's shoulder, still looking for Chad. She thought she was talking to one of the other girls' mothers, Eve realized with a jolt. She was nothing to

Victoria but some stranger making small talk. The girl wouldn't even look at her.

"Tori." One word, a plea.

Victoria's gaze locked on Eve's face at the pet name Chad and the rest of his all-powerful family had hated. Cheeks rosy with excitement a moment before paled.

"Please don't call me that. No one calls me that. My name is Victoria."

"You used to like it when I called you Tori. It was my special name for you. Don't you remember?"

The girl stumbled back a step. She hadn't forgotten, Eve thought numbly as recognition registered in Victoria's eyes.

"Wh–What are you doing here?" Victoria demanded, trying to hide dismay behind the lift of her chin. "You're not supposed to come near me!"

Eve's heart twisted. She struggled to keep her voice steady. "I wanted to see you graduate. You're eighteen, now. The courts can't keep me away from you any longer."

"I don't care about what the courts say! I don't want anything to do with you!" Panic tinged Victoria's voice. Something inside Eve's chest tore. What had she expected? Hoped? That her daughter would be counting off the days, the hours, the minutes as eagerly as she had, until they could legally be reunited? Victoria had been barely four years old when she'd been dragged from Eve's arms. Even now she was so young, confused, maybe even a little afraid. It wasn't surprising, was it, that she would react this way? Eve tried to battle back the wave of disappointment.

She grappled for reason. "How can you be sure you don't want anything to do with me? You don't even know me, Victoria. But now we can change that."

"I know everything I need to know every time I look in the mirror!" Her fingertips brushed her forehead, the thin white scar gleaming. "You disappeared from my life for fourteen years, never sent so much as a birthday card! Just . . . just disappear again!"

Eve felt like she'd been kicked in the stomach. "But I *did* send them!" she started to explain. "Your father must have—" *Thrown them away, kept them from you. He moved you from place to place in Europe where I couldn't reach you, couldn't challenge custody even when I had my life straightened out enough to fight him. Oh, God, if you only knew how sick I felt when I saw your picture in the paper, realized you had been in Boston for the past two years—close, so close—* The words tumbled in a rush through her mind. Words that could only hurt Victoria when all Eve wanted was to give her relationship with her daughter a chance to heal.

"The court ordered me to stay away," she explained instead. "Claimed that if I honored their ruling, I could see you when you were eighteen. The lawyers almost managed to have me banished from your life forever. I did what I could to fight it, but I was terrified that if I disobeyed the ruling, we would never even have this chance. Please, Tori. I love you so much. Let me show you—"

"You want to show me? Just go away before Daddy comes! He's been looking forward to this day forever, and you'll ruin it for him, too!"

Eve winced. *Ruin the day . . . know all I need to know . . .* Victoria's words burned into her. Sick, desperate, she caught hold of her daughter's hand. The girl ripped her fingers away as if Eve had burned her. "Victoria, please! I know you're shocked right now, confused, but I'm begging you, give me a chance . . . just a little time."

"Victoria!"

Eve stiffened at the sound of that voice behind her, so familiar it made her turn ice cold. Once, it had made her pulses flutter. Now it made her want to retch. She could still hear its echo: *I'm only thinking of what is best for Victoria. If only you would, too. . . .*

"You were fantastic!" Chad raved. "Not a dry eye in the— What the hell?" Eve heard the confusion and—

damn him—the concern in Chad's voice. She knew he'd glimpsed the emotions rampant on their daughter's face. "Sweetheart, what's wrong?" he asked, rushing up to the girl. "Are you sick? You look like you've seen a ghost."

Victoria opened her mouth, closed it, and Eve could sense her struggling to find a way to explain. Eve could spare her daughter that much at least.

"No ghost," Eve said, squaring her shoulders and turning to face Chad. "Only her mother."

"Eve."

She should have taken some small pleasure in the fact that he looked like she'd kicked him in the teeth. The last time Chad had seen her she'd been so young, so helpless, as the power of the mighty Tolliver family ran over her like a runaway train. The last time he'd seen her she'd been shattered, begging to be allowed scraps of Victoria's life. He'd left her desolate, more alone than he could ever imagine. She'd wanted to die. She chose to fight. For an education, for a place at the top of her profession. She'd made certain there were commas in her checkbook. What she'd really wanted was to make certain no one could ever hurt her that way again.

But like most bullies, as soon as she was strong enough to fight back, hire herself a good lawyer instead of the dull-eyed, alcoholic public defender who had lost her the first case, Chad had run. He'd scooped up their daughter and taken her to Europe. Hidden her in schools in Switzerland and France—God only knew where—always keeping one step ahead, just beyond Eve's reach.

"Hello, Chad."

His throat convulsed, his cheeks livid. "What the hell are *you* doing here?"

"I came to see my daughter graduate."

"Daddy, I told her to go away. I didn't want to see her," Victoria broke in.

"Tori, please. I never wanted to hurt you."

"So after fourteen years you show up at her graduation and ambush her on one of the biggest days of her life?" Chad snapped.

"You didn't leave me much choice! I rarely even knew what continent she was on! When I saw her picture in the paper I just—"

She had thrown together a few mismatched clothes and raced to the airport, willing to pay any price to reach this chapel lawn. Hell, she would have walked the whole way from New York to Boston on bloody stumps if she'd had to. In all the years she'd hated Chad, tried to fight him, nothing had made her loathe him more than discovering he'd been arrogant enough to put Victoria where she was finally within reach, and Eve hadn't been able to find her.

"Can't you see you're upsetting her?" Chad accused. "For Christ's sake, Eve, can't you ever think of anyone but yourself?"

"Myself?" Eve winced, hating him for the shred of truth in his accusation. "Maybe I shouldn't have . . . have sprung this on Victoria this way, but I was afraid—" Afraid if she waited she would be too late. That Chad would whisk Victoria off to Italy or Spain, or wherever. Tolliver Enterprises had international business interests spread over half the globe. One call to gas up the family jet and Eve would have had to start all over trying to find her daughter. Even so, Eve's sudden appearance had to have been a shock to Victoria—

For God's sake, Eve yanked herself up short, seething. The bastard had done it again! Made her start blaming herself for situations *he* had created! He was the one who had made it impossible for her to see her daughter. He obviously hadn't even given Tori the birthday gifts she'd made with so much love, or the letters she'd written.

And **he** accused *her* of being selfish? In the years she had known him, Chad Tolliver had turned getting what he wanted into an art form, damn the price to anyone else. He'd charmed his way into the role of class president, football captain, but his hardest fought battle was to find a way beneath Eve Danaher's skirts. If she'd been a little older, a little wiser, Eve would have known it was the chase that mattered, the challenge. Charity student, trailer-park trash, with a mind sharper than any of those St. Benedict's wealthy patrons could buy for their own pampered offspring, she'd been something unique in his white-bread world. Another toy to be used, then thrown away once the newness wore off. Chad just hadn't counted on the baby.

Yet even now, angry and hurting as she was, he had her trapped and he knew it. She could hardly say what she wanted to without hurting the wide-eyed, troubled stranger who was her daughter. And she had already unintentionally hurt Victoria enough.

"Sweetheart, go on to the reception with your friends." Chad feathered his fingers with infuriating tenderness across Victoria's cheek. Hot envy ate deep inside Eve. "I'll settle this and join you in a few minutes."

"But Daddy—"

"Now, sweetheart."

They were so natural together it broke Eve's heart. Victoria nodded with complete trust, then flashed Eve a quick, nervous glance from beneath thick lashes before she turned and rushed away.

They both watched her in silence until she wound through the crowd to disappear into the festive entrance to another building, a silk "congratulations" banner fluttering overhead in the wind.

Chad turned back to Eve, scowling. "I never thought I'd see you again."

Eve had to force her voice past the hard, burning knot of anger and pain and loss lodged in her throat. "Did you think that I would just forget my own daughter? You had to know from the packages and the letters I kept sending that I hadn't given up. But you didn't let Victoria have any idea I was still thinking of her, loving her, did you Chad?"

He flushed, irritation and stubbornness flashing in his eyes. "I hoped you would leave her in peace. Leave her happy, busy with the life she was born to."

"I carried her for nine months under my heart when you and your family wanted to kill her!" Eve cried, outraged. "I loved her while you tried to deny you were her father! She was my whole life for four years until you changed your mind and demanded blood tests."

"I'd grown up a little bit by then. Realized that if she *was* a Tolliver, I had a responsibility to see she wasn't raised in the sewer. I needed to know if she was my daughter."

"So you could steal her from me? You knew I'd never been with anyone but you."

"Dammit, Eve, keep your voice down!" Chad glanced uneasily around the crowded lawn. Several graduates and their parents were looking their way. "Do you want to embarrass Victoria even more than you already have?"

"Embarrass her? No! All I ever wanted was to love her! She was born to be in *my arms*, Chad."

"The judge didn't think so. Hell, she could have been killed because you were so damned careless!"

"It was an accident and you know it."

"It wouldn't have made her any less dead!" Chad raked his fingers through perfectly styled hair.

"I lost Tori for fourteen years. Haven't I paid enough to satisfy even you? Just let me talk to her, Chad. I'm begging you. I'm her mother. Doesn't she deserve the chance to know I love her?"

Chad sneered. "If you loved her you wouldn't have stormed into her life like this, destroyed what should have been one of the happiest days of her life!"

"I didn't mean to—"

"Did you see her face? Dammit, Eve! What did you expect? For her to run into your arms?"

No. She'd wanted such little things. Just some hint that her baby remembered something good about her mother, just some tiny flicker of gladness in her eyes.

Some slender thread to hope on. Damned if she'd confess that to Chad.

But he'd always been able to read her too easily.
Suave, handsome Chad, trained from the cradle to use
his charm to manipulate everyone around him.

"You haven't changed at all, Eve, have you? Still
dreaming of fairy tale endings."

The barb stung. "You can't keep me away from her
any longer, Chad."

"I won't have to." She wanted to scream at the
smug expression on his face. "You heard her. She
doesn't want anything to do with you. What are you
going to do, Eve? Try to force your way into her life?
She'll only hate you more than she already does."

"I don't believe it. We loved each other so much before you and your parents—"

"Did what? Committed the unforgivable sin of rescu-
ing her from that rattrap of an apartment you were living
in? Kept her from being dumped into the laps of baby-
sitters who couldn't be trusted? Or dragged into that
warehouse you worked in where she almost got killed?
Look at her, Eve! She has everything any girl could ever
want! The best schools, riding lessons at the finest stables!"

"There was one thing you never gave her, Chad.
Her mother."

"You aren't her mother anymore. Face it, Eve.
You're a stranger. Let her go, for God's sake!"

Eve knotted her hands in the skirt she had chosen
to remind her of her daughter, the navy folds pat-
terned with scenes of a foxhunt in full cry, horses leaping stone fences, manes and tails flying free. She had
dreamed so often of this moment, of being able to hold
Tori in her arms again. It was all she had ever wanted.
Was it possible Chad was right? Was it selfish and cruel
to force her way into Tori's life again?

No. Eve closed her eyes, remembering her own
mother, so cold, always too busy for her daughter,

making Eve feel as if she were an inconvenience, or worse still, her mother's cross to bear. Every child needed to know her mother loved her. And Eve did love Tori, desperately.

"Eve, you have your own life now. I know you're working at a museum, just like you always wanted to—"

"You would know that, wouldn't you? Did you keep track of me so you could know when to whisk Victoria off someplace new so I couldn't reach her, couldn't fight to get visitation?"

"I did what I had to do to protect my daughter."

"She's my daughter, too, dammit!"

"Not anymore. Even you should be able to see that. Just forget about Victoria."

"Never." Eve's chin bumped up a notch. "Maybe you're right in one way. I can't force her to listen to me. But she's not a little girl anymore, Chad. She's growing up more and more every day. Someday she'll want to know what happened. Maybe not today. Maybe not tomorrow. But someday. And when that day comes, Chad, I'll be waiting."

Heart breaking, Eve turned her back on Chad and walked away.

2

*E*ve curled up on the floor of her apartment, exhausted from her ordeal, her heart an aching hole from Victoria's rejection. She should have felt some sense of comfort, returning to familiar surroundings after the disaster at her daughter's graduation. Didn't wounded animals return to their dens to lick their wounds? And yet, there was nothing soothing in the presence of things she'd collected over the years, no sense of coming home. Despite fourteen years and all she had fought to accomplish during that time, Eve still might as well be shivering under the bare light bulb of the tiny efficiency apartment she and Tori had called home. Truth to tell, she would *rather* be in that cramped room. Maybe there were no vibrant Oriental carpets or pieces of original art by up-and-coming talent, but there had been crayon drawings scotch-taped on the cracked-plaster walls—yellow suns with smiling faces, stick-people with triangle skirts, careful printing labeling them as "Mommy and me."

There had been pain and poverty, but there had been laughter, too, and Tori's soft little arms tight around Eve's neck to remind her there was a reason to go on.

Tonight, here alone, it was hard to remember. She was tired. So tired.

At least the phone had stopped ringing. Eve grimaced. Steffie Reklaw, pediatrician, best friend, and the terror of half the administrators of the hospital she worked at could be about as subtle as a Mack truck.

She'd been calling every fifteen minutes for the last four hours, anxious, no doubt, to find out what had happened, though God alone knew how she'd already discovered Eve was home. Of course, the woman had an army of miniature spies all over the city—kids who would march off a cliff for her à la Pied Piper. She'd probably deployed them around the building armed with secret decoder rings.

In the end, it didn't matter how Steffie had pulled off this latest discovery. Steffie always found out, damn her. And, more infuriating still, she was almost always right. Steffie had certainly been right this time.

Steff had predicted disaster, been jumpy as a cat on hot cement. She'd practically begged Eve not to go to the graduation. *Just five more days,* she had pleaded. *By then I'll have browbeaten the hospital board into approving the new wing and I can come with you.*

In five days, Chad could take Tori anywhere! Remember last time I got close? When I learned they'd come back from Europe for Chad's mother's funeral? I just wanted to see Tori, look at her from across the road. Know she was all right. Chad's cousin saw me and they ducked out the back of the church, disappeared again. No, Steff. I can't risk it!

I don't want you there alone! Steffie had argued in her best mama grizzly bear tone, her mocha-dark face so protective, creased with concern. Her eyes, behind the frames of signature bright red glasses filled with that odd blend of empathy and practicality, that under-standing of other people's pain that had been the one warm corner in Eve's existence for the past ten years.

Years Eve had alternately envied and admired how fearlessly the woman took hold of life, her enthusiastic embracing of everything, her ability to laugh off mistakes, forgive other people, and most of all, forgive herself.

Steff delighted in all the crazy messiness and unpre-dictability about living that Eve fought so hard to wall out. Being alone at a time like this was unthinkable to Steff. Tears were only put there for someone who loved you to wipe away. What Steffie, with her gregarious, brawling, unconditionally loving family didn't know was that Eve had always been alone except for those four precious years she'd had her little daughter.

A knock at the door made Eve wince. Oh, God, so *that* was why the phone had finally shut up! But she hadn't even thought Steff was crazy enough to go plowing through New York City alone at this hour of the night! Eve had just wanted some time alone. Was that too much to ask? She scowled as a low voice came through the door.

"Girl, this knock is just a formality," Steffie warned, with gruff affection. "I've got a key and I'm coming in whether you like it or not."

Where the hell had Steffie gotten a key? Eve moaned as the key rattled in the lock. No time even to throw the safety chain. Maybe she could just lie on the floor and play dead. No, she couldn't even do that. With her luck Steff would call in the paramedics. She'd been looking for an excuse to set Eve up with that earnest, cute blond medic.

Eve made some effort to slam shut one of the scrapbooks that littered the floor. But there were fourteen years' worth of magazine clippings, catalogue pages, and travel brochures scattered about. Victoria grinning up at her ribbon-bedecked horse when she was ten and had won her first junior championship—a picture published the month after the event when the girl was already beyond Eve's reach. Victoria's picture cut from among a magazine's glossy pages: Tomorrow's leaders—top 100 teens in this year's graduating class. And the ragged-edged newspaper clipping that had sent Eve racing off to Boston.

The door swung open with a bang that doubtless woke people three blocks away. Garbed in a lab coat spotted with dozens of purple dinosaurs, a stethoscope with bobbly eyes glued on it still looped around her neck, Steffie marched in like Patton chasing down Rommel. Eve felt a twinge of guilt at the dark circles under her best friend's eyes. Somehow, Eve sensed it wasn't a late night kiddie emergency that had been keeping Steff awake this time. It was worrying about Eve.

"You think not answering the phone was going to keep me away?" Steff asked with a wry smile.

Eve glared, bleary-eyed, the sight of Steff's familiar face making her throat constrict even tighter in an effort not to break down. She couldn't start crying. If she did, she might never stop. She tried to fend it off by resorting to irritation. "Couldn't I have you arrested for breaking and entering? I damn well know I didn't give you that key."

"Your super did. You know, that sweet Mr. Brown who took in the kitten I found in the park last February."

Eve grimaced, feeling strangely even more sad and empty. Of course Steff knew everyone in this building far better than Eve did. Even though Steff lived a twenty-minute subway ride across town, she chatted with everyone she met while Eve seldom even made eye contact with her next door neighbors. As for the kitten, Steff had begged Eve to take the scrawny little mite, said it would be company for her. If only Steffie had guessed how terrifying that tiny kitten was to Eve—something to take care of, something to care about, a living thing she could fail. Not to mention a poignant reminder of the night that had cost Eve her little girl.

Eve groaned. "I should've taken the first flight to Outer Mongolia."

"Yeah, well, it would've taken a little while for my leave of absence to go through, but then, I'd be chasing your butt so fast you'd think your pants were on fire," Steff said, striding into the adjoining powder room. Eve heard her rummaging around, water running. Steff marched out again, a damp washcloth in her hand. She handed the cool cloth to Eve. "Come on, honey, put it on your face," she urged. "You'll feel a little better if you do."

Eve didn't have the energy to argue—not when she knew how stubborn Steff could be about stuff like this. Surrendering, she gave her face a cursory swipe with the cool cloth. It *did* feel good. Not that it changed anything. When she was done, Steff took the cloth again, gave it a toss through the powder room doorway. Eve heard the splat of it hitting the sink—another "swish" from Steff's high school basketball days.

Eve winced as her friend turned back, hurt clouding her face. "Dammit, Eve, you promised me you'd call as soon as you got back."

"What kind of cynic are you?" Eve said, trying to brush it off. "You didn't trust your supposed best friend?"

Steffie forced a smile. "I have a very suspicious mind. Besides, I know you too well to believe half the stuff you say." The smile wobbled, broke, chocolate eyes flooding with sympathy as she scanned the floor with its telltale mess.

"Honey, I'm so sorry."

"Yeah. Well." Eve shrugged, unfolding cramped legs and trying to get to her feet. The navy skirt was so crumpled it looked as if someone had jammed it into a horse stall.

"Did you get to see her?"

"She was . . . ah . . . well, let's just say I got the same reaction as the bad fairy when she showed up at Sleeping Beauty's birthday bash." Desperate for something to do, Eve started gathering up the scrapbooks and trying to shove them onto their shelf. She might as well throw them out the sixth-story window. Tori didn't want to see them. Hard as it was for Eve to face, she might never want to see them. Pictures kept so carefully for her daughter, cutouts labeled: "Christmas when you were 10 years old." A picture of the Christmas tree Eve had put up, still decorated with the makeshift ornaments she and Tori had made years ago. Faded tissue paper and construction paper chains. Tin foil stars and white paper snowflakes sprinkled with glitter. She'd wanted Tori to know someday that she'd never forgotten her.

"Evie, you know she's still just a baby. Eighteen is a hell of an age. I'd take a leap from the Empire State Building before I'd ever be eighteen again and I bet you would, too."

"No. If I could turn back time, I'd be eighteen again in a heartbeat. But instead of staying where the Tollivers could reach me, I'd take my baby and run. Instead of trying to think of what was best for Tori and deciding to let Chad come into her life, I would lie like hell. Why should I have cared if Tori never got to know her father? I never knew mine! Besides, Chad didn't want her anyway until it was convenient for him! When he demanded to know if she was his, I should have just laughed in his face and told him he wasn't the only boy I'd ever had sex with. There were dozens of boys, so many that I couldn't possibly guess who might have been my baby's father. Then, when Tori stood in that pulpit, smiling that amazing, loving smile, *I* would have been the one smiling back at her." Eve's voice cracked.

Steffie started toward her, arms outstretched, ready to offer a hug, but Eve knew that if anyone touched her she would shatter into a million pieces. She held up one hand in a silent plea, and hard as it was for Steffie, she respected it. One more compromise they'd reached in their friendship. Somehow, that consideration touched Eve more than any other. Reaching out was as natural to Steff as breathing. Giving someone space to hurt alone was far, far harder.

Steffie bent down to pick up one of the scrapbooks, her long brown fingers tucking bits of paper deeper inside it. "Well, then, things didn't turn out the way you wanted them to. Now what?"

"What do you mean?"

Steff shrugged. "What are you going to do now? You took time off from the museum, didn't you? Decided to make the rookies' day and actually let them touch some of those priceless doodads you restore?"

"Not the priceless ones," Eve said with a wan smile. "I took care of those before I left."

Steff chuckled softly. "Yeah, well, most of them are centuries old, painted by dead people. I doubt they'll hassle you if you're a few weeks late spiffing them up." Steff's eyes got that pleading, "look for the sunshine" kind of light in them that Eve knew so well. "Come on, Eve. 'Fess up. You must've saved a mountain of vacation time over the years."

"I was hoping—" Eve stopped, swallowed hard.

"I know," Steff said with that tenderness so dangerous to Eve's strangle hold on her emotions. "You were hoping you could spend it with your baby. Why don't you spend it on yourself?"

"What?"

"Take the time off. Go somewhere. One of those places you were always dreaming about." Steffie touched the slick edge of a travel folder. "You've been saving these brochures forever, but you haven't gone anywhere just for the fun of it in all the years I've known you."

"I wanted to take Victoria with me," Eve said in small, tight voice.

"That's not going to happen. At least for now."

Anger flared in Eve, ten years of friendship making it safe to let feelings out, at least the sharp-edged ones carving Eve up inside. "Tough love" Steff had always called it when she pushed Eve headfirst into the pain and wouldn't let her back away from it. *Can't heal it unless you feel it,* she'd said more times than Eve could count. There were times Eve could almost hate her for that little quote, and herself for knowing underneath it all Steff was right. But it was too painful, too dangerous, too scary to let those feelings out. It had been too hard to pull herself together in those terrible months after Victoria had been taken away from her. She'd done what she could to protect herself since then, afraid she'd never have the strength to go through that kind of agony again.

"You think I don't know I can't share time with my daughter right now?" she demanded, grabbing on to the safe, clean burn of anger.

"You're always pretty sure you know everything, to tell the truth. But this—somehow you got this all wrong."

Eve could see Steff square her shoulders, bracing for one of her giant-sized emotional shoves.

"I know this sounds hard, honey, but someone has to say it. You want a life with your daughter? No one—not you or I—knows for sure if you'll ever get that. But this much I can tell you, Eve Danaher. If your Victoria came into your life right now, she'd find you damned boring."

Eve gasped, the words cutting deep. "What the—?"

"Maybe instead of dreaming about the life you and Victoria *might* have someday, you could concentrate on the life you've got here and now. Or do you want your baby to find you shriveled up, dried up, and half-dead if she ever comes looking for her mama?"

"You have no right—"

"That's true. I don't," Steff admitted. "I'm just your best friend. Someone who's loved you for years. And someone you actually care about, even though I'd bet right about now you're wishing you'd never let me past those giant walls you've built inside you. Someone has to tell you the truth, Eve. At least give you a chance to fix what's broken inside you. Maybe I'm making a mess of it, but there's no one else who can say this to you and live to tell. Now here it is in black and white. If you want to dry up and let Chad Tolliver and his family suck all the life out of you, that's your decision to make."

"Dammit, he took my daughter!"

"Yeah, he did. But he didn't take your spirit," Steff said softly, her face a reflection of Eve's own pain. "*You* gave that away."

Eve reeled as if she'd been slapped.

Steff's dark eyes filled with compassion, sadness, pleading. "Look what you've done. Picked yourself up off the floor, put yourself through school. Became one of the finest art restorers in the country. And you did it alone, without a lick of help, no family to support you as you went through it. Girl, do you know how many people would have curled up and died if they'd faced what you have? I've been waiting forever, hoping you'd make that last step—take on your private life the way you did your schooling and your career. Get in there with both hands and clean up the stink Chad left there. Sometimes I catch glimpses of what you might have been like if you'd ever found the courage to take your life into your own two hands again and live. But then, it's back to scrapbooks and memories and blaming Chad Tolliver."

"Don't!"

"Honey, I just want you to stop and think. If your baby ever does come to you, wanting to know her mama, Eve, what kind of woman do you want her to find?"

Eve wanted to argue, but Steff was already crossing back to the front door.

"Don't you dare start a fight like this and leave!" Eve cried. "I'm not finished!"

Steffie smiled, wise as Buddha. "As a matter of fact, I think you're just getting started, girl."

Then in a whirl of dinosaur-print lab coat, her stethoscope dragon's eyes bobbling, Steff was gone.

Eve wanted to rage at her, wanted to throw something. Who did Steffie think she was? The great brilliant doctor flying in on her broomstick to stir everything up! Make her even angrier and then just walk out the door! Hadn't things been bad enough before? Tori—no, *Victoria*—had made it clear she didn't want anything to do with her mother. Had no interest in the woman she hadn't seen for fourteen years.

But what if she had reached out to Eve? Steffie's challenge taunted her. What would her daughter have found?

Eve looked around the nondescript apartment. Except for the scrapbooks, it could have been a suite in a posh hotel, expensive but with all the personality of a model in a face cream ad. There was nothing of Eve in these rooms. The apartment had only been someplace to crash when she couldn't be at work, locked in the restorer's lab at the museum. When she couldn't distract herself with the painstaking work of brushing away centuries of dust or repairing paint that was slowly disintegrating after generations of neglect. Success, yes, it was evident whoever lived here had money now, the furnishings tasteful enough not to shame her art background. But where was the woman Eve had wanted so desperately for her daughter to be able to know? Maybe that woman didn't even exist anymore.

He took your daughter away, but you gave him your spirit.

Had she? Her spirit hadn't seemed worth much without the baby she loved.

But Tori wasn't a baby any longer. She was a young woman, full of intelligence and eagerness, enthusiasm and hope despite the hurt dealt her so long ago. What could she possibly have in common with Eve? Thirty-six years old? A woman who had spent her life making sure she had commas in her bank account and was respected in the art world. She was as much a stranger to life as she was to her daughter, just as Steff had said. Consumed by work and with imagining the life bound up in those scrapbooks, a life that was supposed to be hers, a life that never would be.

She'd cursed and kicked and fought, no matter what, to hold on to the life she and Victoria should have shared, but that tenacity hadn't changed a thing. It wasn't fair, what Chad and his family had done to her. It wasn't right. Somewhere deep inside she'd always believed someone would come to their senses and realize that one day, sweep it all away, give her back all the things that should have been hers.

Fourteen years of little-girl smiles, skinned knees, jelly-smeared kisses. First heartaches and prom dresses and unsteady adolescent hands applying lipstick for the first time.

No power on earth could give that back to her now, Eve realized with a sick thud in her stomach. That time was gone forever. She had to stop holding her breath, hoping for the impossible.

She winced, seeing in her memory Tori's face, the rejection, hearing the alarm in her daughter's voice. Something woke inside her, stirred by Steff's words and the stark reality Eve had faced at Victoria's graduation. It swept away forever the fantasies she'd nursed for years. The ones that had paralyzed her with fear that she'd ruin things, make them worse. How could she? Things were as bad as they could get.

She couldn't do anything about what she'd lost with Tori. But maybe, just maybe, there was something she could do for herself—make herself into the kind of woman Tori would be proud to find, if she ever did decide to let Eve into her life.

Steff was right, Eve thought, her chin lifting with new determination. Chad couldn't take her life unless she let him.

But how to begin? Go somewhere, anyplace quiet where she could think. It didn't matter where. Maybe she should let fate decide. She looked down at the papers scattered across the floor, then closed her eyes and picked one, knowing by touch the thick, glossy folder had to be a travel brochure. She opened her eyes, looked down at the folder she held in her hands. *Bridey McGarrity's. . . . Come find rest.* Eve read the print beneath a beautiful picture of seacoast and waves and fields so green she could almost feel them beneath her feet. Rest. Peace. She needed that so badly—a place where she could decide what to do with the rest of her life. What better place to do that than in a little bed and breakfast in Ireland?

Does it really matter where you go? A voice of doubt whispered inside her. *You don't have your daughter.*

"It does matter," Eve said aloud, squaring her shoulders. "It's past time to find out what kind of a woman I want to be when I grow up."

Rubbing away salty grit left by tears, she crossed to the phone and punched in the numbers before she could change her mind. A cheery little voice greeted her. "Bridey McGarrity, *cead mil failte.*"

"Hello. My name is Eve Danaher. I wanted to know if . . . if you have a room available for the next six weeks," Eve asked.

There was a moment of silence, and Eve almost thought she'd lost the connection. "I'm sorry to be telling you this, my dear, but I'll be off to hospital before the month is out. Won't be able t' tend to a soul."

So much for throwing herself to the winds of fate, Eve thought grimly. "I'm so sorry."

"Ach, it's a lot of bother over nothing. They've been expecting my heart to give out for the last six years and it's still ticking along steady as Big Ben. I'll be fit again before you know it, though there are them that thinks I'm going to give the undertaker business. But I've robbed the sour old goat before, an' I'll do so again, so I will."

After the upheaval she'd been through the past few days, Eve could hardly believe it when a smile curved her lips.

"But truth to tell, I haven't taken in boarders for years. What moved you to call me?"

"A brochure I picked up—it must have been from years ago. When I found it I thought it was fate." What was she thinking? Eve shook herself. She'd had a hard enough time confiding vulnerabilities to her best friend, let alone some woman she'd never met!

"Fate, was it?" Bridey McGarrity's voice perked up. Eve could almost see the sudden sparkle of excitement in this total stranger. "So ye were meant to come to us?"

"I know it sounds silly. I just wanted to sit in one place. Stay quiet. Have time to think."

"Smooth out all the ripples in your soul, eh?"

"Something like that," Eve said. "I'm sure I can find someplace else."

"And be defying fate, then? I think ye'd be wiser not to. Never a good idea. Fate can have a temper tantrum worse than any you can ever imagine, treasure. Besides, there is no place like Kilrain in all the world, and if it's calling to you, who am I to turn you away?"

"But you said you were sick." Eve started to protest.

"*I* don't say I'm sick. It's those pesky doctors who keep insisting I am, and what do they know? The whole bunch of them look like babies to me, young enough they should still have their mams running after them wiping their noses."

Eve chuckled, liking this woman already, refreshed by Bridey McGarrity's attitude. It was no wonder. Eve's own mother had played out the death scene from *Camille* every time she'd had a hangnail. She'd convinced herself she was dying so many times that when she really did get sick Eve hadn't been able to make herself believe it was real until she'd heard the final thud of the casket closing. The thought sobered her, saddened her. She'd wanted so much more for her own baby girl, promised herself she'd be the best mother in the world. That every time Tori stumbled she would be there to break her fall, protect her, comfort her, make her feel safe the way only a mother could.

"There, now, don't be thinkin' sad thoughts, Eve Danaher," Bridey said with a tenderness that surprised Eve. "I can feel your aching from clear across the ocean."

Eve's neck prickled in alarm. She'd made a science of hiding her emotions, and this woman God knew how many miles away in Ireland had unearthed her vulnerabilities somehow. "You . . . how did you know—?"

"Why, by magic, of course. Don't you believe in sorcery and such?"

"I think I—maybe this wasn't such a good idea—"

Bridey's laugh rang out. "It was a joke, treasure. A joke! Don't be scared off now, just because an old woman had a bit of fun with you. Didn't take a mind reader to realize you must be sorrowing, dearie. Said you needed quiet time, to think. When that happens, most often a body needs healing. And if you need healing, it only stands to reason there must be hurting. Don't you agree?"

"I suppose," Eve said. But it didn't matter if Eve agreed. Her favorite movie as a child had been *The Wizard of Oz*. And like the wizard, she'd always been damned uncomfortable when someone peeked behind her curtain to find her small and shivering and all too vulnerable. Not at all as self-assured as she seemed.

"I've a proposition that might be the answer for both of us," Bridey continued. "My place needs tending while I'm gone—not much, mind you, but I'd rest easier knowing it wasn't empty. And you, you seem t' need a place t' light. Would ye think of stayin' at Kilrain on yer own?"

Disappointment shifted, and Eve felt a bubble of something like excitement. Alone in a tiny, tidy white cottage in that beautiful green field? It wasn't what she'd expected. What did she know about living in a foreign country anyway? The whole arrangement sounded a little crazy, and yet. . . . Maybe she should believe it had been fate after all. It was perfect. *Too* perfect! A voice inside her whispered. And she'd learned long ago not to trust in too great a helping of good fortune.

"It's a very generous offer Mrs. er, McGarrity, but there must be some—" Some catch, some trap, some snare. In her experience, there always was.

"I swear by the Rock of Cashel it's an honest bargain I'm offering you," Bridey McGarrity said, humor breaking through. "I'm not a tinker trying t' swindle ye. I just hate t' have the place sitting empty while I'm gone. There will be no one else about and ye said ye wanted peace and quiet and time t' rest."

Eve hesitated. It really did seem like an ideal setup. One even better than she'd hoped for. She remembered her favorite art history professor, glowing when he'd come in with the news he was going to "house swap" with a family in Italy over the summer. Surely this was no different. She could still remember Professor Hansen's delight when school opened the next fall and he'd displayed the snapshots he'd taken of his family in front of a charming little villa in Milan.

In spite of it all, the old Eve would have excused herself politely and gotten off the phone. It was too risky, and she never took chances. But wasn't she trying to make a new beginning? Change? What better place to begin than to take this chance?

Heart hammering, she sucked in a deep breath. "All right, I'll do it." Her whole body buzzed as if she'd just bungee jumped off a perfectly good cliff. "Would you like me to send references?"

"We'll not be needing those if Kilrain has beckoned ye," Bridey scoffed.

Eve stiffened, appalled. Did the woman have any idea how dangerous it could be, inviting a perfect stranger into her home? For all Bridey McGarrity knew, Eve could be an ax murderer! If Eve hadn't already accepted Bridey's offer, she would have felt compelled to now. Who knew what kind of looney-toon might call the sweet, trusting woman next?

"So when do ye think ye can come? Take yer time—it'll give me an excuse to stay in my own comfy bed a while longer."

"By Friday if I can get a ticket. But I don't want you to put off going to the hospital if things get tangled—"

"Sure and you won't have a bit of trouble, I'm sure

of it. Look how perfect things have worked out so far for the both of us!"

The woman was far more optimistic than Eve could ever be.

"I'll have a man t' meet ye at Shannon airport whenever ye say, treasure," Bridey said. "We can have a beautiful chat and get ye settled in quite cozy before I have to leave. There is a trick or two about living in my darling wee place, just like in any old house." Bridey chuckled. "I wonder what Michael will have to say to this! I told him you would come. Kilrain always takes care of itself."

"Who is Michael?"

"He's a plague of worry dropped down on my head. But now he can leave an old woman in peace, can't he . . . em, what did you say your name is?"

"Eve Danaher."

"Safe journey, Eve."

Safe journey. Eve hung up the phone, but it wasn't Ireland and plane trips that filled her mind. She was setting out on a journey of a far different kind, and Bridey McGarrity had no idea how far Eve had to travel.

3

$\mathcal{V}$ictoria kicked off white dress shoes that seemed to have shrunk three sizes during this endless evening, glad to be back at the house Daddy had leased to be close to her when she'd come to school in Boston. But even the throb of pain as blood rushed back into her feet couldn't numb the misery of this day. She flung herself onto the vast canopy bed and drew her knees up tight against her chest, as if to ward off a blow. But the blow had already come, and it had ruined what was supposed to be one of the most important days of her life.

The cut-crystal clock on the mantel chimed twelve—far too early to be calling it a night. Dozens of graduation parties still celebrated on, silver trays full of hors d'oeuvres in the process of being devoured, mountainous cakes with white icing decimated. People laughed and danced to hired bands in all the posh restaurants within driving distance of the academy. But if Victoria had been forced to keep a smile plastered on for another minute, she was sure her face would crack into a million pieces.

Forget about what happened, Daddy had urged her with a bracing hug on the way to the party. *Don't let her ruin this night for you. She's just a stranger, sweetheart. She doesn't matter.*

He'd looked so shaken himself, in spite of the way he tried to hide his reaction. And she wanted to protect him. But it *did* matter that her mother had shown up after so many years. It had changed everything.

Worst of all, how could she tell him that it might have been something she'd done or thought that made this terrible thing happen?

Victoria swallowed hard. Was it her own fault? Had she somehow . . . somehow summoned Eve Danaher up like a genie from a bottle in one of those old fairy tales?

Almost never in the weeks preparing for graduation had she let herself admit she had felt left out watching her friends going off with their mothers, picking out the perfect graduation dress, getting their hair done, and giggling over makeovers at the nearest cosmetics counter. Daddy had gone with her to get her dress, but he'd had a business meeting to rush off to and the cell phone hadn't stopped ringing. Patient as he'd been, Victoria had known he was glad when the shopping trip was checked off his list of a jillion and one things to do.

Once the dress had been bought, she had just settled back into the school routine, assuring herself she was glad she didn't have the constant pressure her classmates did, the ringing of the phone as menus were discussed and discarded, guest lists refined, and plans for parties made. It was understood her father's caterers would do a flawless job.

She would never have hurt her father's feelings by telling him that she would have liked a little fussing this time, would like to have had someone lingering over the plans with her, getting teary-eyed, wanting everything to be perfect. She could never tell him about the sinking sensation in her stomach when she answered the phone in her dorm room and heard her roommate's mother laugh. *Melissa is going to want to murder me for calling her again, but I can't decide what color icing to put on her cake. Purple used to be her favorite color, but you girls have grown up so much, changed so much these past few years, I thought maybe she'd choose something different. What color are you having on your cake, Victoria?*

Whatever color Alphonse thinks will go best with

the color scheme he's chosen. It turned out to be black. Everything black and white, sophisticated, with not a single gooey baby picture in sight.

She'd told Melissa's mom she just didn't care much about that sort of thing. She hadn't even realized she *did* until that moment.

It wasn't Daddy's fault she felt so . . . so weird. He was wonderful. She'd always felt so lucky to have him. But she couldn't help feeling things would have been different if she'd had a mother.

Victoria sucked in a sharp breath. How could she even think such a thing? What a miserable, disloyal little brat she was being! She clambered off the bed, and crossed over to glare at herself in the mirror.

She'd been Daddy's whole life forever. Besides, it didn't matter what the other girls' mothers did. *Her* mother wasn't like them anyway. Four years of taking care of a little girl had been too much for the woman. Her mother had just thrown her away, disappeared and not come back for fourteen years.

Daddy had tried to excuse her leaving way back in the beginning. Even then, Victoria had known he wanted her not to hurt so much. *Your mother decided she needed a fresh start after what happened the night of the accident. The judges, your mommy, and I knew she couldn't take care of you properly, and I wanted a chance to love you so very much.*

She'd pictured her mother gobbling up life like a birthday cake, partying and traveling and doing all those things it was impossible to do with a kid hanging around your neck. It hurt a lot at first to think her mother was glad to be rid of her. She hadn't even believed it for a long time. But days passed, weeks, years, and still her mother never came back. What reason could there be for that except that she didn't want to be bothered with her daughter?

For a long time Victoria hadn't even thought of her, blocked her from her mind, until all the graduation craziness opened up the lost, empty place in the middle of her chest again.

Still, nothing in her imagination had prepared her for seeing the woman again. She hadn't been anything like Victoria had imagined. Her face wasn't hard. Her eyes weren't the careless, selfish ones of a woman who had forgotten her little girl. They were painful with emotion, her mouth soft and trembling, voice unsteady. And when she'd reached out to touch her—

Victoria hugged herself tight. She wasn't about to feel sorry for the woman. After fourteen years you couldn't just—just walk back into someone's life as if nothing had happened! She hadn't even bothered sending a single letter, not one birthday or Christmas gift. Apparently putting a stamp on an envelope was one of those things about child-raising that had been too demanding for her to bother with.

And yet, the woman had looked so stunned when Victoria had accused her of it. As if she really had been surprised. Was it possible Daddy had—no! That was crazy. She crushed the tiny spark of suspicion. What was she thinking? Eve Danaher had deserted her years ago while Daddy had always been there, Victoria reminded herself. She should forget all about her. She might even have been able to do it if only she wasn't still so troubled by the look that had been on the woman's face.

Victoria's eyes stung, and she was angry that she could still hurt after such a long time. She had so many questions, and only one person could answer them right now. Swiping away the tears, she glanced at herself in the mirror, then pushed open the door and headed down the hall to her father's wing. Outside his door she hesitated, then knocked softly.

"Daddy?"

She wondered if he was already asleep, but then a voice answered. "Come on in, sweetheart."

She pushed open the door, surprised at what she saw. His covers weren't even pulled back, and he hadn't changed into pajamas. He stood in his tuxedo, jacket and all, staring out the window, a crystal glass of his favorite whiskey in his hand. She couldn't ever remember seeing him so still.

Then he turned and smiled, but it was that smile he'd worn all night, achy and uncomfortable, straining tight about the lips. "How's my little valedictorian?"

"I don't know." She shrugged. "Fine, I guess. Daddy, can I ask you something?"

He looked worried. The smile grew even more brittle. "Sure, sweetheart."

"I thought she'd forgotten all about me. Why would she come to see me after all this time?" There was no need to explain who *she* was. Her father's mouth got even tighter.

"It doesn't matter. You don't want to see the woman. She'll respect that, dammit. I'll make her."

She'd never seen his eyes so fierce. It made her stomach twist. She walked over to his cherry-wood dresser and fiddled with the silver lid of the cologne bottle she'd given him three Christmases ago. "I told her to leave me alone." She hesitated, couldn't keep from probing. "Said she'd never even bothered to send me a birthday card. She said she did."

"And you believed her?" Daddy demanded in a voice she'd never heard before. Tight. Almost a little scared, but she knew that was impossible. "Victoria, the woman neglected you. Abandoned you. The fact that she would tell you a lie shouldn't surprise either one of us."

He was right. Why did that hurt?

"She didn't look the way I . . . I imagined at all," Victoria said. "She looked . . ." *Overjoyed, scared, uncertain, and hurting.* "Like me."

"She's nothing like you, Victoria. That much I can tell you. You're brave and beautiful and intelligent, so many amazing things Eve Danaher could never be. Maybe your hair is the same color. Your eyes and the shape of your mouth are similar. But that doesn't matter. You're completely different in *here* where it counts." He tapped his chest. "Don't let this upset you. By next week, all this will seem like some crazy dream. You'll be riding with the best coach Europe has to offer and, if I know you, you won't be thinking of anything but horses. It will be just you and me and a stableful of horses, just as we planned."

Victoria tried to smile, hugged him to hide it when she failed. He was right, of course. It would be just as they had planned. That was what she wanted, wasn't it? But could anything ever really be the same again? She'd pretended her mother away for fourteen years. Imagined her, selfish, beautiful, taking what she wanted, not caring who she hurt. Forgetting her baby girl even existed because it wasn't convenient to have her around.

But now, those familiar images were gone, and other, more disturbing ones took their place. Was it possible things weren't the way she'd always imagined? That there might be some way to explain—explain deserting your daughter for fourteen years? No. Whatever Eve Danaher had to say didn't matter, she told herself firmly. There was too much hurt, too many questions that could never have reasonable answers. It was too late. She reached up, touched the thin ridge of scar on her forehead, one more reminder of how her mother had failed her. But even that familiar gesture didn't quiet the whisper someplace deep inside her.

She came back.

4

*C*EAD MIL FAILTE—A hundred thousand welcomes—
the sign proclaimed in huge green letters above the
baggage claim in Shannon airport. Eve thought they'd
do better to show diagrams of how to haul ten-ton
suitcases off the baggage carousel without ending up in
traction. But, then, most of her fellow travelers had
probably packed their own bags. Eve had had help.

The two giant-sized suitcases she dragged off the
conveyer belt were so heavy they felt like solid con-
crete thanks to Steffie's insistence she pack everything
except the washer and dryer. Appliances Eve was sure
her friend would have found a way to shove in if it
hadn't been for the difference in electrical voltage from
one country to the other. Eve shook her head as she
started toward a huge papier-mâché castle that stood
across the room advertising a medieval-style banquet
at a castle in County Cork, complete with mannequins
in traditional Irish dress.

Bridey had insisted her friend, Fingall, would feel
more at home picking her up at that display than anywhere else in Shannon airport. All the lights and
crowds and such made him jittery as a cat, the old
woman had confided.

Frankly, Eve wasn't so comfy herself. A sea of faces
swarmed around her, the Irish easy to pick out from
the rest—complexions like cream, pale, yet cheeks
touched with a rosy color she could hardly believe was

real. Freckles sprinkled Puckish noses, kids looking like
they should be sleeping in buttercups, the spitting
image of illustrations of fairies she'd loved in vintage
children's books.

There was every shade of hair from black to silver
blond, but it was that bright, coppery color so rare anyplace else that amazed her, flashing in banners here
and there, while the gorgeous, melting lilt of Irish accents floated around her.

She watched, entranced, as a little girl in braids
and her gap-toothed brother played hide-and-seek
behind the legs of people who were obviously complete strangers, a dapper-looking old gentleman prop-
ping his battered suitcase on its end to give the little
ones a better place to hide. He had such a kind,
apple-cheeked face. Could he be Fingall? Eve wondered. Any friend of Bridey's must be the same kind
of person. But the man didn't seem to be looking for
anyone.

The whole trip felt so strange. Eve moved toward
the castle, feeling as if she should wake up any minute
in her own bed to discover she'd just had another
really weird dream.

The past days seemed unreal, a flurry of preparation, a mad rush of stopping her mail, getting her tick-
ets, fending off Steff, who had delighted in the whole
process with the glee of a woman who was sending a
kid off to summer camp for the first time. She'd
brought over thick sweaters and a rain poncho to
ward off unpredictable Irish weather, travel guides
with sticky notes marking tourist attractions Eve
might find of interest. She'd tucked a copy of Yeats's
poetry into Eve's flight bag along with the latest mo-
tion sickness drug in grape-flavored chews, highly rec-
ommended, Steff insisted, by the Kool-aid crowd. A
gorgeous boxed set of paper came next, tied up with
blue satin ribbon—in case Eve felt like writing letters,
or keeping some kind of a journal about what she saw.

But when Steff bounced in with a mammoth-sized box of condoms "just in case," Eve had tried to draw the line.

You're getting a little too optimistic here. I haven't had sex in years and I'm not about to start now.

Hope springs eternal, Steff had laughed. *Think about those Irish actors we see in movies, girl. If they grow 'em like Liam Neeson and Gabriel Byrne over there even you might not be able to resist. What kind of friend would I be if I didn't send you off prepared? Besides, someone told me once to pack all this kind of stuff when you go to Ireland.* She'd tossed five boxes of tampons onto the pile. *They can be tough to find over there.*

One thing Steff's enthusiasm *had* managed to accomplish was to wipe out any doubts Eve had about leaving New York. She would have been happy to spend her vacation hiding behind a vending machine in Central Park just to get away from all that exuberance.

But her last bit of preparation had been hardest of all. Picking up the phone. Dialing the Tolliver mansion in upstate New York on the off chance Chad would have brought Victoria there after graduation. The ringing of the phone, the cultured, perfect accents of one of the servants. *Mr. Tolliver and Miss Victoria have left the country. No, I can't say where they've gone. What's that? How did Miss Victoria seem? Who is this?* The long pause when Eve said her name. *You should be ashamed of yourself for what you've done to that little girl!* The outraged voice snapped, followed by the harsh click of the phone disconnecting.

Ashamed? Eve had thought, setting the phone back in its cradle. She was ashamed of plenty of things in her life. But not of trying to contact her daughter. Besides, maybe she *had* botched things at Tori's graduation, but she had been right about one thing. Chad had done exactly what Eve had feared. The instant she'd gotten anywhere near her daughter, he'd snatched her away again. God knew how long it would take to find out where they'd gone this time. Or did it even matter?

It wasn't as if Tori would be willing to talk to her even if the girl lived next door. *Give her time*, a voice inside Eve whispered. Tori needed at least a little time to sort things through before Eve could try contacting her again. And Eve needed time as well.

"May I help you?" a soft Irish voice asked.

Eve snapped back to the present, looked into a round, pleasant face, the mother of the two little ones, gathering them close. "Pardon me?" she asked, stunned.

"You look as if you're lost."

Steffie was one of the few people who would have offered help like this in New York and Eve had told her friend more than once that she was crazy. No—don't make eye contact, stride along as if you know exactly where you're going even if you have no idea. Eve had lived by those survival rules so long it was hard to process anything else.

"Uh, no. Thank you. I'm meeting someone. He's supposed to be near that." She gestured to the castle.

The woman smiled. "Well, then—" and was off, fairy children in tow.

The people in this country seemed so—so *nice*. It would take some getting used to, Eve thought, maneuvering her bags toward the castle. If strangers were that nice, imagine someone who was Bridey's friend. She started to relax. The ride shouldn't be so awkward, after all.

"You!" A sharp voice cut through the buzz of sound. "Are you the one I'm to be taking to Kilrain?"

Eve blinked hard. There was nothing soft or creamy-complexioned or kind about the person who had spoken. A giant of a man who must be well past his sixties glowered at her from under a heavy set of brows, his face lined as a map of Manhattan, his eyes piercing over a hawk nose. His shoulders were broad under a thick Aran sweater, making Eve wonder what he must have looked like in his prime. He looked like he'd feel more at home in one of those portraits of fierce clan chieftains or knights rather than this bustling airport. *This* was the driver Bridey had sent her?

"I'm Eve Danaher."

"Then get off with you to the car. Not got all day. Visiting hours will be over soon and then where will you be?"

"Visiting hours?" she echoed, confused. "I don't understand."

"She's in the hospital about fifteen minutes from here, the stubborn old woman. Won't settle down and behave for the doctors until she's had a chance to talk to you."

Eve's heart sank. Oh, God, had Bridey gotten worse because she'd been waiting for Eve to arrive? "Is she all right? I mean, how bad is it?"

The old man looked her up and down, disgust curling his upper lip. "You're about as bad as you could be, from the looks of those bags of yours." He turned and stalked toward the door. Eve grabbed her suitcases. So much for a "hundred thousand welcomes," she thought grimly, her cases careening wildly behind her as she tried to keep up. From what she could see, Bridey's "friend" was perfectly capable of leaving her behind.

Eve peeked into the hospital room, grateful that the surly Fingall had decided to wait in his rattletrap car. She swallowed hard, getting her first look at the woman who had persuaded her to take this completely insane trip.

Bridey McGarrity twitched about in the hospital bed, fretting like a little bird, her gray hair gathered into a pony tail draped over one thin shoulder, her face traced with laugh lines, while bright blue eyes sparkled with an eagerness for life terrifyingly like Steffie's.

Oh, God. Eve thought, wishing she could sneak away quietly and run. What have I gotten myself into? One more barrage of *joie de vivre* and she was going to have to dive for cover. But it was too late to back out now. Bridey saw her, cried out.

"Ah, and there you are! I've been that worried about you! How was your flight, dearie? A terrible long one it can be, I know."

"It was fine," Eve said. "But you—how are you?"

Bridey's hands fluttered skyward. "Out of my mind with irritation! One little tumble and you'd have thought the world was ending. I told those boys I was just having a little lie down when they found me, but they'd not believe it. 'Course I was lying in the middle of the floor!" She chuckled. "But the spell was over, and you were coming and I didn't see why I couldn't wait for just one more day. I so wanted to get ye settled in before I had to go."

"Don't worry about it. I can figure things out myself. Or if it's easier, I'm sure I can find someplace else to stay."

"No!" Bridey piped up. "I won't hear of it! Look at you! You're a lovely girl, completely lovely. I knew you would be. You'll do well enough on your own at my darling wee place, I'm sure. Just be a wee bit patient with the telephone, though you'll not know anyone here to talk to, I suppose. And the lights—well, sometimes you have to talk to them nicely to get them to cooperate the way you want them to. I keep candles around for the times they might be having a fit of the sulks. I wanted the cupboards all filled and everything just so before you came. A proper welcome." She mourned, then brightened.

"But I suppose it won't matter so much. You'll get the welcome of your life when you get there, so you will!" She chuckled. "Ah, and wouldn't I love to see it! Nothing I'd love better." Suddenly her face softened with heartbreaking tenderness, her eyes touched with sadness, almost as if she were lonely. "Poor, poor wee mite."

Eve stiffened. Was Bridey talking about her? Sympathy had always made her twitchy. "I'll be fine."

"You?" Bridey looked almost startled, then smiled, almost as if she had a secret. "Sure and you will be. I wouldn't have trusted you to take care of my darling place if I hadn't been sure of you. You will take care of . . . of everything, won't you?" she asked hopefully. "Seems so strange to be away from Kilrain. In all my years I've not spent a handful of nights outside of my own bed there."

Eve tried to imagine such a life—roots so deep, a home cherished, more familiar than the reflection of your own face in the mirror. A place you loved, longed for, even when you were gone for only a little while.

"Promise me you will stay, Eve, even if it gets a bit . . . inconvenient at times?" Bridey asked, catching Eve's hand tightly with her own birdlike fingers. "They'll be transferring me up to Galway tomorrow, to a heart specialist there. I'll be so far away. I know Kilrain will do you good. And as long as you're there I . . . I can concentrate on getting well. Coming home. I want so much to come home."

Eve didn't want to care so much, but something in the old woman's pleading face grabbed her by the heart. It was sweet, Bridey worrying her little cottage wouldn't measure up to Eve's standards. If only the old woman could have seen the first apartment Eve and Tori had shared it would have calmed her fears in a hurry. Eve had lived with plenty of glitches there.

"I'm sure everything will work out fine," Eve said. Her brow furrowed, and she glanced at the door. She was sure she could hear that nasty Fingall laughing.

"So now," Bridey said. "I suppose I should give you the key, though I can't say I ever lock doors." Bridey motioned toward a bag in the corner of the room. "If you'll just get that for me, dearie."

Eve did as she was told. The instant she lifted the bag, she knew Bridey had gone to the Steffie Reklaw school of packing. Eve hefted the bag up onto the bed, being careful not to crush the old woman beneath it.

Bridey rummaged around and emerged triumphant,

the biggest key Eve had ever seen clutched in both hands. She'd known the electric sockets were different, but nobody had told her about the size of the keys. The thing was a foot long, wrought of heavy iron.

"You're the answer to my prayers, Eve Danaher," Bridey said, pressing the key into her hands. "Don't be forgetting that."

Eve tried to smile, wondering if she'd ever get the answer to her own.

She should have taken a taxi. Eve glanced over at the stern man beside her. As soon as they'd left the city even the road seemed to get inhospitable, barely wide enough for the car. The red compact was so beat up it looked as if it had played bumper cars with every rock from Shannon to Dingle. Little wonder, since the road writhed like a snake, undoubtedly designed by some sadistic civil engineer/serial killer who laid out every hairpin turn solely for the purpose of flinging unsuspecting tourists off cliffs. Ever since she'd left the hospital she'd been saying Hail Marys more earnestly than she ever had in her years under the nuns at St. Benedict's. One thing she knew for certain: even if she lived through this car ride, it would be little thanks to her escort. In the hours since they'd left the hospital, the old man had made it no secret he'd rather be anywhere but driving some "eejit Yank" to Bridey McGarrity's.

"I'm sorry to inconvenience you," she began, hardly wanting to start her visit to Ireland off on such a bad note. "I'm sure I could have taken a taxi or a bus or something."

The old man snorted. "I told the old woman I'd see ye to the lane, and so I will, though what any sane person would want with a place like Kilrain is beyond me." There were moments—like the one when he'd all but slammed the car into a boulder—she'd begun to wonder why she'd come here herself. But then she closed her eyes and saw Bridey's hopeful eyes or saw too clearly the image of her daughter's face—the fear, the confusion, the pain. Heard the echo of Victoria's voice begging her to leave her alone.

Fingall gave her a sly look, no doubt thinking it was his words that made her uneasy. He had probably been one of those hideous little boys who loved to slip spiders down girls' blouses. Eve deliberately fought back the knot in her throat every time she thought of that disastrous meeting on the chapel lawn.

"Tell me, are ye plannin' to get any sleep while ye're in Ireland?" After the turmoil of seeing Victoria again and the wild rush to pack for the trip, not to mention seven hours on the plane and the visit to Bridey in the hospital, Eve figured she could catch a nap on a bed of nails if necessary. "I hope to."

"Hope all ye want, but it's not for you to decide. No, it just depends if himself is up an' rattling around."

"Himself?" Alarm jabbed deep. She'd grown so pleased with the idea of a cottage all to herself. Heaven knew she was never at her best around strangers, a holdover from girlhood shyness made far worse because of the disaster that had followed when she had trusted Chad. The possibility that she would have to face some stranger if she did manage to survive this car ride was almost more than she could take. "Bridey said she lived alone." Though she *had* talked about a wonderful welcome—and it hadn't taken five minutes in the hospital room to know Bridey was the kind of woman who loved surprises.

"Did she now?" He barked a laugh that didn't help calm Eve's nerves.

"She did mention someone named Michael."

"Michael?" he gave a hoot of laughter, braking the small red car as a flock of sheep poured across the narrow road, the shepherd and his border collie following behind. "No. It's the ghost I'm talkin' about. The Dark Knight of Kilrain."

Eve sagged against the lumpy upholstery in relief.

Ghosts. How quaint. Eve tried not to smile. Was this an extra service he gave, spinning tales to get tourists in the mood for Ireland?

"I never even believed in ghosts as a child." She didn't say that the monsters in her closet had been real even then. Shoving thoughts of the past back into the black hole where they belonged, she continued. "I work in a museum back home, and half the objects I restore are supposed to have curses attached to them. I doubt this dark knight of yours will bother me."

The old man slanted her a look. "Have it your way, then. But I wouldn't be saying that too loud round about Kilrain. Five hundred years moldering in his grave haven't done much t' improve his temper."

Perfect, Eve thought. This old crank would probably spend hours now thinking up ways to scare her. But his ghosts could have no power over her. She had too many ghosts of her own.

Astonishingly, the old man lapsed into silence. Eve turned to stare at the wild, breathtaking scenery beyond the window. If there were such things as ghosts, this would be the perfect landscape to haunt—the pitching folds of land, like a raging sea frozen by a magician's spell, tumbled boulders and trees twisted into gnarled hands that seemed to claw at the darkening sky. It was too . . . too powerful, almost alive, as if the very ground felt real emotions, molded them into the land like a sculpture—the face of a life hard-lived. But beautiful, Eve admitted silently to herself. So very beautiful.

No. She wasn't the first woman in Ireland who had felt pain and loss if she believed her mother's version of history, anyhow. Regina Danaher had been fond of recounting the sins of the English in Ireland, as if way back in the seventeenth century Oliver Cromwell was responsible for ordaining that she would have to work in a laundromat the rest of her life.

But did it matter how many other women had felt

this pain? Eve wondered. It didn't make her own any less agonizing, any less fresh or raw.

The old man slammed on the brakes, pitching Eve forward so hard she banged her elbow. She muttered under her breath, rubbing the place where a bruise would soon be appearing. She glanced around. Saw nothing but the pale gravel road winding off in front of them, a clutch of trees on either side.

"Why are we stopping? Did that last bump we ran over break the axle?"

"This is far as I go, lass. Out with ye and grab yer cases out of the boot."

"But—but I don't see any cottage."

He chuckled. "It's up top of that hill. The lane is just a nice walk t' take of a Sunday."

"Can't you take me the rest of the way? It's almost dark and my bags are heavy." And my heart hurts like hell. . . .

"I'm that sorry for you, but the answer is still no. You'll just have to go the rest of the way yourself." He jackknifed his big body out of the impossibly small space of car seat, then stalked to the trunk and yanked open the lid. He dumped her Louis Vuitton bags in the dirt.

"Please, I'll pay you extra—"

"Pay me? Ye want Bridey to skin me where I'm standin'? Ah, and aren't I doing this out of the goodness of me heart and my fear of the old woman's temper! Not one pence will pass between us."

"Isn't there anything I can say that will convince you to drive me the rest of the way?"

"No, nor the car, either," he shouted back at her. "Not been one of his kind that's survived the trip up to Kilrain in the past twelve years, since that rain washed out the drive."

There was no way to reach the place by car? She felt a sudden sense of alarm, then mustered her courage. Bridey had hinted that there might be inconveniences. Maybe this one could turn out to be a good thing after all. She wanted to be alone, didn't she? It didn't get much more alone than in the middle of nowhere where cars couldn't even reach her. She was still trying to decide if this were a good or a bad thing when the first fat drops of rain plopped onto her cheeks.

The old man grinned. "I'd step lively if I were ye. Looks to be a grand soft evening." He tipped his battered tweed hat, his eyes twinkling. *"Pogue mahon,"* he said with a grin, and she wasn't sure if he'd just told her "welcome to Ireland" or "kiss my ass."

In a heartbeat, he was ping-ponging the car down the road again as if it were a lunatic pinball.

If all her neighbors were going to act like him, being so isolated would definitely have its advantages, she thought, jamming the giant key into the side pocket of her tunic. Hefting the bags, squaring her shoulders, and surrendering her leather pumps to destruction in the rocks and mud, Eve started up the overgrown mess that had once been a lane. It would have done the witches' forest in *The Wizard of Oz* proud if a few of the trees had just started throwing apples and wisecracks.

Watching her feet so she wouldn't trip over roots or vines or rocks, she barely noticed when the underbrush began to clear. It was all but impossible to see with the rain blurring her eyes, drenching her from linen tunic to jeans. Especially since she couldn't hold the bags and shove her bangs out of her eyes at the same time.

Just as she was certain that she would need CPR, an ocean away from Steffie's cute paramedic, she broke out of the woods.

"Thank God," she said aloud, letting the bags fall in a heap. Fingers that would probably carry the red strap marks until she was seventy swept up to shove the sodden bangs out of her face. She raised her head. Froze. Looming before her was no tidy white cottage— but rather, a tower castle, complete with parapets and grim arrowslit eyes. The whole crumbling mass seeming just moments from tumbling off a cliff.

"No!" Eve choked out. "There must be some mistake! This can't be—"

The key chose that moment to fall from her pocket onto her little toe. Eve yelped in pain, staring down at it in the growing puddles spreading around her. No. It was no mistake, she realized. This was Kilrain.

Dazed, Eve picked up the key, stumbled to a wooden door massive enough to let half an army on horseback into the Great Hall. Shoving the key into the hole, she meant to unlock it, but the door just swung open. It was pitch dark, cool, and a little damp. She'd probably break her neck just trying to find a light switch.

Eve shoved her suitcases through the door ahead of her. After all, if the castle did come complete with dragon, better he chew on the bags than on her leg.

"Oh, for heaven's sake, Eve! You're being ridiculous. If that—that awful Fingall could see you now, he'd be laughing his tweed cap off." She stepped through the door and groped along the rough stone wall, but there was not a light switch in reach. Still, Bridey had said something about candles. Eve's fingers bumped into something that felt like the edge of a table where she found matches and a bent candlestick. Fumbling in the dark, trying not to drip on the matches, she touched flame to wick just as something flung itself out of the darkness, snarling. Eve shrieked as it grabbed her ankle.

She should have felt pain, blood, but all she felt was . . . slobber. . . . The thing let go, and crawled back into the corner where it had been lurking.

Heart in her throat, Eve grabbed the candlestick— weren't wild animals supposed to be afraid of fire?— and thrust it down so she could see the rabid monster that had attacked her.

A black wrinkled gargoyle with black gumball eyes glared up at her, its expression would have been deadly savage if it had had any teeth in its mouth to bare. Instead, pink gums gleamed, showcasing a single snaggley fang. It seemed Fingall's Dark Knight of Kilrain had shrunk with time. . . .

A sharp, furious burst of yapping almost made her drop the candle as the gargoyle made a second charge. Eve jumped back, slamming into something hard and huge—and human! She wheeled as the figure fell with a hollow clatter, sending her attacker fleeing.

Armor! It was just a suit of armor, and . . . she forced herself to look at the ferocious beast now snarling from what looked like a tattered pillow—

The gargoyle was—*a dog!* That kind that looked like it's face had been hit by a truck. She'd seen plenty of the atrocious things depicted in artwork from the time of William and Mary. What were they called? Pugs. That was it! Eve bit her lip. She would have preferred Fingall's ghost!

The gargoyle/dog was tearing at its pillow with that single fang, as if to say "If I could reach I'd be tearing out your throat."

Oh, lord! Eve pressed her fingers to her lips. Anything but a dog! She was terrified of them! Okay, so she was terrified of any animal not separated from her by a nice, sturdy set of iron bars! If God had wanted animals running around loose he wouldn't have invented cages.

She fought against very real panic. She'd heard they didn't have rabies in England—but Ireland? She wasn't so sure. As if that wasn't bad enough the animal obviously *lived here.* Could *this* be the "poor wee mite" Bridey was talking about? Some welcome!

Breathe, Eve! Bridey can't expect you to . . . to be responsible for this . . . gargoyle! What kind of person would dump their pet on an unsuspecting stranger? She could almost hear that old man's nasty laugh. *What kind of person? The same crazy old woman who invited a stranger to live in her house—and didn't bother to mention she lived in a castle!*

Thunder crashed and Eve all but jumped out of her

skin. For once, she and the gargoyle were in total agreement. It burrowed its nose under the pillow.

Was it the thunder pushing her over the edge? Or was it the low, miserable howl coming from under that wad of fluff? Eve felt a knot tighten in her throat. No, dammit. She wasn't going to cry! She hadn't cried once since she left Victoria and fourteen years worth of desperate mother's dreams on the chapel lawn. She couldn't cry. If she did, she would never stop.

Her eyes burned fiercely. She was wet. Exhausted. Starving.

Miserable.

She'd had a nasty surprise. Things like this—well, *almost* like this—happened to people every day. If she just . . . just got some sleep, surely she'd be able to figure things out in the morning. Like how her life had turned into such a mess and where she'd lost her courage on the path up to this dismal place.

No!

This was supposed to be her fresh beginning. She wasn't going to let one little setback—or five or six or seven—make her lose heart. This might be her only chance to get it right.

The pug set up another wail. That thick, choking feeling lodged in her throat again. Was the animal hungry? Thirsty? What if it died before morning?

She grabbed a container from the table, poured what was left of her bottle of spring water into it. She set it on the floor as far away from the dog as possible. Hey, if it was that thirsty, it could damned well walk a few feet! As for food—all she had left were some peanuts from her connecting flight—the only dinner it looked like she was going to get, since she wasn't about to go through the dog to find the kitchen.

In a burst of benevolence, she sprinkled a few nuts on the stone floor, hoping she wouldn't poison the animal. Although, it would be Bridey's own fault if she did! How was Eve supposed to know what the thing ate—besides people's ankles and pillow stuffing!

She jumped back as the ungrateful pug pulled his head out from the cushion long enough to yap at her. He bared his tooth for another charge! Eve grabbed her overnight case, the wildly flickering candle, and bolted toward what looked like a spiral set of stone stairs, the gargoyle in hot pursuit. Just as his tooth nicked her ankle, she threw him the last of the peanuts and ran.

5

*E*ve woke with a start, shoving a tangle of unfamiliar blankets off, her gritty eyes struggling to focus. She had to be dreaming. But it wasn't her usual nightmare—the one with Tori sobbing, screaming as Chad took her from Eve's arms. This was a new nightmare—stone walls bleeding moisture, grinning dragons' heads snarling down from the top of bedposts thick as tree trunks, and a badly preserved peacock grinning at her under a layer of dust thick enough to stuff a mattress.

No. She realized with a start. She wasn't dreaming. Her eyes focused on a broken piece of Celtic cross leaning in the corner of the room. She was in a castle. In Ireland.

Ireland? It sounded so simple. A name on a map. But from what she'd seen thus far it would be safer to be wandering around in some crazy dream.

She stiffened as the sound that had awakened her echoed up the stone stairway again. What the— *Crash!*

It sounded like something was coming through the wall! Battering the door down! Even the most determined gargoyle-dog in the world couldn't make a sound like that! Something clattered, the hollow thud that followed sending raw alarm shooting through her veins.

Someone was down there!

"Oh, Lord!" she gasped. "I never even locked the door!" Maybe Bridey wasn't overly concerned, but Eve had lived in New York too long not to be terrified. She scrambled out of bed, shoving down the edge of the blue tee shirt she'd slept in, and searched for a weapon. Her umbrella? Hardly threatening enough with its image of the rose window of Notre Dame. But what was that lost in cobwebs by the arrow-slit window? A sword! She tried to grab it and all but dislocated her shoulder. Bracing herself at the sound of another crash, she hefted the weapon and started creeping down the stairs, bare feet freezing on the stone. The only way she had any chance was by surprising the intruder with this ancient weapon.

Ever so slowly, she edged downward. Around the corner she caught just a glimpse of shadow. God in heaven, the intruder must be huge! She swallowed hard, then charged, bellowing at the top of her lungs.

But no gigantic burglar or ax murderer spun toward her; instead, a horse reared up with a fearful whinny.

Horse? A horse?

Eve let the sword drop from nerveless fingers. There was a horse in the Great Hall of the castle. And not your average placid trail variety. No, this one looked strung tighter than the cables on the Eiffel Tower. Dark eyes flashed as it tossed its head, showing a line of teeth almost the size of piano keys. Did horses bite? This one looked ready to take her head off. Nostrils flared, eyes white-ringed, the animal shook its head at her and pawed the floor.

Who the hell did it belong to? The ghost? Eve thought, panic pressing hard on her chest.

Why couldn't she just be haunted by the ghost? The nice, safe, chain-rattling kind!

She looked at the wooden door, saw it standing half-open. She was probably lucky every piece of livestock in the county hadn't wandered in because of her carelessness.

Okay, so the dog was Bridey's fault, but there was no question who'd left that door open last night. She'd just wait for the thing to wander out again. After all, wouldn't it want grass or something? It couldn't just hang around in here forever eating something out of that eight-hundred-year-old Saxon urn—*Saxon urn?* Ohmigod! The thing might be priceless!

Instinct took over, years of fighting to restore priceless objects left to all but ruin. She couldn't stand it as the horse stuffed his nose into the bowl again, setting it rocking on its stone pedestal.

Heedless of teeth, hooves, and tons of equine muscle, Eve dove for the urn, restoring its balance. The gargoyle yapped, spitting out bits of peanut, as the startled horse reared back, shying away. Eve stood her ground, imagining the headlines. *Art restorer dies heroically protecting urn, Pug and horse held for questioning.*

She was getting punchy—or losing her mind. Either way, she had to get this horse out of the castle somehow! There was some kind of rope-thing looped around his head, but there was no way she was getting close enough to touch it. She scooted outside, grabbed up a handful of clover from the side of the door, and returned to dangle it warily in front of the horse's nose.

"Come on, Trigger." She wiggled the green stuff in front of him. "Lots more of this outside."

The horse stared her down, and Eve's knees started knocking. It neighed, tossing its head, and charged toward her. Eve flattened herself against the wall, trapped between two stone pillars, expecting to be crushed by the animal at any moment when the horse veered off, kicking with its hind feet. Eve heard the sickening crunch of hooves making contact, the horse caving in the wooden side of a bog oak chest. Horrified, Eve let out a scream. The animal careened into the pedestal supporting the urn. Eve dove to steady it, the water splashing over the rim, drenching her. Eve ground her teeth, determined not to screech again. She was sure this time *her* eyes were glowing red—a far better reaction than diving for the pug's ragged cushion.

"Dammit, get out of here, you monster!" Eve swore,

waving her arms in an effort to scare the thing. The horse kicked at her, would have hit what he'd aimed for if a flash of blue and buff hadn't streaked through the doorway, a dark-haired man diving for the horse's halter.

"Get back!" Nothing lilting about this Irish voice—it was hard, irritated, relentlessly masculine. The horse reared up, the man dangling off his feet for a few seconds as the animal fought to shake him off.

"Easy, there. Easy, big fella," he soothed. Eve watched, stunned. Too bad Steff wasn't here. The girl always loved being right and it looked like she'd hit the bull's eye again when she'd claimed how delicious Irish men were. If this specimen was any example, they took "mouth-watering meter" right off the Richter scale.

"Perfect fantasy material," Steff would have called him. Good thing Eve hadn't wanted anything to do with any man anywhere since the day Chad had sauntered out of her life. But she had spent her career recognizing artistic beauty and appreciating it. Even she had to admit that this guy would be Michelangelo's dream model.

His shoulder muscles rippled against the soft blue of his riding shirt, long legs straining as he wrestled with the horse. Worn, soft riding boots braced against the uneven stone floor. But it was his face that took her breath away. Tanned from the sun, buffed by the wind, too rough-edged to be handsome, but even more arresting because of the lines and creases, the asymmetrical bump on his nose.

Whoever had hit him in the face had done women all over Ireland a favor. Unfortunately, from the glint in piercingly blue eyes, the man knew it. Shocked, she realized she'd seen that face before—where was it?

Before she could think, the horse made another attempt to get free. Somehow the Irishman held on. "I know she's got no manners," he soothed the horse in a voice smooth as fine Irish whiskey, "but you know how Americans are."

"No manners?" Eve gasped. Damn, why did men always have to ruin things by opening their mouths? "You let this—this thing wander into someone's house and you criticize *my* manners?" She gave a squeak as the big horse rounded on her again, only the dark-haired man hanging on to it keeping it from charging at her.

"I'm going to tell the owner of Kilrain about this and—"

"I'm shaking in my Wellingtons, darlin'."

Smooth, like fine Irish whiskey, his voice mocked her. The big Irishman wrestled the horse to the door, set him free. In an explosion of dirt and hooves, the animal bolted away.

Eve squeaked. "You can't—you can't just let him go! That horse will kill somebody!"

"Already tried plenty of times. Doubt he'll run into anyone on the way to his own pasture. Might as well go back there since you've already ruined his breakfast."

Eve straightened all of her five feet three inches, despite the fact that it pulled the hem of her damp skirt halfway up her thighs. "Breakfast? Have you lost your mind?"

"I'm stunned even you would object to the presence of an invited guest."

"Invited?" Eve huffed, eyeing the door where the horse had disappeared. "You can't be serious!"

"Every time Innisfree slips the gate, he comes over to join Bonaparte for a cuppa tea."

Was everyone in this country mad? "Bonaparte?"

The man grinned, crinkling the corners of his eyes in a way that made them dance as he nodded at the pug. The fiendish gargoyle thumped its tail and meandered out the door after his supposed friend.

"That damned dog curls right up next to Innisfree's hooves," the man said, shaking his head. "Thought Bonaparte here must have a death wish but Innisfree took a liking to the beast. No accounting for taste, I suppose. Besides, Bridey always said she enjoyed having company for breakfast."

Eve shoved her hand through her hair, trying to get the tangled mass out of her face. It was ruining the effect of her glare. "Bridey isn't here right now. Next time you see Innisfree tell him I prefer to dine alone."

Damn him for laughing! "I'm afraid the old woman will be horrified when I tell her. Irish hospitality is legendary, and the door to Kilrain has always been open."

"I'll remember to lock it next time." And pile whatever furniture she could move in front of the door as well. "I've come here for a sabbatical. To sort some things out." If only the washed-out lane had been about three miles longer! "I don't mean to be rude, but I prefer to be alone."

For the first time, the light in his eyes dimmed. "Trust me, darlin', it's a bad idea."

"Excuse me?"

"To be alone. From the look of you, you've been alone too long already."

Instinctively, Eve wrapped her arms around her middle, hating the jolt of discomfort she felt beneath this man's gaze. Surely, he couldn't see—see what? Years of vulnerability, years of walls so thorny and high no one but Steffie had ever dared climb over them.

She raised her gaze, intending to ask him to leave in the most dignified manner possible, but she glimpsed the corner of his mouth tipping up in a smile that made a mockery of that deep, searching moment which had filled her with terror.

"Please, just shut the door on the way out," she said, her heart doing an uncomfortable flip at the way he was looking at her.

"You'll have to lock the door yourself," he said as if he sensed just how edgy he was making her.

She latched on to indignation, her very best art restorer voice. "If that urn is any indication of what this castle holds, Bridey should have a security system to rival the one guarding the crown jewels!"

"Bridey's never believed in locking beautiful things up where people can't see them, touch them." A low burr roughened his voice. "Neither have I."

He was looking at her again, his eyes suddenly darker, hotter, tracing a path down her body.

In a flash, she felt the scant damp folds of cotton clinging to her breasts, a drop of water dripping in a wet path down the inside of her knee, down her calf, to her ankle. Bare feet with absurd bright pink nail polish Steff had insisted on painting on the night before she left. *No woman should go on an adventure without her toes polished, girlfriend! Galahad had the Holy Grail, King Arthur had Excalibur. Maybe it's not much, but a woman's got to have some weapon, and there's nothing like pink toenails to bring a man to his knees.*

Terrific! Just terrific!

"Mr.—ah, whatever your name is. I'm asking you for the last time to leave. And just keep your horse on the right side of the fence."

What the hell had she said? He was grinning like she'd just laid out some double entendre or something. "It won't be easy, darlin', but I'll do my best. By the way, the name is Michael. Michael Halloran."

Halloran. That was the name she'd been groping for a moment ago. *This* was Bridey's "Michael"? Eve thought, dazed. Now she remembered where she'd seen him—in full color glossies in horse magazines. He'd been famous, or infamous, on the circuit when she'd followed it years ago, one more effort to feel close to her horse-loving daughter. No man had been hungrier for victory, or more ruthless in getting what he wanted. Everything that terrified her.

He'd reminded her so much of Chad from the arrogant glint in his eyes to the sneer as he faced cameras in the winner's circle. The similarities she'd been sure she glimpsed in the two men had chilled her even then. It was worse now—now with Chad's face so fresh in her memory, the cutting edge of his voice as he'd raged at her on the chapel green still grating on her nerves.

She could handle crotchety old men, ghosts, gargoyle-dogs hungry for blood, even finding a horse inside the house. But she'd had a bellyful of men like Michael Halloran. Feeling a little sick that she'd felt even that tiny spark of attraction toward the man, she leaned against the wall. Maybe this was all a mistake. Maybe she should leave—Kilrain, Ireland, the planet Earth.

"When Bridey had to go to the hospital early she made me promise to look in on you, Miss Danaher. Help you get whatever food you need from town. Make certain you were comfortable."

"Comfortable? It's a castle, in case you haven't noticed! It's got mold growing on the walls. The lights don't work. There's a dog she didn't even mention! When I visited her in the hospital she promised me a wonderful welcome when I got here. If this morning is any example, that must have a completely different meaning in Ireland!"

"You saw Bridey?" That hard, masculine face softened, his eyes so blue, suddenly worried. Eve didn't want to see them like that. "How was she?"

"She's a lot better than I am at the moment!" she snapped, trying on purpose to drive the disturbing tenderness from his face. She was a little hysterical, the strain of last night, this morning, the past month, and the disturbing sensations this man was creating putting her nerves on a ragged edge.

"Listen," Halloran soothed. "I'm not usually such a bastard, but I've been worried. I have to watch out for Bridey. You've got to admit, it was damned dangerous to invite a complete stranger here. Maybe we should start over, try this again. After all, we've barely met."

He was almost charming, far more dangerous. Eve clung to the only defense she had. "Are you the steeplechaser Michael Halloran?"

The man actually cringed a little, groaned. "The reputation that never dies. That was in the old days. I've changed a lot since then."

"Men like you don't change." Eve froze, aghast at what had fallen out of her mouth. This wasn't Chad she was talking to, after all. This was a perfect stranger.

"Mr. Halloran," she amended. "I'm sorry. Maybe that was uh, a little blunt."

"A little?" His lean cheeks burned. He almost looked hurt.

Eve felt a twinge of guilt, but trying to further soften what she'd said would just muddy things up. She wanted to make sure this man knew exactly where she stood. "I just want to make it clear right from the start that I came here for some peace and quiet," Eve said, deeply grateful Steff was an ocean away. At the moment, she would have been ready to whack Eve over the head. This was a perfectly gorgeous guy, and she'd managed to alienate him in a matter of minutes.

Halloran's smile was hard-edged, brittle. "Well, then, as long as we're being honest, Miss Danaher, I'll tell you this. I wondered what kind of a woman would cross an ocean to stay in the house of someone she'd never met. Hell, someone she'd once barely talked to on the phone. I thought you must be a little crazy. But I guess if you intend to stay away from me, you're smart enough after all."

"It's nothing personal. I don't even know you. I just want to be left alone."

He shrugged one broad shoulder with a lazy, animal grace. "If that's the way you want it, then. Fine. It's a long walk to get groceries, but hey, you Yanks trekked from Boston to Oregon, didn't you? This walk should be a nice one to take of a Sunday."

With that, he strode out of the castle. Eve glimpsed another horse cropping grass in the yard. Halloran grabbed the pommel of the saddle and swung astride its back. Man and beast streaked across the Irish countryside, leaping stone fences—gorgeous, poetry of sinew and freedom. Almost as if he were trying to out-run demons of his own. The insight pricked her. No, more likely his male pride wasn't used to outright re-jection. *Especially when he might not deserve it?* Steff's voice whispered in her head.

Eve winced, staring after them, then buried her face in her hands. All right, all right, she'd made a mess of things already, and she hadn't even had breakfast. Okay, so Michael Halloran had a rotten reputation. She'd read about the accidents he'd caused, people and horses he'd trampled over on his way to victory. Not much different from the way Chad and his money had trampled over a young, helpless girl. She knew what it felt like to be bloodied and battered in the dust, watching someone else ride away with everything that ever mattered.

Maybe she hadn't been fair—or polite. But fair had gotten her nowhere fast in the past. She'd been trying to be fair when she'd let Chad into Tori's life, even agreed to consider marrying him so their baby would have a father. Oh, yeah. She'd been so fair that it made her sick when she thought about it now. Chad had never had any intention of marrying someone like her. He'd just used her vulnerabilities to weasel his way into their lives. He'd watched like a predator, waited for her to make a mistake so he could move in for the kill. And she hadn't disappointed him. But was it fair to make a complete stranger pay for Chad's sins? Or her own naiveté. Did "fair" matter if it kept Halloran at a safe distance? Her head ached.

She dragged the castle door shut, leaned her back against it, fighting the instinct to run as far away from the uncomfortable feelings the Irishman had stirred in her as possible. Damn Bridey for making her promise to stay—for looking at her with those pleading old eyes. Damn her own bloody conscience!

Eve sucked in a ragged breath. In spite of every-thing that had happened, she wasn't going to break the old lady's heart by leaving. Kilrain wasn't what she'd expected. And Halloran was about as welcome as a dragon moving in next door. But she could get through this. She didn't even have to go outside for the next six weeks if she didn't want to. She could just stay in the castle and do what she loved best—sifting through dust and neglect to find things other people had forgotten. Things lost . . .

Wasn't that what she was good at? Except when what was lost had hurt gray-green eyes and blond hair curling around a soft heart-shaped face and a valedictorian's speech tucked into the sleeve of her graduation gown. Except when what was lost didn't want to be found.

"Come on, Eve," she said aloud, trying to brace herself. "You're making a new beginning. That means you're going forward, it doesn't mean all the pain you're leaving behind is going to stop hurting all at once." *More like never.*

She went over to the urn, grabbed the hem of her tee shirt, rubbed away the worst of the grime. It was beautiful. She waited for her heart to soar, her pulses to race. Maybe it would take time. Time.

She had forever. But wasn't that what she was afraid of?

Forever alone. Bad idea, Michael Halloran had said. But then, from what she'd read he was the kind of person who took what he wanted, damn the cost. Desperate as she was for a relationship with her daughter, she wouldn't force Tori, hurt her even more. Maybe being alone was a bad idea, Eve thought, her heart aching. But what did that matter? Sometimes you just didn't have any other choice.

6

$\mathcal{I}$t had been a long time since he'd been on the receiving end of one of those "you're lower than pond scum" kinds of glares—especially coming from a pretty woman, Michael thought, reining his big gelding over the green hills toward his own land. But there had been no mistaking the look in Eve Danaher's eyes.

It chafed—that flash of automatic dislike, that rush to judgment based on God knew what. One thing that was certain was that he hadn't even had a chance to defend himself.

Poor Michael, Bridey's voice teased in his ear. *To think someone would be so judgmental to you, and you always so fair, waiting to see before you jump to conclusions. Do you think the lass sensed you've been accusing her of being a tinker ready to take advantage of a poor old woman? Not once had you seen Eve, talked to her, but you were determined to dislike her from the moment you first heard her name.*

"That was different," Michael muttered, as if the old woman was right in front of him. "Somebody has to watch out for you. You sure as hell don't bother to watch out for yourself."

No. Bridey just wandered around talking about fate and destiny and journeys as if life were some sort of movie and she had the script, knew everything that would happen on the way to "the end." But Michael had learned the hard way that often as not, fate dumped bricks on your head instead of good fortune, unless you kept your wits about you.

Three years ago, Bridey had claimed fate had been responsible for making a distant cousin drop a lawsuit in which the sonofabitch had tried to prove her incompetent so he could take over the castle. She'd claimed it was fate when land developers had surrendered their fight to buy her seafront property and left her in peace after a grueling few months. Fate? Michael snorted. More like he'd charged into the situation like a wild boar, cutting all the knots, straightening all the tangles, keeping the ugliness from touching Bridey as much as he possibly could.

Once, in an effort to urge Bridey to caution, he'd pointed out his part in driving back the wolves. Bridey had smiled tenderly, patted his cheek until he felt as if he were about seven years old. And in that voice she used only for him she'd said, "But wasn't it fate brought you to me, Michael-my-heart?"

What the hell was he supposed to say to that? Not that it would matter if he'd written a three-hour dissertation on the subject. Bridey wouldn't listen. There was no arguing with the old woman, especially once she'd insisted that this Eve Danaher was coming to Kilrain at fate's invitation, just as Michael had.

As Michael saw it, the biggest problem with fate was that the only one it seemed to want to chat with was Bridey. But then, for an old woman who lived alone, Bridey had always managed to attract plenty of company. Fate. The ghost. Bonaparte, the most spoiled rotten dog in all of Ireland; Sean, who laughed with the old woman. And Michael himself, who adored her, worried about her, frequently wanted to strangle her. Now she was fussing over a woman she'd only talked to for about ten minutes on the phone. Michael had made no secret from the beginning that he thought the whole idea of inviting this woman to the castle was crazy. Dangerous.

Be honest, boyo. You've not given the lass a ghost of a chance up to now. But tell me, what do you think now that you've seen her? Is she a hardened criminal? Pushy, shrill like the people on the American programs we get on the telly? Or is it possible she is just what I said she was—a lost lamb needing shelter from the storm?

Michael grimaced. What did he think of her? Okay, so she was pretty. Blond hair tousled with that "just got out of bed" look that made a man itch to sweep the strands back from her cheeks. A pale, cameo kind of face at odds with the flash of defensiveness in eyes the green-gray of mist over the glen. Her nose, small, up-turned, lightly freckled. Unmistakably Irish. Pink toe-nails on bare feet an impossibly sexy contrast against scarred centuries-old stone floors. And that tee shirt that should have had all the sensuality of a feed sack had been transformed by the damp spots that made it cling in all the right places.

All right, so there were probably men enough who would be tempted by the lady. But if they wanted to touch, they'd have to risk pulling back a badly scratched hand, at the very least. The woman was prickly as hell.

And you were just charming to her, weren't you, Michael? He admitted to himself. Maybe he *had* been a little distracted—wrestling a panicked horse, comparing the woman's face to people on "America's Most Wanted," trying to prove she had all the flaws he'd been giving her in the days before her arrival.

But the truth was, Eve Danaher was nothing like he'd imagined her. And that made him mad as hell.

Or had that really been the reason he'd reacted so badly? Michael asked himself ruthlessly. No. Truth was, when he'd seen Eve Danaher standing there in Kilrain's Great Hall, he'd felt like he'd been kicked in the stomach. He hadn't been able to bear walking into the castle and not finding Bridey there, her silvery hair like mist in the dim light, the shadows hiding lines and creases in her face, making her seem younger, as if some magic in

Kilrain could hold back the advancing years. Somehow, in Kilrain, Bridey had always seemed younger—like the bare-footed free-spirited young woman Michael had adored as a boy. And when Bridey laughed—always, always, it had been the laugh of a young girl. Michael's throat tightened as he remembered the last time he'd seen her, so small and fragile in the hospital bed, the harsh light carving the years deep into her face no matter how hard he tried to close his eyes to it.

Truth was he would have hated to see anyone taking Bridey's place at the castle, no matter how temporarily. But what really ate at him was the knowledge that, while Eve Danaher's stay might be temporary, the time was coming when Bridey's absence would be real, forever. Already the doctors shook their heads, hedged answers (though his best friend, Sean Murphy, insisted Michael himself was the one who was dodging, trying to keep from hearing what the doctors were saying).

Michael had wanted to knock Sean across the room for saying so. It was harder to deflect the wisdom that had come from a sweet-faced ten-year-old, little Theresa, who'd been riding at the farm for months now. Theresa, who would always be "Joy" in his eyes.

What was it the little girl had said, her eyes so wide, too wise, too old from too much pain? *Sean said Bridey's clock is running down and that's why you're sad. I've been thinking, Bridey's heart is just too big, has to work too hard to take care of everybody. It's just wearing her all out. An' it's hard to keep going when you're tired.*

Little Joy had learned that the hard way in the last year, ever since the accident in which she'd almost lost her life. Michael's heart had constricted when she had reached up, squeezing his hand. *Don't worry, Michael. You'll always have me.*

It was a damned good thing he did have Joy, the farm teeming with animals no one else wanted, rejected creatures loved and cared for by the steady stream of kids in need of special therapy—that love, encouragement, acceptance, only animals could give them. Thank God he had the farm, the kids, the animals. A life worlds away from the self-centered, driven one he'd had before.

If he had the courage to be honest, he'd admit that the only real sin Eve Danaher had committed was being in the place where Bridey belonged. Making him face changes he didn't want to face. Catch a glimpse into a future he couldn't even imagine. A future without her.

But he'd picked a hell of a way to honor his friendship with the old woman. Bridey had begged him to take care of Eve, her last request before they'd carried her away to the hospital. He'd done the bare minimum with a rotten attitude.

Maybe he should just step back, give things a chance to settle down. Try to be better with Eve later. There were no real issues standing between them, after all. He'd just managed to play right into her preconceived notions of him and she'd done the same thing. Thought he was the arrogant jerk who'd been publicized by the press. Unfortunately, his actions had proved her right.

He crested the rise of the hill, disturbing emotions fading. Three horses trotted in a circle in the front paddock, kids in helmets riding on their backs. Another two kids worked with their parents doing physical therapy, getting ready for their reward—time on the horses—the children's eager faces distracted for once from the pain of stretching tendons and muscles to the limit.

Raider, the black and white border collie, loped over, herding Michael and the horse toward the "flock" of kids and horses and therapists the dog thought it his responsibility to guard.

"Michael!" Joy called out, pausing in a leg stretch to wave frantically at him. "Wait till you see what I can do!" She flexed one of her injured legs, raising it higher than he'd ever seen it before.

Michael grinned. "You're beautiful!"

Beautiful. And she was. If a ten-year-old could wrestle through the kind of difficulty Joy had, surely he could tolerate Eve Danaher for a few weeks for Bridey's sake, couldn't he?

"Michael?" He stiffened at the sound of his best friend and partner's voice coming from the direction of the stable. "The boy is at it again." Sean's Murphy's ruddy face was creased with worry. Michael sighed, bracing himself.

"What now?"

"Innisfree came back about fifteen minutes ago. I told the boy not to get in the paddock with him when he's like that—raw as hell, dangerous. He got kicked a good one in the ribs."

"Bloody hell. Cracked ribs?"

"Don't think so. Worse still, one of the little kids was near the gate. Lucky he wasn't trampled."

"Thank God."

"You have to do something, man, or someone will be injured if Rory keeps this up. The kid's got the bit in his teeth, Michael. Even you can't do anything with him."

"I'll take care of it," Michael ground out between clenched teeth.

"You've been trying to take care of it for three months now. Sometimes it doesn't matter how much you try, you just can't break through."

"I said I'll take care of it!" Michael snapped, swinging down and tossing his reins to Sean. The smaller kids were quiet, and Michael could feel them watching him as he strode away, mad as hell.

They were all waiting for the explosion, Michael thought grimly. Around here trouble had a name. Rory. But the one he was really mad at was Sean. He was scared, damned scared that this time Sean might be right.

Things were finally looking up! Eve smiled across the car seat at the benevolent driver who had taken pity on her—a bedraggled, hopelessly confused but determined tourist trying to decipher a road sign a ways back. Quietly handsome in a forty-something, faintly balding way, Dennis Moran could have been a poster boy for that Irish hospitality Eve had heard so much about—and begun to believe that, away from Shannon airport, was as imaginary as the fairies. He'd offered her a ride to the grocery store and back, and, to allay her New York suspicions, had shown her that he was some sort of government official on business. She'd been laughing ever since she'd gotten into the car.

Laughing? She could almost hear Steff scoff in the back of her head. *Girl, that is grade-A, high-class flirting you're doing!*

Maybe it was, Eve admitted to herself. But what harm could there be in it? Dennis was safe enough—thoughtful, amusing, good-looking. Besides, once she'd gotten some food to beat back the snarling in her empty stomach, she'd probably never see him again.

Always your first priority in a man.

Blast, Eve thought. Wasn't it bad enough that Steff harassed her in her own living room? Did she *have* to keep it up when she was an ocean away?

"I appreciate your coming to my rescue, Mr. Moran."

"Dennis."

"Dennis." She smiled. "This morning someone told me we Americans had trekked from Boston to Oregon with no problems. I should be able to find my way around here. Unfortunately, I lost every drop of my ancestors' sense of direction and every place on the map is Bally-something." She didn't add that the rest of the words looked like random letters a three-year-old had filled into crossword puzzle squares.

He had a straightforward laugh, not like that low, disturbing chuckle of Michael Halloran.

"It's a common point of confusion for tourists, I'm afraid. Bally is 'town' in Gaelic."

"It would've been kinder just to use the name of

the place, let us figure out it's a town for ourselves. The shops and sidewalks would be a great clue."

He laughed again. What a nice man! Steff was right. She should trust her instincts more. Maybe if Dennis Moran asked her for a date, she'd stun herself and say yes. Had she actually packed lipstick? Maybe Bonaparte had some tucked away she could borrow. Did she and the pug use the same shade?

She looked out the window, pleased with herself. But even that rare emotion vanished as her gaze snagged on the countryside rippling past beyond the car. It had been far too gray when she'd arrived yesterday and she'd been too exhausted, frazzled and distracted by Fingall, her crotchety driver, to pay much attention to the scenery. Which just went to show that sometimes Steffie was right. With the possible exception of rusty old museum relics, Eve *didn't* notice the beauty of what was right in front of her unless it bit her in the nose.

She stared, mesmerized by the stone fences and green fields of the loveliest farm she'd ever seen. Even the animals looked picturesque from a nice, safe distance. Horses of every shade from russet to chestnut to gray cantered around their pastures, elegant manes and tails rippling in the wind. Long-legged foals kicked up their heels in games they alone understood while soft-eyed mares looked patiently on. Sheep grazed the hillside in fluffy clusters, bright patches of paint on their rear ends instead of the brands Americans used on cattle. Comical, but pretty, their white fleece was splotched with color until they looked a little like the confetti angel food cake Victoria had loved.

The memory thudded hard against Eve's heart, reminding her that her daughter should be here, sharing this adventure with her, laughing over the "Bally" maps, her eyes bright and eager as she stared at the horses. Her little girl would have been so thrilled. Irish horses were among the finest in the world.

"Miss Danaher?"

Moran's voice brought her back to the present with a jolt. Her smile was only a little forced as she turned back to him. They were turning beneath a freshly painted sign. GLENAMMURA FARMS.

"My business will only take a few moments," Dennis said. "I apologize for the nuisance."

"It's not a nuisance at all! I could look at this place forever." She swallowed hard, an unexpected knot in her throat as she gazed over fields a myriad of rich greens, neat stone fences. She'd lived in cities all her life, and even as a child she'd far preferred holing up in her room with a stack of books to playing outdoors. Why did she suddenly feel as if she had spent all those years parched with thirst for these colors, the sweet freedom of the wind?

Dennis parked, then exited the car, some official-looking documents in his hand. Farm stuff, no doubt. Eve grinned as he disappeared among a cluster of farm buildings. Top secret governmental business. Vital stuff like checking to make certain the paint on the sheep was color-coordinated so they didn't clash with the landscape.

She meant to stay in the car. Might have, if the wind hadn't smelled so heavenly through the open window, or if she hadn't caught a glimpse of an object that looked like an ancient standing stone in the middle of a grassy knoll a dozen yards away. Intrigued, she climbed out of the car and started to wander over, amazed at the grace of swirling figures carved in the face of the stone ages ago. She would have enjoyed her discovery if it hadn't been for the sudden burst of sharp, angry voices.

What in the world was the matter? She tried to make light of the situation. The farmer didn't like the sheep-color allotted to him? But her attempt at humor didn't work. She caught her lip between her teeth, feeling damned uncomfortable. Wanting the argument to be over. Whoever Dennis was arguing with sounded furious.

She'd hated conflict as long as she could remember,

fled from it whenever possible—a holdover from her mother's explosive temper. And Chad had used her reticence to his advantage. But there was something in these voices that made her nerves even more raw than usual.

A third voice, pleading, desperate. A voice young enough to make her cast dread and her manners aside. She strode toward the sound, intending to take whoever was shouting by the scruff of the neck and shake them until their teeth rattled for upsetting the boy so badly. As she rounded the corner of a stable, what she saw almost made her knees give out from under her.

Michael Halloran, his face flushed and furious, his eyes blue fire, bare inches from grabbing poor Dennis by the throat from the looks of it. Halloran didn't seem to give a damn about the boy who stood directly in his line of fire.

Hollow-cheeked, eyes dark-circled and haunted, the lanky teenager's face was white, terrible in its stillness. Hay clung to shaggy russet hair. Hands that looked like they hadn't been washed in a month shook beneath the cuffs of his dirt-smudged flannel shirt. Eve felt a horrible moment of déjà vu. Her own face had had that haunted look in the mirror the day they had taken Tori away—utter helplessness, hopelessness.

"Take your papers and shove them, Moran!" Halloran raged. "I'll be damned if you're going to take him!"

Take him? The boy looked exhausted, battered. What had Halloran done? Tried to work the poor child to death as some sort of stable hand? Was that Dennis's business? To rescue him?

"Sir, please. I'm begging you to listen." The boy's voice almost broke on a tremor as he appealed to Dennis. "You don't know what he'll do to me if you make me go!"

What *he'll* do? The boy could only mean Halloran. Eve could taste the boy's fear in the back of her throat.

"Rory, I want you to listen to me—" Dennis began, but almost impatiently. Didn't he see the monsters in the boy's eyes? Eve couldn't bear it. To hell with her usual policy of never getting involved. She burst in on them, her resolve to do better around Halloran forgotten, all the anger and frustration she'd been swallowing for a lifetime breaking free.

"Don't be afraid, Rory. Halloran can't hurt you."

All three wheeled to stare at her, and she almost faltered as Halloran's blazing gaze slammed into her. No wonder the boy was terrified! Her spine stiffened.

"*I* can't hurt him?" Halloran shot back so fiercely Eve had to remind herself to breathe. "Lady, you have no idea what I'm capable of right about now!"

"Maybe I don't, but it's obvious this poor boy does! What's the matter, Halloran? Not tough enough to trample other steeplechasers anymore, so you've decided to beat up on teenaged boys? We *Yanks* have a saying back home: Pick on somebody your own size!"

"Miss Danaher, I could have predicted Halloran would make this difficult," Dennis said in a controlled voice. "I think it would be better if you waited in the car as we agreed."

His tone needled right under Eve's skin. She was as angry with Dennis as she was with Michael Halloran. Dennis had been laughing with her in the car, *flirting* with her, knowing he was coming into a situation like this? He considered a boy torn apart, a victim of God knew what kind of cruelty and abuse, *business?* So much for trusting her intuition!

"Stay the devil out of this, Miss Danaher," Halloran snapped. "You play all high and holy about my past when you've already hooked up with him? I won't be bothering to set things right, then." The laugh that tore from his throat was as ugly as she'd ever heard. "You Americans have a reputation for sticking your noses in where they don't belong. Got this whole scenario all figured out, do you?"

"It doesn't take a degree in rocket science to guess what's going on here! All it takes is one look at this boy's face. Can't you see he's terrified? What kind of man are you, bellowing and raging and scaring him this way?"

"Tell her what kind of man I am, Moran." His voice dripped sarcasm as he turned back to glare at her again. For once Dennis was silent, a muscle twitching in his cheek. Halloran finished for himself. "I'm the sonofa-bitch who is trying to keep your bureaucratic asshole of a boyfriend here from handing Rory over to—"

"The boys own parents," Dennis inserted.

Halloran might as well have stamped his boot heel down on an open wound. Eve could feel Rory's mother's empty arms, the gaping hole in her heart. "You're trying to keep this boy away from his parents?" Eve gasped. "How dare you!"

"It's easy enough for a cold-hearted bastard like me!"

"You have no right!" Eve cried out, words she'd screamed a thousand times in her dreams. "A child belongs with his mother!"

"Not if that child's mother is an irresponsible, miserable failure of a human being."

Eve froze as if he'd cut her with something sharp and cold.

"Halloran, we've all had about enough of your temper tantrums," Dennis warned.

Halloran cursed. Dennis didn't flick an eyelash.

"This is the last chance I'll be giving you. Hand this boy over now, or I close Glenammura Farms for good."

"No! You can't do that!" Tears glittered in Rory's eyes. "Michael, don't make me—"

"You know I have the legal authority to do it, Halloran." Dennis brandished his handful of papers. "One stroke of a pen."

Eve stared as Rory's fingers clutched at Halloran's arm, the boy suddenly looking as if the ex-steeple-chaser was his last hold in a stormy sea. Something was wrong. Out of kilter. Rory's appeal to Halloran didn't make any sense. What in the world was going on?

Dennis folded his arms across his chest, waiting. Too

calm, unaffected. Shame burned the boy's cheeks, but he couldn't stop the tears. Seconds stretched into eternity, agonizingly painful.

"I don't want to go back!" Rory pleaded.

Eve's stomach plunged, Rory's sharp-edged features shifting into delicate ones, red hair suddenly blond, the wisps fluttering against Victoria's soft cheeks as she begged Eve to leave her alone.

"Your father is sober now," Dennis said. "Come, now, Rory, be fair. Your da has worked hard. Been a glowing success in the program. Don't you think your da deserves another chance?"

"That sick bastard has had seventeen years!" Halloran raged. "How many more chances are you gullible eejits going to give him? You want to talk about *fair*, Moran? What about Rory? Doesn't he deserve some kind of chance himself?"

"You're only making this worse for the lad, Halloran. Stretching out his misery. For pity's sake, just put him in the car and get it over with!"

Halloran swore, slammed his fist against the stone wall. Eve sensed he wanted nothing more than to slam Moran's balding head into the stable wall with the same force he'd used to bruise his own knuckles.

"You promised, Mick." Rory's voice cracked, so small, suddenly so young. "You promised I could stay here for as long as I wanted. Like it was—was home."

Home. Was there any word more powerful? How many times had Eve felt her own heart twist with envy when she'd heard it? Home. That place where you belonged. Were safe. That place filled with the laughter of people you loved. One so many people took for granted. One Eve had wished for, even though it was always beyond her reach. But wasn't it possible Rory could find it when he returned to his parents? If Eve had ever had the chance his parents now had, to create a home for the child she'd almost lost, she would have done anything, everything in her power to make it perfect, a Norman Rockwell dream.

"There's nothing I can do." Halloran's voice grated raw, rough, stone against steel. "For God's sake, lad, try to understand."

Betrayal contorted the boy's face, as if his worst fear had come real.

"You have to go with Moran for now," Halloran allowed, "but I'll fight for you. We'll go to court. I swear I'll make them see—"

"The court has already ruled in his parents' favor," Dennis said. "Come along, Rory. You're making this nice lady wait. She's had nothing to eat since yesterday."

No matter how right she felt it was to return Rory to his parents, Dennis's methods disgusted Eve. Dennis talking to this shattered boy about her growling stomach as if it were more important than Rory's devastation.

"Dennis, don't—" she objected. She wanted to reach her hand out to Rory. Didn't dare. "Rory, give this a chance. Maybe things will be better than you think. Your parents love you. Want you back."

"What the *hell* do you know about his parents?" Halloran snapped. For an instant she thought it might be *her* head slamming into the wall. But he turned his back on her, facing Rory.

She couldn't see Halloran's expression, only the iron-hard set of his shoulders beneath his wind-rippled blue shirt. But Rory's emotions were pared to the bone in his thin face. Fear. Loathing. Betrayal. Helplessness. Would Victoria's face have held the same torment if someone had taken Eve's side over the years? Forced Tori to come back to her mother? Eve had known there would be adjustments to be made, but she never guessed Tori might hate her for it. At first—Eve assured herself fiercely. Only at first. Tori would have softened given enough time to heal, enough patience on Eve's part, and enough love. And the one thing in her life

Eve had never questioned was the love she had for her daughter.

But whatever Rory's future held, right now the boy's pain burned real.

Halloran reached up slowly, and she felt the tearing inside the boy's chest as the ex-steeplechaser gently disentangled Rory's fingers from his sleeve. Rory jerked away, fear and pleading changing to outrage.

"You said I'd be safe here! You promised I'd never have to leave! Liar! You're a liar just like everyone else!" Sobs ripped from Rory's chest. Jagged, awful sobs from a boy Eve knew instinctively had rarely cried before.

Dennis grabbed for his arm to lead him to the car. The boy shook free. Sobs choked into hard silence. "The hell with you then, Halloran!" Rory snarled. "The hell with all of you! You think I was trouble before? You haven't seen the half of it yet."

"Dammit, lad, don't do anything stupid!" Halloran pleaded. "Give me a little time—" But Rory climbed into the car and slammed the door shut hard enough to break the hinges.

Mission accomplished, Dennis turned to Eve. His mouth curled in an apologetic smirk. "I'm sorry this got so ugly. Of course, I could have predicted that it would, with Halloran about. It won't take long to deliver Rory to his parents. We'll be filling your grocery order before the hour is out."

Eve felt sick as she looked at that bland face. "I'd rather starve."

Moran's eyes widened in surprise.

"Could you have made this any more difficult for that boy?" She demanded.

"I do my job."

"But it's not a 'job' to Rory. It's his life! Even if what you're doing is right, even if it's your *job* you could show a little compassion. How dare you try to use me to make that boy feel guilty! As if it were his fault I hadn't had any breakfast and his pain was nothing but an inconvenience."

Moran's cheeks reddened. He glanced over at Halloran. It was the first time any hint of anger sparked in Moran's face. "If that's the way you feel."

"You haven't seen the half of it yet," she echoed Rory. She was afraid she was going to throw up as the red compact zipped around in a circle, carrying Rory away.

"Well, at least you're not completely blind," Halloran snarled as the car vanished in a plume of dust.

She felt battered, broken, so raw she couldn't bear it. She wheeled on Halloran. "I could see well enough to know you're as bad as Dennis, making it so hard on the boy!"

"*I* made it hard on him?" Halloran exclaimed. "In case you didn't notice, the lad wanted to stay with me."

"That doesn't necessarily mean this is the right place for him to be."

"He's seventeen. Old enough to decide for himself."

"Let's see. Great decisions made by seventeen-year-olds. Getting your navel pierced. Dying your hair blue. Driving a hundred and ten miles an hour on a dirt road just because your buddy dared you to." Or making love with a boy on a starlit summer night, risking everything you'd worked a lifetime to achieve. Respect you'd wanted so bad you could taste it. A future where you could use your mind, open doors, travel to all the exotic places you'd read about in the library books you'd carried home by the armload. It was so hard to see past the moment at seventeen. To glimpse consequences behind all those delicious experiences you wanted to guzzle down. And afterward? Eve often wondered how many people at thirty-six could look back with no regrets over decisions made when they were so young. Decisions made in such haste, such blind, childish arrogance. Decisions like refusing to speak to a mother who had waited fourteen years to see you.

Halloran's eyes narrowed. "Don't judge Rory or me, Miss Danaher. You still don't know a damn thing about what just happened here."

"I know he's a child. A confused one, an angry one, yes. But still a child. And you're trying to keep him away from parents who love him. Who want him back."

Halloran's lip curled in disgust. "Giving birth to a child is a matter of biology. It has nothing to do with whether or not someone is fit to be a parent, Miss Danaher."

Eve's fists knotted at the memory of what that "biology" had meant to her. Not cold facts of science, but the soft flutter of new life beneath her hand as she laid it on her swelling stomach. Singing lullabies late in the night to let her unborn baby know it wasn't alone. Loving her daughter long before Victoria had fought her way out into the world. Quiet times alone late at night as she nursed her little girl, feeling as if just for that moment she could give Victoria everything she needed, keep her happy, safe in their own little universe. What could any man know about the power of that bond or the magic in it?

"And just who is going to sit above us all, the great high judge, deciding who is an acceptable parent and who is not? You? What do you know about being a parent? Have you ever sat up all night, trying to bring down a fever? Have you ever listened while a child poured out all their hurt believing that somehow you could make things right?"

Have you ever tried to calm your little girl, holding back your own screams of rage and heartbreak and helplessness while you handed her over to the man who had stolen her from you? Have you ever told her you loved her and prayed she wouldn't forget it in the eternity before they allowed you to see her again?

Halloran's hard laugh shattered images so real her palms were slick with sweat. "I doubt Rory's parents ever let him 'pour out' anything besides their bottles of gin."

"You heard Moran. They went through some . . . some program. Got themselves straightened out."

"How convenient!"

"You don't believe it's possible for people to change? You don't think people ever deserve a second chance?"

His jaw clenched, gaze dark, fierce. "How many chances should an adult have to turn a kid's life into a disaster? Isn't once enough?"

"Even in baseball you get three strikes before you're out. Haven't you ever made a mistake, Mr. Halloran?"

His face paled. He hesitated for an instant, but his eyes burned blue. "We're talking about a child's life here, not some stupid game!"

"You're talking about a *family*. Do you know what that word means?"

"Contrary to popular belief, Miss Danaher, I didn't crawl out from under a rock, though Rory's father may well have. Besides, what do *you* know about any of this? It *is Miss* Danaher, isn't it? I doubt you have six kids and a Mr. Danaher back in the States. If you did, you wouldn't be running away from home."

Running away from home. Eve winced, glad this arrogant, self-centered, judgmental hypocrite didn't know the truth. She had no home to run away *from*. She closed her eyes, seeing all too clearly the sterile walls of her apartment, feeling the sense that she didn't belong there. Sometimes she thought if Steffie hadn't insisted on helping her unpack, she'd still be living out of boxes. No. Her place wasn't a home. It was a shell of four walls filled with regrets where memories should have been.

"You and Moran and all the bureaucratic assholes in the world can debate social issues all you want," Halloran snapped, "but only one thing matters right now. I failed that boy, Miss Danaher. Failed him." Broad shoulders sagged, and for an instant stark vulnerability filled those eyes too full of energy, fierce emotion. "And if I live to be a hundred, *damned* if I'll ever forget it."

Halloran turned, walked toward the stable. Eve expected him to disappear. Just leave her stranded. But he crossed to a phone just inside the building. Lifting the dusty receiver, he pressed a red button. "Sean, I need you in front of barn three," he said.

After a long moment, a man limped from the direction of a cluster of other farm buildings. Handsome, with reddish blond hair, he was compact where Halloran was long-legged, bright and direct where Halloran held fierce secrets. This man, Sean, had the most honest eyes Eve had ever seen—not that she had much faith in her intuition after the fiasco with Dennis Moran and Michael Halloran.

"This is the woman who is staying at Castle Kilrain," Halloran said.

Sean's grin was wide as the sweep of Irish sky. "Bridey's American! Welcome to Ireland!" the man started to say, then stilled, obviously registering the expression on Halloran's face for the first time.

"Mick, what's wrong? Is it Bridey? Did something happen to Bridey?" Dread shadowed Sean's eyes.

"No. It's Rory."

Sean looked almost relieved, as if this was a problem he'd expected, one he was used to dealing with. He rolled his eyes heavenward and gave a long-suffering sigh. "That boy is worse than the seven plagues of Egypt. What has the lad done now?"

"Rory's done nothing. Nothing out of the usual anyway."

"Then why do you look as if you're carrying the Slieve Mish mountains on your shoulders?"

"Dennis Moran took him."

Sean swore in disbelief. "How the hell did the little weasel manage that?"

"Said he'd close Glenammura down if I didn't turn Rory over."

"Turn Rory over to whom? Nobody on earth wanted him! Hell, Moran was practically frothing at the mouth he was so eager to dump Rory somewhere, anywhere he didn't have to deal with the lad!"

"The courts awarded custody to Rory's parents." Eve felt compelled to say.

Sean groaned. "Aw, Jesus, Mary and Joseph! Mick, I . . . We'll get him back. We'll fight. Moran won't have Rory for long. We'll get the best lawyers in Ireland. Damn the cost. We'll fight as long as we have to, Mick. And that won't be long since Rory's father barely has two shillings to rub together."

Eve felt her hands tremble at Sean's words as the two men set up a dynamic she was far too familiar with. Courts and lawyers. Poverty and helplessness versus money and power as the attorneys battled over things that would change your life forever. Destroy it if you let them.

"Fight?" Halloran gave a broken, hard-edged laugh. "Do you think that will matter? I broke my word to Rory. It was a miracle he'd trusted me as much as he did. He wouldn't have bothered at all except for that man-killer of a horse—" Halloran drove long fingers back through his unruly dark hair.

"God, man, I'm sorry. Tell me what to do. Anything! I'll call the lawyers—"

"I'll take care of that. You give Miss Danaher directions to town. She can borrow the blue Jetta."

"That isn't necessary. I'll work something out on my own." Exactly what, Eve had no idea, but the last thing she wanted was to accept help from men who were from the same mold as Chad and his parents. Men who believed money could buy anything, even children.

"Don't be stubborn," Halloran said. "The shop is too far to walk to and you have no car."

"A car wouldn't do me much good anyway," she admitted, cheeks burning. "I don't drive. At least, not since I was twenty."

At Halloran's expression, she snapped defensively.

"I live in New York City. You have to be insane to drive there! I take taxis, the subway."

"I guess you'll have to drive her to the shops, Sean. You know Bridey. Not a scrap of anything fit to eat left on the shelves at the castle. Never have figured that old woman out. Does she expect serfs to come offer Kilrain tribute or something?"

"I suppose so, since we've been doing it for years. There's no point in taking Miss Danaher to Dougherty's shop, Mick. You know as well as I do Castle Kilrain objects to modern appliances." Sean shot Eve a wry glance. "Best repairmen in the county can't keep them running in the castle for more than two weeks together."

"Another thing Bridey didn't quite mention."

"Bridey insists it's the ghost," Sean explained. "If you're real polite, 'his lordship' will cooperate. I suppose she figured he'd be on his best behavior with a guest."

"I said I'll figure something out on my own."

Halloran's eyes narrowed in vague surprise. "Sean's right. The appliances at Kilrain are purely ornamental. Damn Bridey anyway."

Sean flashed her a forced smile. "Can't have a guest at Castle Kilrain starving to death, although it wouldn't be the first time. Nasty stories about a siege at the time of Cromwell. Only one solution to the problem, as I see it. Miss Danaher, you'll just have to join us for meals at Glenammura."

Halloran looked as if he'd just swallowed one of his riding boots.

"No," Eve protested, glancing from one man to the other—Halloran, red faced and glowering, Sean wide-eyed and innocent as a baby. "I couldn't possibly—"

"It's only an hour until lunch anyway. Besides, Bridey ate here every day until she got sick. It only makes sense for you to do the same. Tell her, Mick!"

Halloran's glare could have melted lead. "What?"

Sean blinked, completely bemused. "The cook makes enough to feed a football team. With Rory gone—"

"He's not gone, dammit!"

Sean stopped, flushed, appalled by his blunder. "I know that, Mick. I just meant—"

"The last thing you need at the moment is a dinner guest," Eve said. Besides, she would rather join the roll of castle inmates who'd dined on rat fricassee than spend her mealtimes listening to these two plot against Rory's unsuspecting parents.

"Sean is right," Halloran growled. "You'll have to eat at Glenammura. Things are such a mess right now, what difference can it make anyway?" With that, he turned and stalked away.

What difference could it make? Not much besides giving her chronic indigestion and splitting headaches, Eve thought as she watched him disappear. It would be like looking through a time warp, sitting across the table while Chad and his parents talked strategy. Except this time she would know what they were capable of before it was too late. This time she might have a chance to somehow change their minds.

What wouldn't she have given to have such a chance fourteen years ago when it could have made such a difference? The difference between kissing her daughter's soft cheek each night while Tori lay sleeping, or lying alone in the vast emptiness of an apartment that never knew the delightful clutter of toys and storybooks and childish laughter.

But she had never met Rory's parents. Perhaps they *had* made very real mistakes. But this—this *program* Dennis spoke of wouldn't have graduated them, or whatever, if they weren't cured, would it? No one could love a child the same way a parent did. Nothing could replace the need for that love in the heart of a child, could it?

Didn't Rory's parents deserve the chance she had never had? To heal? To love? To make memories with their child? But hadn't Halloran already said he'd do anything in his power to get Rory back? And he was willing to pay to win, just as Chad had been. But there was one vital difference between Rory's case and her own battle with Chad. Chad had had biology on his side. Halloran wasn't related to Rory at all.

Eve stole a glance at Sean, wincing at how honest, how open his face seemed. "What do you think your chances are of . . . of beating Rory's parents in court?" she probed.

"If there's a way to reverse the court's decision, Mick will find it." Sean sighed. "Not a man in Ireland born more stubborn than Michael Patrick Halloran. The first day he brought Rory here I figured it was proof Mick had landed on his head one too many times while he was jumping fences. I'm not proud to admit it, but even now, part of me wonders if it might be for the best that Rory's been taken away."

Eve started in surprise. "But you said you were going to help Halloran fight. I don't understand."

"I wish I didn't . . . didn't understand, didn't know things in my gut that Mick does his best to ignore." Sean shrugged, turning his gaze out across the fields. "There is something in Rory's eyes. I've seen it before in horses that have been abused. Rage so deep they don't care who they kick out at, just as long as somebody hurts as much as they do. You may not know when they're going to explode, but you know damn well that they will. And when that happens, people are going to get hurt."

Of course he was hurt, angry, Eve reasoned. He'd been taken away from his parents. It was natural enough. But he would heal. With time and love, he would heal. "Rory is just a boy," she said. "He can't be that . . . that—"

"Dangerous? Do you ever pick up a newspaper back there in New York, Miss Danaher?"

Eve swallowed hard. She'd read far too many headlines about kids lost, lashing out. What did she know about Rory except for the pain in his eyes? "He's not like those other kids. He's just confused. Hurting." *Once he was back with his mother, where he belonged, he would be all right.*

"Bet every parent of every one of those headliners said the same thing to themselves in the weeks before their kid exploded. Don't get me wrong. I like Rory— when I'm not ready to strangle him. And I hurt for the boy. There are just . . . just some wounds you can't fix, no matter how much you want to, no matter how unfair it is that you can't do it. Sometimes it's too late. It's that way with horses, and with boys like Rory."

A knot of panic tightened in Eve's chest, Sean's words giving form, substance to her greatest fear. Too late. If it could be "too late" for Rory, it could be "too late" for Victoria and for Eve herself. "I don't believe that," she said fiercely, then more softly, "I can't believe that."

"Neither can Mick. Which is why I'm going to fight like hell to bring Rory back here, hoping Mick will prove me wrong."

Fight like hell . . .

She'd learned plenty during her years fighting Chad and the court system for her daughter. She'd learned that respecting authority and trusting that everything would be handled fairly was as practical as believing in Santa Claus when you're in the sixth grade. She'd learned that sometimes being "a good girl" only gave people another weapon to use against you, and by the time you realized it, it was too late. How many times in the past had she wanted to turn back time, do it all again. Enter the court kicking and screaming and fighting with every bit of rage she could find. Scoop her little girl into her arms and run, the hell with consequences.

The last thing she needed at the moment was to get embroiled in a mess like this in a country whose legal system she didn't understand. But even if Rory wanted to stay with Halloran, he belonged with his parents, didn't he? If there was a chance she could help Rory and his parents, didn't she have to try? For Rory. For Victoria. For herself. To prove that there was still a chance, always a chance to heal?

She'd been so sure she needed quiet time, peace, rest when she'd come to Ireland. Instead she needed something entirely different. *To fight like hell*—the same as Michael Halloran—except that she'd be on the opposite side.

7

*M*ichael leaned against the fence, feeling as if every stone in the barrier that stretched across the pasture were piled on his chest as he stared out at the lone horse lost in that field of green. Powerful muscles sheathed legs graceful as any dancer's, every move the animal made poetry. So much beauty, so much strength, endless possibilities etched into every line and curve of the horse's body. Had there been a time when Innisfree's breeder had glimpsed those qualities? Felt delight? Anticipation? That heavy surge of instinct that this colt was special?

Had the breeder's delight been overwhelmed by despair years later when he saw Innisfree, confidence shattered, promise destroyed, the glorious future once glimpsed in a colt's awed brown eyes seemingly snatched away forever?

Maybe Michael had never seen Rory when he was still unbruised by life. Had never seen the boy when there was still wonder in his eyes. But dammit, he knew there were still flecks of gold all but hidden under the rubble of the boy's life. Courage. Tenacity. Without them, Rory would never have survived. And strength. God, there was strength. Strength that could heal wounds or dig them deeper. Destroy Rory and, if he lashed out like Innisfree, wound everyone around him.

One thing Michael knew for certain—whatever direction Rory chose, he would bolt down it headlong, plunging over every obstacle in his path the same way he charged fences when he was astride a horse, not caring if he broke his neck or anyone else's in the process.

Michael shifted, his boot snapping a twig. Innisfree's head jerked up at the sound. The gelding shied and pranced away. Glaring at Michael with suspicious brown eyes, the animal tossed his mane, pinned back his ears, and pawed at the ground as if to say "You again? Go away! Where's that boy? If I'm going to give anyone a black eye today, I'd prefer it was him."

Yet, even though the gelding's thoughts were so clear to Michael in the threatening stance, the way the beautiful horse all but dared anyone to tame him, there were other emotions, more subtle ones, layered beneath those piercing dark eyes. Vulnerability where there was once only fury. A sense of waiting, of expectation, where once the horse had wanted to drive everyone away. And what had made such a change in the animal every other horseman in Ireland had agreed should be put down before he killed somebody?

The boy.

The boy who was every bit as fascinated by Innisfree as the horse was fascinated by him. The boy who had spent weeks standing at this fence crunching on apples, sucking on sugar cubes, snapping off chunks of carrots. He'd claimed that he was just bored and hungry, that this fence was as good as any to rest his arse on. But Mick hadn't needed anyone to tell him the truth—that Rory was trying to lure the skittish horse close. And if Mick lived a hundred years, he would never forget the expression on Rory's face the evening the lad finally discovered that the one treat irresistible to Innisfree was a palmful of grapes.

Magic shone for just an instant in eyes that had been so hard, so jaded. Rory still acted as if it didn't matter—the horse's trust. It was just a way to while away boredom in "the middle of this worthless bog." But after that first, magic afternoon Mick made sure there were always grapes on the table, and Rory never left the house without taking a bunch with him.

For the first time since the sullen seventeen-year-old had come to Glenammura Farm, Mick had felt real hope. Sean's enthusiasm had been more guarded. Innisfree had put three grooms in the hospital before he came to the farm. The horse was responsible for more cracked skulls and broken ribs than any animal who'd lived to tell. It was madness to let a boy near him, especially a city boy who hadn't even been up on a horse six months ago. Michael knew anyone with a grain of common sense would agree that Sean was right. And yet—somewhere in his gut Michael had known the truth. It would be far more dangerous to keep Rory *away* from Innisfree.

Maybe it would've made more sense for Rory to reach out to the farm's sweet-natured border collie or one of the gentler horses that would let him groom them and stroke them and bury his face in their manes when the pain got too fierce. But the human heart wasn't so easy to maneuver, and bonds like the one forming between Rory and the horse were something beyond anyone's power to control. The boy needed the horse. The horse needed Rory.

Michael gave a bitter laugh and Innisfree skittered back with a glare. It made perfect sense, this argument. He knew it was the simple truth. But how could he explain that to a judge? Tell the court about the grapes? Show them the scar on his elbow where he'd landed the first morning he and Rory had tried to cinch a saddle around Innisfree's barrel? Would any barrister or social worker or court official care that the horse had kicked Michael so hard his ears were *still* ringing, but that while he was trying to remember to breathe, Rory had managed to climb up on Innisfree's back?

What value would a man like Dennis Moran put on the fact that Rory had come to the table that night and mentioned that he was going to show Innisfree, ride the gelding in the cross-country event at Glengarry by the end of this summer. And win.

Sean had choked on his slice of bread, and later, begged Michael to forbid Rory even to try. That at best steeplechasing was dangerous enough. On a horse like Innisfree, it was suicidal. The priest who had come for dinner that night had begun reciting Hail Marys and planning Rory's wake. But Michael had merely looked at the boy steadily and realized that for the first time, maybe in his life, Rory had a dream. He'd vowed then and there to do everything in his power to make it come true.

They'd worked. Bloody hell, they'd worked, the two of them. Michael and Rory had fought with Innisfree until they had bruises on top of bruises, and were so stiff and sore at chore time they moved like old men.

But it had been worth every ache to see the changes in Rory. He might still hate the world. But dammit, he was starting to love that man-killer of a horse. And if Rory could love the horse—wasn't it possible that some-day he could learn to love another person? Given time and patience, a safe place where Rory could breathe?

But now, the courts were trying to snatch that chance away from the boy. Throw him back to the place that had hardened him, withered his sensitivity, made his eyes so weary and cold: Dublin with its crowded streets, poverty thicker than peat smoke in the neigh-borhood where Rory had grown up. Hopelessness that ground away men's souls, let alone those far younger.

He'll be with his family.

Michael scowled, the American woman's voice whispering in his memory. He could see those too-wide eyes so earnest, so angry. Hell, it must be won-derful to be so damn sure you were right. He ground his fingertips against eyes irritated by the dirt, but the woman's face just painted itself on his eyelids. Heart-shaped, too pale, framed by wisps of hair the color of new wheat. A mouth full and pink, a perfect bow in the upper lip. Eyes that should have belonged to a fairy

seemed too old in a far different way—not that time-
less wisdom and understanding that would go with her
fairy face. Determined eyes. Defiant eyes. Eyes that
looked at him as if he were something unpleasant she
needed to scrape off the bottom of her shoe.

If Bridey had set out on purpose to find the kind of
woman who would irritate the hell out of him, she
couldn't have chosen any better. But then, the old
woman had always loved complicating his life. About
now, he would be grateful for a simple thief, someone
trying to con the old woman out of the treasures in
that moldy old castle. Someone he could toss out the
door into the mud. But no, Miss Danaher was only a
meddling, opinionated, judgmental pain in his bum. A
stinging burr he couldn't quite reach to get rid of.

The last thing he needed right now was some
stranger sitting in judgment over him while he tried to
untangle this mess with Rory. But damned if he'd let her
distract him. He might have to put up with her during
meals, thanks to Bridey and Sean, but he wouldn't let it
distract him. He'd learned the hard way to keep women
from getting under his skin when the stakes were high.

Michael closed his eyes, remembering too clearly
the scene when Moran had taken the boy away, Eve
Danaher's outrage that Michael had tried to keep the
boy from his parents. So much for trying to tolerate
Bridey's American. The woman had butted headfirst
into that argument, arrogant, superior, as if he were
the monster and Moran the white knight. She hadn't
had a clue what was really going on—what kind of
lowlifes Rory's parents were, how much they'd already
cost him. She hadn't any idea how far Rory had come
since he'd been at Glenammura, or the risk it had
taken for the boy to care about the horse.

So much for worrying about getting things on a better footing with Bridey's guest. Even Bridey wouldn't
fault him for being less than attentive to the woman
now. Eve Danaher was obviously capable of taking

care of herself. Rory wasn't. He had a hell of a fight on his hands, something far more important than seeing that an interfering stranger was cozy at the castle, even if she was pretty enough to make badly neglected parts of his anatomy tingle. The woman had better just stay out of his way.

Innisfree, objecting to being ignored, made a charge toward the fence. For a moment, Michael feared the horse would sail over it. But at the last possible moment, Innisfree dug in his front hooves, splashing up some mud left in a shady place from last night's rain. Cold and wet, the mud splattered Michael's riding breeches. Innisfree glared at him and gave a snort of displeasure.

"I know," Michael said thickly. "I miss him, too."

Ever so slowly, Michael reached out his hand, palm up. Innisfree stretched out his neck and sniffed for grapes. Tactical error, Michael thought in disgust, and promised himself that next time he wouldn't be too distracted to bring Innisfree's favorite snack. Teeth flashed white, only Mick's quick reflexes keeping him from getting a nasty bite. Fury and frustration flashed in Innisfree's eyes. The horse spun around, his hooves kicking out clods of turf as he raced around the pasture like he was possessed.

Michael figured he should be grateful the horse had even come near him. He doubted Innisfree would make the gesture again soon. With Rory gone, it wouldn't take long for Innisfree to go wild again.

Michael swallowed hard. Closed his eyes. Remembered Rory, time after time, dragging himself out of the dirt, dusting off his riding breeches. Time after time, Michael saying they'd done enough for the day. Time after time, the lad moving to capture Innisfree's reins again. Soothing the powerful horse with careful touches and heartfelt words. Then, though Michael knew every muscle in the kid's body had to ache like fire, Rory would climb back into the saddle to try again.

Dammit, no matter what happened, Michael couldn't let those afternoons be in vain. There would be time for lawyers, for planning legal strategy, in the days before they went to court. Innisfree wouldn't be so patient.

Michael turned and entered the tack room, grabbing up Innisfree's bridle and saddle. Both gleamed, polished to a brighter sheen than any other in the stable. More of Rory's amusing himself in this "boring bog." Michael carried the gear out into the sunshine, under Innisfree's challenging glare.

There were a thousand things Michael needed to do for Rory, but somehow, at the moment this seemed the most important. Leaving the saddle balanced on top of the fence, Michael let himself through the pasture gate, bridle in hand. Even if Innisfree kicked him into the next county, Michael wasn't about to let the animal lose the ground Rory had gained. The horse would be ready and waiting when Rory came home.

She was following him again, shapely jeans clinging to her legs, a pink cotton sweater outlining breasts that looked far too soft and inviting for a woman as hard-edged as Eve Danaher. That determined walk of hers warned Michael he'd better think fast if he wanted to get rid of her. In the past two weeks, he'd turned avoiding the woman into an art form. Not that he'd been very successful.

She'd been across the table from him three times a day, sitting in the seat that had been Bridey's for so long. She'd added new smells to the kitchen in the morning—the flowery, soapy scent of freshly bathed woman, that scrubbed-clean glow that warmed her cheeks creamy smooth. She'd added sounds, too. Laughter at Sean's jokes, excited chatter about the treasures she'd found while exploring the castle. Stories about helmets worn by Cromwell's roundheads in the 1600s, bundles of old letters written between a Protestant heiress and her Catholic lover a hundred years ago. A short sword whose blade was battered from who knew how many battles. And portraits by Sir Joshua Reynolds, the corner of canvas nibbled on by an art-loving mouse.

By the time she'd return for lunch she'd be a little more bedraggled. When dinner time came, she'd be exhausted, the satisfaction of all the treasures she'd uncovered plain in her eyes.

He'd almost gotten used to the bustle of her helping to set the table, dry the dishes, peel the potatoes, and the sighs of pleasure as she breathed in the smell of the warm brown bread Sean had just pulled out of the oven.

It was a miracle anyone else at the table even got a slice of the stuff. She'd practically lived on the bread until finally, yesterday morning she'd chosen something softer, admitting that the coarse, delicious bread had made the roof of her mouth raw.

Michael hadn't wanted to be amused by the sheepish look on her face, or the longing glances she kept casting at the slices of bread he and Sean were eating.

He hadn't wanted to notice the way she ducked her head, hiding behind a soft veil of blond hair when she was thoughtful or shy. Hadn't wanted to notice that she looked a little overwhelmed by the chaos of their bachelor household, muddy wellington boots, riding jackets strewn about. Bits of equipment in boxes near the kitchen's old fireplace, where he and Sean could sit and get warm and mend them when the weather got soft. Rain slickers and the empty pen they hadn't had time yet to disassemble, where an orphaned lamb had spent part of his day until he'd been put back with Glenammura's small flock the day before she had arrived.

He almost could have liked having the woman around except for two small problems. First, the way she'd reacted when Sean invited her to see the workings of the farm, the sessions of physical therapy they did with the kids. Okay, so Sean said Michael was always overly sensitive when it came to the kids they worked with. Protective to a fault. But he'd seen people before who couldn't stand to see disabilities. Eve had looked like he was trying to drag her into some kind of nightmare. Almost sick as she scrambled to get out of the invitation. She'd made plenty of excuses and Michael had forbidden Sean to even suggest that she go out to the paddocks again. The last thing he needed was one of his kids picking up on her hesitancy, some woman with a weak stomach recoiling from them.

The second barrier was as irritating as a burr underneath a horse's saddle. That the woman wouldn't stop trying to argue with him about fighting for custody of Rory. Seemed like at least twice a day she was trying to pin him down, trying to corner him, trying to wheedle or cajole, threaten or mentally bludgeon him, argue until she was blue in the face that he was doing the wrong thing with Rory, taking the wrong stand.

Never in all his years had Michael met anyone as tenacious as this American. Hell, she made a whole pack of Jack Russell terriers look like mild-mannered old biddies by comparison. Maybe he should be glad she was scared of horses. He sure would never have wanted to face her as an opponent on the riding circuit.

He gritted his teeth and stalked into the dirtiest stall in the barn, pitchfork in hand, in hopes that mucking out the mess would make it too unpleasant for her to hound him for very long. He should have known better. The only place he really found peace was when he went into the paddocks with the horses, worked at the far end with the animals. Then she'd hang near the fence, watching with wide eyes, trying to hide her terror of the big animals. It was the only thing that held her at a sanity-preserving distance.

Mr. Halloran, if you could just listen for a moment— those words in that feminine American accent were enough to send him diving out the closest window.

Miss Danaher was great at asking him to listen. Unfortunately, she wasn't willing to listen much herself.

"Miss Danaher, I'm busy right now. Unless you want to help?" He eyed her white tennis shoes, then the dirty straw.

"You're not going to get rid of me that easily," she said, hands on hips, her posture pulling the sweater tighter against her breasts. "For the past week I've been trying to pin you down."

"And you haven't been able to? I wonder why? Could it be that I don't want to talk to you? This business with Rory is between the courts, the boy, and me."

She was going to crack her tooth enamel if she didn't stop clenching her jaw so hard, trying to be reasonable. "Don't you think Rory deserves a chance to know his parents love him? To see things have changed if they have?"

"They don't love him. Things haven't changed. How many times do I have to tell you that?"

"You can't know that for sure. When was the last time you saw his parents? Talked to them?"

"They were drunk on their arses the day I picked Rory up and brought him to the farm. That was enough for me."

"You don't believe people can change?" she demanded, eyes flashing fire.

Michael rounded on her, glaring. "*You* obviously don't think that, since you're still convinced I'm exactly the same as I was twelve years ago on the riding circuit."

"This isn't about what I think of you or you think of me. It's about Rory's future—"

"Which has nothing to do with you, Miss Danaher. As for your question—do I believe people can change? Sometimes. But people like Jamie and Oonagh Fitzgerald? Never."

"Don't you owe it to Rory to be sure?"

Halloran scooped up a forkful of filthy straw, threw it out the stall door into the wheelbarrow, narrowly missing the woman. She dodged out of the way—*decent reflexes,* he thought.

"I have nothing to say to you, Miss Danaher. I wish to God you'd quit hammering at me."

"I've been trying to get information from the social workers' office. When the castle phone is actually working."

"Remind me to cut the lines entirely; Rory's case is none of your business. Rory deserves some privacy. The poor kid hasn't had much else. I'm not going over this with some stranger who doesn't even belong in Ireland, period, let alone poking around in the kid's custody battle, and there's an end to it!"

"I have to do something! You don't understand!"

This time Michael pitched the soiled hay onto her foot.

She sputtered indignation, her mouth irritatingly soft, kissable in spite of the sharp edge of her tongue. A crime, that kind of mouth on a woman who could argue St. Patrick into bringing the snakes back to Ireland.

"You do have to do something, Miss Danaher," he said. "Clean off your shoe." That ought to slow her down a little, he hoped, as he stalked away. Damn the woman—why couldn't she just take her shapely little arse back to the castle and dust off more of Bridey's trinkets? Sean said she'd been head over heels in delight over the junk. Why couldn't she just quit trailing after him, stinging at his nerves like a nettle shoved down his riding breeches?

One more week and the case would be over, thank God, Michael thought. In fact, maybe he'd leave for Dublin in the morning. Sean could follow later. After all, there were things Michael wanted to get straight with the barrister arguing their case and, if he was lucky, maybe he could catch a glimpse of Rory, see how the lad was doing. Sean could handle the farm for a few days with the help of the kids who rode here. It made sense, the decision to leave early, for all the most logical reasons.

Not the least of which was the faint hope that maybe if
he was clear across the country Eve Danaher would
give him a little peace.

Thank God for Sean Murphy, Eve thought, ner-
vously fingering the top button on her prim white
blouse. She never would have found her way from the
west coast to this grimy Dublin courthouse on the opposite coast of the country if the man hadn't stumbled
over his own generosity once again.

Why shouldn't she be having a trip to Dublin? Sean
had insisted over elephant-sized helpings of shepherd's
pie. She'd been here three whole weeks and had seen
but little of the country. Mick was already in the city,
and Sean had to drive alone anyway. She'd be company for him, Sean had reasoned, and at least if she
came *someone* would enjoy the trip.

It had seemed almost too good to believe—a ride to
Dublin, to the courthouse, and a chance to argue her
case in front of someone who might actually listen.

The only sticky point came every time she looked
into Sean's face and feared he'd leave her behind if
he'd guessed the truth—that she planned to argue for
the opposite side. That she'd taken the only measure
she could think of since no one would listen to her—
not Halloran or Sean or the social workers she'd tried
to talk to during those times when Kilrain's capricious
telephone service decided to work for a little while.
Desperate measures, yes. Ones that made her edgy,
even though she'd really had no choice—either act or
give up, and giving up wasn't an option.

Still, even this much deception wasn't natural to
her. No matter how just her cause, any hint of dishon-
esty pinched her like shoes that were too tight. Maybe
Chad and his parents had been sly. Maybe Halloran
would stoop to plot and plan. But Sean Murphy had all
the guile of a three-week-old puppy—one very proud
of the tricks he was showing her.

She tried to smile as Sean made his way around the parked car, but her face felt like it was about to crack as he held out a bright-colored pamphlet marked in red. "Map of the city," he said almost shyly. "Marked some things you'll not want to be missing. The National Museum has mountains of Celtic gold. Even a wee longboat with oars. Working at the museum like you do in the States, I knew you'd not want to be missing it."

Eve took the map, realizing Sean must have gone to some trouble. She looked down at the maze of lines and place names. "It was so thoughtful of you. Thank you. But I'm meeting someone else here."

Sean grinned. "I didn't realize you knew anyone in Dublin!"

She sucked in a deep breath. "I don't. Not exactly. But—"

She was going to tell him the truth as gently as possible. She would have, except that Halloran chose that moment to storm down the stone stairway, murder in his eyes. She took a step back, survival instinct at its most basic.

"Don't worry yourself over Miss Danaher," Halloran snapped. "She has plans of her own."

Eve's stomach plunged.

Sean flushed, rising to her defense. He turned back to Halloran. "She's free to do whatever she cares to."

"Oh, aye, she is that!" Halloran's scornful gaze burned through her. "Why don't you ask her what she's been up to the past few weeks."

"You didn't leave me much choice," Eve said in a small voice. "I tried to talk to you."

Sean must have sensed the pain in her voice. He scowled, angling his body so he stood between them. It was a protective gesture that cut Eve to the heart. "Dammit, Mick," Sean growled in a show of temper Eve already knew was rare, "you're jumping up and down on my last nerve with this surly attitude o' yours."

"Surly? That's right, I'm surly. And Miss Danaher,

here, she's a regular angel, that she is. Just ask Rory's mother."

Eve braced herself against the fury in Halloran's voice.

"Rory's mother?" Sean echoed. "I think the strain of all this has gone to your head. I've heard you make more sense after five pints of Guinness."

"She's on their side, Sean. She's even paid for their shark of a lawyer somehow, though damned if I can figure out how she managed it."

Eve winced. It was the truth. The simple truth. Why did it sound so ugly?

"You've lost your wits!" Sean scoffed, so certain Halloran was wrong that Eve winced. "The strain has broken you, man."

She couldn't look at Sean, couldn't bear the puppy-dog trust in his face knowing that the moment he knew the truth it would shatter forever. Trust was so easy to lose, so hard to regain. Not that she'd even try once this was over. Sean would have every right to hate her. She was surprised how much that knowledge hurt.

"Go on," Halloran dared her. "Tell him."

Sean cocked his fist, his face crimson. "Mick, you're going to feel the back of my hand if you don't apologize."

"No." Eve grabbed Sean's arm. She swallowed hard. "What he says is true."

Sean stared at her, dazed, as if the sky had fallen on his head. Eve knew she'd never forget the instant he realized what Halloran had said was true. Bewilderment, disbelief flashed across his face. His voice cracked. "I don't understand. Why would you help those people?"

"I tried to talk to you, but you wouldn't listen, so I contacted Dennis Moran when the phones were working. He caved in to 'hammering' when Halloran wouldn't. Moran gave me the Fitzgeralds' number and the name of a good attorney. I told the attorney to get the Fitzgeralds whatever they needed. Paid the fees with my credit card. Rory needs his parents. And they . . . they need Rory."

"No. Ah, Eve!" Sean groaned.

"They need Rory all right," Halloran sneered. "It would be a damned shame if they had to steal for themselves."

"Steal?"

"You mean Rory's sainted mother forgot to mention the fact that she had the boy stealing as soon as he could walk? Had to get the drink money somehow, after all. Did she mention the fact that they'd leave him in their junk-heap of a car outside of pubs until two in the morning? Not so much as a jacket to keep him warm?"

Eve felt sick. "No. I didn't know. But . . . but they're . . . Dennis said they're . . . better now." Was it possible for someone that careless with their child to get better? Eve wondered wildly. "I talked to them. They seemed so . . ." Normal. Grateful. They'd been treated unfairly because they were poor. She'd heard the stories. All of them except the one about the little boy huddled, cold and alone in the back of a car while his parents were drinking.

"Maybe I shouldn't have bothered protecting Rory's right to privacy. Maybe I should have given you a peek at this." Halloran shoved a thick manila folder at her. "Maybe then you would've thought twice about what side you were on."

Dread thick in her chest, Eve eyed the folder as if it were alive. "What is it?"

"A full history of Rory's childhood, at least what we know of it. Times his parents were reported to the authorities. Times he ran away. Times he was put in what you Yanks would call foster care. One woman even wrote down what he screamed in his nightmares."

"All kids have nightmares. Nightmares aren't real." Eve recoiled at the magnitude of how wrong she might have been.

"Rory had scars in all the places he screamed about. I'd say his nightmares were real."

"Nobody told me. Why didn't—"

"It wasn't your business to be poking in where that boy was hurting, then just walk away from the mess! The kid has more pride than anyone I've ever known, and more grit. Rory deserves some goddamned dignity!"

A thin, harried-looking man of about thirty pushed open the building's heavy door. "Michael, you and Sean need to get in here. It's about to begin."

"Our barrister, Gerrard Egan," Halloran told Eve, then turned back to Egan, who was wrestling with the knot of his tie. "Gerry, this is Eve Danaher. She's been a big help in this case."

Gerrard surrendered the mangled knot and gave a weary smile. "We can use all the help we can get, Miss Danaher. I knew winning custody of Rory would be a long shot from the beginning, but I never expected this. His parents brought in a barrister who could sell an angel real estate in hell." He turned back to Halloran. "How could they possibly afford him?"

Eve's cheeks flamed. Her fingers knotted. Hiring the lawyer had been the one tangible thing she'd felt she could do for Rory's parents. She'd wanted them to have a level playing field at least, a fighting chance against Halloran's power and money. It had seemed like the right thing to do. But now . . .

"I didn't know." She whispered the words again, sickened, appalled. Good God, what had she done?

"Be sure to tell Rory that when he loses the only chance he had to be safe. Cared for." Halloran spun on his heel and stalked into the courthouse. Sean gazed at her mournfully for a moment longer.

"I'm sorry. I'm so sorry, Sean," she breathed. He didn't reproach her. He didn't have to.

"What's done is done," Sean said, then trailed after Gerrard and Halloran, shoulders already bowed in defeat.

Sean was right, Eve thought grimly. There was no way to fix what she'd done. She wanted to slink off to some dark hole, never to have to face Sean Murphy again, or Michael Halloran. Or Rory, with his angry, wounded eyes. But she wouldn't add cowardice to the list of her mistakes. Swallowing hard, she followed the three men into the building. She only prayed it wasn't too late to make things right.

BY KIMBERLY CATES

8

*R*ory looked like hell.

Michael's jaw knotted as he searched the boy's taut face. Not that Rory even glanced at him. Hands shoved deep into his pants pockets, shoulders hunched, chin almost touching his chest, most people would've judged Rory to be just what he seemed—a delinquent who didn't give a damn about anything. A lazy, sullen troublemaker who would spend most of his life in courtrooms and jail cells and rat-infested flats with other kids as lost as he was.

For an instant, defeat punched Michael in the gut. It was just as he'd feared the day Moran had taken Rory away from Glenammura. The boy had turned bitter, the hate crystal-hard in his eyes. Every move Rory made screamed that he'd bloody well never trust anyone again.

But damned if Michael would let him give up, no matter how bad the odds had become. Michael approached the boy, refusing to let Rory ignore all that was going on around him.

"Rory."

The boy flashed him a glance so full of blame and pain Michael had to brace himself against it. Lips twisting in a dismissive sneer, Rory started to turn his back on him.

"Just wanted to tell you I've been exercising Innisfree for you."

Rory hesitated, then sagged back into that surly

stance. "Wasting your time. He's no good for anything. Nobody's ever going to be able to ride him."

"You already have. You told me Innisfree is going to jump again, take the crown in cross-country."

Loss streaked across Rory's guarded features, then hate, the kind reserved for someone who's dangled food in front of a starving boy's face, let him smell it, almost taste it, then snatched it away. "Joke's on you, then. I didn't give a damn about the horse. I just liked seeing you get thrown on your arse. It was great fun to see the famous steeplechaser Mick Halloran out there day after day getting the hell kicked out of him because some kid who didn't know shite about horses said he wanted to ride an animal that should've gone to the knackers long ago."

Rory looked so fiendishly pleased with himself that for a moment Michael wondered if he'd just told the truth. At least a half truth. Maybe their struggle with Innisfree *had* started out as a nasty prank on Rory's part. Maybe Rory had needed to believe that to protect himself, somehow. And Michael had no doubt at all the boy was just ornery enough to enjoy seeing him hit the dirt. But he couldn't have been totally wrong, could he? He'd seen the communion between horse and boy. He'd seen the rare softness in Rory's eyes, heard the unfamiliar gentleness in his voice.

"Know what, lad? You're a damned fine liar. Maybe even good enough to fool me. But there's no way in hell you could fool that horse."

Rory looked at him sharply. "Stupid animal! All but got himself shot, he was so stupid."

"Maybe he did. But along the way he fought enough rotten sonsofbitches to know one when he sees one. And you can ask all those grooms he put in hospital whether or not Innisfree knows what to do when he's facing down someone unworthy of his trust."

He could have been talking about the boy instead of the horse.

Rory shrugged. "Think what you want."

"I just want you to know that that horse is waiting for you. Looking for you every day. Whatever happens with this case, I'm not going to let Innisfree lose all the training you've given him. Or the love."

"Love?" Rory spat the word. "I don't give a damn about that flea-bitten nag." Michael might almost have believed him if he hadn't glimpsed the terror in the boy's eyes, vulnerability so stark, so raw, Michael could see it bleed.

"No, Mick, no more mucking out stalls for this lad. I'm back on my home turf now, and the gang from the street missed me. That glad to have me back, they are. More bollocks than brains, they've got, and without me they couldn't think of new ways to entertain themselves. But all that's changed now that Rory's back in Dublin."

Michael caught a glimpse of three people he sensed Rory had been aware of for some time.

Completely uncomfortable in new clothes Eve had probably paid for, Oonagh Fitzgerald was a washed-out version of her son. The rich color drained out of her hair turned it sickly orange instead of russet. The planes and angles that made Rory's face so powerful, so intriguing, were obscured by sags and wrinkles, as if years of drink and cigarette smoke had sucked the life out of her. Or had that task fallen to the man who stood beside her, bull-thick body stuffed into clothes some other man might have worn to mass?

No question Jamie Fitzgerald had ever darkened the door of any church in Ireland. Last time he'd seen Rory's parents they'd been half-soused and raging, wanting to wash their hands of their son. It seemed Moran was right about one thing. They had changed. There was a smugness in Jamie's eyes, a "kiss my arse" pleasure in the prospect of winning today, beating one of the "rich bastards" Jamie perceived had ground him down. With men like Jamie, failure was always someone else's fault.

The thought that Rory might turn into a man like

his father if someone didn't help him was too terrible to imagine.

The only time Rory had ever let Michael touch him had been when he'd been helping him with the horse. But Michael couldn't stop himself from putting his hand lightly on the boy's arm. "You don't belong here anymore, Rory. You know it. I know it, too."

"It's up to the court to decide where the lad belongs." Andrew Hill, the barrister Eve had retained for Rory's parents, strode toward them, flashy, intelligent, so confident it turned Michael's stomach. As they called the court to order, Michael had no choice but to return to his side of the room, join Sean and Gerrard Egan. He'd expected to find them waiting. He hadn't expected the white-faced woman sitting behind them.

Eve gripped the mahogany rail in front of her, the wood worn light and smooth from other desperate hands that had grasped it over the span of a hundred years. The white blouse could've belonged to a schoolgirl if it wasn't for the swell of Eve's breasts beneath the layer of cloth. Yet even the prim clothes couldn't hide the fact that she looked like she'd been hit by a truck. No small trick since she'd also been the one driving it, Michael thought with a bitter edge. Damn her for looking so wounded when *she* was the one who had turned this into such a mess.

Michael met Eve's gaze for just an instant, wishing he could shove her back onto a plane bound for New York, where she belonged, then turned his back on her and slid into his seat beside Egan. He hated the defeat already etched in the lines around the barrister's eyes, hated Sean's helplessness.

It wasn't over yet! Damn if he was giving up!

Michael braced himself for the fight of his life.

He was stunned when he felt the light touch of a feminine hand on his shoulder. He turned to glare at Eve.

"I want you to . . . to put me on the stand. Do you do that here? I mean, let people testify?"

"No. The judge reads the verdict in tea leaves." He

was being nasty, but she deserved it, didn't she? Then why did he feel like such a jerk?

Color burned two hot spots in her cheeks. "Please. I need to . . . to tell the truth. Why I did what I did. Why it was a mistake."

"It's too late now. It won't matter—"

Egan turned. "It couldn't hurt, Michael. I'm desperate enough to try anything."

Hell, the woman looked so miserable he doubted she could stand long enough to say three sentences. He grimaced, then shrugged. "It's your call, Gerry. If you think it might help."

As it turned out, Eve had plenty of time to regain her strength. Seemed like Jamie was going to talk forever. Without the slick barrister courtesy of Eve Danaher, there was little doubt Jamie would've stuck his foot in his mouth and his case would've gone into a tailspin. But Hill managed to make Jamie look repentant, if a little thick in the head, someone to be pitied rather than someone to scorn. Oonagh could've won a Golden Globe award for the performance she put on, complete with tears the size of the Hope Diamond.

Face buried in her hands, she claimed that she loved her boy. She wanted him home. Even Michael might have believed it if he hadn't caught a glimpse of a smirk on her face as she peeked out at the judge between her fingers.

Egan might as well have been shadowboxing from the moment he began arguing the case. He never got close enough to land a real punch. Michael's own testimony was so raw he felt like the words were being torn from somewhere inside him. Rory deserved a chance. Rory deserved a home.

Everyone was exhausted by the time Eve stood, fingers knotted together. Even so, Michael could see them tremble.

The judge peered down at her through a forest of bushy eyebrows, disapproval blatant in his craggy features. "You've barely been in our country for three weeks, young lady. What could you possibly know about what is in the best interests of this boy?"

"Nothing, sir." It was obvious Eve felt the judge's distaste toward her—someone meddling in business that wasn't her own. "I knew nothing except what I thought I saw."

"Did you or did you not hire this barrister on behalf of the Fitzgeralds?"

"I did, for all the wrong reasons. And now, now I'm afraid Rory will pay for my mistake—" Her voice caught. "Rory wants to remain with Mr. Halloran on the farm. I heard him begging to be allowed to stay."

"You now think Rory should be allowed to remain with Mr. Halloran? I'm confused, Miss Danaher. Did you or did you not contact the boy's parents as his father testified? Did you or did you not find Mr. Hill to represent them? Had you ever met these people before?"

"Yes. I mean, no. I'd never met them before but I did hire Mr. Hill to help them."

"At no small cost."

"No."

"And now you have changed your mind? Are you mad, Miss Danaher? Some kind of social crusader? Or do you just like poking your nose into places it doesn't belong?"

The judge had merely echoed sentiments Michael had felt over his brief but eventful acquaintance with Eve Danaher. But suddenly, she looked small. Fragile. Determined. Michael forced himself to stare down at the pad of paper on which he'd been scribbling notes throughout the proceedings.

"When I heard Dennis Moran and Michael Halloran arguing about Rory, whether he should go back to his parents' custody or not, it struck a raw nerve," she continued. "You see . . ." she paused, sucked in a deep breath. "Fourteen years ago, I lost custody of my own daughter."

What the hell? Michael's gaze snapped up. Sean straightened.

The judge's gaze sharpened. "If my understanding is correct, mothers rarely lose custody in the United States except in cases of extreme parental negligence."

Michael saw her slender throat work. She gave a raw little laugh. But she faced the judge, unflinching, completely vulnerable. "I've heard that so often. You said it carefully, but everyone here knows exactly what you mean. I must have done something terrible to deserve losing my little girl."

Michael's gut tightened. What had it cost her to say those words, lay herself open to the judgment in people's eyes, the scorn she was obviously so familiar with?

She shrugged one white-clad shoulder stiffly, as if working out aches from some old and painful wound. "Maybe I did deserve to lose her. I still wonder if I could have stopped it. But in the end, it doesn't really matter. It happened. It's over and done with. I can't change it."

She raised her eyes to the judge. "I just wanted to try to make you understand why I did what I did, hiring Mr. Hill. I lost my daughter in large part because her father's family was wealthy and I was not. Because they were powerful and I was alone. I thought Mr. Halloran was using the same tactics with the Fitzgeralds. And I jumped in, headlong. I didn't stop to think that just because I wanted my daughter back, because I would have . . . have given anything to be able to tuck her into bed at night—doesn't mean other parents feel the same way."

Hill stood up, gesturing with one manicured hand. "It's already been established that Jamie and Oonagh are eager to renew their relationship with their son."

"Not that you'd notice," Rory drawled. "Haven't seen them a night since you dragged me back here."

"If I ever had the chance to see Victoria, nothing and no one would take me away from her." Eve's eyes glistened for a moment. She hid them beneath lowered lashes.

"Me an' Oonagh were out lookin' for work!" Jamie cried, indignant.

"At two in the morning?" Michael snapped back. But it was Eve who pulled his gaze. His throat tightened, reluctant empathy lodging in his chest. She'd lost her daughter. That was the aching empty place he saw in her eyes. That was where her pain and passion about Rory had come from. Why she'd pushed so hard, argued so fiercely, battered against Michael's nerves until he'd been half crazy, until he'd shut her out entirely. Why in hell hadn't she told him the reason why she'd cared so damned much? Made him understand? Because it hurt too much. He'd been too hard on her. She'd protected herself the way he'd tried to protect Rory's privacy.

Michael cursed under his breath, so many things making sense. Her pleading, her arguing, that last threat—she had to do *something*.

And yet, no matter how much sense her behavior at the farm suddenly made, what the judge said was true. Michael knew firsthand how difficult it could be to win custody away from a mother.

What really *had* happened? He could see how much the loss of her child had cost Eve, but what price had her daughter paid? Michael didn't want to feel too sorry for the woman. In all his years working with kids, he'd known plenty of parents ready to pass blame for their own problems off to someone else: It was the ex-husband's fault, it was all about money; it was anyone's fault but their own.

"I don't think Rory belongs with his parents," Eve said quietly. "I'm afraid my interference in this might cost Rory his future. I just wanted to tell you I made a terrible mistake when I interfered the way I did. With Victoria gone, I've thought a lot about what *I* lost, what *I* needed. I'm just learning maybe that doesn't matter as much as what *she* needs right now. I hope you'll think of what's best for Rory when you make your decision. And I'm sorry for any confusion I've caused."

She sank back into her seat with a quiet dignity Michael couldn't help but respect. Hell, he'd been furious with the woman, but she'd moved him with her painful confession. Was there any chance she changed the judge's mind? He glanced at the older man, saw gnarled hands shuffling a pile of legal papers. Killing time so he could think, Michael knew instinctively. He held his breath, almost daring to hope.

After a long moment, the judge looked up. "This is a question of what is legally as well as morally right," the judge said slowly. "Rory's parents have graduated from a program we put great faith in. They are no longer drinking. We must support the success of this program and we must do what we can to preserve the family unit. Custody is awarded to Jamie and Oonagh Fitzgerald."

Michael's stomach dropped like a stone. He braced for Rory's outcry, wanted to bellow and rage at the judge himself. But the boy went death-quiet as his oblivious parents and their barrister rejoiced. Michael turned, saw Eve frozen against the backdrop of the dark-paneled courtroom, her face stark, her shoulders sagging.

It had all been for nothing. Exposing her painful secrets, admitting to costly mistakes. She'd stripped her vulnerabilities bare—worst of all, in front of him. No small sacrifice since he'd made sure she knew exactly what he thought of her outside the courthouse.

No matter what else he thought of her, the woman had courage. He wished he could think of something to say to her, but Sean was the one who turned and grasped that pale, slender hand.

Michael couldn't hear what Sean murmured to her, only saw her raise grateful, remorse-filled eyes to his. Michael felt an odd sting of envy. Sean always knew just what to say. But did that really matter this time? Even if Michael *could* think of something to say?

FLY AWAY HOME 113

Gerry tapped him on the shoulder. Michael turned, looking into the barrister's tired, strained face. "I'm sorry, Mick. Wish I could have done better for the boy."

"You did more than anyone could ask."

"It's not over yet. You know Jamie and Oonagh will trip up. They'll have a run-in with the garda, Rory will get in trouble, or they'll just get sick of him the way they did the last time and let him run wild on the streets. When that happens, we'll be waiting."

Michael nodded, then kneaded his throbbing temple. "You're right, Gerry. I know you're right. It's about all we can do." But would that be enough? Would Rory understand?

He glanced over to where the boy had been moments before, sitting motionless in the shadow of his parents and Hill. The chair was empty. Had any of the three gloating adults even noticed Rory was gone? Maybe it was better if they hadn't. Let the lad steal off to some quiet corner where no one could see him grieve. Because, no matter what Rory had claimed in those moments before the hearing began, Michael knew he would be grieving. Rory had lost something far more important than a roof over his head, three square meals a day, and a clean bed to sleep in. He'd lost the only thing he cared about. Innisfree.

Michael leaned over to Sean. "I'm going to go find Rory. Tell him not to give up. We'll keep fighting."

"Halloran, wait."

Michael started at the sound of Eve's voice, soft, so changed he felt as if he'd never heard it before.

She peered up at him with haunted eyes. "Sometimes hope has . . . has edges that cut as well as heal."

Michael searched her face. What hopes had Eve Danaher had? They had cut her. He could hear it in her voice, see it in the tender curve of her mouth.

"She's right, Michael," Sean said. "Enough."

Familiar anger prickled at the nape of Michael's neck. "What the—"

"We've lost. It's time Rory started to accept that."

"Damn it, Sean—"

"We can't keep setting him up when we know he'll probably fall, build false hopes when we know it'll damn near take a miracle to bring him back to Glenammura. Dammit, Mick, it's cruel."

Michael reeled at the accusation. "I'd never willingly hurt that boy!"

He felt the brush of Eve's hand, hated feeling so raw when he looked down at her. "Of course you wouldn't hurt Rory if you could help it," she murmured in that soft, pained voice.

"What do you want me to do?" he demanded, looking from Eve to Sean. "Give up? Abandon him?"

"Of course not," Eve said. "Just don't make promises you may not have the power to keep. Don't let him spend every minute waiting for you to ride to the rescue. Maybe Jamie and Oonagh aren't the people you'd choose to take care of the boy. Maybe this isn't the life you'd wish for him. But for now, maybe forever, this is the life he's got to live."

"But it's wrong! At Glenammura he had a chance!"

"A chance," Sean affirmed. "But that's all, Mick. Even at Glenammura, there were no guarantees Rory would be able to stay out of trouble."

"Of course you'll keep working to bring him back to the farm," Eve broke in, a tiny tremor in her voice. "But hasn't Rory suffered enough? Don't let him spend every moment holding his breath, waiting, hoping. It will eat him alive inside if you don't come through."

He wanted to dismiss what Eve said, wanted to scoff at her. What did she know about Rory? He wanted to rage. But it was obvious Eve Danaher knew plenty about suffering. Being eaten alive inside by hope. Despair.

"Listen to her, Mick," Sean urged. "Jesus, Mary, and Joseph, listen to her."

In over thirty years of friendship Michael never

wanted to punch Sean more than he did at that moment. But it was bad form to blacken someone's eye
just because he was right. One more glance at Eve's
face and Michael swore low. "Have it your way then,
the both of you. The boy can think what he likes, but
damned if I'm going to give up on him just because
some brainless judge doesn't have the guts to do
what's right. I want you to hire someone to keep an
eye on the boy, Sean. At the first sign of real trouble,
I'll snatch him out of that flat so fast Jamie's and Oonagh's heads will be spinning without their usual liter of
gin. I don't give a damn what the courts say."

Sean nodded. "I'll go talk to Tom O'Hara. He's the
garda who first told Mick about Rory," he explained to
Eve. "If he still patrols the same area, maybe he'd be
willing to keep watch."

"That's it. Tom will do what he can. He's as sick of
losing kids to the streets as I am."

Sean heaved an audible sigh of relief. "I hope you
don't mind, Eve. It means staying overnight somewhere in the city. By the time I arrange things, it'll be
too late to drive back. Unless Mick wouldn't mind taking you with him?"

Unless Mick didn't mind? Mick damn well *did* mind!
He wasn't the eejit who'd come up with the bright idea
to invite the woman to Dublin. He'd even driven to the
city a week early to get some peace, and considering
the outcome of the day in court, he wouldn't want to
talk to St. Patrick himself.

He opened his mouth to make excuses, but he
made the mistake of glancing at Eve. The once crisp
blouse wasn't half as wilted as she was, her skin so
pale he could see the tracery of blue veins beneath it,
her eyes lost in bruised circles. What was it Bridey had
insisted? Kilrain had called to Eve?

She was exhausted, worn down. He'd be a real bastard if he let Sean drag her around Dublin for the rest
of the night. Knowing Sean, once morning came, he'd

try to take her to see the Celtic gold at the museum in an effort to distract her. More often than Michael cared to remember he'd been tempted to murder his best friend at times like these. No matter what disaster had occurred, Sean Murphy always bounced back, resilient, while Michael wanted nothing more than to crawl deep into a cave where he could be miserable and angry all alone.

Whatever mistakes Eve had made, she *had* tried to make things right. She'd fought for Rory from the very first, no matter how misguided she'd been. For that, alone, he owed her a ride back to the castle, didn't he? Bridey would sure as hell think so. Michael could imagine the blistering scold he'd be in for if the old woman ever found out what a surly sonofabitch he'd been toward her houseguest.

Michael shrugged. "I suppose I could make room."

Eve brushed a strand of hair away from her cheek with a weary hand. "You don't want to ride hours in a car with me, Halloran. We both know that. I'll just . . . just check into a hotel until Sean is done with whatever he has to do."

Why did the image bother him? Eve sitting alone in a cramped, unfamiliar room in some nameless hotel.

"Great!" Sean piped up. "Then maybe I could take you to the museum in the morning—"

Michael groaned inwardly. Sometimes it was terrifying to know somebody so well. Eve looked as if she were about to drop.

"I can understand why you wouldn't want to ride back with me," he admitted. "But you wouldn't have to say a word. Just . . . close your eyes. Think about something else."

He'd meant to lighten things up a bit, put her at ease. Instead, pain streaked across her face. She swallowed convulsively, and for a moment, her eyes filled with tears. Was she thinking of her daughter? Michael

was almost certain of it. Wouldn't anyone think of
wounds they'd just ripped open wide?

"I would like to go back to the castle. If you're
sure . . . ?"

"It's settled, then," Michael could still hardly believe
he'd not only agreed to it, but even given Eve a verbal
shove or two to get her to ride with him. But he didn't
have time to figure out how he'd ended up in this
predicament. An uproar behind him made him turn
just as Sean and Eve did.

"He's gone!" Oonagh shrilled. "Rory's gone!"

Michael rushed toward the cluster of Rory's parents, Hill, and a half-dozen other court officials drawn
by Oonagh's shriek.

"What did you say?" Michael demanded.

"My boy is gone!" Oonagh glared at Michael as if
she suspected he'd hidden Rory in his pocket.

"What do you mean 'he's gone'?" Michael asked.
"He just slipped out to go to the loo or something."

"When I went to find him he'd vanished."

"He has to be somewhere in the building," Michael
said.

"And does he then?" Jamie's mouth twisted, ugly.
"The lad told us what you said! You'd do anything to
get him back. What is this, Halloran? Some trick you
and that fool of a boy plotted out in case you lost?"

"What the hell are you talking about?" Michael
stared at Jamie as if the man's hair was on fire. Some
part of him wished he *had* thought to make some sort
of plan with Rory, but he hadn't even been able to
consider that they might lose. It had been too painful,
the consequences to Rory too grim.

The judge approached from the far side of the
room, scowling. "That is a heavy accusation you make,
Mr. Fitzgerald. Surely Mr. Halloran understands the
danger of tampering with a court decision. The legal
consequences he would face?" The judge turned to
Michael. "You do understand how foolish, not to men-

tion dangerous, it would be to defy a court order, don't you, Mr. Halloran?"

Michael wanted to sneer at the judge, tell him the word "dangerous" had never made him back down from a fence before. But losing his temper wouldn't help find Rory. "I don't know where the boy is, but we damn well have to find him! Stop wasting time. Start looking. He's angry. Hurting. He's just . . . just gone someplace quiet to—" *Cry. Rage. Ache.* Halloran couldn't say it aloud, wouldn't strip Rory's vulnerabilities bare before these people. The boy deserved more dignity than that. Michael dashed off, heart pounding. Rory was desperate. God only knew what the lad was capable of.

Rory flattened himself against the door in the loo, the knob poking hard into his back, panic a knot in his belly. They'd won. Jamie and Oonagh had won. The words kept screaming through him, unbelievable, stomach wrenching, a verdict that hit him harder than he'd ever believed it could have.

Hell, he'd given up expecting happy endings when he was about five years old. He'd stopped hoping things would get better. Hoping just made it harder to deal with the way things were. The way they'd always be for Rory Fitzgerald and the other kids who hung out all night on Dublin's darkest streets.

Maybe those streets had been ugly, but at least they were *his* streets. His parents were drunk, but they stayed out of his way most of the time. And he was finally too big for Jamie to hit. The bastard had quit after the first time Rory had really been able to hit back.

Everything had been familiar, rotten, but expected, his life all mapped out in the faces of the hopeless older men who wandered the neighborhood trying to kill their pain with cheap liquor. He'd known what to expect, been determined to take at least a little of what he wanted, even if he had to steal it. He'd had power with the other kids because he never backed down, would risk anything, fight anyone. He'd had a place on that rotten corner of his until Michael Halloran had charged in and ruined everything!

Rory ground his teeth until his jaw ached, trying to hold back the rage in his throat, the hopelessness, the despair, thicker than any he'd ever known. What right had that bastard Halloran had? Taking him to Glenammura, letting him smell the fresh air, walk without expecting a knife in the back, giving him just a glimpse of something clean and decent, promising Rory could have it, then snatching it away?

Halloran hadn't snatched it away, a voice inside Rory insisted. The man had fought—fought for him. He'd looked like he'd been gut-kicked when the judge had ruled, cried out in denial. But it hadn't mattered. Jamie and Oonagh had won. No matter how hard Halloran had fought, no matter what that blond-haired lady had said to the judge.

That lady—she'd been tearing herself apart, pleading—for what? She didn't even know him. If she had, she'd have run away, scared, just like every other clean, pretty lady on the street who got one look into his eyes. Saw the ugly stuff in there.

Rory closed his eyes tight, his chest knotting hard. He couldn't stand it anymore. Couldn't go back with his parents, back to that street. He couldn't stand seeing men's eyes narrow in suspicion every time they passed by him or ladies like that Eve Danaher cringe away, like they were scared of him.

God, if only they knew how bad he scared himself sometimes—the anger in him so dark it felt like he was drowning in it, the future looking so hideous, so hopeless, like prison without the bars.

What was it Jamie had said last night? *You think you're better than me, boyo? You'll end up just like this—on the dole, with a broken-down wife and nothing but a bottle of whiskey to give you comfort. Halloran and his sort will look*

*down their noses at you, wipe you off the bottom of their boots
like the shite you are.*

"No!" Tears burned his eyes, running down his
cheeks. He swore viciously, punched the door on the
toilet stall. "I can't go back there. The judge will
make me—"

You'll end up just like me, lad, Jamie's jeer raked
through Rory's memory. *Just like me.*

"I'd rather be dead!" Rory cried aloud. His eyes
caught a glimpse of light—a window. In a heartbeat he
was shoving it all the way open, climbing through it,
leaping two stories without even looking what was
below. He crashed into a pile of cardboard boxes, the
wind knocked out of him.

"Hey, there, you crazy?" a little boy demanded.
"You a criminal? A real bad one?"

"Tell anyone you saw me and you'll find out!" Rory
snarled, giving the kid a glare that scared him white.

Rory scrambled to his feet and ran.

Within moments, the courtroom emptied, people
taking off in different directions to search for the missing boy. Michael rushed around the unfamiliar corri-
dors, stopping, asking everyone from clerks to other
judges to sanitation workers if they knew of someplace
quiet, out of the way. A place for a boy to hide. Almost
an hour had passed by the time Michael entered a
water closet tucked out of the way on the second floor.
The window was open so wide it nudged his suspicions. In his experience most water closet windows
were only opened a discreet hand's width for privacy's
sake. This one was jammed open as far as it could go.

Leaning out of the opening, he saw a stack of what
had been boxes below, the cardboard crushed in one
place, as if something heavy had landed on them. Or
had the two boys playing with a Gaelic football below
been jumping on the boxes for fun?

"You there, lads!" Michael called down.

The smallest of the two nearly jumped out of his skin, the older boy looked up as if he expected God Himself was giving him a scolding. When the boy's brash eyes fixed on Michael, bravado replaced fear. "Not doin' anything wrong, sure an' we're not! Free country, 'tis. Can play on the street if we want to."

"That's right, lad, though I wonder what your schoolteacher would have to say about that." Bull's eye. The little one paled, grabbed the bigger one's hand. In a second they were going to make a run for it.

"Wait!" Michael called, cursing himself for his blunder. "I was just hoping you could help me. I'm looking for a boy. About this tall." He approximated Rory's height with one hand. "Red hair."

"What's he done?" The older lad asked eagerly, scratching his freckled nose. "Housebreakin'? Stealin' a car?"

"Nothing like that." *At least not yet.* Michael's blood ran cold just thinking of it. Who could guess what Rory would be driven to try, now that he thought all hope was gone?

The lads looked disappointed.

"How long have you been out here?"

Guilt flushed the oldest boy's cheeks, the littler one tugging on his arm. "Don't tell 'im, Patrick! He'll tell Brother Bernard, an' we'll be cooked."

"I won't tell Brother Bernard a thing as long as you tell me the truth."

"Alphie, here, claimed 'e was sick an' I was a good brother takin' him home t' mam. It's just we took the long way. We'll get home soon."

"Exactly how long a way is this?"

"Hour or so. Just got here when your man with the red hair dropped almost on Alphie's head. Ran that way." Patrick waved a grubby hand. Michael's heart thudded. An hour ago. Rory had jumped through the window an hour ago.

"Alphie wanted to go in an' tell on him, but I

wouldn't let him," the older boy continued. "What if yer man was some kind of . . . of spy or criminal or something. We'd be famous for catchin' 'im, and Brother Bernard would be sure to find out we were playing football when we should've been studying catechism."

"The boy with the red hair. He didn't hurt himself when he jumped?"

"Ran out o' here like his pants were on fire. Don't think he could've if he'd banged himself up."

Michael blew out a breath in relief. He wasn't hurt, but God only knew how far the boy could've run in an hour. How would they ever find him in a city the size of Dublin?

Michael returned to the room where Rory's fate had been decided. He'd obviously been the last to admit defeat. Everyone else milled about, Rory's parents ranting and raging, court officials pacing in agitation, Sean and Eve leaning against a table. Eve's hair was tousled, a smudge prominent on her left shoulder. What had she done? Searched the courthouse attic?

Sean raised his eyes, shook his head. "Not a sign of the boy," he said. "I'm sorry, Mick."

Michael opened his mouth, ready to tell what he'd found. He stopped as Oonagh sobbed noisily into a handkerchief. "How could that brat do this to us?" she wailed. "We've no time t' be tearing apart the half of Dublin!"

Jamie's fists clenched, unclenched. Michael could only pray Rory's father wasn't the one to find the boy. He stalked over to Michael, lips drawn back in a snarl. "Tell you this much, boyo, when I find that lad, he's going to learn right from wrong, at the end of my fist if need be!"

Any thought of sharing what he'd found vanished. Let them run around in circles for a while, hopefully long enough so that he could find Rory.

Jamie's neck swelled, his face brick red. "And if my son is anywhere near that farm o' yours, Halloran—"

Dennis Moran, still pristine in his gray suit, held up a hand. "No threats, Jamie. They're not necessary," he said. "Mr. Halloran knows exactly what would happen if he spit in the court's eye that way. No child would ever set foot on his property again."

"Moran, for God's sake, let's quit this bickering," Michael urged. "Let's just find the boy. Damn, he's so upset he could do anything."

"Like run whining to you?" Jamie sneered.

Michael's fists knotted. "Hell, I'm the last one Rory would run to! Did you even look at your son's face during this hearing? He's furious with me! I let him down!"

Moran eyed Michael with stark suspicion. "Or you set things up so that it didn't matter whether you won or lost custody? I know you, Halloran. I know how far you'll go to get your way when it comes to these kids."

"I barely had time to talk to Rory!" Michael protested. "Stop being an ass, Moran, and make yourself useful! Let's just find the boy."

"We'll find him. I promise you that," Moran said. "And don't think you can just break the rules and do as you please, like you have so often. Until Rory is back in the custody of his parents I'll be so close to you, you won't be able to sneeze without me saying 'God bless you' in Dublin! One hint you've had contact with that boy and didn't report it to me, Halloran, and Glenammura Farms will be empty as a graveyard after a famine. Mark my words."

Michael slammed his palm down on the mahogany table. "This isn't about you and me, Moran, and the fact that I beat you as captain of the football team at St. Malachy's! It's not about playground fights or winning or losing even if you've hated me since you could barely wipe your own nose! It's about finding a kid who is so desperate, God knows what he's going to do."

God knew . . . or did *he?*

Michael went still. His heart skipped a beat. Maybe it didn't matter so much what Rory had run *from.*

Maybe it was more important to figure out where he might run *to*. Michael turned away from Moran, feigning frustration, trying to conceal the tiniest flicker of hope in his face. He had to get out of here. Fast. And without Moran caught like a burr in his saddle blanket.

He caught a glimpse of Eve out of the corner of his eye. Damn, the last thing he needed was Eve with him. What if he *did* guess right? Find Rory? Eve would be breaking the law if she didn't report it to Moran.

But all Michael was doing was offering her a ride to the farm. He could dump her at Kilrain, and go from there. Michael grimaced, and turned to the cluster of people.

"Moran, I'm sure you'll call in the garda, and Oonagh and Jamie will be searching the streets night and day, devoted parents that they are. But someone has to get back to the farm. There are chores to get done."

"You're leaving?" Suspicion sparked in Moran's eyes.

"Someone has to take Miss Danaher back." His story was easy enough to believe. Eve looked like a gust of wind would topple her over.

But her gaze flashed up to his, defiant, so damned stubborn he almost took a step backward. "I'm not just leaving that boy out there somewhere alone! I—"

In that instant, Michael knew he'd have to choose. To trust her, or to find some other way to get out of here. And he'd already seen what not trusting her had cost him, cost her, cost Rory.

He met her gaze, mouthed the word *please*. In that instant all could be lost. One question from her and Moran would be on him like a dog on a T-bone steak. The guy was suspicious enough already.

Deep, soft, gray-green, her eyes searched his.
Please.

"I have to get back anyway," Michael explained. "Horses expect to be fed, and there's at least one of them that would kick the teeth out of anyone but me. Sean can stay here, help all he can with the search for

Rory. Take care of that business we discussed. I'm sure Rory will turn up. He's just mad as hell, and determined to make us as miserable as he is. What do you say, Eve?"

He'd said her name without bite, without an edge, without some shred of resentment. Her eyes widened in surprise and confusion.

The judge stepped over to block his way. "Do you swear you don't know where that boy is?"

At least the judge hadn't asked if Michael knew where Rory would *go*. "I swear," Michael said.

"Don't be forgetting what Mr. Moran told you. Interfere with my court, young man, and I'll make you wish you'd never stepped through this door."

Michael's lip curled. "Too late. I already wish that. More than you'll ever know."

He was surprised when Eve touched his arm. "Mr. Halloran," she said softly, "I'm tired. If you would take me home. Please." Her eyes were heavy with weariness, her face lined with strain, yet there was something else in that heart-shaped face that unnerved Michael. A kind of street-wise, hard-won intelligence, signs that she'd understood, and a kind of trust that made her reach out to help him.

Determined to carry off the illusion before Moran or the judge or Hill, the shrewd barrister, caught on, Michael took Eve's hand in his. For a moment she looked bewildered, let him lead her out of the dark-paneled room.

They'd barely gotten out of earshot when she leaned toward him, whispering. "Just tell me what we're going to do," she insisted as he pulled her along.

"Let Moran and Rory's parents chase their tails around Dublin for a while. It'll keep them busy while I figure out what to do."

"We can't just leave Rory to them! He's so scared and hurt and angry!"

Her gaze sharpened, her brows drawn down in deep

thought. For an instant he felt as guilty and cornered as the truant boys he'd seen beneath the water closet window.

"Halloran, you know something."

It wasn't a question. It was a statement of fact.

He started to deny it, but she wouldn't be put off.

"Don't lie to me. I saw you with Rory before Dennis Moran took him away. I heard you every night over the dinner table. I know you wouldn't just leave that boy. You have to know I care about Rory. I'm afraid for him. I want to help."

She'd "helped" Rory right off Glenammura, Michael thought, but that paled in comparison to what she'd risked in an effort to win it back for him.

"I know we disagree probably on almost everything. Except that Rory can't go back to those . . . those people." He saw her face twist, knew she couldn't begin to call Oonagh and Jamie "parents" without retching. "But couldn't we try to trust each other—for Rory's sake?"

Trust.

She'd trusted him in the courtroom when he'd mouthed the word "please." She'd understood he needed cooperation and had given it to him blindly. Without her he never would have gotten the hell out from under Moran's nosy gaze. She'd fought for Rory. Taken risks to try to help the boy. And yet . . .

Michael chewed at his bottom lip. What did he really know about Eve Danaher except that she lost her daughter, that Bridey thought she was seeking shelter and rest, and that she had the courage to admit mistakes and the tenacity to stand up for what she believed was right? That she had cared enough about Rory to make herself completely vulnerable in a way Michael sensed was far more painful to her than Moran's simple threats of legal action.

He slanted her a glance, trying maybe for the first time to see what lay beyond those large, dark-fringed eyes, that tender curve of lips, that determined thrust of chin. She'd already proved she would do whatever she thought right if she believed in a cause strongly enough. If there was to be a fight, he'd damned well rather have her on his side.

Michael took a deep breath, felt like he was stepping off a cliff, didn't know if the ledge below would hold him.

"I don't know where Rory is right now," he said slowly, "but I have a damned good idea where he's going."

Her face lit up with hope. "Will he be safe? Can we help him? I don't even think he has any money to . . . to buy food. Where, Halloran? Where is he?"

It didn't make a damned bit of sense after the day he'd had, but somehow, for the first time since he'd entered the courthouse that morning, Michael felt like smiling.

"Come with me," he said, guiding her to his car. "I'll show you."

9

Why did everybody in this country have to drive cars the size of sardine cans? Eve wondered, crowding so tight against the passenger side door of Halloran's tiny vehicle it would be a miracle if the thing didn't pop open, sending her sprawling onto the narrow road. But maybe if she did fall out it would be a blessing in disguise. Halloran wouldn't notice—his eyes were riveted on the road as if he were Han Solo navigating his spaceship through the asteroid field.

What had she been thinking when she'd accepted Halloran's offer of a ride? She'd just wanted to get away from the courtroom and the memory of Rory's stricken face, the images of her own past, wounds raked raw again during her futile testimony before the Irish judge. As for Halloran, she had no delusions. He'd used her as an excuse to get out from under Moran's sharp eyes so he could search for Rory without interference. If Halloran had been able to think of any other way to escape, she was sure he would have used it.

The last thing Halloran needed right now was for her to give a jumble of explanations, try to make him understand why she'd done what she'd done. But why should the man bother listening? Why should he be anything except furious with her? Because of her interference, he'd lost custody of Rory and now the boy was wandering out here somewhere, alone, desperate. How could she hope Halloran would forgive her for the mistakes she'd made? She doubted she'd ever really forgive herself.

As the tires ate up the seemingly endless winding roads, she'd curled up so tight inside herself her whole body ached in misery, though not half as brutally as her heart. It was terrifying enough for her to expose vulnerabilities to anyone at all. But to do so in front of a man like Halloran . . .

She'd handed Rory over to his parents by hiring a barrister so slick he was even able to make a jerk like Jamie Fitzgerald look sympathetic to a judge. Then, as if that wasn't bad enough, she'd gotten up and spilled out all her darkest, most painful secrets, her shameful failures, and worst inadequacies. She'd told the world and Michael Halloran that the courts in America had judged her unfit to mother her baby girl. And, as the judge—and anyone else who heard of that loss—had said, it was almost impossible for the courts to take a child away from its mother.

She'd seen the reaction in other people's faces too many times to be surprised by it—suspicion, discomfort, doubt, a sick curiosity. *What was it that she'd done to deserve to lose her child?* The question always burned in their eyes. Along with the certainty that whatever it was must have been terrible. A terrible act by a terrible person. Someone they shouldn't get too close to, must avoid as if they could . . . could *catch* something from her.

In view of Halloran's reaction to Rory's parents—no matter how well-deserved—it was obvious that he was quick to judge when it came to raising children, had set a rigid standard of what was right and wrong. He was a man who saw things in black and white. He'd never understand how easy it could be to get lost in the gray spaces in between.

Even so, it was hard to swallow the fact that he could now justify every nasty thing he'd thought about her.

His thumbnail was ticking against a loose string in the leather wrapping the steering wheel, a nervous gesture that was slowly driving her insane. He was as uncomfortable as she was. But then, it wasn't every day a White Knight Savior of Abandoned Children like him had to be trapped in a car with a parental reject like her.

But it's not what it looks like! she wanted to scream at him. *I'm not what you think I am. I love my baby. I never meant for her to get hurt! I was so desperate, so afraid, so alone. . . .*

Her eyes burned, and she turned her face pointedly to the view outside the window, the sheep grazing beyond it smears of white against a blur of green. No point in even trying to explain, she thought. Not that it would matter even if she tried. He'd made up his mind about her—even *before* he met her. Besides, everything she'd done since she'd arrived in Ireland had merely confirmed his bad opinion of her. What could she say that wouldn't sound like lame excuses? The same kind Jamie and Oonagh had thrown out in the courtroom a few hours before.

"Do you need to stop for a minute?" His voice almost made her jump out of her skin. "Grab something to eat on the way? Use the ladies'?"

Eve fought to control the rawness in her throat. "I'm fine." Fine? She was so "fine" she wanted to throw up.

She hoped he'd lapse back into his surly silence now that he'd taken care of asking about necessities—a bit of consideration she had to admit surprised her. But that thumbnail was tick, tick, ticking against the steering wheel at a rate that made her think of somebody winding a clock until the spring was about to break. The man was thinking far too loudly. Maybe it was better to fill the silence on her own terms.

"Are you sure that Rory is heading this way? Shouldn't we have seen him on the road? A boy alone, on foot?"

"Rory is too street smart to use the main road when he knows we'll be looking for him. He's spent a lifetime learning to stay out of sight when he wants to avoid being caught—by teachers, the garda, his parents, or me." Halloran's voice dropped a little at the last, a kind of sadness tugging at the corner of his mouth. "Besides, Rory won't spend much time on foot." Halloran grimaced. "He'll charm every tourist and farmer he passes into giving him a ride."

"Hitchhiking?" Eve asked, alarmed. "That's so dangerous—taking rides from strangers!" She winced, remembering how she'd justified taking the ride from Dennis Moran.

"This is Ireland, Eve, not New York. Rory's safe enough here."

Safe enough from the crazed lunatics every American kid was warned about practically from the cradle. All the "stranger/danger" shadows that made the world seem like a darker, scarier place. But Rory hadn't been safe from his own parents, or from a bad ruling by the court system that was supposed to defend him. He hadn't been safe, no matter how hard Halloran had tried to protect him.

Maybe "safe" was always just an illusion. Eve had imagined she would feel safe if she and Victoria had been together, if they'd shared a home. If she had been stronger, wiser, a better person.

Did Rory ever think about what it meant to be "safe" the way she had, late at night, alone? Setting up rules and regulations, like the monster-under-the-bed rules she'd made as a child. *Monsters could only come out between midnight and four in the morning. They couldn't get you if you tunneled under the covers, but if you let an arm or a foot dangle off the edge of the bed you were monster chow.*

"You're right," she admitted, glimpsing two children delivering milk to a frail-looking old woman at a cottage beside the road.

"Right?" Halloran echoed, looking bemused. How long *had* she been lost in her thoughts?

"When you said this isn't New York," she explained.

The kids hopped back on battered bicycles, pedaling off. Back to whatever game they'd been playing.

"Do you think that's their grandmother?" Eve had never known her own.

"I doubt it. Just someone who needs help getting fresh milk now and then. The wee ones are glad enough to help her. And later, when one of them skins a knee or gets teased, some little heartache, they'll just happen to come back to the cottage, all by accident, of course. The old woman will give them chocolate biscuits and tea and listen to them when their own mams and das are too busy with work or taking care of the rest of their brothers and sisters. Bridey was like that for Sean and me growing up. It's the reason I always knew once I was done riding the international circuit I'd come home to Ireland."

Eve's throat tightened. Home. Something Halloran had always taken for granted he could come back to. Knowing that home would always be there must have made it so much easier to wander around the globe, chasing after horse races and glory and wealth and women. She envied him his smugness, his certainty. One more reason to dislike him. But she was too tired to do anything except ache.

She hoped Halloran would lapse back into silence, knew she should encourage him to do so by being quiet herself. But she couldn't resist asking one more question.

"How can you be certain Rory will come this way? He already knows he can't stay at the farm. Besides, it's the first place Moran will look. Rory would have to know that. If he wants to run away—"

"There's one thing Rory doesn't want to run away from."

"You?" The ache pushed harder against Eve's heart. What would it be like to have a child trust you like that? Love you? The way Victoria's eyes shone with unshakable faith in her father.

"Not me. It's too risky yet for Rory to care about a

person. But for some reason God alone understands he loves that damned horse."

"The horse?"

"Innisfree. Your houseguest that first morning."

Eve started, remembering the gigantic horse, its thick muscles flexing beneath its red-brown coat, huge, red nostrils flaring in warning. Something not right in its eyes. Okay. So she was terrified of horses. Anything on four legs. But she hadn't been crazy that first morning at Kilrain. There was something nerve-wracking about that horse, something dangerous.

"Should a boy be allowed . . . I mean, that horse. There was something wrong with the horse. Even I could see that."

"By rights, Innisfree should've been shot a year ago, crazy bastard that he is."

"Then why—I thought you were supposed to know horses. Why would you bring a horse like that to the farm, let a boy like Rory near him?"

"Rory was never meant to get near Innisfree. None of the kids were. It's just that, well, sometimes I need a little adrenaline rush. A speed junkie fix." He sounded almost sheepish. For the first time the thumbnail stopped fiddling with the leather string. "Innisfree was supposed to be my . . . er, challenge . . . when I needed to work out some frustrations. Besides, the horse was so beautiful. There was something in his face, pain, abuse, neglect, I just couldn't forget. Sean thought I was crazy. So did anyone else who knew the horse. But it wasn't Innisfree's fault he ended up the way he did. Trainers hurt him. Riders abused him. He was . . . how can I explain? People thought the horse was stubborn, mean, needed a heavy hand. What he really was was more sensitive. Things hurt him more deeply than most other horses, and he lashed out. I wanted to try to—"

Eve glanced over at Halloran, saw his cheeks darken. With what? A strange kind of embarrassment?

"He deserved a chance. I didn't even know Rory then. And then when Rory came to the farm I sure as hell didn't expect the lad to get attached to a man-killer like Innisfree. But once it happened, it made a strange kind of sense, the two of them together. Both wild. Wounded. All but given up on."

All but given up on—but Halloran hadn't given up on either one of them, Eve thought, torn between fierce admiration and a dragging sense of loss. How ironic. She'd spent every moment since she'd met the man coming up with a thousand reasons why he was insufferable, arrogant, obnoxious. Now, when she feared it was far too late to win his good opinion, she was suddenly aware that there was something *fine* under all Michael Halloran's rough edges. Something she wished she could learn more about.

"I think I . . . I'll try to sleep," she said, unable to bear talking anymore. Silence fell, thicker than before. But not with strain and anger this time. Instead, with a raw sort of hopelessness, loss. She'd come all the way to Ireland, tried so hard to give herself a fresh start, but she'd done it again, made mistakes, missed opportunities, gotten it all wrong. Maybe she wasn't so much different from the uncertain girl who had lost her daughter years ago. Maybe she never would be. Once this was straightened out and Rory was found, maybe it was time for her to go back . . . not home, never home, but back to a place where she could at least pretend she belonged.

The isolated stable was dark and still, smelling of fresh hay, manure, sweat, and body heat from the restless horse that paced the stall below and from the man sprawled next to her. Eve's muscles ached from holding still, her throat scratchy with hay dust and rigidly enforced silence. They'd hidden Halloran's car where no one coming to the farm could see it, then Halloran had led her up a makeshift ladder into the tiny loft above Innisfree's stall.

Eve shifted, easing the pressure of old barn wood against her hip bone. She and Halloran had been lying next to each other for almost three hours now, belly down, peering over the wooden ledge so Rory wouldn't see them when, or *if,* he entered. One thing Halloran was sure of was that if Rory thought anyone was here, he'd take off so fast even Innisfree at a dead run would never catch him. Because once Rory knew that Michael had guessed his secret—his love for the horse and his choice of hideaway—Rory would feel too vulnerable, too exposed. His only goal would be to get away from Michael, the farm, and the horse that had made him that way. If Rory *did* manage to elude them then, no one at Glenammura would ever see him again.

Eve shuddered at the thought of the lanky teenager wandering someplace all alone, his experience at Glenammura no longer healing him, but rather, one more wound. Proof that what Rory feared was true—to care about anyone or anything was too painful ever to risk again. What would it mean to the boy if Halloran failed to find him now? What would it mean to Halloran?

She glanced over at the man lying so still beside her. He seemed to take up the whole ledge, fill the small space with long, thickly muscled legs, wide shoulders, a broad chest. Dark hair gleamed despite the dimness, sucking up any light that strayed through narrow cracks between boards or crude windows. He'd seemed so strong, so smug, so invincible during their brief acquaintance. Arrogant, certain of himself in a way Eve had never been. But now, in the dim light of the stable, she saw something new in his features. Strength. Compassion. Courage. It had to take courage to dare to love a boy like Rory. The odds that he'd break your heart along with his own were great. But Halloran had risked that kind of hurt for the boy.

Is that why she suddenly felt so strange? Because she'd never known a man who would have taken on the challenge of Rory? Bet his own peace of mind against a half-crazed horse and a wild, wounded boy who wasn't even his own son?

Whatever the reason, it seemed as if she could sense his worrying, his uncertainty, the slow, steady throb of his heartbeat in the silence of the stable.

She'd eaten at Halloran's table, argued with him, even reluctantly bared her darkest secrets in front of him, but she'd never been physically this close to him—or for that matter, any man since Chad. But as she lay on this bed of musty straw, she was close enough to feel warmth from Halloran's long thigh mere inches from her own. She couldn't help remembering the hard texture of his arm when she'd touched him at the courthouse, or the work-roughened surface of his hand abrading her fingers as he led her out to his car.

Eve had to admit, his touch had felt good, too good. After all, hadn't that been Chad's secret weapon when he'd gotten her into bed so many years ago? She'd never known her father. Her mother had touched her as seldom as possible. Perfunctory tugs on wayward curls or skirts that didn't lay quite right. She hadn't even known how terribly she missed being touched until Chad had held her hand, stroked her cheek.

Even after her world fell apart, she'd had her baby. She'd barely put Victoria down. Couldn't get enough of her downy curls, her rose-petal cheeks, the little creases in her arms and chubby knees. Most wonderful of all, Tori had wanted to be in her arms as much as Eve wanted to hold her.

Then, Chad was gone. Tori was gone. No one but Steffie had since dared cross the ice-queen boundaries to touch Eve. Steff would have been thrilled Eve was even talking to a man like Michael Halloran. And it made Eve damned uncomfortable to think of how gleefully her friend would react to knowing Eve had been crammed into this tiny space with him.

Girl, you'd have to be dead not to feel anything lying alongside a fine man like that.

Eve could almost hear Steffie gloat. *And no matter how hard you try to pretend otherwise, I damn well know you're not dead!*

Maybe not, but it would be easier if she were. She chafed inside to feel *anything*, even the tiniest stirrings about this man. Especially when she knew that at best he held her in a kind of benign disgust, if such an odd mixture of emotions were possible.

Halloran shifted, his elbow just brushing her rib cage. Instinct urged her to move aside, but if she did, she'd tumble ten feet down into Innisfree's stall and she was *almost* more afraid of the horse than of Halloran. Besides, she didn't want Halloran to think she was, well, paranoid. That she thought—what? That he was attractive? That he could unsettle her so much without even trying? Maybe she and Halloran had struck an unsteady truce, but that didn't mean she was about to trust the man with any more of her secrets, her private, raw places. She wasn't even going to notice how silky his dark hair looked, how good he smelled, like outdoors and new-mown grass and wind.

If only this was Oz or someplace where she could click the heels of her ruby slippers together, she'd wish she could erase everything that had happened between them up until now, all the strain, everything that had gone wrong. Then she could just relax, enjoy his presence, no danger, no consequences. She'd wish for a nifty magic spell to set things right even if she succumbed to temptation and—and what? she asked herself sharply. Touched him, the same way she'd been drawn to touch other beautiful things she'd found. Saxon urns, bog wood harps, Etruscan jewels, and Michael Halloran. Somehow, the image just didn't fit, but then, it showed her exactly how ridiculous she was being.

All Halloran had done was made a little small talk since they'd gotten here, let her know he didn't hate her. But what *did* he feel for her? Pity? Probably. She was too scared to hope for understanding.

She was just exhausted, emotionally ragged. Yes, dammit, and *lonely*. All this waiting, all this uncertainty about Rory was making her lose her mind.

Was Halloran as uneasy as she was? No way. He had nothing to be ashamed of. Nothing he'd done would make him feel small and shabby next to her, while she had blown things completely.

Stop it! she told herself. *It isn't going to help to keep beating yourself up this way.* Not that knowing that bit of wisdom had ever done much to stop her before.

Innisfree, knowing his prison was being observed, tossed his head up to glare at her. He kicked out at the stall door, cracking one of the boards with his hoof. Eve gasped, startled, nearly toppling off the ledge. Halloran's arm shot out to steady her.

"Easy, there! Guess I should've taken the side near the edge," he murmured. "I just wasn't thinking."

Don't let it bother you, she felt like saying. *I haven't been thinking since the moment I decided to pack up and fly off to Ireland.*

She expected him to let go the instant she'd got her balance again, but his arm tightened, drawing her closer to him. She gritted her teeth against the sensation as he dragged her full length against his side. Warm. He was so warm. Hard. She could feel the corded muscles of his thigh against the softer curve of her own. His breath ruffled the fine hair at her temple.

"I don't blame you for wanting to stay as far away from me as possible, but believe me, I'm not worth your falling into that stall."

"I . . . I wasn't—" she started to protest.

"I know I've been a bastard to you, Eve. Maybe if I hadn't acted that way things would have been different." He stopped, shrugged, his shoulder shifting against the curve of her breast. But it seemed Halloran was suddenly almost as uncomfortable as she was. Ever so carefully, he loosed his arm, still keeping her from falling off the ledge, but gingerly, as if she were made of spun glass, something he was afraid of breaking.

Color crept into his cheeks again, making him look . . . younger, somehow. More boyish. Nothing like the polished, suave, glittering jet-setter she'd been instinctively wary of in all those horse magazines.

"Rory can ride him," he said unexpectedly.

The words jolted Eve from sensation, emotion she didn't want to explore any more than Halloran did. "What?" she asked.

"He can ride Innisfree. The horse almost killed everyone who got near him. But in the end, he let Rory get on his back. Even if you could've seen it, you wouldn't have believed it."

"How could you let him try something so dangerous? I mean, Rory's just a child."

"Rory's a lot of things. But he's never been a child. It's strange; the reason I brought him here was the same reason I bring all the wee ones to Glenammura. I was hoping he'd bond with one of the animals. Hell, the place is crawling with dogs and cats and stolid old stable ponies who adore kids. People even bring us wild animals that are hurt. I thought maybe he'd take to a hawk or a fox cub. And the lambs orphaned at lambing time—I doubt Ebenezer Scrooge could resist them with their wee winsome faces. But it was Innisfree who intrigued him. Innisfree."

"Sean said this was a fine therapy farm. You must be proud of the work you do."

"The kids are the ones who do the work." Halloran's brow arched, his eyes warming with the first spark of amusement she'd seen since the day he'd found her at the castle. "Glenammura belongs to them far more than it does to me."

"What exactly is it you do?"

"Animal-assisted therapy. It's amazing. The power in it. Hard to believe until you've seen the miracles happen. When Sean got hurt eight years ago, he wasn't expected to walk again."

Were the shadows in the stable playing tricks on her, or did the Irishman's chiseled features darken?

"It's impossible to imagine Sean not . . . not . . ." *able to get around on his own feet, independent, almost swaggering despite his limp.* "How did he . . . he get hurt?"

She could have bitten her tongue when she saw Halloran's face haggard with old pain. Of course it hurt him to think of Sean's accident. If she'd learned one other thing in her ill-starred venture, it was that the affection between the two men who ran the farm was warm and deep and real.

"I'm sorry. I guess you're right about my tendency to pry into other people's business. It's just so hard to think of Sean so badly injured. He's so . . . so *alive.*"

Halloran was silent for a long moment, then Eve met his eyes. Was there trust in them? A willingness to expose something still aching in his own chest? It made Eve hope just a little that things between them could heal. "The only thing that got Sean through rehabilitation was contact with horses."

Eve winced. She'd probably move too if they brought an animal in to help her with therapy—she'd run as fast as she could in the opposite direction!

"He'd do things . . . things we'd all thought impossible, just to feel a horse beneath him again. And the look in the mare's eyes when Sean crossed some new barrier—it was like the horse understood the magnitude of what Sean had done, and understood her own part in it. Felt joy in it. Fulfillment."

Halloran paused, his gaze far away, as if he weren't in the barn lying beside Eve, but rather, watching a miracle. "I'd been around horses all my life. The finest the world has to offer. I thought I knew everything about them. I'd seen more courage, more drive, more will to win in a horse's eyes than most people see in a lifetime. But I'd never seen anything more powerful, more *real* than I saw between Sean and that therapy horse."

He'd been with Sean while Sean was in therapy? Eve mused in surprise. Overcoming injuries so severe didn't happen overnight. What kind of man took a chunk out of his own life in order to watch over a friend? She tried to reconcile the articles she'd read, the pictures she'd seen of Michael Halloran, steeple-chaser, with what he was telling her now. Closing her eyes, she could still see the hard, driven glow in his eyes, the ambition, the arrogance in his smile. Who was it who had said that the eyes never lie? No man could live the way Halloran had in those days without it showing in his face. From everything she'd read it seemed the world had been something to trample be-neath his feet on the way to the finish line, nothing more. Or had she merely judged him unfairly even then because of those vague similarities to Chad she thought she saw?

But she'd picked up the undertones every time any-one had written about him—the thinly veiled jabs about his womanizing, the edge of dislike at Halloran's supposed arrogance, flaws leavened by the writer's grudging admiration as Halloran took the cup again and again and again.

"While Sean was recovering, I watched his therapy, and the other patients working at the facility," Hallo-ran continued. "Most of them were in pain beyond any I could imagine, their bodies broken up from car wrecks, accidents, diseases that disabled them. When no human therapist could get them to work through pain, make them try harder to push back the bound-aries of their limitations, they would bring an animal in to help. It was amazing. Kids with cerebral palsy taking their first steps to feed a dog a biscuit. Adults who'd grown bitter from constant pain, crooning to the horse they were about to ride to stretch their muscles."

He chuckled. "If one of their human therapists had put them through the paces it took to get up on that horse, the patients would have told them to go to hell. But with the horses around, they just gritted their teeth, so damned determined to walk or ride or cinch a saddle girth themselves. And when they'd get discouraged, all it took was a nuzzle from the horse, a minute to lean against their warm flanks, bury an aching hand in their mane, and the patient was ready to try it again."

"But Rory—was Rory hurt? Physically, I mean." The thought of the boy suffering more than he already had sickened her.

"No. He wasn't hurt on the outside, where you could see it. But I hoped that if the animals could heal physical pain, maybe they could also cure pain in kids' hearts. Not only teach kids how to walk, but maybe how to trust."

Eve lay silent for a moment, eyes closed. What Halloran described seemed amazing. Impossible. Not that she would ever be able to experience it or understand it the way he could. She had barriers of her own—built of her fear of the very animals Halloran insisted had worked such miracles. But some people never got miracles when they were dished out, it seemed. Eve never had. And what about Rory? The courts had just snatched away any hope of miracles for him.

She fell silent, looked down at the horse pacing in the stall below. Her eyes burned—straw dust, no doubt. Or was it the feeling she'd always had of standing outside of life, peering in through a window? Not able to touch it or taste it the way other people took for granted.

She started to speak, wanting to fill up the silence, pretend the emptiness inside her away. But at that moment, Innisfree froze, the restless horse statue-still, ears pricked, eyes wide. Halloran's fingers touched her lips to silence her, the Irishman every bit as taut and alert as the horse below them.

Eve swallowed hard, held her breath at the stealthy sounds at the main door of the stable. The door creaked open on protesting hinges.

Rory. It had to be Rory.

10

~

$\mathcal{S}$ilence again. Rory was being careful. So careful. Like a wild animal, so desperate, so hungry he was daring to raid a farmer's flock. And yet, this boy didn't need to fill his stomach. He was hungry to fill his heart.

Innisfree scented him. Any doubt as to who it was got swept away. Even Eve could see recognition in the animal's eyes. Innisfree tossed his immense head, whickered softly. But as footsteps neared the stall, the horse changed, deciding now that his boy was back, it was time to show displeasure at being abandoned.

Innisfree pranced about the confines of the roomy stall, keeping his head turned decidedly away from the shadowy figure approaching. The horse stopped at the far end of the stall, seemingly absorbed in a dark knot in the wood, ears back, muscles taut under his gleaming coat.

Eve's heart stopped as Rory stepped into a narrow beam of light, dust motes wafting around him, making the boy seem only half-real, as if she'd conjured him up herself in desperation. His face was smudged with dirt, his eyes hollow with despair, but his chin thrust out in defiance, determination, like a child shouting down a storm.

"Ah, then, don't be showing me the hard side of your temper!"

Eve's throat tightened. She had never heard Rory sound that way—vulnerable, open, tender. She wondered if anyone but this horse ever had.

"I know I've been gone a long time, but you knew I'd be coming back, now, didn't you?" Rory coaxed.

Innisfree slanted the boy a glance over one massive shoulder as if to say "Oh, it's you. Who cares?" The horse did its best to look bored, but failed miserably. Chocolate brown eyes glowed welcome.

Carefully, Rory slipped up the latch on the stall door. Eve felt Halloran stiffen as Rory eased inside, securing the door behind him. Eve's fingers dug into the straw in fear as she saw the horse paw the ground. Rory looked so small, so uncertain, the horse so big. She glanced at Halloran, saw that even he was nervous for the boy.

"Sure and what was Michael thinking, leaving you in here? He knows it puts you in a surly mood. But maybe it's for the best if you stay inside just now, boyo. This way, I can steal in and see you from time to time and no one will be the wiser, eh? Damned if they're going to keep me away from you."

Rory stretched out his hand, and Eve was stunned to see a small mound of crushed grapes against his palm. "Look what I've brought for you. All right, so I stole them, but they'll taste just as good as the ones from the table, I'm thinking."

Rory edged nearer to the horse, hand outstretched. The horse reached out its neck and took one of the grapes so delicately it amazed Eve.

"There, now." Rory sighed, shoulders sagging in relief. "So I'm forgiven, then?" He leaned against Innisfree, pressed his face against the horse's mane. "I'm tired, boyo." Tears roughened the boy's throat, breaking Eve's heart. Rory sank down into a corner of the stall, lost in mounds of clean straw. He leaned back against the rough wood planks, eyes closed. Innisfree stepped near him, nuzzled his cheek.

Eve's throat ached, her own eyes teary. She remembered all too well what it felt like to be so young, so alone. Halloran's hand closed gently over hers. She glanced up and he cautioned her to silence again.

With impossible stealth, he eased over her to where the ladder led up to the loft. Rory's eyes stayed closed by some miracle as Halloran made his way down to the stable floor, avoiding the rungs he knew would creak. But Innisfree wasn't so easily fooled.

The horse pricked his ears, jumped away from the boy. Rory's eyes snapped open. Eve bit her lip, trying not to cry out as hooves slashed terrifyingly close to Rory's face.

"What the—" Rory scrambled to his feet, dread and fury in his eyes, like a wild thing, hunted, cornered, betrayed.

Michael opened the stall door, blocked the only escape with his broad shoulders. "Easy, lad." He could have been speaking to the boy or the horse, his voice so low, so rough with emotion.

Rory glared at him in surprise and fury. "How—how did you find me? How did you know . . . ?" Terror filled Rory's eyes. He flattened himself against the wall, gaze darting around, searching for any way out. But the square stall was unbreakable, the only one on Glenammura strong enough to hold Innisfree. Sensing his boy's terror, the horse reared and pawed, kicked at the boards. Glimpsing the indoor arena beyond Michael's shoulders, the horse charged the door. At the last moment, Michael moved aside, letting the half-wild animal out into the arena beyond. Rory tried to charge after the horse, but Michael slammed the door shut before the boy could get away, locking both himself and Rory in the stall.

"Get out of my way!" Rory snarled, scrabbling again in his pocket. This time, he came out with a nasty-looking knife. Eve stared in horror, appalled, as if Rory had transformed into something dangerous before her very eyes. Michael took no notice of the gleaming blade pointed at him.

"I'm not goin' back there!" Rory swore. "The judge can stick my parents up his arse!"

"Sounds like a good place for them."

Desperate hope sparked in the boy's eyes. "Just . . . just pretend you didn't see me, Mick. No one will ever know."

Michael frowned. "I'll know. I'll know you don't have a roof over your head. And you have to eat, boy."

"Slept outside before, and as for food, I managed to get the grapes, didn't I?"

"You want to get yourself in more trouble than you're already in?"

Rory snorted in disgust. "What does it matter? I ran away already, didn't I? Besides, Moran and the judge have to catch me before they can punish me, and that they'll never do."

"You don't think so, eh? The judge was mad as hell when we left Dublin, and your man Moran is going to hunt you down like you're one of Ireland's most wanted. He doesn't like to be made to look like a fool, especially around me. We had a rivalry when we were kids. I could ride. He couldn't. His father was a grand old horseman who knew it. When he had a stroke, he gave me the best horse he owned. That horse started me on the road to riding professionally. Moran never forgave either one of us."

Rory scoffed. "Well, I don't give a damn about any of you, so you can all go off and fight with each other. Keep me out of it."

"It's too late for that." Halloran's voice gentled. "He knows what you mean to me, boy, and he knows I'm not going to give up trying to help you."

Startled, Rory took a step back. He hadn't been afraid of the half-crazed horse, Eve realized with a jolt, but he was terrified of the caring in Michael Halloran's handsome face.

"Hell with both of you, then," Rory sneered.

"I'm just trying to warn you, lad. They're not going to be letting this go."

"They haven't found me yet."

"They're still looking for you in Dublin. But it won't be long before they come around here."

"They still won't find me," Rory scoffed. "Like I told you when I came to Glenammura—I can take care of myself. Always have."

"That's so, Rory." Sadness crept into Halloran's voice. "You *have* always taken care of yourself. And you've done a better job at it than any of the adults who were supposed to be watching out for you. I guess I'd just hoped you wouldn't have to take care of yourself anymore."

Eve could see just how much Rory had hoped that, too. It showed in his eyes, despite the nasty curl of his mouth and the dangerous blue light dancing along the blade of his knife.

"I don't need you," Rory said through clenched teeth. "I don't need anybody. I just have to stay out of the way for ten more months. I'll be eighteen then. Nobody can make me go back."

Bravado, pure and simple. Eve had used it to shield herself once a long time ago. But she hadn't forgotten how small and scared and alone she'd felt inside where no one else could see.

"Rory, do us both a favor, lad," Halloran said quietly. "Put the knife away. Only one of two things is going to happen with it out in your hand, boy. You'll hurt yourself, and you'll have to be taken to the surgery. They'll have to report it and Moran will be down here on your back quicker than you can sing 'Rose of Tralee.' Or you'll slip by accident and cut me, and then you'll be torn up about it no matter how far you run or how well you hide."

"The hell I would!" Rory scoffed. "I don't give a damn about you. Why should I?"

Halloran didn't even flinch at the loathing in the boy's voice, but Eve knew how much it must have hurt. He cared for Rory as she loved Victoria. To be rejected by a child you loved—nothing could cut deeper.

Halloran shrugged. "Maybe you don't care about me, but you do care about Innisfree. And you know damned well no one on this farm besides me and you can take care of him. Without me here, with you on the run, there'd only be one thing left for Sean to do."

Rory blanched.

"Be a shame after all your hard work," Halloran said, shaking his head in regret. "Especially since that man-killer seems like he's finally coming around."

Betrayal contorted Rory's face. For an instant, Eve feared Halloran had pushed the boy too far, that Rory was going to lash out with the knife, pushed past the edge.

Even Halloran seemed braced for action underneath that cool exterior. And if something did happen, what could *she* possibly do? Eve thought wildly. She couldn't even get out of the stable and run for help with Innisfree charging around loose.

"You'd let Sean shoot him?" Rory seethed. "You sonofabitch!"

"I am a sonofabitch," Halloran admitted. "But at least I'm honest."

Rory swore, his fingers white-knuckled on the tape-wrapped hilt of his knife as his wild eyes flicked from the restless horse beyond the stall door to Halloran's impassive face, then back again. Eve could see the agony of indecision in the boy's face. It seemed forever, then slowly Rory's fingers loosened and the knife fell with a soft thud into the pile of straw. "I hate you."

"I know." Halloran ran his fingers back through his hair. "But that doesn't change anything here, lad. We've still got a hell of a tangle in front of us. We still have to figure out what to do."

"Let me go!"

"I can't do that, any more than you could open that gate and let Innisfree run free. Try to understand."

"Then I might as well be dead! I can't go back there and I can't stay here." Rory eyed the knife.

Halloran pinned the blade down with his boot sole. "Give us a chance to work things out. We'll think of something, Rory. I know it's hard, but try, lad. Try to trust me just a little."

"What can you do? You going to risk closing down the farm?" Rory shot him a wild, hopeless, childlike glance, full of desperation and disbelief. "No, Mick. I know you can't do that."

"I wish to God I could. If it weren't for the other kids I'd do it in a second, lad."

"You remember the first day I came here? You told me there was a place for everybody. That . . . that maybe there was a place for me here at Glenammura?"

"I remember."

"It was a lie! There's no place for me. I should have figured that out a long time ago."

Eve peered down over the ledge, hating the pain in the boy's eyes, understanding it completely, down in the very marrow of her bones. Oh, God, she remembered it all—believing everyone else fit somewhere, except her, and that she never would. Wishing she could just close her eyes, and never have to open them again to see what everyone else took for granted—the love, the belonging, that she could never have. Hadn't Victoria shown her those few weeks ago that her greatest fear had been right? It never stopped hurting.

She was stunned to hear the sound of her own voice. "Maybe there is a place for you."

Rory cried out in surprise, Halloran's face jerking up to glare at her. She struggled to a sitting position, swiping a strand of hay away from the corner of her mouth.

The boy, distraught enough when he'd thought only Halloran and the horse had seen his emotions stripped bare, went wild when he realized *she* had been spying down on him.

Any flicker of trust toward Halloran vanished, Rory's face turning hard and ugly.

"Didn't want to wait for me in the hayloft alone,

Halloran?" Rory sneered. "Or maybe you weren't waitin' for me at all. Maybe I just stumbled in on you shaggin' the pretty little Yank."

Eve's cheeks flamed.

Halloran scowled. "Watch your mouth," he snapped. "She was worried about you almost as much as I was. For a kid no one gives a damn about, lad, you sure have a lot of people damned desperate to find you."

"She helped my parents," Rory accused. "You should've heard Jamie and Oonagh bragging about their expensive lawyer, their new clothes. And, hey, lady, when this is over, they'll be able to get something besides rotgut gin to celebrate."

"Rory—" Halloran started.

Eve shook her head. "No, Halloran. Don't. Everything Rory said is true. I thought I was helping. I made a terrible mistake. And Rory, you are the one who's had to pay for it."

Rory made a harsh sound low in his throat.

"But maybe, just maybe, I've come up with a way to make things right."

"What way is that?" Rory mocked. "Flash more of your American money around under the judge's nose? No thanks. You've already done enough."

"You need a place to stay," Eve said. "You can't stay here on the farm. But maybe you could stay with me at the castle."

"Eve, you can't be serious!" Halloran looked as if she'd dropped a bale of straw on his head. Rory just laughed.

"You not right in the head, lady? You just saw me pull a knife on Halloran."

"I did," Eve said in a small voice. "You must have been fr—" She stopped. The worst thing she could do was to let the boy know she'd guessed he was afraid. "—pretty desperate to do that," she amended.

"I won't be trapped. Not by a judge, my parents, or even you, Halloran."

"Then it would be perfect, you're staying with me, I

mean. If you wanted to leave the castle I certainly couldn't stop you. Besides, the place is huge. You'd never even have to see me if you didn't want to. But at least it would be a roof over your head. I could bring food enough from the farm everyday. You'd be safe there, until . . . until you decided what you wanted to do. It has to be better than hiding under hedgerows, looking over your shoulder every minute, just waiting for someone to catch you."

"Eve, wait," Halloran warned. "You can't just rush into this without thinking."

Halloran shifted his feet as if the straw beneath them had suddenly caught on fire. Eve wasn't sure what reaction she'd expected from Halloran, but this wasn't it. Edginess, uncertainty. Concern so deep it carved lines at the corners of his mouth. Hadn't he wanted to find something to do with the boy?

"I'm offering a solution to the problem," she reasoned. "A place for Rory to stay. A way to keep the work you do here at Glenammura safe."

Rory's eyes narrowed with just the slightest spark of hope. "I'd be close enough to see Innisfree," he said slowly.

"It's not that simple!" Halloran snapped.

"I'm not going back to my parents," Rory said. "You don't know what to do with me. Only thing you do know is that you don't want me wandering around alone. She's willing to take me in. So, if she's crazy enough to do it, why not?"

"Because she . . . she doesn't understand. Doesn't know—"

"About what a lost cause I am? She saw me pull the knife, didn't she? Heard all the stuff they said about me in court."

"It's not that, dammit! She couldn't even—I mean, her own daughter—"

Eve felt like Halloran had tossed her Rory's knife, and she'd caught it, blade first. Halloran didn't trust her with Rory. Who could blame him? After the disaster at Victoria's graduation, she didn't have much faith left in herself when it came to kids.

Halloran's lean cheeks went brick red. "She could get in trouble with the law," he fumbled, obviously knowing he'd hurt her. "I don't know—"

Eve pushed back the hurt, got a grip on her own pain. "So what could they do if they caught me with Rory?" she demanded. "Send me back to America? I'm willing to take that risk."

"It may be more than—" Halloran stopped, cast an unsettled glance at the boy standing a few feet away from them. "Rory, just—stay here for a moment. I need to talk to Miss Danaher." Halloran bent down, retrieved the knife, then grabbed Eve's arm and maneuvered her out of the stall. It was obvious he still wasn't sure Rory wouldn't bolt. He fastened the door from the outside, locking the boy in those four sturdy walls.

Eve cringed against the boards. Innisfree was pacing the open area, looking huge and mad and dangerous. Hating the stranger who obviously had upset his human friend.

Sensing her terror of the animal, Halloran scooped Eve up and sat her on a high ledge in the adjoining tack room. He crossed to the main stable door and opened it, letting Innisfree charge out into the paddock beyond.

Through the open door Eve saw a blur of red-brown as the horse streaked out into the fresh air, the rich green of the field. Free in a way Rory couldn't be for now. For a long time.

Halloran stalked back into the tack room, shut the door so Rory wouldn't hear them. He drove Rory's knife into the crack between two boards, then turned and came back to Eve's ledge. She looked down on him through shimmering dust motes, the waves of rich coffee-colored hair, the piercingly blue eyes, the rugged planes of his face drawn taut over a bone structure Michelangelo would have killed to capture in marble.

Strength, goodness, compassion—all three were carved deep into his face. They pulled at chords deep in Eve's heart.

"Eve, this is mad," Halloran growled low in his throat. "You can't have any idea what you're leaping into."

"I was there at the court hearing the same as you were. I heard everything they said. And, as Rory pointed out, I did see him with . . . with that knife. I guess I know everything I need to."

"What you don't know is that odds were Rory would use the knife on me. The only thing that stopped him was the threat that his horse would have to be put down if I weren't well enough to take care of Innisfree."

"But you were gone all last week in Dublin."

"Rory doesn't know that, thank God."

Eve's chin tipped up. "I still don't believe he would have hurt you."

"Then you're a lot more optimistic than I am."

"I don't believe that either." Eve crossed her arms over her breasts and stared Halloran down. "If you thought Rory capable of hurting someone, why would you bring him here to the farm? You had other children to think of. He wasn't your responsibility. You didn't have to take him on."

Halloran grimaced. "I thought we'd already established that I'm an adrenaline junkie. There are plenty of people—including Sean, by the way—who would swear I'm dead crazy when it comes to taking risks. Rory is just one more."

"Bullshit," Eve said.

"Pardon me?" Halloran's brow arched.

"Bullshit." It felt good to say it, good to mean it—to be so certain of something for maybe the first time in her life. "I don't believe you for a minute, Halloran. I saw you with that boy, watched you fight for him. Nobody fights that hard for a cause he doesn't believe he can win."

Halloran looked a little sheepish, still plenty desperate. "Maybe not, but dammit, Eve, just because I'm crazy enough to think—hope—I might be able to get through to the lad doesn't mean I'm right. Even Sean didn't want to bring Rory out to the farm. Sean's worked with kids for almost seven years here, rehabilitating them, and there was something about Rory that made him back away, want to let go."

"I know. Sean told me that first day."

Halloran's eyes widened in surprise.

"Sean said he wasn't sure it wouldn't be best for you and the farm if Rory was taken someplace else."

"Sean's got the biggest mouth in Ireland. But at least he's not as crazy as I am, or as dead stubborn. I was mad as hell about everything Sean said about Rory. I was mad because I knew damned well he was right."

Halloran slapped the flat of his palm against a ladder rung in frustration. "Rory has so much . . . so much built up inside him. Hate. Distrust. Anger. I can't promise he won't explode someday and it won't all come pouring out. And if that time comes, I don't know what's going to happen to the person unlucky enough to be in Rory's reach."

Eve couldn't doubt the tension in Halloran's eyes, the very real fear for her. Was she crazy to even consider taking responsibility for this boy she'd barely met? This boy even Sean was concerned about? If Sean couldn't handle him, if Halloran couldn't handle him—what possible hope did *she* have of doing it?

"Not being able to handle the boy is nothing to be ashamed of," Halloran said softly, obviously sensing her doubt. "In the horse world, there are some mounts everyone can ride, others only the best trained riders can even get on. The only chance I figured Rory had here at Glenammura was in working with someone with years of experience, a good, steady, practiced hand."

"You mean *you.*"

Halloran winced. "Maybe so, but—"

"If Rory was at the castle, he'd have a roof over his head and food to eat. As for the danger you're worried about, trust me, I'm a card-carrying coward. There's no way I'd ever be brave enough or stupid enough to get between Rory's knife and the door."

He stared at her, disbelief in his face, uncertain, but desperate enough to hope just a little. "It's insane. Have you ever even been around kids?"

Halloran flushed, the question zinging Eve. "God, Eve, I'm sorry. I don't mean to hurt you, but I have to ask. Even someone used to a whole pack of normal, healthy kids would have a tough time with Rory."

Eve swallowed hard, knowing Halloran was telling the truth. He hadn't wanted to hurt her. He'd had to ask the question anyway. "No. I haven't been around kids much. Truth is, I haven't been around them at all. After I lost Victoria, I—it hurt too much to be reminded of everything I was missing. Even so, what does it matter if I've been around no kids or a hundred? Can you think of a better solution?"

Halloran swore. "I wish to hell I could."

She managed to smile just a little. "I wish you could, too."

Blue eyes sparkled, warmed. No wonder women had been pursuing him over five continents. "It will be all right. The place is so isolated and the road so overgrown there's almost no risk anyone will stumble across Rory. Even people who would have liked to visit Bridey couldn't face the trek toward the end."

"Try it hauling two suitcases in the dead of night."

"I'm glad it didn't scare you off."

Glad? His voice made Eve tingle.

"One look at this place and plenty of women would have run, screaming, in the opposite direction."

"It wasn't until morning that I was tempted."

"You've got bottom, Eve."

"Bottom?" she echoed, confused.

"Courage. I'm damned grateful for it right now." He

looked down. "You won't be alone in this. I'll slip over when I can to help you. No one will think it suspicious. I've been helping Bridey with the place for years."

"Who would have guessed I'd ever be glad at the prospect of seeing Michael Halloran?" she asked.

He chuckled, then surprised her and himself by reaching out to close her hand tight in his own. "Eve, what I'll owe you—I can't begin to explain."

"Don't thank me yet. I'm perfectly capable of making a mess of things, no matter how good my intentions are. You, above anyone, should know that. I'm not going to lie to you, or to myself. I'm scared. Might as well have Innisfree knocking around the castle as Rory. It would be just about the same."

Halloran's hand tightened, bruising the bones in her fingers, a low curse tearing from his lips. "Damn. The horse. I wasn't thinking."

"What is it?" Eve asked, genuinely alarmed.

"There would be no point even trying to hide Rory at the castle. He'd be chasing over to see Innisfree every chance he got."

"Innisfree?" Eve might as well be calling out the name "Lucifer." It frightened her just about as much.

"Someone would be bound to see Rory hanging around the stable yard," Michael explained. "Moran is going to be watching, just waiting."

"Won't he be in Dublin? I thought—"

"Couldn't be that easy. No, Dennis Moran lives just on the other side of the mountain. Plenty close enough to be a thorn in my side. I'm sorry, Eve. This just won't work."

Eve swallowed hard. She could sense Rory's agitation in the locked stall. She could hear Innisfree beyond the stable, trumpeting his displeasure. She wasn't sure which of the two terrified her more at the moment—the wild horse or the boy who teetered so close to being lost forever.

God above, what was she thinking? She was crazy

enough to consider taking on Rory—what did she know about kids that age *period*, let alone one as brittle, as fragile, as deeply troubled as Rory? And now— she must have completely lost her mind. She couldn't possibly be thinking. . . .

She gulped. "Is there someplace on the castle grounds we could keep the horse?"

Halloran's eyes snapped up to hers, widened with surprise and something more, something that set a netful of butterflies fluttering inside her.

"Eve, you can't be serious."

She shrugged. "Rory would be taking care of him. I . . . I wouldn't have to go near him . . . would I?"

"I suppose not, but—"

"Then it's settled."

Halloran stalked away from her, swore, then stalked back. "You know how much trouble you could get into for doing this? There's no way anyone could convince a judge you didn't know exactly what you were doing in hiding Rory from the authorities. No one in that courtroom this morning could ever forget you."

No, Eve thought. *People had a terrible habit of remembering word for word things you would sell your soul to have them forget.* "I want to do this, Halloran. Besides, it's the only way."

Maybe he admired her, respected her just a little for offering to take Rory. But he didn't have much faith in her. She could see it in his face. But then, she couldn't blame him, since she didn't have much faith in herself.

She could see the moment he surrendered despite his better judgment.

"I'll be doing everything I can on my end, trying to find some way to overturn the court decision," he said. "It won't be forever."

"I know that." It would only *seem* like forever.

"I'll try to get the phone working more reliably."

"You mean you could've done it before and chose to just let me stew without it?"

"Maybe. Maybe not." He flushed, looking younger suddenly, abashed.

"In other words, it wouldn't do to make me more comfortable when you were hoping I'd surrender and head back to America, would it?"

If Halloran had been an American, he'd be muttering the word "busted" about now. "I'll only be a short walk away," he said.

A half-hour away, Eve thought with a sudden jab of fear. Anything could happen in half an hour. She closed her eyes, remembering that disastrous night with Victoria. *Anything* could happen in five minutes. Panic knotted in her throat. Reality hit hard.

She was going to be trapped at the castle with an explosive teenager who'd just pulled a knife and a horse that put people in the hospital for fun. She could still change her mind. Dive into the hay and hide. Jump down from the ledge and sprain her ankle. She couldn't possibly take care of Rory if she had a sprained ankle, could she?

"Eve, are you sure?" Halloran asked.

She grasped the edge of the ledge tight and nodded.

His brow furrowed in concentration. "I could leave one of the cars at the bottom of the castle drive, but Moran would be sure to notice it. I'm not sure he's smart enough to connect it with Rory—"

"Absolutely not. We couldn't take that chance."

"But you need some way to . . . to get to the farm. If anything should happen—"

Eve didn't need him to tell her the possibilities for disaster.

"Damn, I wish you rode a horse."

"I'd rather be trampled by a herd of elephants," she said with feeling. "I don't mind knife-wielding teenagers, and I can always run up the tower stairs if Innisfree decides to storm the castle again, but there is no power on earth that could ever get me near one of those things."

He scowled at the wall for a moment, swore low. "I

don't like this. I don't like it a bit. But dammit, I can't see any other way."

"Neither can I," Eve said.

Halloran's big hands spanned her waist, burning warm palm prints into her skin beneath its thin barrier of cotton blouse. Eve shivered at the sensation of being touched—a sensation so strange, so unexpectedly welcome. Was it her imagination or did Halloran's hands linger a little longer than necessary before he lifted her down from the ledge. Eve's breasts brushed a path the length of his chest as he slid her down until her feet touched the floor.

Her knees wobbled for a moment, oddly unsteady. No surprise, she reasoned desperately, after the strain of the past few days, the hours lying still in the loft, hours trying to hold herself away from the hard muscled temptation of Michael Halloran's finely honed body. She'd been right to be so careful, she admitted. It was even harder than she'd imagined to pull away from that warmth, that exotic masculine scent of hay and leather and spicy after shave.

Halloran's eyes burned into hers with fierce intensity for a long moment, a disturbing spark in his eyes before he turned to open the tack room door. He crossed to the stall in which he'd locked Rory minutes before. Unfastening the latch, he swung open the wide, splintery wooden door.

"Took you long enough," Rory griped, hands on hips, feet planted firmly. One look at Rory's face doused the unfamiliar sensations Michael had made Eve feel as thoroughly as if he'd tossed a bucket of cold water over her. Eve wanted to turn, run. She'd spent years mothering an imaginary child, dreaming of what it would have been like to have Victoria with her, to touch, to love, to comfort and give strength to. In those dreams, Eve had always known just what to say, just what to do. Perfect, like a picture by Mary Cassatt. A serene, loving mother, a child with painted-on smiles. Perfect. Until she'd come face to face with a flesh and blood daughter—seen fear and anger and something close enough to hate to crush her heart.

"Rory?"

Eve could hear the warning in Halloran's voice, the tension, knew he was going to lay out rules, regulations, things he hoped would protect them both, things Eve knew instinctively were too brittle, too weak, too harsh to help either one of them.

She caught hold of Halloran's wrist, felt the throb of his pulse beneath her fingertips. When he glanced down, perplexed, she could see the confusion in his eyes.

Let me. Her eyes pleaded with him for a long moment. *Rory and I have to begin sometime.*

She turned back to the surly boy. "Rory, you're coming home with me," she said softly.

"Halloran didn't talk you out of it?" The tiniest crease in Rory's forehead showed just how much he feared Halloran had.

"Dammit, Rory, you know I—" Halloran started to argue, stopped.

"No," Eve answered. "He didn't talk me out of it."

Rory shook his head. "Lady, I can't figure you out. You're either really brave or really stupid."

At that moment, looking into Rory's eyes, so angry, so bruised, Eve would have bet her life on the latter.

11

$\mathcal{I}$t should have been perfect, Victoria thought, smoothing out an imaginary crease in the folds of her black silk skirt as she peered out at the party that filled what had once been the ballroom in the three-hundred-year-old Irish manor house. Graduation was over. She'd almost managed to put that disaster behind her. And since the moment they'd stepped off the plane in Ireland early this morning, the strange new lines in Daddy's face had almost smoothed away.

She was free from school, she'd had the finest education available, and was finally done with the rigid routine she'd had to follow since she was old enough to be sent away, first to Switzerland, then France, then the Academy at Boston. Most miraculous of all, she had the chance to chase the dream she'd had from the time she was a little girl.

Any other father from her class at the Academy would have had a heart attack if their daughter had done what she did, she reminded herself a dozen times a day. Thrown prime placement in Ivy League colleges at least temporarily out the window to ride horses.

It was a dream come true—living in Europe, where the finest trainers could be found, starting lessons with a man who had more wins to his credit than anyone since Ireland's Michael Halloran. What could be more wonderful than searching for the perfect horse, the horse that would help her become the best rider in the history of the sport?

And this house—it was like something out of a fairy tale. So old, so elegant, like a set from one of those movies the BBC made out of Jane Austen novels. And tonight it looked even more magical.

Paper lanterns dangled from the trees beyond the windows like pale, glowing moths, lighting formal gardens that had been planted when James the Second had sat on the throne. The rambling gray stone manor overflowed with treasures from all those historical periods her teacher, Miss Bane, had delighted in lecturing on. But far more important, beyond the screen of darkness lay the finest stables Victoria had ever seen, tucked like a jewel into the green Irish countryside.

There, in that stable, impossibly beautiful, brilliantly trained horses were even now being groomed to look their best, grooms putting them through their paces, getting ready for morning. For *her*. Because morning was when she and her father would go down to the arena so Trevor Butler could start giving her lessons. Then, she could choose the most promising horse they could find to carry her on to the goal they all hoped for—Grand Prix silver, maybe even Olympic gold.

Yes, Victoria thought, this trip to the most famous stable in Ireland should have been perfect.

It *would* have been perfect except for just one thing. Eleven children racketed around Butler House, tromping over carpets with muddy boots, whole packs of dogs trailing in their wake. Nobody, not their horse-trainer father or their mother with her worn riding breeches and laugh-lined face seemed to care that the whole place was in a constant state of chaos that would have made an attack by Oliver Cromwell cozy by comparison. The decibel levels stayed somewhere between road construction work and a rock concert. And the Butler kids—they were always looking at her like she had a giant red spot painted on the end of her nose, Victoria thought with an inward shudder.

As if things weren't bad enough, Mrs. Butler had wanted to make "our new visitor's first night in Ireland one to remember!" The woman had invited everyone in Ireland between the ages of seventeen and twenty to a party tonight so Victoria could "start getting acquainted." After all, Mrs. Butler wouldn't want the "poor girl" to feel lonely.

Lonely? Victoria thought grimly. She'd be grateful if she could just hear herself think!

No, in all the time she'd been dreaming of this trip to Ireland, she hadn't once envisioned it turning out quite this way. Horses she'd imagined plenty of. The wind in her face, the dizzying slam of her heart against her ribs every time she landed a perfect jump. She'd pictured just how it would happen—that immediate fierce bond she'd feel when she found the right horse—that sense of *destiny.* The way her father's eyes would shine with pride when she won. She'd pictured it all a thousand times. But never once had she imagined being crowded in by so many people. People who were always watching her, making her hands feel too clumsy, her feet too big. People who all knew each other while she was alone.

Wistful, Victoria peered out into the packed room from her hiding place behind a bronze statue of William of Orange at the battle of the Boyne.

I know 'tis hard at first, the all-knowing, wise Mrs. Butler had attempted to soothe Victoria earlier, *but these kids all ride at our stables and they're as horse-mad as you are. You'll be grand friends before you know it. Just grand.*

Victoria doubted it. Most of these kids were riders who'd known each other forever. The last thing they needed was a new friend. They already had plenty. Fit in perfectly. They knew the inside jokes and all those secret codes that got you into the cliques that had always left Victoria an outsider. And if that wasn't a big enough obstacle to her fitting in, there was an even worse one. Competition. These kids wouldn't appreciate a new rider taking over turf they'd worked a lifetime to win.

Victoria winced, shrinking back into the shadows a little deeper, trying to hold back a twinge of hurt. No. The truth was that the last thing these kids would want to do was give her a chance. She wished Mrs. Butler had just left her alone the way everybody else always had. Let her fend for herself. Figure things out on her own. It made her jittery inside knowing that a complete stranger had guessed how nervous she was. After all, she'd fooled Daddy for eighteen years.

He'd been all smiles when Mrs. Butler had scooped him away from the party with a wise nod. *Time for us to leave, let the young ones get to know each other on their own terms.*

And he'd never once doubted she'd be great at plunging in headfirst. Or that the whole world would adore her as much as he did.

"Have you seen the new girl ride yet?"

Victoria stiffened as a girl with hair the color of ginger asked the oldest Butler girl.

Victoria looked for someplace to slip away unnoticed, but she was trapped by William of Orange, no place to escape. The last thing she wanted was to hear herself being discussed by strangers.

"You know Da," Dara Butler said with a shrug. "He never rushes anything. Wants her to be rested so he can get an accurate opinion of how she can ride. First impressions, and all that. But they can buy any horse in the stable, they've got so much money."

"Money doesn't mean she can ride. Besides, the best horse is mine. Your da said I could ride him and I'm sure not giving him up." The ginger-haired girl made a face. "I suppose your mam is pushing you to be best friends with her."

Dara Butler shrugged, tossing her head so her dark

hair shone. "You know how mothers are. She says I'm to feel sorry for Victoria."

Victoria cringed. Sorry for her?

Dara's voice changed to mimic her mother's. "You can take a few moments to be specially kind to Victoria, Dara. Think what it would be if you had no mother to love you. Poor little thing."

Victoria dug her nails into her palms, hating the sudden stinging in her eyes. Her cheeks burned with humiliation. It was hard enough being in a place with so many strangers, but to feel like they were all whispering behind her back about the fact that she didn't have a mother made her chafe.

"How old is she anyway?" the ginger-haired girl asked.

"Mam said she's eighteen like us."

"Eighteen?" the snotty girl scoffed. "She acts lots younger than that. Maybe we should send her upstairs to play with your sister Katie."

Katie Butler was about five years old. The words stung, tightening a knot in Victoria's chest, a panicky feeling of needing to escape. Victoria shoved it down. She couldn't let them know the words had cut deep. Even embarrassing Dara and her snit of a friend was far better than being trapped here, having to listen to any more of this. All she had to do was get past them, make a run—or more like a *walk* for it. She swiped the unexpected moisture away from her eyes with one hand, then stepped out from the shadow of the statue, all but bumping into the two girls.

"Oh, excuse me," she said, trying to slip past the girls as hot color spilled into Dara's cheeks. "I was just looking at the statue. Your mother was saying it's been in the house three hundred years." She almost made good her escape, but a cluster of boys goofing around with each other blocked her way.

Dara looked like she wished she was buried under the statue's bronze base. Victoria wanted to dislike her, but it was hard when the girl looked so genuinely miserable. "V–Victoria, I'm sorry. I didn't see you there."

That was obvious, Victoria thought, trying hard not to blush.

"Can I get you some more punch?" Dara said, obviously scrambling to make things better. "There are some other people I wanted you to meet. This is my best friend, Clare."

Clare was easier to dislike. Victoria had never seen anyone quite so smug. "Welcome to Ireland," the girl said. "I'm that anxious to see you ride. Will you be having a go at it in the morning?"

The thought of Clare watching her on her first morning on a new horse with a new trainer was too grim to consider.

"I'm pretty tired from the trip. I'll probably wait until the afternoon," Victoria said. Hopefully that way she'd have found the horse she'd been looking for and would have ridden out her first-day jitters.

"Oh," Dara forced a smile. She was probably terrified her mother would find out about what she'd said.

Maybe Dara and Clare thought she acted young, but Victoria wasn't about to run tattling to Dara's mother. It wouldn't hurt anything to let them sweat it, though.

"I'll tell Da," Dara offered. "I know he planned on going to the stables early."

Tell Trevor Butler? Victoria knew a moment's panic. Let him think she was too much of a wimp to make it out of bed early in the morning? No way. She knew how important it was to make a good impression on the trainer. Show him she was serious about winning. After all, hadn't Daddy reminded her a dozen times on the plane? She only wanted to buy herself a little time without witches like Clare staring daggers at her.

"I'll tell Mr. Butler myself on the way up to my room," Victoria said. "Good night."

"But you can't leave yet. Mam will kill me if she finds out." Dara plucked at one of the buttons on her blouse. "I mean, she wanted you to meet everyone. I haven't been doing a very good job introducing you. Clare just got back from England. She won the Ferringer Cup and we haven't had time to talk yet."

Too bad, Victoria thought, hating the fact that *she* was the main topic of conversation.

"My father and I will be here all year," Victoria dismissed Dara's concern. "I'm sure I'll meet everyone at the stables."

I'll be the one everybody is staring at, watching, waiting to see make a mistake, Victoria thought, hiding a grimace. *If I do screw up, some of these kids might even decide to like me, but if things go the way Daddy and I plan, they'll be shaking in their riding boots by the time I leave the arena.*

"Your father is staying here with you while you train?" Clare asked sweetly. Victoria flushed, knowing the girl was making fun of her. "But Dara said you were eighteen."

"Daddy's got plenty of business he can do here in Ireland. He loves to watch me ride. Said he wouldn't miss it for the world."

"Isn't that . . . lovely. Well, Dara, I'll not be distracting you from doing your duty by er—what was your name again? Ah, yes! Victoria. Dara, you'll have to come over sometime and help me find someplace to fit my new trophies. Every shelf in the house is positively stuffed with them." Clare laughed, turned her back pointedly on Victoria to talk to a tall boy with perfect teeth.

Dara turned even redder. "I really am sorry." She looked so guilty it made Victoria squirm. Dara might have rotten taste in friends, but it probably wasn't every day she accidentally slammed a "poor motherless little thing."

She wasn't motherless, Victoria had almost said, hating their pity and the flash of an image in her memory. Soft honey-blond curls, wide, pleading eyes, a face that looked uncomfortably like her own. No. She wasn't motherless, no matter how hard she and Daddy tried to pretend that she was. She was just nervous.

Miserable. Rotten at fitting in. She had to get out of here. Now.

Her face felt like it was going to crack when she smiled. "Good night. The party was lovely." One more "lovely" nightmare.

Victoria set her punch glass on the edge of a table and wove through the crowd, head down, striding so purposefully few people tried to stop her. She ignored the one boy who called out her name, pretending she hadn't heard him.

She just wanted to get away, to be quiet, alone. To be able to sag down into a chair instead of sitting up straight, to not have to think up something to say to people she didn't want to talk to.

She sneaked past the room where the adults were laughing and chatting over their brandies, relieved when the eagle-eyed Mrs. Butler didn't catch her. Victoria sighed in relief as she rounded a corner, *home free*, she thought, as she neared the suite of rooms Butler had given her and her father.

Victoria frowned. She didn't remember leaving her door open. She always took care to keep it closed. Shut everyone out of her private space. She opened the door, stunned to find the bed already occupied by three red and white spaniels and Katie Butler, aged five.

Victoria hesitated, gripping the door handle. Had she made a wrong turn? The house was like a maze! Had she entered the wrong room? The thought of traipsing through the endless hallways trying to find her room made her brain ache. She'd rather stay lost forever than admit to Dara she'd forgotten where her room was. Besides, if she wandered around on her own, someone was sure to see her and start asking those questions she hated.

Is something the matter? Aren't you having a good time? You can't possibly be tired yet, go join the party!

She glanced around the room one last time, confused. It looked like the one she remembered. True, she'd barely been in it any time at all. She'd been in too much of a hurry to get to the place that was really important—the stables. But the little desk under the window looked familiar and she was sure she'd seen the Stubbs print of a horse. In one of the reams of horse books she'd collected over the years? Or had she seen it this morning through a haze of jet lag?

Katie Butler had lived here her whole life. The little girl would hardly make a mistake. She started to back out, meaning to close the door again, when she froze, her gaze lighting on a pair of riding boots tucked under a chair.

Victoria might not remember the color of drapes and bedspreads, but there was no way she'd miss her lucky riding boots. They stood at attention, the way her riding boots had in every room she'd ever lived in. Waiting, ready for the moment she could escape to the pastures. Worn in all the right places, the supple leather scratched where her old horse, Bottom Line, had scraped her leg against a tree, the boots were one of the few things she'd bothered to unpack when she and Daddy had arrived. The rest of her stuff was still in her opened suitcase, which looked a lot messier than she remembered leaving it.

Terrific, she thought. This *was* her room, but that didn't make things much better. What was she supposed to do now? She couldn't even get away from the Butlers in her own bed!

Just then one of the spaniels lifted its head, giving a cheery yip of welcome. Not even a dog should be that cheerful when wakened from a dead sleep. The little girl stirred, sat up, rubbing the curls out of her eyes.

"Mammy?" Katie Butler asked, groggy. "Did you bring my cake?"

Chubby fists fell away from cornflower blue eyes, Katie's mouth forming a surprised O as she saw Victoria in the doorway.

"You're not s'posed to be here!" the little girl accused, giving Victoria a wounded glare.

"Um, this is—I think this is my room. My boots are over there."

It didn't seem like she had a very strong claim on the bed compared to Katie, what with her pack of dogs sprawled all over the covers.

"I mean you're not s'posed to be here *yet*. There's a party, you know."

Victoria resisted the urge to roll her eyes. If only she *didn't* know. "I got tired."

"I got tired, too. When you get tired, you go to bed. Mammy and Da are always telling me that. 'Katie, you're tired. Go to bed.' So I did."

"Don't you have your, uh, your own bed?"

"Don't want crumbs in *my* bed. They stick me when I'm trying to sleep."

Victoria stared at her. She'd never been around little kids—well, not since she'd been one herself. Even then she'd preferred the company of horses. "Crumbs?" Victoria repeated, hoping it might get the kid to start making sense.

"Mammy always brings me a plate with things on it since too many people 'round makes me all itchy. I'm 'lergic to parties."

Allergic to parties? Victoria almost had to smile. Next time she wanted to duck out of somewhere, maybe she'd try Katie's excuse. Poor kid. If lots of people around made her "itchy," she must be miserable in this house.

"My mammy was 'lergic to parties when she was my age, so she never makes me go. But I'm not 'lergic to cake. Since I don't like crumbs in *my* bed, she always brings the plate here."

Victoria twisted a button on her blouse, uncomfortable. "Maybe she left it in your room, since she gave this one to me."

"Maybe." Katie fished under the coverlets and came out with a raggedy stuffed horse. Victoria winced. She might be dumb enough to drag the thing with her, but that horse never saw the light of day. Nobody else had set eyes on it since she was about eight years old. She took a step forward, tried to act nonchalant.

"Where did you get that?" she asked.

"It was hided under your pillow." The little girl examined the little horse's faded patchwork body, its bedraggled rainbow-yarn mane. "Isn't this yours?" she asked, poking at the stuffed animal's one remaining black button eye.

Victoria's cheeks heated. Oh God, what if this little blabbermouth goes running off to her big sister and tells Dara that the new American rider sleeps with a stuffed horse under her pillow? Wouldn't that snit Clare just love that bit of information? "I . . . I, uh—"

"Maybe it's Tara's," Katie mused. "Tara's my friend an' she stayed overnight. Maybe we played hide and seek an' she hided it, but I thought I knew all of her babies."

Katie tucked the horse under her arm with a frighteningly proprietary air. "I'll just take him to my room an' ask Tara at school."

"It's not a . . . a him," Victoria almost choked on the words. "She's a her. The horse, I mean." Victoria couldn't resist another second. Cheeks on fire, she crossed to the bed and took the horse. She tried hard not to look like she was cuddling it in her arms. She just nonchalantly pressed it against her heart.

"Oh! Your horse is a secret," Katie crowed with terrifying understanding. "What's her name?"

"Fly," Victoria said, running her thumb over a raveled wisp of mane.

Katie frowned. "Like the bug fly? That's not a very good name. I'd call her Sally if I were you."

"No. Not like a bug. Fly—like flying through the sky. Like a bird flies."

"I thought Da said you'd rided lots and lots. You should know horses don't fly."

"But I always knew *I* would." She felt so silly, admitting this to some kid she barely knew. "When I was really tiny I knew that if I got on a horse's back, it would be just like flying."

"Why did you stick Fly under the pillow? You know she can't breathe under there. Nobody but me ever comes in here, and I won't tell. Nobody else will know."

Victoria nibbled at her lip. If only it were that simple! Someone else *would* come in here. And Fly was one secret she couldn't let him know about. "Fly likes it under the pillow. She's lived there since—ever since I was really little."

Katie seemed satisfied with that. But suddenly the little girl's eyes narrowed, too shrewd for a kid the size of a hay bale. "'Toria, you don't look like you had very much fun downstairs."

"Wh–what?" Victoria asked, unnerved.

"Are you 'lergic to parties, too?"

What was it about that round little face that made Victoria confess? "I am, but don't tell anybody."

"It'll be a secret." Katie climbed out of the giant old bed, dropping barefoot onto the floor, the three dogs scrambling down after her.

She looked funny. Kind of cute. Her nightgown was twisted around her like a toga, her hair sticking up all over her head. For the first time all night, Victoria felt like smiling. A *real* smile. She hugged Fly close.

"I love secrets," Katie said. "I know another secret, too."

"Secrets can be fun."

"Mammy says we're not to talk of it. But I just keep thinking an' thinking an' thinking. An' then I get tempted to be asking an' the boys say I'm stupid."

"My teachers used to say the only question that's stupid is the one you don't ask."

"Then maybe I wouldn't be *too* bad a girl if I asked." Katie sucked in a deep breath. "Does it hurt lots not to have a mammy?"

Couldn't these people talk about anything else? Victoria felt like she'd been slugged in the stomach. She fought to keep her face frozen, didn't want to let Katie see. The flash of hurt she pretended didn't exist, the empty place she fought to hide, the thousand questions she could never ask because the few times she'd tried she'd seen something that scared her in her father's eyes. She blinked hard and squeezed Fly so tight the stuffing bulged out of one of the tears in her seams. Something to hold on to, to keep her balance. Inside, not outside.

Katie's mouth pulled down in a frown. "I think the boys were right an' your teacher was wrong. You look all funny."

"No. I . . . I just felt like I was going to sneeze for a minute. There. I'm better now."

Katie seemed to buy the excuse. "I didn't mean to be poking around, even though Owen says I always do."

Owen? Wasn't he the nine-year-old Butler who looked like he was always looking for trouble?

Katie shrugged. "I just wanted to know who maked you wash your face and who taught you to ride bikes an' who told you you were pretty even when your nasty brother said you had a rabbit nose?"

"I don't have a brother."

Katie stared, incredulous.

"And I didn't need a mother," Victoria rushed on. "I was away at school most of the time. I guess that . . . that my teachers taught me. And my dad. He—"

"Daddies are different," Katie said, hitching up the hem of her nightgown. "You can't tell daddies you're 'lergic to parties."

Curiosity satisfied, Katie trailed out of the room, her dogs pattering along behind her. Victoria closed the door before the kid could turn around and come up with any more questions. But instead of going to the rumpled bed, Victoria went to the huge old window that opened up onto the formal gardens.

She snuggled Fly against her, feeling just a little silly as she aimed the little horse's button eye so it could see out the window. "Look, Fly. Isn't it beautiful? You can almost see the stable from here. That's where I'm going to find everything I've ever wanted."

At least, everything she'd ever let herself *admit* she wanted.

She looked down into Fly's threadbare face, her embroidery floss mouth still frozen in its familiar grin. What would it be like to have someone like Mrs. Butler always there to run to? To cry to, to tell secrets to when you slipped and fell and made mistakes and wanted to admit it and get it off your chest? To be forgiven?

Not that she couldn't run to her father, Victoria thought with a sharp surge of defensiveness. It was just . . . complicated. He wanted her to be the best she could be. Didn't every parent want that? Only he believed in her so much she never made mistakes. Not in his eyes. That made her lucky. Didn't it?

It wasn't *his* fault she was too scared to let him know the truth.

Victoria hugged Fly tight, staring out into the darkness. Things should have been perfect, she thought one last time. But Katie Butler was right.

You couldn't tell a daddy you were allergic to parties. You couldn't tell him you slept with the stuffed toy you fished out of the garbage after he'd thrown it away. Not when he thought you were perfect.

If you didn't have a mother, you couldn't tell anyone.

12

*E*ve shifted restlessly in a chair that looked like it had belonged to the Queen of Hearts when she'd yelled "off with their heads," the griffin carvings on the arms some of the finest she'd ever seen. It was easy to fall in love with Kilrain, every nook and cranny stuffed with delicious artifacts that still echoed with the pulse of lives long faded away. The very pulses that had drawn her to the career she loved so much, preserving what had been before.

But now the place felt oppressive, as if the gray stone walls of Castle Kilrain were about to tumble down on top of her at any moment. From bits of history she'd picked up from aged letters strewn about the castle, she knew Kilrain had withstood siege and famine, occupying armies and the rebellions that had come and gone over the centuries almost as regularly as the change of Irish seasons. But she wasn't sure the castle could withstand the invasion it was facing now.

One rebellious seventeen-year-old boy with the hardest eyes Eve had ever seen.

A knot of panic lodged beneath Eve's breastbone. It was just the enormity of the responsibility she was taking on that made her feel so strange, she knew. And yet, it seemed like every old portrait, every suit of armor, every stuffed animal head that crowded the castle rooms as if they were ready for a rummage sale was following her with doubt-filled eyes.

At least she could put one concern to rest now, she thought wryly—the rumor that the castle was haunted. It would be haunted by a pale, desperately unhappy Rory. And if Halloran had been directing a horror movie, he couldn't have found a more perfect place to hide his vampire.

She squirmed inwardly as she glanced through the secret opening to the tiny room hidden in the stone wall. She would have been helping Halloran and Rory clean up the place, but there was barely room for the two of them to fit.

They filled the small space, Halloran swiping down centuries old cobwebs while Rory moved in what few belongings he'd left at Glenammura since Moran had been in such a hurry to drag him away the day he'd been taken back to Dublin. Riding clothes, still looking fairly new—doubtless gifts from Halloran. Horse gear, high quality, but worn and well used, but so precisely cared for that the leather and metal and wood all gleamed. There was nothing that looked like it came from Rory's life before—as if the boy was trying to pretend that his life with Jamie and Oonagh had never existed.

Eve had heard plenty at the courthouse about where Rory had slept as a child, in cars all night, on floors. She could hardly stand it that even here, at Kilrain, he was being crammed into this stone shoebox.

"Halloran, are you sure he has to stay in *this* room?" she asked, a little shaky. "There must be half a dozen other ones in the castle. Rooms with windows. Doors you can actually tell are doors. This is like—like a dungeon in here, even if it does have a bed and a table."

"It's one place I'm sure no one will be able to find," Halloran said, tossing an empty cardboard box out the door to give them more room. One cardboard box. It held everything this boy had in the world. Eve might have been able to bear it if she'd known he had riches in his heart—love and security, faith in himself and the world. But the secret places inside Rory held even less than the box had.

"Besides," Halloran said, "it's not a dungeon. It's a priest hole."

"A what?" she asked absently, sorting through the piles of old books that had been on the bed.

"A place the priest stayed when he came to the area."

Eve grimaced. "Ireland has always been mostly Catholic. You're supposed to *like* priests, not trap them behind walls." She shuddered. "Didn't you ever read Poe's *The Cask of Amontillado?*"

"They liked their priests just fine at Kilrain. In fact, they could have lost the castle—not to mention their lives—for giving the priest this little room. In the seventeen hundreds it was against the law to hold mass, so the castle lords would hide the priests here so they could go to the surrounding countryside and do their priestly things. Baptisms. Marriages. Funerals. Of course, the priest hopped around a lot from place to place, so you just hoped you'd get lucky if you needed last rites."

"The history lesson is lovely, Halloran, but the room's charming past doesn't make me like the idea of locking a seventeen-year-old boy up in here any more than I did before."

Rory glanced up from where he was sorting through his riding gear. He gave her a strange look. "It's bigger than my place at home."

"I suppose that shouldn't surprise me," Eve said unhappily. "It's just—"

"Listen, lady, don't start acting like this is supposed to be some five-star hotel or something. I don't care where I stay. I won't be here long, anyway."

Eve tried not to think about how little she'd be able to do if he decided to take off, or how miserable she'd feel, worrying about where he was, if he was safe, had food, shelter. The most she could do was to try to make this arrangement work so he wouldn't want to leave. But she knew less about teenaged boys than she did about pugs and felt about as comfortable around them as she did around Innisfree.

She searched her mind, trying to think of something to say that might soften the edge of grimness from Rory's face. "I'll be glad to have somebody staying with me in the castle—somebody human, that is. Every time I turn around, somebody's telling me this place has a ghost."

Rory grimaced. "It's not the ghosts you have to worry about. It's the real people."

She hated the cynicism in his voice. "Rory, I—"

"Bloody hell, can't you just leave me alone? I don't want to talk about nothing. The room's just fine, except that you and Halloran are in it."

Eve flinched, hated the fact that Halloran saw her do it. She wasn't used to being snapped at that way, wasn't used to seeing so much emotion in anyone's face when they were relating to her—not anger and not joy.

"Listen, boyo," Halloran warned, "you and I had both better be damned grateful to this lady. She didn't have to pull either one of our arses out of a jam and let you stay here."

"I *will* be grateful if the two of you will just leave me alone!" There was enough child in his cry to make Eve suck in a steadying breath.

"Rory's right, Halloran," she said. "It's his room. If he doesn't want us in the way while he's getting settled we should respect his wishes."

Rory froze, shock obvious in his face.

"When you're hungry, come down to the kitchen," Eve offered. "I've got a few things down there that don't have to be refrigerated or cooked."

Hot light flared in Rory's eyes. Hunger. God, why hadn't she thought to feed him first? Because she'd thought he'd already eaten. After all, he'd had the grapes for Innisfree. Was it possible the boy would steal treats for his horse, but wouldn't take something to eat for himself?

She wanted to urge him to come downstairs immediately. Wanted to open every can or jar or package of food in the place and make sure he ate until he couldn't hold another bite. Worst of all, she could feel tears threatening again. But she couldn't let him know she'd figured out another of his secrets, and she couldn't let him see she pitied him. Rory would hate that. Fear it. Maybe enough to run away. Instinctively, she knew that much about him.

She got up, trying not to let either Halloran or Rory realize how unsettled she was. She went down the spiral stairs, blinking hard. Bonaparte made a yapping charge from his pillow beneath the table, but for once she didn't care if the dog gummed her to death.

Down here, two weeks of work had made a dent in the dust and tarnish and neglect it would take a lifetime to completely sweep away. She'd taken out her frustrations on the treasures Bridey had stuffed on every surface. It had distracted her, given her something to do with her hands in the long hours she'd spent alone at Kilrain. She'd loved restoring the old things. But now, she was too restless to sit inside. The problems she faced she couldn't wipe away with a soft cloth.

She went to the castle door, stepped outside. Sweet and cool, the breeze teased her cheeks. Fences of stone flowed in gray streams across the bed of green that fell away from the castle yard, cutting the countryside into sections like a cake. Tomorrow, there would be a horse in those pastures. Horse, the animal her little girl had always loved.

She crossed to the fence and leaned against it. She'd be sharing her time in Ireland with a teenager, but not with her own daughter. She'd be facing her terror of horses, but not with any hope of winning Victoria's approval. Everything was mixed up, backward, and inside out. Everything was *wrong*, a part of her wanted to wail.

Where was her little girl now? What was she doing? For so many years, Eve had tried to imagine

Tori going about her life. Picturing her in pinafores, imagining the first time she put on lipstick, or her excitement the first time she'd gone to a sleepover at one of her friends' houses. But now it was harder to imagine what she was doing. Her life was open, her wings full grown. It was time to fly. . . .

Fly . . . She closed her eyes. Tori had always wanted to fly. She'd run around the house, clutching her little stuffed horse, her eyes shining as she crowed. *Watch me, Mama! Watch! I'm flying!* But then, Eve had been there to scoop her up when she fell. Then, both Eve and Tori had thought she always would be.

"Eve?"

She jumped at the sound of Halloran's voice behind her, and tried to scrub away the tears that had sprung to her eyes. But the man was too quick, damn him. Strong fingers curved about her wrist. He drew her around to face him, worry dark in his eyes.

"It's not too late to change your mind about taking Rory on," he said quietly. She knew just how much it cost him to say it.

There wasn't much point in trying to hide the fact that she was crying. The damned tears wouldn't stop. They ran down her cheeks, chilled by the wind, leaving raw places on her skin and in her heart.

"This isn't about Rory," she admitted. "I was just thinking . . . Innisfree will be in this pasture tomorrow."

"You won't have to get near him."

"I know. It's just that . . . my daughter loves horses. I was just wondering what she's doing right now. If she's happy."

It was supposed to be Halloran's cue. He was supposed to say something to distract her from feelings too harsh to bear. But he only cupped one finger under her chin to keep her from looking away from him, his thumb brushing a gentle sweep across her chin. Blue eyes stripped away layers from her face, masks she'd gotten so good at hiding behind.

"Was she happy the last time you saw her?" he asked.

Eve laughed, raw and hurting. "Happy? Yes. She was happy and proud and so beautiful I couldn't even breathe. Then she saw me and . . . she wasn't happy anymore."

"Eve, whatever happened, I don't believe it was your fault."

"The courts said different. I was raising my daughter in a shabby apartment, barely keeping my head above water. Sometimes I didn't know how we were going to eat at the end of the week. Victoria—she never knew. I just told her I wasn't hungry. Made a game of it, playing airplane with her spoon, feeding her the last of whatever I'd managed to scrape up. I made sure she had what she needed. Fruits and meat and milk. I made sure—but it was so hard."

He was staring at her, his eyes burning with empathy, outrage on her behalf. Listening, just listening to things she hadn't spoken of for so long. She hadn't known they were still inside her, hard lumps like stones pressing on her heart.

"You said the girl's father and his family had plenty of money. Surely they would have helped—"

She gave a bitter laugh. "Chad wanted custody of Victoria by then. The harder things got, the closer he figured I'd get to letting her go."

"The rotten sonofabitch."

"There were times I almost thought of it—thought maybe Chad was right. That Victoria deserved a better life than I could give her. But then I'd listen to her laughing, see the way her eyes would shine whenever she looked up at me. Maybe she didn't have lots of things, but as long as we had each other she had everything she really needed."

"Love is what all kids want most. Love and time."

"She was my whole world. Hard as things were, she was worth every scrap I had to fight for. One night when I was getting ready for work my baby-sitter got sick. I had to go to work. It was the dead of winter and they were going to turn off the heat. I thought if I just took Tori with me, I could keep an eye on her until she went to sleep, then run around the warehouse, stacking boxes, processing orders. I thought it would be all right. She was sound asleep when I left her. I swear. I was just gone a few minutes. Then I heard her scream. Boxes falling. Blood. There was so much blood."

"Eve, I'm sorry."

"It was just the chance Chad had been waiting for. Proof that I was a failure. But it doesn't matter that I failed once. I'm not going to fail this time, Halloran. I'll do whatever I must to make it come out right."

"Whoa, there, Eve. Rory's not your daughter. You can't fix what's broken between the two of you by using that boy."

"Do you think I'd do something that . . . that reprehensible?" she snapped, stung.

"Eve, I just—the boy is more fragile than he looks and so are you."

"I know I can't fix things between Victoria and me through Rory. I didn't mean it the way it sounded." She'd be damned before she admitted even to herself that somewhere some part of her *did*, and it scared her to death.

Halloran looked away. They stood silent for a long time. "You asked me once if I'd ever made a mistake. Do you remember?" he asked softly.

She nodded.

"I've made plenty of them, Eve. Maybe one of the worst was what I thought about you."

She looked up at him, astonished.

"I was right about one thing. You *are* crazy. No sane person would take on a kid like Rory minutes after he pulled a knife. And you're stubborn. Hard-headed. Reckless."

"That's ridiculous. I've only been reckless once in

my life. And I learned—God, how I learned my lesson. Besides, I thought you said you were wrong about me."

"I was. You see, darlin', I've finally seen the truth about you."

That she was afraid? That she'd bargained away really *living* her life to be safe? She cringed to think that Michael Halloran had discovered that bleak secret. "And the truth is?"

"I think you may be the bravest woman I've ever known."

"No, Halloran, I'm not. When they took Victoria away from me, I was scared to death they'd make it so I'd never see my baby again. I tried to be a good girl, obeying every stupid condition they put on me, hoping that if I did what the courts said, they'd do what was fair, what was right. I sent her gifts—birthday presents, wrote her letters telling her how much I loved her, missed her. I wrote, begging Chad to let me see her. He never answered. And when I tried to sneak a glimpse of her, he took her and ran to Europe, knowing I was too poor to follow. It hurt so bad, that empty hole where Tori had been. I hid in my job, in my life."

"You were fighting to survive the only way you knew how."

"Maybe so. I thought Tori had my letters, but Chad must have thrown them away. I believed she would remember how much I loved her. I didn't know she would forget. That when 'someday' finally came, it would be too late."

"It's never too late. It's never over until you're dead. And even then, I'm not so sure."

They were words, just words, she'd told herself a thousand times. Why were they easier to believe when they came from Halloran?

"There's only two things you can be sure of in life," he said. "You are going to screw up, make mistakes. Everyone does. But real love is never wasted. Whatever went wrong between you when they took her away, the love you gave your daughter is still alive, somewhere in her heart."

Eve peered up into the face of the man she'd been so determined to dislike. She wanted to pull away, felt so vulnerable it terrified her. But she held her ground. He deserved that much.

"Halloran, thank you for that," she said.

He looked as if he wanted to say something more. His lips parted, his gaze warm, rich with something unexpected as he peered down at her mouth. She flinched, instinctively frightened by what that look did to her, how much it made her want.

Want Halloran to hold her. Just hold her. Let her sink into his chest, feel someone else's heartbeat, know that they could ache as much as she did.

But she couldn't risk it. It would change everything. She'd never be able to forget what it felt like for that moment, to be safe, cared for just a little. In the end, she'd have to let him go, but she'd never be able to let go of the *knowing*. Knowing what it felt like to be held. Knowing she was so very alone.

She started to turn away from him, was stunned she couldn't do it. The wanting was too much. Halloran cupped her cheek in his callused palm, tipped her face up. Ever so slowly, he lowered his mouth to hers.

Hot silk, moist, indescribably tender, his lips searched hers, as if he were groping his way through her hidden shadows, finding his way through her secrets, her pain. He tasted it, soothed it, shared it as no one had shared it before. The sensation made Eve's hands shake, her heart pound. With fear? Vulnerability? Attraction or surprise? She wasn't sure. She flattened her palms against the beat of his heart, intending to put distance between them. Instead, her fingers curled tight into the folds of his shirt, holding him close.

Halloran's mouth moved to the corner of her lips, traced kisses along the salty path her tears had followed. She felt his breath, warm on burning eyelids, the brush of his lips on the fragile lids, soft, tender, his fingers stroking her hair. She choked back a sob. Couldn't bear the closeness another moment. It was too much. Too soon. Too good.

Halloran stepped away from her, and she shivered at the understanding in his face. That intuition, that empathy that seemed to read bruised hearts—Rory's and Innisfree's and maybe . . . maybe hers.

The thought terrified her. She clutched her arms tight against her stomach. "That shouldn't have happened. I don't . . . don't want it to happen." She was lying. Her voice cracked. "It was just . . . talking about Tori. It made me—" Weak. Needy. Made her take risks too dangerous to dare. "Halloran, I can't—" She shook her head, feeling like a fool. "I'm sorry."

Did he look hurt? Or was it only regret that glimmered in his blue eyes?

"It's all right. No wonder after everything you've gone through." He touched her cheek one last time. "I'll be back first thing in the morning," he said, then started down the lane to where they'd left the car.

Eve pressed her fingertips to her tingling lips and watched him go. He would be back. To watch over Rory. Watch over Innisfree and Bridey's castle. To watch over *her* with the incredible tenderness, protectiveness she'd felt in his kiss. She'd never had anyone do that before, she realized. Take care of her. She'd always been the one looking out for her mother, breaking her falls instead of the other way around. Chad had been funny and charming, exciting, forbidden. But he'd never given her shelter. Any time Steffie had tried too hard to shield her, Eve had shoved her away. But Michael Halloran wouldn't let anyone shove him away.

Eve stared at his broad shoulders until he disappeared around a corner choked with gorse. She had to be careful. Halloran was already way too tempting with his whiskey-rough voice and his reins-callused hands, his knee-melting smile and hard, lean body. But there were things about him far more terrifying. Courage. Loyalty. Compassion.

She shivered, reliving the sensation of his kiss. It would be far too easy to want to belong to him. And that was impossible. Halloran had had women lined up halfway around the world just dying to get their hands on him. If he'd wanted a woman in his life, all he would have had to do was shine that amazing smile at them. While she—her experience with Chad had left her uncertain, wounded. She'd frozen the soft places inside her, the only way she could survive the hurting. Michael Halloran deserved everything that was warm. He was whole and she was broken. One kiss could never change that.

Dream, girl! She could almost hear Steffie plead with her. *What can it hurt to dream?*

But dreams had sharp edges. Eve had cut herself too many times to risk it again. Steffie would argue. Halloran would disagree. But Eve had learned the truth both of them would deny. Sometimes it *was* too late if you didn't dare to believe.

*M*ichael paced the farmhouse, naked except for the riding breeches that hung on his hips, half fastened, his bare feet cold on the scuffed kitchen floor. It wasn't the first time he'd had insomnia. He'd spent plenty of nights like this over the years. When he was riding the circuit, he'd rarely gotten to sleep before three in the morning, no matter when or with whom he'd gone to bed. When race days drew near, his blood had been too hot in his veins, his drive to win battering him from somewhere deep inside, craving his next fix of adrenaline and triumph. He'd been hungry and more than a little dangerous. And women had scented it, the way a stallion scented a mare in heat halfway across the county.

He'd loved the way they looked at him, fascinated, intrigued, turned on. Even more, he'd reveled in the envy in the eyes of the other men and the resignation that he would always ride faster, harder, and that the most desirable woman would always be waiting for him at the end of the course. He'd guzzled the sensation of being wild and reckless and young until he was drunk with it. In the end it had almost killed him. At least, killed anything decent inside him.

Then Sean had been hurt, and he'd found out the hard way there was another kind of sleepless night. One that left you exhausted and ragged and hating yourself. One broken by cries of pain and images rolling over and over and over in your head: horses pounding toward a stone fence, the need to win thundering in his veins, turning him savage. The horrific crash of horses colliding, the snap of bones, the taste of dirt and blood. Opening your eyes to a world changed forever.

The passage of years had given him many more sleepless nights. But then there had been other things to keep him awake: children to worry about, Bridey to tend, the farm to manage.

It had been grim sometimes. Exhausting often. But never, since the day he'd left Ireland with nothing but dreams and riding boots, had he ever paced away a night like this one. Never before had he been entirely alone.

He crossed to the electric kettle he'd turned on during one of his earlier passes around the room, then poured himself hot tea, his gaze probing beyond Bridey's lace curtains. Mist curled along a dark silver stream of sky, the moon perched on the crest of the hill. Was that same mist veiling Kilrain? He pictured the castle on its wood-tangled hill, isolated, alone.

Had Rory fallen to sleep yet? He wondered. The boy had been dropping with exhaustion when he'd stolen into the stable earlier that day. Surely he was dead to the world. But he'd wager half of Glenammura that someone else wandered about Kilrain tonight. Someone he was certain was used to sleeplessness, and, he thought with a fierce tug in his chest, even more used to being alone. Someone who might be restless in the aftermath of an unexpected kiss just as Michael himself was.

Eve. He'd seen the doubt in her earlier, the dread at knowing she'd be responsible for Rory. He'd seen the glint of something broken in her eyes. Burned with outrage when he'd heard her shaking voice describing everything she'd been through, everything the wealthy bastard who'd fathered her daughter had put her through.

Damn, but he'd like to get his hands on that son-ofabitch and—

Michael's fingers tightened on his mug, hot tea splashing over his fingers. He swore, set the mug down, turned on the tap and thrust his burned hand under cold water. He clenched his jaw, anger surging in the pit of his stomach. He felt off balance, out of focus, unsettled, feelings he hadn't had about any woman since Gail.

But then, Eve Danaher was as different from Gail as any woman could have been. While Eve was going hungry, Gail had been drinking champagne. While Eve had battled to hold on to her daughter, Gail had been taking delight in playing coy little games.

Michael winced. Not with the pain of the hot water burn. Not anymore. Just fierce embarrassment and disgust that he'd ever been so stupid. Young and dumb, his body in control far more than his heart. Maybe things would have been different if he'd been the only one who'd lost his head over Gail. But Sean had been head over heels about the woman as well.

Damn, why was he even picking around that raw place in his memory? He was only edgy because of everything that had happened in the last twenty-four hours.

He was reacting to stress.

If only it were that simple. He was really mad as hell. Outraged that Eve was so alone. That was all it was—these unnerving feelings. No one deserved to be so much alone. Not even if they'd made mistakes.

He turned off the tap, swabbed his hand dry with a towel. You shouldn't have to pay for mistakes forever, not even if you deserved to, he thought. God knew if anyone had deserved such a grim sentence, he had deserved it long ago.

He closed his eyes, seeing her again so clearly it nearly blinded him. Waves of golden hair against pale cheeks, full peach-pink lips still trembling, green-gray eyes shimmering with tears. She'd tasted so sweet, so fragile, so lost when he'd kissed her. She'd looked like a fairy that had strayed too far from her ring of stones.

A wanderer, lost in the mist, waiting for someone to find her.

Michael grimaced. He should have known Eve would bring the Irish out in him. Romantic, impractical, head filled with fairy dust. He'd wanted to shelter her, hold her. Wanted to drive away the pain and fear and loneliness in her that hurt his heart. But he had to keep things in perspective. She was Bridey's houseguest. The woman who was taking care of Rory. She was someone willing to help fight against Moran and Jamie and Oonagh and the courts. And she was scared, damned scared to let anyone get close. Not that he could blame her after what had happened with the man who had taken her daughter. Bottom line was that as soon as Bridey got out of hospital, Eve would be gone. Sooner, if he wasn't careful not to spook her. And his kiss had come damned close to doing just that.

That thought was enough to sober him. No matter how good she'd felt curled up in that loft beside him, no matter how her lips had felt under his, no matter how good her hair smelled, he had to stay in control. No attraction to a woman was worth putting Rory's hideaway in jeopardy. And this was a woman whose wings had been beat to hell. Any relationships Michael had had in the years since he'd come to Glenammura had been casual. Eve Danaher would need something far more. She was too fragile, too fine, too brave, too wounded to handle carelessly.

The thought was scary as hell, blindsiding him in a way that shouldn't be possible for a forty-four-year-old man who had seen as much of life as he had.

He needed to keep things strictly business between himself and Eve Danaher for Rory's sake. She was the boy's only hope. Michael could be her friend, yes. Jesus, Mary, and Joseph, the woman needed friends. But he couldn't risk scaring her off. Any sweet, uncomplicated summer romance between them—that was out of the question.

Nothing with Eve Danaher would be simple.

The phone buzzed, nearly making him jump out of his skin. Alarm knotted the muscles in his stomach as he looked at the clock on the wall. Any phone call at three in the morning meant trouble. Something was wrong. In an instant possibilities flashed through his mind. Eve? Could things have gone wrong already? No, the odds of her phone working were slim at best. Bridey? The old woman had looked better when he'd stopped on his way to Dublin to visit her in the hospital a week ago. But he'd told the hospital to call him if her condition changed for the worse. Sean from Dublin? He dove for the phone.

"Hello?" he barked into the receiver.

"Michael?" How could any voice have so much energy after eighty-five years?

"Bridey? What is it? What's wrong?" Panic squeezed his lungs, telling him in no uncertain terms just how much the old woman meant to him.

"Wrong? Why should anything be wrong? You worry too much, lad."

"It's three in the morning."

"Is it, then? Well, you know how 'tis when I get caught up in the 'craick.'"

That was true enough. No one loved hashing over the news as much as Bridey. The old woman adored gossip. Sometimes when he was most afraid for her, he'd reassure himself that was the reason she'd hung on so long in spite of heart problems and failing eyesight, arthritic joints and osteoporosis. She wasn't about to die. She might miss some tasty bit of news.

"You called me at three in the morning to tell me you've been gossiping the night away?" He couldn't stifle a smile, even though part of him wanted to shake her until her false teeth rattled out of her head for scaring him that way. His smile widened. If he wanted to rattle her teeth, he'd most likely have to go rummaging in the back of her nightstand drawer. She only wore them for "fine company." He wondered if the poor nurse she'd conned into a conversation in the wee hours of morning had merited Bridey donning her pearly whites.

"I knew you would be awake, treasure."

"If I wasn't before, I would be now. You scared the life out of me."

"You're made of sterner stuff than that, boyo. Besides, Kilrain told me to call, and you know I've not argued with his lordship in eighty-some years."

Michael sank down in a chair and rubbed his temple. He should have performed an exorcism in that castle years ago. But it was damned hard to get an old woman to allow even the best kind of psychic charlatan to drive away a castle ghost when she'd been in love with said ghost since she was a child. In love with the ghost, in love with the castle—somehow they'd blurred together until after so many years even Michael was too tired to try to untangle them.

"So, Kilrain told you I wouldn't be sleeping, eh? You didn't just figure it out yourself because you guessed Rory's court case might be settled?"

"Sometimes you grieve me, lad. You've no Irish soul, not believing in ghosts."

"You believe enough for both of us."

"Well then, tell me, what happened with the boy? Is it over?"

"Over? Moran would say so. We lost."

Bridey made a clucking, mournful sound. "Oh, Michael!"

"But you know how stubborn Rory is. The kid ran away. Managed to get all the way back here to see that horse of his. Then, I don't know where he planned to run."

"But you can't let the lad run wild! He's done too much of that already, poor mite! There must be something can be done."

"I can't say much, but I promise you, he's safe."

He could actually hear the old woman smile. "I

knew you'd not be letting the boy down. Those babies of yours—they're all you ever think about."

Not all, Michael thought ruefully. He'd spent most of tonight thinking about Eve Danaher's soft skin, her eyes, haunted with old pain, so much need, the way her mouth had trembled, then opened under his. He wasn't about to tell Bridey that, though. No, time to change the subject.

"How are you feeling?" Michael asked. "And how did you get hold of a phone? There isn't one in your room. Did you bribe some poor nurse? You'll get her in trouble! The doctor said complete bed rest, Bridey. That means in bed *all* the time."

"One would think you had no spirit of adventure left in you. I may be an old woman, Michael Patrick Halloran, but if I choose to make a phone call to my boy then I will, and Cromwell's whole army won't stop me."

It was true. Michael chuckled. Maybe Bridey *shouldn't* be on the phone. Maybe he *should* be chasing her back to her bed, irate, but he had to admit, it was good to hear her voice. It helped him to catch his breath, his balance. Distracted him just enough to drive back his fears for Rory and the disturbing memory of Eve Danaher's kiss, at least for a little while.

"One thing I can guarantee you, old woman," he said. "No matter what spit Cromwell is roasting on in hell, he's thanking his lucky stars you were born three hundred years too late to put him in his place."

"There, now!" Bridey crowed. "That is the first time you've tormented me for three weeks! I was beginning to fear you hated me, you were treating me so *polite.*" She said the last word with the distaste of a duchess eating three-day-old bread.

"I was trying not to worry you, dammit!"

"Well, next time be your obnoxious self and I'll not guess anything is wrong. That's the ticket, Michael-my-treasure. Irritate me and tease me and I'll never have a clue what's ailing you—until, of course, his lordship sees fit to inform me. And I'd not be calling *him* a tale-carrier if you want to sleep anytime in the next month. He's very sensitive of his honor, you know."

"I'll try to keep that in mind."

"I've been worried about you, lad." Her voice warmed the ragged places in Michael's chest. "You had better take care of yourself or you'll answer to me."

It had been a serious threat when he'd been a scabby-kneed boy climbing over the fence to raid Kilrain's orchard. A tangle of half-rotted trees and fallen branches, just enough red apples clinging to life to tempt a small boy to climb after them—and probably break his neck in the attempt. But Bridey had been wiry then, small and fast as a rabbit, with a tongue that could sting worse than any switch the good brothers at St. Malachy's had used on his palms. Now the memory made him ache, Bridey so long ago, hair still red, skin only faintly wrinkled, skirts hiked over her knees as she chased him and Sean. Caught him by the tail of his shirt just as he'd been about to scale the fence after he'd boosted Sean over.

Now Bridey could only run in her dreams, but she was still chasing after both him and Sean, trying to keep them from falling.

Bridey's voice softened. "And what are you going to do about your Rory? Can you go back to court again? Fight the decision?"

Michael hesitated. The last thing he wanted to do was worry Bridey or put her in a position where she could get into trouble. And yet, hadn't he been pouring out his heart to her for years? That was when her aging hurt him the most, when he feared her shoulders were too frail, her mind too delicate to bear up under the weight of his problems. When he sensed that she knew he was holding back from her, secrets he once would have told. And that holding back hurt her.

"What did his lordship tell you I was going to do?" he asked carefully, stalling for time.

"You tell me, and I'll tell you if he was right."

Michael laughed. "I'll keep fighting. Do whatever I have to do. You know that."

"But you can't do anything more about it tonight, I'm thinking, can you?" Bridey said. "So then, why aren't you sleeping?"

"It's . . . complicated."

"Oh," she sputtered, offended. "And I'm too much of a simple old woman to understand your explaining it?"

"Yes! I mean, no! I—"

She sounded hurt enough that Michael couldn't stand it. "The castle. Didn't, er, his lordship tell you about his visitor?"

A long pause. He could almost see the glow from Galway as the light flicked on in Bridey's head. "Ah!" she cried, relieved. "That's what you—" She stopped, and for an instant he thought his luck was finally turning and a nurse had discovered Bridey and would chase her back to her bed before he had to explain further.

No such luck. "But my poor wee American—" Bridey demanded, concerned. "Michael Patrick, what did you do to her?"

Kissed her. Tasted tears on her cheeks. Saw her eyes flash with fury, her chin set all stubborn. Got mad as hell at her until I saw the hurt so deep inside her it broke my heart. He searched for the words to explain, knew he couldn't. Eve was fragile as hell, and he—he didn't have the damnedest idea what he was going to do about the feelings the woman had stirred in him. He opted for humor in a desperate attempt to distract the old woman.

"You said she wanted to experience life in an Irish castle, so I locked her in the dungeon."

"I'm not laughing, Michael Patrick. I know just how stubborn and overprotective you can be. You pestered me to a frazzle when I told you I was flying Eve over to stay at the castle! If you did the same to that poor girl I swear I . . . I'll—"

"Easy, Bridey, don't get upset."

"I'm not the one who's upset. My American, she's the one who's upset. Sounded like a wee bird blown through a storm. It's a safe place I was trying to give her, Michael, and much as I love you, aye, and care for Rory, I'll not have you tormenting my houseguest! There's still such a thing as hospitality in Ireland, you know, and—"

Michael surrendered, hearing the strident tones in Bridey's voice, knowing she'd get herself in a lather over this, and that was the worst thing she could do for herself. "Bridey, Eve is keeping Rory for now."

"And why would she be doing such a thing? She doesn't even know the boy and between bits Sean's let slip and your attitude lately I'd wager you've been so biting mean to her, you'd think snakes had come back to Ireland!"

"I don't know why she's doing it. Maybe that's why I'm still awake, trying to figure it out. Trying to figure *her* out. She . . . She surprised me."

"And *that* must have put you in a fine mood. I would have thought you'd be kind to her, Michael. You've always been tender to wounded creatures."

"She's not a horse or a rabbit, Bridey. She's a woman."

"You've noticed that much at least, have you?" Bridey snapped.

Michael groaned. Yeah, he'd noticed one or two things about Eve that made him pretty sure she was female. The soft pillows of her breasts against his chest, that sweet, woman-smell of her skin, the way her jeans hugged her round little bottom. And the way she made his groin ache every time he thought about the kiss they'd shared.

"Well, you've never been a good judge of women, Michael. Horses, yes. No man I've ever seen finer at reading what lies between a horse's ears. And children—you've the gift with them as well. Which is why, I might add, you should have been brightening my morning tea with a half-dozen of your own babies these past fifteen years."

"I've got enough to do with the farm. We've gone over this before. My work is too important to get distracted—"

"It's a fine thing for a grown man to be hiding behind a bunch of hurting babies. And what is it you're supposed to be teaching them at Glenammura, anyway?"

"To be healthy. To be happy. To be whole. To see that they can have a life as full as anyone else's."

"Then you might try being a good example to them. While you're busy arranging Rory's life, and Sean's life, and the lives of the rest of those babies, try having a life of your own."

Michael winced, the words stinging. "I have everything I want. Everything I need. Besides, who are you to preach? You never married."

"But the man I love is a ghost."

It would be cruel to argue with the sorrow in Bridey's voice. Besides, he'd given up fighting over "his lordship" years ago.

Michael closed his eyes, weary. "Don't I have ghosts enough of my own now?" he asked softly.

"Michael." Bridey hesitated. "Much as I love my Bonaparte, I don't want to see you, years from now, with no one but a pup to hold. He can't really talk to me, you know. He can't hold all of my stories and remember. Is it so wrong to want something better for you?"

Michael stiffened, a coldness settling in is stomach. She sounded so tired, suddenly, so vulnerable. So old.

"Go to bed, Bridey," he pleaded.

Was it the worry in his voice or the weight of regrets decades old, regrets she'd never shared, he was certain, with anyone until now? He wasn't sure. He only knew she stunned him by surrendering.

"Good night, my treasure," she said, sounding too far away. He was still astonished when he heard the phone line go dead.

The cold in his gut deepened as he hung up the receiver. He was realist enough to know that someday

Bridey wouldn't be as close as a telephone call or a quick gallop over the hill to the castle. Nothing in his life had ever terrified him more than that looming silence.

A warm, wet nose nudged his hand, and he reached absently to scratch behind the collie's ears. What was it Bridey had said? That she didn't want him alone, with no one but a dog to love him? But he had the kids he worked with. Sean for a friend. Plenty of people in his life. It wasn't as if he were hiding. His life was full already. What could a woman add?

He remembered the tremble of Eve's lips, the warmth of her hand, the way her eyes brimmed with emotion that got too close to his own heart.

Had Bridey somehow guessed the change in his feelings toward Eve? That was one thing Sean couldn't have told her. Sean didn't know.

He winced, remembering the eager, puppy-dog light in his friend's eyes as he'd handed the map of Dublin to Eve. Another complication. Was Sean interested in her? Or was it just Sean being Sean? Rollicking and eager to please, like a setter pup. When he'd called his friend to tell him Rory was found, Sean had asked if Eve had survived the trip back to Glenammura without doing Michael well-deserved bodily harm. But then Sean had let the subject go, promising to be back in a few days, once he took care of some business, and paid a visit to his sister in Drogheda. Siobhan Murphy's brood of eight adored their Uncle Sean, and there would be outright rebellion if any of them found out he'd been close as Dublin and hadn't stopped long enough for a good roughhousing session.

Michael closed his eyes for an instant, picturing Sean's sister's crowded kitchen, the mayhem of lads with footballs and girls with their dolls. Wondered what it would be like to throw open that door at night, look across the sea of dirt-smudged faces to find a wife smiling at you. It was a future he'd taken for granted once—one he hadn't even thought of in a very long time. One he certainly hadn't felt the lack of. Why was it suddenly he could picture it so clearly?

Michael brought himself up short. Damn, what was he thinking? He had to be careful. Real careful. He couldn't afford to muck things up with Eve, and had to do what was right for Rory's sake. Sweet as her kiss had been—and God knew, it was sweeter than anything he'd ever tasted—there was too much at stake to risk pursuing it further.

It had been easier to keep his distance when he disliked the woman. Now . . . Bridey was right. He'd always had a weakness for wounded creatures. That was plenty dangerous enough.

He just hadn't realized until he'd looked down at Eve Danaher silhouetted against the stone fence and twilight sky that he'd had another weakness. One for green eyes, soft and aching with secrets too heavy to carry alone.

It was taking too long. Victoria tried not to stiffen up as she put the magnificent Dutch Warm Blood gelding through his paces. She couldn't help glancing over at her father, his crisp shirt a little wilted, the top button of his collar unfastened. Tiny signs she knew meant he was getting impatient. What could be the problem, after all? He'd presented her with the best horses money could buy, she could almost hear him say. She only had to pick one.

She drew rein on the gelding, the horse stopping with the precision of a surgeon's scalpel. What was wrong? Victoria worried. Whatever was *off* had to be *her* fault. It couldn't be the horse's. The gelding was perfectly trained, with talent deep as the muscles in his chest. Any competitor with dreams of winning events should be doing cartwheels at finding such a mount. But she only felt a sinking sensation in her chest, a feeling worlds different from the bright enthusiasm she'd started out with when she'd begun riding at dawn.

"Well, sweetheart, what do you think?" her father asked for the tenth time that day. "You've ridden every horse the farm has to offer. Which of Trevor's beauties gets the privilege of belonging to the next winner of the Glengarry Cup?"

She pasted on a smile for his sake. The Glengarry event was in just two and a half weeks. A small show, but fiercely competitive. One she'd figured she could use as a test flight for whatever horse she chose. But that was when she'd expected to find a miracle horse, the horse she'd dreamed of all her life. She'd believed in destiny and magic, that indefinable connection between horse and rider that made champions.

How hard could it be to find that perfect horse? she'd thought grandly as she'd dreamed away her last semester at the Academy. Daddy had promised she could have any horse she wanted.

She just hadn't imagined it was possible that here, at the finest stables in Ireland, among horses trained by the greatest trainer she'd ever ridden under, she wouldn't find the right horse.

"I've never seen anyone ride Puck better," Mr. Butler said with satisfaction. "He's a fine lad, is Puck. And I think between the two of us, Puck and I should be able to teach your daughter a wee bit about winning."

"That's why we came to Ireland, isn't it, Victoria?" her father said with satisfaction. "To win."

Not to win, she wanted to say. To find the horse that can teach me how to fly. But there was no point telling him that. Her father didn't understand about flying. But winning, *that* was something every Tolliver understood.

"She's a fine rider," Butler said.

Victoria knew she should be glowing at the trainer's praise. She'd spent enough time at the farm to know just how rare it was. She was earning his respect, at least. She should be elated at that. But would his opinion change if she was honest enough to admit she just wasn't connecting with the horses he'd spent years perfecting? She could just imagine Dara's friend Clare's gleeful outrage—that Trevor Butler's horses weren't good enough for the spoiled little American brat. There were plenty of other riders·on the farm who would just love to believe Clare, too.

Victoria winced. It wasn't like that. It really wasn't. She just . . . it wasn't right. She felt it in her gut the way she felt it when a horse could jump a higher fence than it ever had or run a course at a faster time than anyone had ever clocked it at before.

She knew it like she knew it wasn't over between her and her mother.

Her fingers tightened on the reins, the big horse shied, dancing about on its hooves in bewilderment, trying to figure out what command she was trying to give him. She thought she heard somebody snicker from the direction of the stable doors.

Butler hustled over, took Puck by the reins. "There, now. What's this about? You're not done paying attention, Victoria, until your feet are on the ground."

Her cheeks burned. "I know. I'm sorry. I—" How could she possibly explain? She couldn't say she was thinking about her mother, wondering not *if,* but *when* she was going to look up from her dinner or at a horse show or at her wedding when that time came, to see those anxious green eyes that were painfully like her own.

" 'Tis all right, then," Trevor said. "No wonder you're a bit edgy. Been a long day, it has, and you've a big decision ahead of you, don't you, lass?"

Victoria nodded.

"So which one do you want, sweetheart?" her father prodded.

Victoria groped for something to say that wouldn't disappoint him or insult the trainer. How could she possibly explain what she was feeling to her father or to the great horseman stroking Puck's nose with such pride and satisfaction? Victoria glanced over in the distance to where a crowd of teenagers who had been at the party lounged around the stable door, trying not to look as if they were watching her.

So much for fibbing to Clare and Dana, telling the girls she wouldn't be riding until afternoon. She'd hoped it would give her the morning to work with trainer and horse in peace. She'd figured she'd be done riding by the time they came to the stable, or at least that she'd already have found the perfect horse and could dazzle them with her brilliance. But Trevor Butler was thorough, the right horse hadn't presented itself, and the audience she had dreaded had gathered on the edge of her horizon like a bunch of storm clouds in riding boots.

"I—it's been a long day," Victoria hedged. "This is such an important decision that I don't want to rush it."

Butler's eyes narrowed in surprise. "You're taking the fence carefully then, are you? Watching you ride, I would have thought you one to throw your heart over."

He was subtly saying she was scared to make a decision. It made her cheeks burn.

"What do you think of Puck?" her father prodded. "Can't say when I've seen such a fine animal. Or that black one—you looked beautiful on her. Just pick whichever you want."

Victoria glanced toward the stable door, appalled as she saw Clare double over in an effort to stifle laughter. Victoria swallowed hard. When she realized she couldn't choose one of these horses, she'd thought this couldn't get much worse. She'd been wrong.

She winced at the edge she always dreaded hearing in her father's voice. "Victoria, Mr. Butler is a busy man. He's got lessons to teach, horses to exercise." In other words—make a decision. *Now.*

Her stomach tightened. She wanted so badly to please her father, after everything he had done for her. Giving her this chance, offering her any horse she wanted. She was ruining it for him. She could tell. Presents should be greeted by jumping up and down and clapping hands and cries of delight, not doubts and nervousness and indecision.

She turned back to the trainer. "Puck is . . . is the best horse I've ever ridden," she began, ready to surrender. After all, how horrible could it be to ride a mount like Puck? "Maybe I should—"

"That's my girl." Her father beamed. "We'll take—"

"She'll not be taking any horse today, Mr. Tolliver," Butler broke in, then turned back to Victoria. "Don't be rushing to choose now, no matter how much other people want you to. Remember, you're the one who has to go over the fence. Take it in your own time. That's what makes you the fine rider you are."

She almost sighed in relief. "It is a big decision and I . . . I want to be sure to make the right one."

"And so you will. Take all the time you need," Butler said with a brisk nod. "But while you're thinking, maybe you could do me a favor, lass."

"Anything," Victoria agreed.

"I'm looking for someone to exercise Puck, ride him at Glengarry. Would you be willing?"

A reprieve. Victoria latched on to it eagerly. Her father couldn't be pressuring her to make a decision if she was working Puck. It would buy her some time at least. Time to figure out what to do. Time to maybe, just maybe, make a friend or two around the stable. *Thought you didn't care about friends. Didn't want them. Didn't care about anything but winning,* a voice in her head taunted. Hadn't she thought that all out the night before? Did a part of her really envy the kids hanging around, watching her? Secure in knowing where they belonged?

"I'd love to work Puck," she said, still surprised she was actually *wanting* to be part of that crowd. "He's a terrific horse, and I could use the practice after the school year."

"Who knows?" Butler said. "You may fall head over heels in love with my fine lad, mightn't she, Puck?

Well, take him off and groom him now. I'll be off to tell Clare the news."

"Clare?"

Butler shrugged. "I was thinking about letting her take him on, but he works better for you and he needs the points he can earn there."

She'd bumped Clare out of the top spot as best rider at the stable? Part of Victoria soared. She glanced over at the crowd of kids, tempted to give the girl a well-deserved cutdown. But you didn't make friends at a stable that way.

"Mr. Butler, let Clare ride Puck. She knows him a lot better than I do, and—"

"Absolutely not, Victoria," her father interrupted. "You heard Mr. Butler. He needs to win and Puck should be ridden by whoever is the best. You never have to apologize for being the best."

"I know you would make a better showing on Puck," Butler explained. "Clare wanted to ride him, but there just wasn't any spark. No connection, you know?"

Victoria slumped. She knew only too well.

"So, Victoria." Butler smiled. "Are you and Puck here a team, then? Can I count on you?"

"Of course you can," her father began, but Butler cut him off.

"It's not your fence to jump, Mr. Tolliver. It's hers. What do you say, girl?"

She glanced from her father to the trainer, then at Puck. "I came to Ireland to ride," she reminded herself aloud.

"It's settled, then. We'll start work again after lunch and see if we can't put you in the winner's circle."

She watched the trainer stride toward the cluster of kids, feeling like she was watching an ax fall.

She'd told herself she didn't care about fitting in because she'd known it would be hard. Knew she'd have to prove herself. Strange that, awkward as the party had been, shy as she was, in her heart of hearts she'd wanted to finally fit in. Belong in a way she couldn't at the Academy. Sure, it was easy to be valedictorian, she wanted to shout at her father, when you'd been dragged from school to school so often you felt awkward coming out of your room. Different. Always different, no matter how many girls acted like they wanted to be friends with you. Because you knew the truth. That you could pretend all you wanted, but you didn't quite fit.

"Did you hear him, sweetheart?" Daddy beamed up at her. "He's the finest trainer in Ireland and you knocked his socks off! That other kid won't know what hit her!"

Oh, yes she would, Victoria thought with a strange mix of triumph and despair. Clare would know—and hate her for it. She pasted on another smile, like she had so many times before, surprised at the stirring of resentment she felt.

What was wrong with her? It was stupid to blame Daddy for not knowing she was upset. After all, wasn't she *trying* to hide it from him? She could just tell him the truth if she wanted him to know it, couldn't she? Tell him how she felt?

She heard angry voices at the stable door, looked over to see Trevor Butler and Clare in fierce conversation. The girl's face turned red right up to the roots of her hair, her arms waving wildly. Victoria wished she could melt right into the saddle as the crowd at the stable door buzzed, their eyes flashing from the two people arguing to where Victoria still sat astride Puck, completely exposed.

"It's not personal, lass, and you know it!" Butler's voice raised above the uproar. "It's about what is best for the horse, aye, and the stables. You can ride the mare. You do well on her."

It was over as fast as it began. Clare stormed off in tears, Dara in hot pursuit. The other kids filtered into the dark door of the stable, going off to whisper and complain and probably bash the snotty American who had caused all the problems. Victoria's ears burned.

Daddy grinned up at her, gloating. "What a terrific day!"

"Terrific." Victoria let a tiny quaver into her voice. But her father didn't notice. Visions of silver trophies danced in his head.

14

*N*ow he knew what it felt like to be hung, drawn, and quartered, Michael thought with grim amusement, at least the drawing part. He wrestled to control two horses at once—Tristan, the long-suffering therapy horse he was astride, and Innisfree, fighting like a sonofabitch on his left. His left arm felt like it should trail down past his knees once this ride was over. Innisfree had struggled against the lead from the moment he'd let the gelding out of his pasture at Glenammura.

He'd figured the horse would fight him every step of the way, but as soon as Kilrain was in sight, Innisfree stopped pulling backward, resisting and trying to run back to familiar pasture. This time, the gelding was battling to race ahead to Kilrain.

Michael knew the simplest solution: the smartest, least painful thing to do would be to unsnap the lead from Innisfree's halter and let the horse dash ahead to have tea with Bonaparte at his own speed. It would be easy enough for Rory to catch the horse once Innisfree clomped into the castle's Great Hall. But even with the boy there, Michael didn't want to risk frightening Eve, or, he thought uneasily, risk Innisfree hurting her. The horse had made strides over the past three months, but Michael had no illusions. Innisfree was still capable of putting someone in traction, especially someone as in-experienced around animals as Eve was.

No, better to fight the big animal all the way to the

castle himself, Michael thought, and then turn him
over to Rory. The boy could work off some of that ex-
cess energy he had wrestling Innisfree into his new
quarters. That is, if anyone in the castle was even
awake after everything they'd gone through the last
few days.

Eve.

Michael winced, his imagination far too vivid for his
own good. It was nothing short of a miracle Innisfree
hadn't kicked her that first morning at the castle.
Nothing short of a miracle she'd managed to stand up
to the pressures she'd been under since she'd arrived
in Ireland. Nothing short of a miracle she'd survived
the loss of her daughter so many years ago. She was so
vulnerable, so wounded, so hurt by all that had happened to her. Michael wondered if the woman had any
idea that she was also strong. Strong and so beautiful it
made him ache inside. Generous enough to take Rory
into her care and at least try to help him. Stubborn
enough not to give up on the boy.

Had she given up on herself? a voice inside him
whispered. Given up on happiness, on loving someone?
She had been prickly as hell, ready to do battle the first
time Michael had seen her. Defensive, defiant, scornful,
judgmental as hell. He'd wanted to wring her pretty
neck that first day at the farm when she'd jumped into
the fight between him and Dennis Moran. And at the
courtroom, when he'd first found out she'd hired the
Fitzgeralds a five-star barrister, he'd almost hated her.

Then she'd taken the stand, told truths that devastated her, admitted mistakes that were still carved into
her face, told of losses that still haunted her eyes.
She'd done everything in her power to make things
right, but it hadn't been enough. Even when it looked
like the battle was lost, she'd kept fighting. Then last
night, she'd finished the story. Told of her being cold.
Hungry. Of being manipulated by someone far more
wealthy, more powerful than she. Of being tired, des-

perate, backed into a corner so tight she'd had to take her daughter to work where the little girl had gotten hurt. Then, instead of caring about her, supporting her, her daughter's father had moved in for the kill. Taken her little girl and left her alone.

And she'd stayed that way. Michael could see it in her face. How careful she'd been, how afraid under all that bravado. The slightest smile of appreciation from a man, the barest hint he was interested would send her diving behind walls thicker and higher than any Kilrain had to offer.

Who could blame Eve after what her daughter's bastard of a father had taken away from her? Love wasn't supposed to steal from you. It was supposed to make you stronger, better, fill you up, not empty you out. The way that kiss had filled him last night.

Not that he loved Eve Danaher, he amended hastily to himself. He just—just admired her. Felt a need to protect her the way he did anything wounded. He just wanted her to have a little shelter from the storm—

Damn, wasn't that what Bridey had said the first time she'd told him about the American stranger who was coming to Kilrain? The time he'd nearly lost his mind and his temper and done his best to convince the old woman she was crazy? How could she know the truth about Eve Danaher when Bridey had never even looked into her eyes? Michael wondered. Because it was the truth. Eve did need somewhere to land. She was tired and sad and trying so hard to do better. Maybe it was time he tried to help her instead of hindering her at every pass.

As he rode into the castle yard, he found that the place was silent. Quiet, the way it had been the morning he'd ridden over with Bridey's breakfast to find the old woman lying stone-still on the floor.

It was crazy to feel that low throb of alarm, but he couldn't help it. The thousand and one disasters he'd imagined could happen at the castle all through his sleepless night reared up in his mind. He scrambled down from his own patient mount and tied him to the hitching post he and Sean had erected as boys. But there wasn't a hitching post in all Ireland strong enough to hold Innisfree when there was the prospect of tea to be had. Surrendering to the inevitable, Michael snapped off the restless gelding's lead and opened the castle door.

Bonaparte leapt up from his cushion and rushed to meet Innisfree with doggy delight as the horse entered the Great Hall as if he owned it.

"Eve?" Michael called out softly. "Rory?" No answer. Everything was fine, Michael reassured himself. They were both just sleeping. But he had to tell Rory the horse was here. Innisfree would need to be soothed, eased into his new domain. No one could do that as well as the horse's boy.

Leaving the two unlikely pals to complain about the service, no water, no dog food, and no grain set out for munching, Michael set out up the spiral stone stairs, fully planning to go to the top floor where the priest hole was.

But it seemed Eve Danaher hadn't slept any sounder than he had. He was just reaching the second level when he heard a soft, feminine voice. "Rory? Rory, is that you?"

He almost forgot to feel relieved as the swift stab of awareness jolted through him. He could picture her, too damned clearly the way she'd been that first morning—tousled and heavy-eyed, the tee shirt she'd slept in melting into every curve, her legs long and slender, her feet bare, so dainty, touched with color on her toenails. He'd been lucky then. So damned distracted he hadn't realized she wasn't just sexy enough to get any man's blood pumping. That there was something more to "Bridey's American" than met the eye. Something beyond sunshiny hair and a kissable mouth, skin smooth as cream just before you skimmed it from the top of the milk pail. There was something more than breasts so high and firm they'd made him wonder what it would feel like to cup his hands over them, feel her respond beneath that thin, time-worn layer of cotton.

Yes, dammit, then he'd been too much of an ass to realize that there were deeper layers to Eve Danaher.

Michael swallowed hard. "It's me. Michael."

But the warning came too late. She was already pushing open the bedroom door. For a heartbeat he couldn't breathe, in an instant taking in every part of her from the worried crease between her pale eyebrows to the soft blond curls that looked as if fingers had tried to comb out the tangles. Michael wished those fingers had been his.

Worse still, she wasn't in the old tee shirt. She stunned him with a floor-length nightgown with about a million tiny tucks in the front. A wide satin ribbon held it closed just where the shadow of her cleavage started to show.

"Michael," she said, staring at him, big-eyed and drowsy.

Had she ever called him by his first name before? He couldn't remember. Every rational thought in his head seemed to have flown south the instant he'd seen the barest hint of the cleft between her breasts. "You're—um—not wearing your tee shirt." He sounded like a complete idiot.

She flushed, and Michael could see the instant she remembered the kiss they'd shared the night before. Something like fear flickered into her eyes. It would have twisted his heart if he hadn't also glimpsed the barest hint of wonder. He could see her make a mental dive to try to change the subject. "The tee shirt was so short. I wanted to be decent to go after Rory if I needed to."

She thought this nightgown was better to chase down a seventeen-year-old boy in? She obviously had no understanding of male hormones. Michael's blood was pounding so hard it was pure luck the zipper on his riding breeches was still holding. Maybe she should start sleeping in one of his old sweat suits. She'd be swimming in them. It should have calmed down his arousal, but the idea of Eve's body in something that had touched him all over was almost more than he could take. He looked down at the stone floor, trying to distract himself. His gaze collided with those shell-shaped pink toenails. He'd promised himself he'd give her space, he'd be careful, wouldn't muddy the waters with wanting her so badly when so much was at stake: Rory's hiding place, Bridey's health, his own sanity—

"Michael, why are you here? Is there something wrong?"

Plenty. But he wasn't about to tell her what it was. He tried to defuse the tension for both of their sakes with humor. "I brought Innisfree over. He's downstairs with Bonaparte. I have to say, he's not thrilled with what you did with his water trough."

"I just got the worst of the dust off. It's a Saxon urn. It's priceless."

"Well, there's no water in it. That's all Innisfree cares about."

She raised one hand up to rub the sleep from her eyes, the fabric of her nightgown pulling taut over her breast. He could see the darker circle of her aureole against the thin fabric. His mouth went dry. "Do you want me to go get Rory?" she asked.

"No!" Michael snapped.

She drew back, startled.

"Not dressed like that, anyway," he tried to explain too hastily. "I've got enough problems controlling the poor kid. You'd give him a heart attack." He'd just made things worse. So much for cherishing, protecting—and keeping his distance!

A hot blush rose from the dusky cleft that half-hid the ribbon tie from her nightgown. She turned sunrise-pink from breasts to cheeks. "I just—it covers more than most of my clothes!" she defended. He hated the hurt that sparked in her eyes and the uncertainty, as if she'd made a mistake just as she'd been terrified she would.

"It's not that. It's just—" He hesitated. He might not be able to taste her again the way he was tempted to, but that didn't mean he was willing to hurt her more than she already had been. "Eve, you're . . . you're a beautiful woman. I'm a grown man, and looking at you makes me . . ." *Hungry.* He couldn't say it aloud. "I'll go up and get Rory myself. You go back to bed."

Wrong thing to say. Worse thing to think. He glanced past her to where the giant Jacobean bed was a tangle of sheets and coverlets and pillows still hollowed out in the shape of Eve's body. Every romantic fantasy he'd ever had of a knight and his lady fair flared up in his mind. She looked so much like she belonged here, in this room, in that bed. All she needed was a man to sweep her up in his arms, carry her across the room, lay her down and—

"Michael, you have to wake up the whole county? Even the roosters would like to kick your arse for it!" Rory's surly voice shattered the images. Michael had never been more grateful for the kid's bad temper.

"You've got a horse to tend to," Michael hollered up to the next floor. "Some things don't wait until it's convenient."

Things like horses and troubled boys. And like fairy maidens in long white nightgowns. He curled his fingers tight into the palms of his hands, wishing he couldn't already feel the slick, cool silk of that ribbon against his skin, imagine the contrast as he untied it, his knuckles brushing against the warm cream of her breasts.

Unable to resist one last, heavy stare at her, Michael turned and started back down the stairs. "Hurry up with you, then, boyo!" he yelled as he went back down the stairs, feeling as if he were being pursued by one of those invading armies Bridey liked to talk about. But this time the enemy was inside *him.* Needs he'd pushed aside because he'd been too busy, wants he hadn't even realized he still had, that thirst for something dangerous he could so seldom resist. And Eve Danaher was dangerous, no question. A tempting blend of need and inner strength, beauty and pain, stubbornness and generosity. But Bridey's ancestors had withstood sieges in this castle before. Surely he could manage to do so, too, at least until Rory was safe.

Eve closed the bedroom door and leaned her back against it, trying to remember how to breathe. The nightgown that had seemed so sensible to wear last night might as well have been a black lace negligee the way Halloran had looked at her. She'd long ago accepted that she had all the allure of Little Miss Muffet. Why did one look from one man suddenly make her feel so strange in her own skin?

Because he'd kissed her last night when she was hurting so badly? When she felt so damned alone and sad and the memories had come too fast for her to hold them at bay? Tender, searching, healing—she could still feel the gentle movements of his mouth against hers, still feel the way his touch had driven back the cold, smoothed the sharp edges, bridged the yawning chasm of loneliness that had opened up in her heart.

He'd made her feel not so alone, even just for that moment, and that moment had given her a chance to catch her breath, regain her balance, strengthen the weak places inside her. He'd been tender, caring, comforting. Kind as he was to so many people—Bridey and Sean, the kids he helped at the farm. It was second nature to the man, she was starting to believe. But there was nothing as mild as kindness behind the look she'd seen on his face moments ago.

Eve, you're a beautiful woman, the memory of that whiskey-rough brogue shot right through her, raining sparks in its wake. Michael Halloran had looked at her like he was the big bad wolf and he wanted to gobble her up. No man had ever looked at her that way before. Not because they didn't want to, Steffie would argue, but because she wouldn't give them the chance. She'd freeze them out or stonewall them or run like hell, Steff had always accused. But this time, there was nowhere to run and Halloran had already seen all the holes in her defenses.

No. No man had ever looked at her the way Halloran had, Eve thought, her heart fluttering in panic and in an unexpected trill of excitement. Chad had been smooth, polished, a master at manipulation to get what he wanted. Every move calculated for best effect. But Halloran was as earthy as the land he lived on. All man, from the toes of his scuffed riding boots to the thick waves of dark hair that tumbled over his forehead. Unfortunately, what scared her was every inch in between.

She heard Halloran's footsteps get fainter, fade to silence, then Rory's boot soles pounding down the stone stairs with enough noise for a whole herd of boys. She hesitated for a moment, not sure what to do. Halloran had told her to go back to bed, but if she stayed in her room too much longer, she might never have the guts to come out.

She threw on her clothes, dragged a brush through her hair and knotted it at her nape with the blue denim-colored scrunchie she used to keep her hair out of her eyes when she was working. Slipping into her tennis shoes, she charged down the stairs. It had only taken her a few minutes to change, but Rory was already in the middle of the pasture, Innisfree fighting the lead as if the boy were trying to force him into a burning barn. Eve would almost rather take her chances with the flames than face the unexpected fire in Michael Halloran's eyes.

Halloran stood, legs braced apart, hands on hips as he watched the boy struggle to quiet the horse. Eve would have lashed out at him for abandoning the boy with that dangerous horse except for the fact that Halloran's knuckles were white. She could sense that every muscle was tense with the need to go out there and try to help Rory handle Innisfree.

"That horse is going to kill him!" she gasped as Innisfree reared up, tossing his head, jerking Rory off balance. The boy scrambled back to his feet, his voice low, soothing, as he talked to the horse. Eve knew she'd be so scared she'd be screaming her bloody head off!

"He can handle the horse," Halloran said between gritted teeth. "He has to. He'll be the only one here to do it. Unless you want to volunteer?"

"I agreed to watch Rory. The horse is on his own."

Halloran's breath hissed between his teeth as a hoof came too close to Rory. Rory turned his back on the horse, walking slowly away.

"Halloran, tell him to turn around! He can't even see Innisfree to jump out of the way!" Eve cried, grabbing the rigid muscles of his arm. But Halloran only shook his head.

"Watch," he said..

The horse wasn't fighting so hard, in fact, Innisfree looked like a toddler who had lost its audience during the middle of a temper tantrum. Eve stared in amazement as Innisfree put all four hooves on the ground for the first time. The horse whickered, gave his head one last toss, then started after Rory, one step at a time. Rory stopped walking. Innisfree got within a nose's length of the boy's back and gave him a little nudge.

Eve's heart stopped. For the first time since she'd met the troubled boy, Rory's mouth was curved into an angel's smile.

"Easy, boy. Easy." Rory soothed the big animal, running his hand up under the horse's forelock.

Eve's eyes burned. Her hand trembled, fell away from Halloran's sleeve.

"*That* is why I let Rory work with that horse." Halloran's voice was reverent, almost a prayer.

Eve whispered, "It's like a miracle."

"No." Halloran turned toward her, blue eyes heart-full, voice choked with emotion. "It isn't *like* a miracle, Eve. It *is* one."

"Is it always like this?" she asked shakily. "What you do, I mean. With animals. With kids."

He smiled. "Not always. But often enough that I know I'll never do anything else with my life."

What was it like to feel the way he did about the work you did? The passion? The certainty that you were making a difference? Making the world a little bit better place? Not that Eve didn't love her job—she did. But centuries-old canvas and metal and paint couldn't smile up at you the way Rory had. They couldn't run and laugh and get a second chance to embrace life.

Eve felt something close to jealousy. And regret. Regret that she'd brushed aside Sean's invitations to show her the workings of the farm. Regret that she'd held herself aloof from it all and missed—missed moments like this. But Victoria's rejection had still been so fresh, so painful. She hadn't had the strength to see happy children, children with parents smiling and laughing and overcoming life's toughest hurdles together. She surprised herself when she spoke.

"Remember that morning you and Sean were talking, and he asked if I wanted to go out to the paddocks with you?"

"Can't say I blame you for running the other way. I hadn't been the most charming of company when you were around."

She smiled. "For once you had nothing to do with it. It was the kids—seeing them. I'd caught glimpses of them when I'd come for meals, enough to feel how much it hurt. It was like watching everything I'd missed with Victoria, somehow."

Empathy filled his eyes. "It must be so hard not to see her."

"You know, I never even go to the park back home. When the school kids would have tours at the museum I'd practically barricade myself in my workroom.

Even when I'd pass kids on the street, I'd walk faster, looked over their heads, tried not to hear those high little voices. But sometimes, I couldn't help myself. The worst was when I'd hear some little girl calling for her mommy."

He took her hand, squeezed it. She was glad of that warm strength enfolding her. "I'm so sorry, Eve." And he was. It was there in every line of his face, the curve of his mouth, the shadows in his eyes. "It wasn't fair to you. *I* wasn't fair to you. When you said you weren't interested in the kids, I—"

"Figured I had all the warmth of Cruella de Ville. Can't say I blamed you. I wanted you to think I was hard, cold. It made me feel safer than having anyone know the truth. How much I hurt inside. How much I miss my baby. How scared I am that I can never make things right with her." Eve's voice lowered. "How I failed her."

"You didn't fail her. You did what you could to fight back. But how could you fight that much money, that much power? Someone that ruthless?"

"How can you know that for sure?"

"Because I saw you fight for Rory in that courtroom. And yesterday in the barn. I saw the pain in your eyes when you spoke of your daughter. I know you'd never just let her go. That losing her has hurt you forever, every single day since the one she was taken from you."

Understanding. Compassion. Not the slightest hint of blame. He surprised her. Humbled her. Scared her.

"I was so stupid. Scholarship kid at a ritzy academy, working so hard to get away from being poor, stuck in the dead-end jobs my mother was always griping about. Thought I was so smart. So determined. I could never get trapped the way she had." Eve shook her head at the girl she'd been, so sure of herself so long ago. She hadn't realized how quickly one bad decision could sweep everything away.

"All teenagers think they're bulletproof. It's damned terrifying to watch them once you get to the other side. But everyone makes mistakes. You shouldn't have had to pay such a high price for this one. Losing your daughter. Being too hurt to—" He stopped, flushed, rubbing his fingers against her knuckles.

"Go ahead and say it, Michael. It's true. Running away from anything that could really touch me. Avoiding everything but work. Hiding from other people's kids because mine was out of reach. Thinking all men were bastards because the one time I'd slept with a man he'd turned out to be one."

"I feel sorry about that—sorry—not just because you missed out on having someone in your life, but because—" He stopped, his throat working. "Because some man who might almost deserve the kind of love you've got locked up inside you is missing out on his chance to . . . to have you in his life."

The words were too much—too kind, too caring—she wanted to hear them too much. She pulled away from him, suddenly shy, completely off balance. She struggled to change the subject. What was it she'd wanted to say before Michael had cut to her darkest secrets with those incredible blue eyes? The kids. It had started with Michael's therapy kids.

"I wish I could see—more of how the animal therapy works, I mean. I know I have to stay at the castle, but—"

Halloran's brow swept up. "I never said you had to be chained to the castle or to Rory when we made this bargain."

"But if Rory decided to run—"

"You wouldn't be able to stop him even if you were here. If he really decides to leave, nobody will be able to stop him. He stays because he wants to, for however long he wants to. All three of us have to accept that. But we've got a bit of a secret weapon on our side now, Eve. He's not going anywhere now that he's got that horse to look after."

"I hadn't thought about it that way," Eve admitted.

"Actually, I could use some help. Rory can't be seen

at Glenammura. And when I called Sean last night he asked if it would be okay if he didn't come back for a few days. Would you like to see how my farm works, then, Eve Danaher?" Halloran asked so softly she trembled.

He was short of help at the farm? Eve thought numbly. She'd be about as much "help" as a three-year-old cleaning a china cabinet, but surely Michael had to know that. She hadn't made any secret of the way she felt about animals. That very first morning he had seen her at her worst. He couldn't possibly have forgotten after she'd made such a fool of herself.

She hesitated for a moment longer, still nervous by the unexpected closeness between them, trying to get used to looking at a man as anything but dangerous. But Michael had done his best to make her feel safe, hadn't he? Even when he'd kissed her.

Wasn't that the most dangerous thing of all? a voice whispered inside her. No. He'd backed off when she'd needed him to. He'd been unbelievably understanding. He'd keep his distance if she asked him to.

It would be fine, she reasoned. Anyway, what could happen surrounded by a bunch of kids and a farm full of animals? She'd probably be such a wreck around Halloran's menagerie she wouldn't even notice Michael had eyes like a summer lake and a mouth strong, hard. Heaven help her now that she knew it could also be tender.

"Will you come with me, Eve?" he asked again.

She took a deep breath, feeling like she was stepping off the edge of a cliff.

"I will."

He grinned, suddenly, like sunshine bursting through clouds, almost too bright to be real. "I'm holding you to that."

"I said I would go, didn't I?"

"That was before you realized you'd have to get to Glenammura on the back of my horse."

Her eyes widened, her hands palm up as if fending off a blow. The thought of the horse drove back confusion, tenderness, left no room for fear of anything except the gigantic monster of an animal he was trying to get her to ride. "No way, Halloran. You ride. I'll walk. The exercise will do me good. Besides, I'm supposed to be seeing some of the country anyway. I'm on vacation, believe it or not."

"It's a long way back to the farm. You'll be begging me for a ride before we're halfway there, Yank," he teased her.

"My forebears walked all the way to Oregon and back, Irish. Let's get one thing straight. I'll do whatever I can to help you once we get to the farm, but I'm keeping my own two feet on the ground, thank you very much. End of discussion. I don't get near horses."

He pointed out to the pasture where Rory and Innisfree were facing each other now, gently butting heads. "You didn't have anything to do with teenage boys either until yesterday," he reminded her, so smug she wanted to hit him. She groped in her mind for the perfect comeback but before she could find it, Halloran climbed over the fence and started toward Rory and Innisfree, three creatures, beautiful, wild, dangerous, each in their own way.

She stared at them, irritated, intrigued, trying not to laugh. A witty comeback was impossible, she realized. Especially since Halloran was right.

15

What was that song her mother used to sing? Eve tried to remember. "It's a long way to Tipperary." Maybe that was true, but if the view was anything like the one she'd seen as she made her way to Glenammura, nobody in their right mind would have regretted the walk. There were moments she was so enchanted she almost—*almost*—forgot about the mountain of equine muscle and sharp hooves trailing three yards behind Halloran, linked to the Irishman by a pair of reins that didn't look half strong enough to hold it.

Halloran certainly seemed to ignore the animal—what had he called it? Tristan?—as he strolled along beside her, taking no more notice of the animal than if it had been one of the gauzy-winged dragonflies circling the pasture.

This place would be easy to love, Eve thought. The turf beneath her feet was thick and soft as a down comforter, the color so intense it seemed like it should stain everything it touched green. Wildflowers nodded bright faces at her, gorse and heather, kingcups and azaleas, and the fuchsia! Bushes of it, taller than her head, branches weighed down with flowers rich as jewels.

She'd never understood her mother's melancholy longing for the "auld sod," nor the obsession of people whose ancestors had lived in America since the time of the Revolutionary War still insisting on calling themselves Irish-Americans. Okay, so St. Patrick's Day was a good excuse for a party if you were into green beer.

But she'd never been able to figure out what it was about Ireland that made people's eyes fill with tears during a ballad at a mock Irish pub in Manhattan, their faces haunted with homesickness for a place they'd never even seen.

But now, as she walked along with Halloran and his horse, she wondered what it must have been like for her ancestors to leave this green and magic place where the wind whispered of fairies and poets and enchantment. What had it been like for those people to be dumped into the teeming, stinking slums of New York City? Or to trek across country through deserts and badlands where the land was shrunk to hot bones, and soft rain and tender green things were as far away and impossible to touch as the moon?

"Feet hurting yet, pioneer woman?"

Halloran's voice startled her out of her thoughts. She gave the horse another wary glance. Maybe she and Michael had managed to make peace, but she'd walk all the way back to Manhattan in high heels before she got any closer to that thing.

"My feet are just fine, thank you."

Halloran's brow furrowed with something like worry. "Something's wrong. You were making a damn sour face."

"I was just thinking that if some man had dragged me away from here, across an ocean to New York City in the old days, I would have killed him. How could anyone have chosen to leave this place?"

The hard planes of Halloran's face softened, pensive. "Most didn't choose. It was leave or die. When your children are starving, you do what you have to if you want to survive."

"I know that's true," Eve said. "But—you can be hungry for other things besides food. Hungry for—" Green. Wind. Sky. Jagged rocks and piled stone fences. The smell of peat smoke and air sweeter than anything she'd ever imagined. The touch of someone who loved you. She stopped. It sounded ridiculous.

Michael shrugged. "I never could have left here if I hadn't known I could come back whenever I wanted to. I can't imagine stepping onto a ship knowing I'd never see this place again, hear the sea breaking on Clogher Point, see the Blasket Islands floating in the mist. No wonder they gave people wakes when they were going to America. Part of them was dying. They'd never see their parents again, their brothers and sisters and friends. Or the land."

It was such an unexpected discovery—that people could be homesick for a *place*. Maybe she'd never been able to imagine it because she'd never really called anywhere home. But what if she *had* had a home? What if it had been a place like this? A forever place where she'd expected to live and grow old, where her children's children would still tend the same pastures and mend the same stone fences her great-grandparents had once cared for? What would it be like to feel that chain of generations upon generations break? To be cast adrift with nothing to buoy you up but desperation and hope? Someone in her family a hundred and fifty some years ago had faced that kind of loss. Someone who might have given her the color of her eyes, her hair, the shape of her face. "I don't know anything about my great-grandparents except that they were from the ring of Kerry. But my mother never stopped wishing to come here."

"Maybe it's born in you, that hunger in the blood for green places. The brothers who taught me as a boy said everyone with Irish blood has it. That need for the greening. I remember when Sean and I were at St. Malachy's we were damned disappointed when we studied Irish saints. The Italians, they had grand martyrs—tortured in the Inquisition, and the Spanish ones, sliced up by infidels. Deliciously gruesome, they were. But when Christianity came to Ireland, we didn't have any blood martyrs. No Irish saints dying dramatically with a million arrows sticking in them or skinned alive or broken on the wheel. It was embarrassing to all of us kids in the religion class, grisly little buggers that we were."

She smiled, trying to imagine Halloran in his school uniform—pants and white shirt, blazer and school tie. She had a feeling that with him and Sean in the same class, the brothers had had their hands full. "I studied saints in catechism. The pictures in Sister Agatha's big book gave me nightmares. I mean, St. Lucy standing there with her eyes lying on a plate!" She shuddered in remembrance.

"Ah, and wouldn't Sean and I have loved *that*? But no. We had Brother Thomas—so old we thought he was on a first name acquaintance with St. Patrick himself. You should have seen how solemn his face was the day he told us the worst thing that could happen to any Irish saint. We were hoping for some lovely meat hooks or burnings at the stake. Brother told us that the worst fate was the green martyrdom."

"It sounds grisly enough."

"Not for ten-year-old boys. Green martyrdom was to be exiled from Ireland. Sent away, never to come back. It was a great disappointment to me when I was a lad, but now . . ." He fiddled with Tristan's reins, something honest and vulnerable and more than a little shy curving his mouth. "Sometimes, when I look out over the farm at dawn, I think being stretched on the rack would have been far kinder."

Eve couldn't pull her gaze away from him. Who would ever have guessed that Michael Halloran, that handsome, polished face that had grinned so smugly out at her from so many magazines, would feel so deep? Love things like these? Land and half-crazy horses, broken children and angry boys, wind in his face, and an old woman who lived in a castle that had seen better days when it was under siege?

She shivered. Halloran said he'd gotten Innisfree so he could have his adrenaline fix. In his own way, the man was still hurling himself over fences designed to break someone's neck. Maybe he wouldn't be physically hurt, but emotionally, the risks he was taking terrified her, fascinated her. It took a lot more guts to risk your heart than it took to risk bruises and broken bones.

He crossed to a rusted metal gate, unfastened the chain that held it shut. "You can see the farmhouse from here," he said, pointing. She strained on tiptoe, seeing the whitewashed stone of the farmhouse's walls. Sun struck something metal on the gravel road. A car?

"Is Sean back?" Eve asked, but the color was all wrong. Red. Moran's car was red. Her stomach turned inside out. "Halloran, is it Moran? Do you think he knows about Rory? Guessed Rory would come here?" How fast could she run back to the castle to warn Rory? Could she possibly reach him in time?

Did her panic show in her face? Halloran surprised her by brushing her cheek with his knuckles. "Whist, now. You're skittish as Innisfree, Eve. It's not Moran's car you're seeing there. It's Joy come for her session."

"Joy? I didn't know that was an Irish name."

"It isn't. Not exactly." He flushed just a little, looking sheepish. "Her real name is Theresa. I just . . . just call her Joy because—well, watch and you'll see for yourself."

His step had new spring in it as he strode toward the visitors, and Eve was curious enough to hurry to keep up. They were only halfway across the pasture when a little head popped up over the edge of the stone fence. Blond pigtails ruffled by the wind framed a face that was too pale and thin, but Eve only noticed that for an instant before she fell into the widest, most sparkling blue-gray eyes she'd ever seen.

Eve's heart lurched at the memory of another blond-haired little girl, angel-fine hair she'd once brushed into pigtails. *No!* Pony*tails, Mama*, she could hear Victoria insist in her most determined tone. *Pony-tails, like the horsies I'm going to ride.*

"Tristan! Tristan!" a little piping voice cried out, waving frantically. "I've been looking an' looking for you!"

Michael grinned, approaching the little mite. "And what about me, Joy of my heart?"

"Oh, I was looking for you, too, Michael," she said earnestly, then her baby-pink lips curled into a mischievous grin. "I need you to saddle my baby, don't I, Trissy?" For a moment, the little girl was so enraptured at seeing the horse she didn't even notice Eve was standing there. Good thing, Eve thought, since she was trying to squeeze down the knot that had formed in her throat.

"Theresa Mary, aren't you going to say hello to the nice lady?" a feminine voice chided. A breathless woman of about thirty with a freckled face and sad eyes poked her head up from something she was doing.

"Oh." Joy looked up, surprised, as if Eve had just materialized out of thin air. "I'm sorry, um, nice lady, but you're not a horse, an' Michael always says I never see anything 'less it has a mane and a tail."

Eve's smile was brittle around the edges. "Some little girls are like that." She swallowed hard, admitting wistfully, "My *favorite* little girls."

Halloran's eyes caught hers, his gaze probing, his own grin fading just a little.

Eve brought herself up short. She wasn't going to ruin things just because a memory stung. She'd wanted to see what it was Halloran did with the kids who came to Glenammura, and little Joy was obviously thrilled at the prospect of her session. It wasn't *her* fault she had blond hair and that incredible light in her eyes. It wasn't her fault she reminded Eve so much of a little girl from long ago.

Michael gestured to the girl's mother. "Eve, this is Majella O'Hara, one of the finest women in the glen, if you ask some men around this farm."

Majella's cheeks turned pink. Eve tried not to notice a tiny jab of envy. But Joy was already chattering on.

"Michael, is this lady going to help with the horses 'cause Rory can't anymore?" Joy asked, a shadow in her eyes.

"The lady's name is Eve, Joy, and she's from America. She's going to help some, but not with the horses."

"I'm afraid of them," Eve confessed.

Eve wasn't sure what she'd expected, but it wasn't the nod of understanding she got from the little girl. "I was 'fraid of horses, too, until Michael helped me. 'Cause they're so big an' my legs hurt real bad. But Glenammura's like magic. Tristan would never ever hurt you, an' Michael will always catch you if you fall."

What would it feel like to be so certain? That no one would ever hurt you and that someone would always catch you when you fell? Eve wondered. But then, Joy was a little girl. Life hadn't shown her its rough edges yet.

"I can't catch you if you ride too fast ahead of me, young lady. Remember we talked about that last time." Michael chuckled, and opened a smaller gate, letting Eve through it. For the first time she saw beneath Joy's head and shoulders. She tried not to let her shock show. Miniature leg braces lay in a tangle of metal and Velcro and plastic on the ground beside a child-sized wheelchair.

Eve felt as if Tristan had kicked her in the stomach.

Michael scooped the little girl up in his arms, placing her high up on Tristan's back. Joy winced as her legs stretched to sit astride. She wriggled determinedly in the saddle, trying to settle herself as Michael shortened the stirrups. Her shirttail was pulled out, and Eve glimpsed a scar slithering like an angry red snake across the little girl's baby-soft skin.

"Shall we show Eve how to ride, Joy?" Michael asked. "Then maybe she won't be so afraid." The little girl gave a bounce of sheer delight.

"I can do it myself, now," she said, fiercely proud as she took the reins in her small hands. "Well, almost by myself," she felt compelled to amend, glancing over at her mother.

Majella smiled, so tender. Eve could sense how hard it was for her not to let her worry show.

"Be caref—I mean, have fun, little one," Majella said with a brave smile, then knelt down to gather up the braces.

Eve's heart bled for her.

"Your little girl is . . . is beautiful," Eve said, remembering how she'd glowed years ago when she and Tori had been going through grocery store aisles or through the park and someone had stopped to say something like that. "She's so . . . so happy," she couldn't help adding in amazement.

"That she is, now, thanks to Michael and that horse. Before—well, I don't even want to think about what it was like before we found them. Joy was so small and so weak and everything they did to try and get her back on her feet after the accident hurt her so badly."

"An accident did this to her?" Eve asked, nodding toward the wheelchair. She couldn't imagine the damage it had taken to hurt the little girl so badly. She closed her eyes, picturing the terror of finding out your baby had been hurt, the astringent smell of hospital rooms, the waiting and waiting and waiting while doctors tried to fix what was broken. And then, the sick horror when they told you that the little girl who had skipped out your door that morning, so full of life, might never be able to walk again.

"She was riding a bicycle. I didn't want to let her do it. But I was trying not to be overprotective. She's my only, you know. These roads are so narrow it's hard to see around the corners. Most people who live around here know that and are careful, but if you're not—" She shrugged. "Someone new to the area hit her. They said she would never walk again. But now . . . now they aren't so sure. Michael is, though. He says he'll walk her down the aisle at her wedding someday."

Eve did a double-take. Wedding? What would Halloran be doing walking Theresa down the aisle at her wedding? That was a job for Joy's own father, wasn't it, unless—

He'd said "some men" thought Majella one of the finest women in the glen. Could he have been talking about himself? Maybe he had no children of his own. But hadn't he already shown he was quick enough to love other people's children? And if that was so, why not their mothers as well? The thought pricked her. But there was no mistaking the adoring light in Joy's mother's eyes.

"Are you and . . . and Michael—" Eve stopped, appalled at herself. So Michael had kissed her once—that didn't give her the right to go prying around his personal life.

"Michael is just a good friend. Joy's father left when she was three. It's been just the two of us for so long. Michael helps where he can. He never says anything, but I know he just doesn't want me to feel all alone."

God, what would it have meant to Eve if there had been someone like Michael to turn to when her life was falling apart? When she had half a bowl of Cheerios in the house and the utility company was getting ugly. When Tori had a fever and she was scraping in the cracks of the worn out couch to try to scrounge up enough lost change to buy her medicine? What if Michael had been with her at the emergency room when Chad had come charging in, the picture of parental outrage while underneath he was probably gleeful that she'd given him an opening, a chance to take her baby away for good. She fought back a jab of envy.

"Are you and Michael optimistic then, that your little girl will recover?"

"What's more important, Joy is. When she's up on that horse, she feels like she can go anywhere. Do anything. The other day, she said it was better than walking. It was like flying."

Echoes of Victoria again. Eve turned to watch Halloran work with Joy. Saw him challenge her, praise her, help her reach for her dream to walk again.

No wonder he couldn't let Moran close Glenammura down, not even to protect Rory. What would it mean to Joy to come up to the farm's main gates and find them locked? Her horse gone? She'd be chained to the wheelchair again, with no chance of flying. . . .

An hour seemed to pass in moments, the lesson over all too soon not only for the little girl, but for Halloran as well. And even, Eve realized, astonished, for the horse. No animal had ever looked less threatening than Tristan as Joy buried her face in handfuls of his mane, her feet flopping out of the stirrups, her arms hugging the big horse's neck. If she fell, Eve was certain the little girl would break into a dozen pieces. But Halloran didn't even put an arm out to steady her. He stood aside, respecting whatever healing magic lay between the child and the horse. Knowing that this moment, this triumph, was just between Tristan and Joy.

At last Joy straightened, her face sunshine bright. "See, Eve?" she said. "There's nothing to be 'fraid of. After I got hit by that car, I was scared all the time. But it doesn't hurt inside anymore when I'm here."

Eve couldn't even remember what she said to the little girl, but Joy was obviously satisfied—or maybe she was still too fascinated by the horse to notice much else. Eve made some excuse and dodged into the nearest barn. She'd wanted a few minutes to catch her balance, but as she breathed in the scent of hay and straw and grain, leather and sweat, she knew that now they wouldn't just remind her of Victoria. They would remind her of Michael Halloran, too. The solid warmth of his body as he lay next to her in the loft. The contrast of a strand of hay clinging against the dark waves of his hair. The way he'd gentled a wild horse, a shattered boy, and helped a little girl to fly.

She wasn't sure how long she stood there, with

only the soft shushing sounds of horses' hooves stirring in their beds of hay. She heard footsteps, knew before she turned it was Halloran, Tristan in tow.

It was harder to be afraid of the big horse now. Eve could still see the way little Joy had held him tight.

"Are you all right, Eve?" Halloran asked in that gentle voice she was coming to like way too much.

"I was just thinking . . . Joy's mother told me how much you've helped her."

He sobered. "There's nothing between us if that's what you're getting at." Honorable Michael Halloran. He'd not want Eve thinking he'd kissed her when he'd had feelings for another woman. The thought squeezed her heart.

"Do you have any idea what it means to her? Not to feel so alone? To have someone to turn to?" Her throat constricted.

"A friend."

"Yes. A friend. God, I'm so jealous. Isn't that sick? Jealous of a woman whose child is in a wheelchair."

"Maybe it's not so hard to understand. Even though Joy is hurt, her mother can tuck her in at night."

"Read her bedtime stories," Eve said in a trembling voice. "Even though Joy is hurt her mother can still hold her and love her and have Joy love her back. Not that I'd wish Victoria hurt. Not ever. Not even if it meant I could have my daughter back in my arms."

"I know that. I just wish I could have been there for you. Nothing I'd love more than to get my hands on the bastard who did this to you."

Eve disguised the depth of her emotions with a ragged laugh. "Chad pays someone to take his beatings for him—you know, like princes in olden days had whipping boys who got the lashes for them when they got into trouble."

"Eve—" His voice was too probing, too tender.

"Please, Michael." She needed space again from all she was feeling. Asked without saying so for Michael to give it to her. He sighed, silent for a long moment. Plucking a long straw out of a bale of hay, he twirled it between his fingers.

"So what did you think of my wee one?" he asked, honoring her wishes.

What did she think of his wee one? Blond ponytails and blue eyes, a smile glowing with possibilities. A future not even leg braces could dim.

"You were right," Eve said, trying not to let her voice crack.

His eyes widened in teasing surprise. "That's the first time you've said that to me since you arrived in Ireland, Miss Danaher. And just what was I right about?"

"Joy is a perfect name for her. The way her eyes shine, the way she flings herself into life. I've never seen such . . . such courage. She's . . . she's so little but . . . but even with all that, Halloran, she's still brave enough to fly."

Halloran nodded. "Every time I see her I remember what a miracle it is just to be alive."

Alive—the word reverberated through Eve, so deep, so far, it touched every part of her, even that part she'd forgotten long ago. There had been a time she'd been happy, too, so eager. She'd run in to her mother, a letter in hand. Every dream had seemed possible. Her whole life changed the instant she broke the envelope's seal. *It's a scholarship, Mama. I've won a scholarship to St. Benedict's!* Away from crowded classrooms in a school where half the class couldn't read, the other half didn't want to. Away from battle-weary teachers and kids who would trudge into the same dead-end jobs their parents had. But not Eve. Not her. She was going to escape, fling herself into the world with every bit of passion she'd saved up during years she'd hidden away in her room, nose in a book. She was finally going to *live*, not just *dream* about it.

Eve closed her eyes, picturing so clearly the girl she had been. For that little space in time she'd felt so strong, so sure, so eager. She hadn't loved horses like Victoria. She wasn't injured like Joy. Eve had never known the words to use to describe the scrabbling, restless, ready-to-burst feelings inside her—until little Joy had given them wings.

What would you say if I told you I want to fly, too? she wanted to ask Michael. *I'm just not sure how to start. If I asked you to help me, would you catch me if I fell?*

Suddenly it was too real, too close, too frightening. She hid herself the only way she could, by reaching out to touch Tristan's mane. It was coarse, bristly, warm. Halloran's eyes almost popped out of his head.

"I think I need to get back to the castle now," she said.

"I have more sessions to do."

"I know the way back. First castle on the left." She tried to make light of it, hide the heaviness in her chest. "Michael, would it be too much to ask—I mean, I just—"

Just what? Needed time. Needed to sort things out. Needed to retreat into her cave where she felt safe. Where gentle blue eyes didn't peel away layers of her soul, where a sensitive mouth didn't keep saying things so tender she felt ready to burst into tears. It was as if she'd had gray film over her eyes, couldn't see the sunlight, the colors. Michael had ripped the film away. But he'd left everything too bright, too fresh, too intense. She needed to shade the most tender places in her heart for just a little while until she got used to a world that seemed so new.

"Anything, Eve. Whatever you need. Just ask."

Even if it hurt this man's feelings? Even if it meant asking him for space? How could she explain that the reason she needed it so much was because she needed to see him even more? That *needing* scared her? That she needed to work up her courage to—to what? What was she thinking? Of taking the risk? Of letting Michael get close enough to touch her? Not only her body—that would be the easy part. But her spirit? Even the places that were ugly and scarred and afraid?

Her heart pounded hard against her ribs. What was it her psychology professor had called that reflex? Fight or flight? But what did it mean when you finally, might actually stop running? Fight for what? Affection? Companionship? Trust? The kind of relationship other people took for granted?

"Trust me, Eve. Tell me."

I have trusted you, that's what's so scary. But I don't want to hurt you. You deserve better than that. I have to search deep, see if there is enough of me left to give you. If you want me. . . . She flushed, looked away, remembering the heat of attraction that had shimmered in his eyes. One thing she knew for certain. Michael Halloran deserved a woman who could give him everything he deserved. Her heart. Her trust. Hope. For a very long time Eve hadn't felt hope about anything except healing things with Victoria, and that hope had been bruised at best.

Sucking in a deep breath, she raised her eyes to his. If she hurt him, she at least wanted to know it. "I think it would be best if you didn't come to the castle for a few days."

He'd been so close, she could tell he'd wanted to touch her. Instead, he leaned back against the stable wall.

"I just thought it would be best if you let Rory and me figure out how . . . how to deal with each other alone. We can't do that if you're running interference. Besides, we don't want to make anyone suspicious."

She expected him to balk at the idea. God knew, if she didn't really trust herself with Rory, how could she expect Michael to trust her? But she needed time so badly.

Halloran hesitated, looking deep into her eyes. What was it she saw in his? Reluctance and relief? Bewilderment and certainty? Patience and restlessness? So many conflicting emotions, echoes of things she was feeling herself. They made a separation harder somehow, and all the more necessary.

After a long moment, Halloran shrugged. "If that's what you want. You know where to find me. If you need me—" He didn't finish. He didn't have to. She knew he'd be there for her, as certainly as Joy and her mother did. Maybe Halloran did have a gift for teaching children to fly, but the reason they dared was because they knew that no matter how far they sailed, he would be there, solid, constant, unfailing as the earth below. To fly, you had to be certain you had someplace safe to land.

She reached out to squeeze his hand. "Thank you for introducing me to Joy," she said.

He closed both his hands over hers, the work-callused roughness wrapping her in Halloran's warmth, in Halloran's strength. He looked a little sad, his gaze clinging softly to their joined hands. "I wish I *could* give you joy, Eve. Takes but a look in your eyes to see you've had far too little of it."

She started to protest, too vulnerable, too exposed, his words too true. He shook his head to quiet her.

"Maybe the hardest thing I've ever learned is that happiness can't be a gift from someone else. No one can give it to you, no matter how much they want to. You have to find it for yourself."

Eve looked away. Could he guess how hard it was to feel happiness when your child had been stolen from you? Could he understand how wrong it felt to be happy at all? As if any pleasure was a betrayal of Victoria, as if she'd forgotten her little girl. And that was the most unforgivable of sins in Eve's eyes. Was that the reason it was still so hard to make a new beginning?

If only there was a way to show Victoria she hadn't forgotten her, even as she found a way to go on with her own life. If only she could tell her daughter all she was feeling. But Victoria wouldn't even speak to her. Might never be willing to. Even the letters Eve had written to her daughter over the years had been thrown away as garbage by Chad. Could Michael Halloran ever understand—

Yes. That was what made him so rare. She raised her face to his, looked deep into his eyes.

"You're a good man, Michael Halloran," she said softly.

Color burned into his cheeks. "I wish I was half the man other people seem to think I am."

Her heart ached at the sincerity in his eyes. She raised up on tiptoe, kissing him on his cheek. He tasted of sweat and fresh air and healing.

It was harder than she could have imagined to pull away.

"What was that for?" he asked hoarsely.

"For reminding me that . . . that a man *can* be good. That the sky can be beautiful even when you have to walk a long way. For showing me that an end can be just a beginning."

His throat convulsed. His eyes darkened. "Eve, I—"

"It was just . . . thank you."

He watched her for a long moment, then sucked in a deep breath. "I'll come to the castle on Friday morning, then, unless you need me before."

It felt far too good to know he would be there. He watched her as she started back across the pasture. She could feel his gaze on her. Taste him on her lips, the imprint of his hands still warming her own.

What had Halloran said? You had to find happiness in yourself, on your own? Wise words. She'd just never suspected the other part of the puzzle. You had to let happiness in. Maybe there was a way. . . .

For years she'd cut out pictures for Victoria, made scrapbooks to show her little girl how much she loved her, that she hadn't forgotten her. Images were safe— an artist's tool. Words were far more painful. And yet—pictures of other people being happy weren't enough. Not anymore.

She turned her face into the wind, remembering one of the treasures she'd stumbled across in the castle—not gold or precious stones, great art or the elegantly crafted weapons that had been stuffed in every corner. Rather, a bundle of letters tied up with a faded ribbon. Letters from people who had lived in the castle a hundred years ago, every emotion still preserved. Love and laughter, sorrow and regret even time and death hadn't been able to erase.

What if she wrote to Victoria? Letters that would keep forever, until Victoria was ready to read them. Even if it took until her little girl was eighty they would always be there. Waiting. Even if Victoria was too hurt to see Eve, talk to her face to face, she'd still be able to know how her mother had felt, how much her mother had loved her, missed her, thought of her every day.

It wasn't perfect. It wasn't everything she wanted—the feel of Victoria in her arms, the smell of her hair, trust in her eyes. But it was something real, something Eve could have right now.

A place to begin.

Eve hurried faster, her footsteps lighter. She'd been trying so hard since she'd come to Ireland, wanted so much to turn her face to the future. But now, as she made her way toward the castle, she felt as if maybe she wasn't just *trying* anymore.

Maybe her future was about to begin.

16

~

*E*ve put down her pen and paused for a moment to rub an ink stain from her aching right hand. The stack of pages on the scarred Elizabethan table had been growing during the past day and a half. Words that had started to come out haltingly picked up speed until they poured out at such a great rate she'd begun to wish for the laptop computer she'd left in her apartment in New York. This was supposed to be a vacation, after all. How could she have guessed she would be doing more writing than she ever had in her life? Or that she would have a castle full of rare *objets d'art* she was dying to catalogue and research, cut off from on-line access to international libraries she'd taken for granted for years?

But even if she'd had her computer, she knew she wouldn't have used it to write to Victoria. She wanted her daughter to see her handwriting, let the shape of the letters—sometimes careful, others rushed with emotion—carry with them everything she was feeling. Subtle expressions like the curve of a smile, the wistful dip of lashes over eyes, expressions Victoria might not be able to see in Eve's face, but could sense in the curl of the letters she'd written.

No. No cold typeface would tell Victoria what Eve wanted her to know. Love letters to her daughter written by hand—those were the gifts she wanted to give to her little girl.

Eve caught her lip between her teeth, signing her

latest letter. *Love, Mama.* Was it all right to do that? She
wondered. Mama was the only name Victoria had ever
called her. They'd missed that stage when childish dignity would have changed the tender little name to the
far cooler "Mom." At least out in public. Then "Mama"
would have become a precious secret between them,
taken out when they were alone and Victoria was tired
or sick or troubled.

Eve added the letter to the pile, hoping that when
she came back, they might actually be the way she left
them instead of having pages out of kilter the way they
had been when she'd first sat down this morning. It almost made her think that there might be a ghost, the
way things kept shifting, just a little out of place from
where she remembered them, although a simple draft
was far more likely. The castle was full of them, full of
cobwebs and damp patches on the walls. Things that
should be either inconveniences or irritations, but that
were slowly becoming oddly endearing to Eve, like the
laugh lines on an old person's face, ghostly footprints
that life had left behind.

She sighed with the strange mixture of exhaustion
and elation that had become so familiar since she'd
begun writing messages to her daughter. Exhaustion
from digging out real emotions, not only admitting to
them, but writing them down with the intention of
sharing them with someone else. She was rusty at feeling anything that wasn't close to the surface. Aggrava-
tion at not getting a taxi when it was pouring rain was
safe enough. So was pleasure when she saw a painting
she'd painstakingly restored.

She'd locked away anything deeper, afraid that if
she ever let herself feel the loss and anguish, all the
pain of losing Victoria, she'd start crying and never be
able to stop.

But, painful as it had been to sift through the memories, it was even more healing. Almost what she'd always dreamed of—sharing things with her daughter,

telling her how much she loved her, how much she missed her. Telling Victoria stories about the baby she had been, her first words, her favorite toy, the way they'd decorated their little Christmas tree with tin foil ornaments and paper stars.

Strange, she'd never realized the scrapbooks had been about everything the two of them were missing. But the letters were about what they shared. The more she'd written, the less she remembered the loss of Victoria, and the more she remembered the four years they had been together. No one, not even Chad or the all-powerful Tollivers could take that away from her—or her daughter. Somewhere, deep down, Victoria remembered, too. She was counting on it.

She leaned back in her chair and worked the kinks out of her neck, finished for the day. The past fell away, the castle spinning lazily into focus again, a place familiar, warm, welcoming in a way she'd never experienced before.

The soft rain that had dampened the morning had vanished. Afternoon sunlight slanted through the wavy glass in the leaded window that brightened the cozy alcove Eve had claimed as her own. A nook filled with the small table, a Jacobean chair upholstered in dusty red velvet, a tall brass candlestick topped by a white candle as big around as her arm. Bridey must have loved writing here, too, because a small inlaid box on the table's corner held everything needed—pens and thick sheets of white paper, stubs of what must have been dark red sealing wax, and the brass seal you pressed in it to make a design.

There were letters in it, too, tucked under the paper. Letters in the spidery hand of an old woman on top, then others farther down in the pile, the script close enough to be written by the same hand, but a stronger hand, a steadier hand. A younger one.

Eve put the pen she'd been using back into its place, unable to keep herself from wondering about the woman who owned the box. Bridey McGarrity had changed Eve's life in so many ways by inviting her to come to this place, falling in love with green hills she'd never seen, and finding a part of herself there she hadn't known was missing.

With each day she spent in the castle, she was starting to feel more and more as if Bridey wasn't a stranger she'd barely met, but a friend. What had once looked like clutter and neglect had become treasures, whispers of the woman who made this place her home. She'd always know that *things* could drink in the spirit of the person who had once loved them. Paintings where every brush stroke still seemed alive with the power of the hand that had made them centuries before. Stone that still bore the images the sculptor had seen in its rough-hewn bulk, miracles no one else could have brought into being.

But she'd never had the chance to learn that a *place* could do the same thing. Bridey was everywhere, from the tattered letters to the reminder notes from a year ago that Michael had posted on the useless refrigerator.

Eve had felt so much the outsider when she'd first come here. But in the past few days, even Bridey's dog had decided to call a truce. She slid back the chair, careful not to squash the bundle of fawn-colored fur that was curled in a wayward sunbeam near her feet.

She waited, still half expecting an explosion of high-pitched yaps when the dog realized she wasn't Bridey, but Bonaparte just lifted his smashed-in face and looked up at her with black marble eyes. The old dog gave a long-suffering sigh.

The old Eve would have remembered the peanut incident, when the little brat had taken the only food in the castle and left her to starve that first night. But now— Who would ever have believed that pint-sized gargoyle could look so—well, so forlorn? Bonaparte looked about as miserable as his namesake must have after he'd met his Waterloo.

She wished she could tell him what little she knew

to comfort him—that Michael insisted Bridey was
looking better every time he visited her. That Eve had
talked to the old woman herself on the phone, back at
the farm, explaining she couldn't visit right now, felt
uncomfortable leaving Rory for any length of time.

Explain things to a dog? Eve grimaced, remembering Steffie's crow of laughter when she'd checked in
with her friend and told her about the menagerie she
was now in charge of. A dog, a horse, a boy . . . Steffie
had been so delighted at the situation that Eve had
considered strangling her. She'd opted for laughter instead. So here she was again, face to face with a dog
who was a bundle of misery. She had to do something.

How was it Halloran managed wild horses and
wilder boys? By knowing when to be still and listen,
by telling them they were safe, not only with his low
murmuring words, but with his eyes, his face, every
movement careful and slow.

She held her breath and reached down toward the
pug, half expecting to be bitten. But, after all, how
much damage could that one snaggle tooth do? The dog
only looked up at her so mournfully, she would have
had to have a heart harder than Simon Legree's not to
at least attempt to scratch behind his raggedy little ear.

Bonaparte snuffled. Obviously he didn't like it. But
as she started to pull away, the pug nuzzled its head
into the cup of her palm and gave a low whine.

"I know you miss her," Eve said. They claimed Ireland inspired either poetry or madness in people—she
was obviously suffering from the latter. She was actually talking to the dog. She would have regained her
senses and stopped, except that Bonaparte's mouth
formed a perfect O and he let out a little howl reminding her of just how it felt to be lonely. Was Bridey
missing her dog as much as Bonaparte missed her?

"I'm sure she'll be back soon." How could anyone
stay away from this place any longer than they had to?
Eve thought, then felt a twinge. When Bridey came

back, it would be time for *her* to leave. She wasn't ready to. Not yet.

She winced. How could she look the dog in the eye—or herself in the mirror, as a matter of fact—when she wanted a little old woman to stay in the hospital longer for her own convenience? It wasn't that she wanted Bridey sick! She just wanted—needed—a little more time for herself. Time with wind that told stories, green that healed winter-burned spirits, and the man who had opened her eyes to both of them. Besides, there was Rory to think about. There was no way Bridey could handle the rebellious teenager *or* his horse. Bridey couldn't be left alone with Rory. It was too dangerous, not to mention illegal.

"Way to soothe your conscience, Danaher," she muttered to herself. Anyway, shouldn't she be checking on the boy just to make sure he hadn't broken his neck? He'd spent every minute with that horse. Eve had made it a practice periodically to make sure he was still breathing. It was the least she could do, since she was supposed to be in charge of the kid. Not that Rory did much to acknowledge she actually existed. He acted like he'd be out fifty dollars for every word he spoke.

The pug scratched at her shoe, as if to remind her that he was still there and waiting for his mistress to come home. She would've given a week's salary for a bag of airline peanuts. She tossed her old sweater down for him to lie on, then beat a hasty retreat out the castle door.

At least she didn't have to go searching for Rory; the boy was constantly hanging around Innisfree's new pasture at the rear of the castle. At first she'd been a little nervous, afraid that someone—namely Dennis Moran—might see him. But Rory had laughed at the very idea, showed her how the field was sheltered, its edges overgrown by trees and giant shrubs. Moran would never ruin his shoes walking up the lane, Rory insisted. Besides, Rory had grown up on the streets, was damned used to looking out for himself, as wary and instinctively alert in his way as Innisfree.

But it was the horse that had helped Eve start to relax about it. Even if someone *had* approached, Rory would know right away. Innisfree would scent a stranger and act up like a three-year-old boy who'd just heard the dreaded word "bath."

Eve had fidgeted and fretted until she'd seen the horse in action. It had taken Innisfree a day and a half not to start his little "stranger alert" act whenever she came anywhere near the pasture. She'd decided to leave things in the horse's hands—er, hooves.

She crossed straight to the pasture Innisfree had made his own since he'd arrived. Hadn't taken the horse long to crown himself king of the pasture. No conquistador could have staked claim on a new world more completely. He chased out ravens, threatened bunnies who dared to sneak through holes in the stone fence. And every so often, he took a run around the perimeter, as if alert for invading forces. He wasn't showing off for his boy—no. Innisfree did all he could to make certain no one would think that. But every time Eve approached the pasture, she saw the way the horse's liquid brown eyes watched him. And when Rory was up on Innisfree's back, she could see old fear in the horse's eyes driven back by trust.

It had been lovely to see. But what met her eyes now wasn't lovely at all. It was terrifying. Rory had lost his mind! He was racing on Innisfree's back, full speed toward a pile of rocks and wooden boards that came up past the horse's back. Eve's breath caught. Wasn't this the part in the movie where Bonnie Blue Butler broke her neck before the horrified Rhett?

"Rory, stop!" she croaked. "Don't!" But even if Rory *had* been able to hear her over the pounding of Innisfree's hooves, nothing could have stopped the horse or the boy now. Innisfree charged the fence with fierce determination, as if he were trying to outrun every trainer or rider who had ever mistreated him, while the boy leaned low over the horse's neck, nothing but knees and stirrups and pure guts holding him on.

The horse bunched its powerful haunches, launched itself into the air. Boy and animal soared a good two feet over the obstacle, landing on the other side at a dead run. Eve had watched jumping on television in her quest to feel closer to Victoria, but she'd never seen it through anything but the camera's flat lens, that safe distance with people who weren't any more real to her than Batman on a soda commercial. This was different.

Rory swung the big horse in a circle, his head thrown back in triumph as he slowed Innisfree to a canter. "Beautiful," he crowed. *"Beautiful!* And Michael said you'd never be ready in time for the show in Glengarry! Sure, you're the finest jumper in all Ireland! Won't we show them all!"

Eve leaned against the stone fence, wistful. So Rory *could* smile. He *could* laugh and feel close to another living thing. It was a glimpse of the boy who might have been if Jamie and Oonagh hadn't damaged him.

She started to turn, intending to sneak away, not wanting to spoil the moment for Rory. But the boy saw her. She expected that surly mask to fall across his face, that hard edge to roughen his voice. But it seemed this triumph was so great Rory couldn't hide his pleasure.

His chin lifted to that who-gives-a-damn angle, but he couldn't keep his eyes from shining. "I haven't run off yet if that's what you were wondering. You can report it to Michael when he comes by today. And while you're at it, you can tell him Innisfree will be kicking the arses of every horse at Glengarry. I'd bet my life on it." Rory's chest swelled with pride.

"I believe you. You cleared the jump with two feet to spare. And you scared the life out of me."

He bristled. "Innisfree was ready. I'd never push him if I thought he'd get hurt."

"It wasn't Innisfree I was worried about."

Astonishment streaked across Rory's face, then changed to disbelief, and something sharper, more painful. "Michael says you're scared of everything. Even that one-toothed dog."

Eve tried to ease Rory's discomfort by resorting to humor. "Well, the thing I was worried about a moment ago was that I hadn't kept up on first-aid. I figured I was going to need to put a splint on something." She wanted to keep it light, but she couldn't keep herself from going on with real feelings—loosened by the letters she'd written?

"But then all I could think of was how beautiful the two of you looked going over that fence. Like you were born to do it. I knew that, even if you did get some bumps and bruises, either you or Innisfree, it would be wrong to make you keep your feet on the ground."

Rory's eyes narrowed. "It was good then?" She could see how hard it was for him to ask.

"No, Rory. It was the most beautiful thing I've seen in a very long time."

Rory sat on the horse, silent for a moment. "You think he's . . . he's beautiful? I thought you were scared of horses."

"Terrified would be a more accurate description."

Rory transferred both reins to one hand and with his other stroked Innisfree's sleek neck. "He's not like they say he is. Innisfree. He's not mean. He's just—he's scared, like you."

One thing about Rory—the kid called 'em as he saw 'em. Blunt was too mild a word. She smiled, trying to imagine she and this mountain of a horse having something in common after all. "He didn't seem scared a minute ago."

"I think he'd do whatever I asked him to." A hint of wonder gleamed in Rory's eyes.

Eve tried to steady herself. The boy hadn't strung more than three words together since he'd come to

Kilrain. Had he forgotten, for just a moment, that he was supposed to stay angry all the time? The last thing she wanted to do was remind him. She couldn't screw up. Searched for the right thing to say. The horse. Talk about the horse.

"Innisfree trusts you. Do you think that's why he can trust himself when you're riding him?"

Rory frowned, wistful. "Guess he's not as smart a horse as I thought he was, if he trusts somebody like me. It's a bad idea. Ask anybody."

"I don't think Michael would agree."

"Been kicked in the head too many times, has that one. Even your man Sean looks at me like . . . like he expects me to break all the plates at any minute." Rory stunned her with a rueful chuckle. "Can't say it wasn't without good reason, though. I did break most of them the second night I was at the farm. My night for clean-up duty. Sean said he didn't want to see those dishes again until they were clean. Didn't say I had to *wash* them. Just said he didn't want to *see* them. I figured I'd solve the problem for him. He'd never have to look at those dishes again."

Eve all but choked on a laugh. She'd heard coworkers complain about the shifty way the teenage mind worked, wriggling out of things because of the minutest details.

"Took me a week to earn enough money to pay for the buggers," Rory added ruefully.

"Pay? How did you manage that?"

"Michael gave me a salary first thing, said the money was mine to use on anything I wanted except liquor or drugs. Should have warned me about breaking dishes."

She grinned. Too much. Rory stiffened, startled. Why? Because she'd laughed with him? Listened to him? Or because she was starting to actually like him and was reckless enough to let it show? She had to think of something fast.

"My little girl loves horses, too, but I've never seen

her jump." She tried not to wince at her choice of subject, but it was too late to retreat. How could bringing up something that was so painful to her, so personal, help this boy who had more than enough problems of his own?

Rory dismounted, then unsnapped the chin strap of his black riding helmet. He fiddled with the strap, looking oddly uncomfortable, almost guilty.

No, Eve thought, he was just uneasy about discussing any emotions, but he needed to learn how nonetheless. "I would have given anything to be able to watch her clear just one fence the way I watched you." Did her voice quaver just a little? She wasn't sure. But Rory was watching her too intently.

"So what's stopping you?" he asked. "Thought America was supposed to be a free country."

Lord, she didn't want to talk about this! Not now. Not to anybody. Especially not to him. But there was no way to retreat gracefully. "Remember what I told the judge at your hearing? The courts decided I shouldn't see her. Her father won custody."

Rory grew quiet. "You said there was an accident. I was always having 'accidents' when I was a kid. But you don't look like you'd beat anyone. Don't have the eyes for it."

"Thanks." She meant it, from the bottom of her heart. "But you can hurt people in other ways. When I helped your parents get that lawyer, Rory, I didn't understand how they'd hurt you. I just kept remembering what it was like to . . . to lose my child forever because I didn't have enough money to fight someone richer, more powerful than I was. I should have found out the whole story before I jumped in. I made things worse for you, and I'm sorry."

Rory shrugged away the loss of Glenammura, and what might have been his one chance at a decent life as if it didn't matter. "Sooner or later I would have wrecked things anyway. Always do." He flipped off the helmet, revealing coppery bright hair. "What happened with your little girl?"

"She's not so little anymore. She's eighteen and . . . and so grown up." Her voice dropped low. "I've only seen Tori once since she was four years old. Maybe that's why I wanted so much to make sure things turned out right for you."

"Bet she was mad as hell at her da for keeping you away."

Eve's chest throbbed with all too familiar hurt, that instinctive need to feel Tori *had* grieved, had missed her, been angry at everything they'd lost. But those feelings wouldn't have changed what had happened to her little girl. They would only have made it harder for her to go on.

"I think Victoria loves her father very much," Eve said. "I . . . I'm glad she does, since I can't be there. A child needs somebody—" She stopped, appalled at her blunder, not wanting to hurt Rory. The last thing she wanted was to point out to the boy just how alone he really was. She scrambled to cover her mistake. "Watching Innisfree, I guess a horse does, too."

Rory stiffened, but he couldn't hide the fear in the back of his eyes. "Who would love a stupid horse? It's just an animal, it is. I just . . . just ride him because there's nothing better to do."

She could have backed down. Let him escape feeling, retreat to where it was safe again as she had herself so many times. But she couldn't bear the thought of this boy living in the emotional wasteland she'd lived in for so long. She looked Rory straight in the eye, shook her head. "That's bullshit."

She'd wanted to shock him. She had. His eyes bugged out. His mouth fell open. He couldn't hide the beginnings of an all-out grin, forgetting to get all prickly because she'd amused him. A little foul language was well worth it.

"The hell you say—" he sputtered, still completely off balance.

"That horse loves you. And you love that horse. Look at what he'll do for you."

"What? Go over a fence? He's been doing that since he first found his legs. Did it for the trainers who hurt him, too. He just threw them off once he got over."

"No, Rory. You have a gift. Deny it all you want, but I know what I just saw. What I've seen every day I've looked out the castle window to see the two of you together."

"You're mad, you are." His smile turned brittle. "Now, if I could get *you* anywhere near him, *that* would be something to brag about."

She was crazy. Insane. A complete, card-carrying lunatic, a voice inside her screamed. A straitjacket would be too mild a way to treat her. At least she couldn't break her neck in a padded cell, could she? What on God's earth was she even thinking?

"If getting me to work with Innisfree would be something to brag about, why don't you do it?" It was a joke, just a joke, but the second the words slipped out of her mouth she was cursing herself.

Rory gaped at her, but his eyes shone with possibilities. "Michael would kill me. He never lets anyone but me near the horse."

"It's not up to Michael. One of the conditions I set when you came here was that I'm in charge."

"That was his first mistake, agreeing to that," Rory scoffed. "You'll kill yourself."

She probably would. She should have put Victoria's address on the letters so they could send them to her posthumously. But if she was going to be crazy, she might as well go all the way.

"Maybe I don't trust horses," she said, "but I do trust you."

Rory's face tightened in disbelief, hard, edgy—be-

cause he didn't want anyone close enough to trust him
or because he wanted it too much?

"Trust me?" he scoffed. "You don't even know me. If
you did, you'd take off running like everyone else does."

I'm not going anywhere.

Eve wanted to push him, but she didn't dare. She
might just have goaded him into doing something to
prove just how unworthy of trust he really was. She
might already be too late, might have triggered God
only knew what kind of acting out. Time alone would
tell. Best thing to do was to beat a hasty retreat, hope
for the best. That, and leave him something to think
about while she was gone.

She plucked the longest blade of grass she could
find—the better to avoid Innisfree's teeth—and held it
out toward the horse. The animal looked as if she were
trying to feed it arsenic. She dropped the grass, and
shook back a strand of her hair.

"Whenever you're ready to give me that riding lesson, let me know," she said, trying to act casual. "You
know where to find me."

"Up in that corner where you sit all the time, writing stuff down."

So he'd noticed. He hadn't been as oblivious to her
presence as he liked to pretend.

She glimpsed something canny in his eyes, something
that was too wise, too old, too sharp in a boy this young.

"Sean said you were supposed to be on holiday. Some
holiday. Your face stuffed in a bunch of papers, working."

He was probing, she could tell, but there was no
harm in satisfying his curiosity.

"I'm not working, they're letters for my daughter,
just in case she ever wants to read them."

"You said she's eighteen. Why not just talk to her?"

"I tried. She . . ." Eve paused. How could she explain to Rory the agony of rejection? The hint of *fear* in
her daughter's eyes? The way Victoria had begged her
to leave her alone? "Maybe it's been too long."

She expected Rory to dismiss the whole subject, but his gaze sharpened, intent.

"She doesn't want to talk to you, then?"

"No." Would it ever stop hurting so much to admit that, even to herself?

"They told her bad things about you, didn't they?" Street kid. He'd always seen too much. Too damned smart for his own good. And hers. "Bet they lied to her," he said.

"They wouldn't have had to lie. At least not much. The last time Victoria and I were together, she got hurt."

"I bet it wasn't your fault."

"If a parent's around when their baby gets hurt, it's always their fault. In their own mind and in almost everyone else's."

Rory thought for a moment, his brow creasing underneath the imprint still there from his helmet. Something tic-tic-tic-ing in his eyes made Eve nervous as all get-out. "Someone should *make* her talk to you," he said. "I could."

The offer touched Eve almost as much as it terrified her. She could picture Rory all too clearly striding into the castle with a wriggling burlap bag slung over one shoulder, dumping her daughter out of the sack with great satisfaction. At least he'd given her one reason to be glad Victoria was back in America.

"Nobody can make anyone talk to someone else if they don't want to. You, above anyone, should know that."

"So you keep writing letters she'll probably never read?"

"I keep writing letters hoping that she will. Maybe by the time that happens, we'll have something to talk about. Me, learning how to ride after all this time."

She turned, waded back through knee-deep wildflowers that laid siege to the overgrown path. She could feel Rory's eyes on her back until she closed the castle door behind her.

Bonaparte charged out to drive off invaders, saw it was her, and sat down on his wrinkly little haunches watching her with black eyes.

"Easy for you to look so blasé about this whole horse issue," she accused. "Innisfree only wants to have tea with you, and you can do that keeping that curly little tail of yours on the floor. I know where this horse thing is going. First I touch the thing. If I survive, then I'm supposed to get on its back. Think you could talk to your buddy the horse and ask him not to break my neck if I'm stupid enough try it? Mention the peanuts I gave you that first night to soften him up."

Bonaparte looked decidedly unimpressed.

Eve grimaced. "Maybe I'll get lucky and Rory will have amnesia. Forget everything I just said," Eve told the dog hopefully. "Maybe he'll just blow it off, never call me on it. Ignore it as . . . as the harebrained idea it was. Aren't all teenagers dying to show they have better sense than the grownups in their lives? This would be Rory's chance to prove it. Or maybe I'll trip over you, you little gargoyle, and sprain my ankle or my wrist—or hit my head and come to my senses."

The pug peered up at her, far too wise for a dog who looked like he'd been hit in the face by a truck.

Or maybe you'll just have to take a leap of faith for once in your life. Those big eyes seemed to mock her. *Maybe you'll learn how to fly. What would your daughter think of that?*

She shivered, closing her eyes. If only Victoria could see her—Eve Danaher on a horse—surely her little girl couldn't ignore her then, could she?

No. Victoria had always been tender-hearted to animals. She'd probably come running over in desperation, trying to save the poor horse.

A knock sounded on the door. Eve nearly jumped out of her skin. In an instant, she imagined Moran waiting outside, every hair in place, his mouth sour with disapproval. An army of garda, the Irish police, ready to drag her off to jail. But when she opened the door, it was Michael silhouetted in the arched opening.

How long had it been since she'd seen him? A few days? Too long. Not long enough. She wanted to touch him so much. That hadn't changed in the few days he'd stayed away. He was just as she remembered him. Dark hair wind-tossed during his trip from the farm, his eyes warm, his mouth sensitive. But he wasn't wearing his usual riding breeches. It was obvious he'd taken pains with his appearance for the first time since she'd met him. A soft Irish tweed sport coat in heather and gray encased his shoulders, gray flannel slacks unable to disguise the muscular legs that had held him on the back of countless horses as they plunged across racecourses all over the world.

He was devastatingly masculine, mouth-wateringly sexy. That only made it all the more amusing that he reminded her of a schoolboy about to make his first communion—pressed to the point of discomfort, a tie knotted at his throat. Surely he hadn't dressed that way just to come check on Rory. But the idea that this man might care enough about her to want to dress that way was heady stuff.

Did he still smell as good as he had when she'd kissed his cheek in the stable? His jaw had been satiny warm, the faint roughness of his beard under her lips making her tingle. What would it feel like for him to kiss her beyond the hurt, beyond comfort and gentleness? Kiss her with the kind of passion Eve had never known? Hot with that underlying sensuality, that recklessness, that passion for life that always bubbled just beneath the surface with Michael Halloran.

He was looking at her, too, as if he could gobble her up with his eyes, as if he'd missed her the way she'd missed him.

Eve averted her eyes. She tried hard to swallow. "Michael."

His eyes searched her face, his voice low, sending shivers down her spine. "How are you, Eve?"

How was she? She felt like she'd just plunged down a hill on a rollercoaster, thrilled, scared, wanting even more. "Fine," she said. Fine, except for being uncertain, fine, except for hoping too much. Fine, now that he was standing in front of her so she could look into his eyes, see the strength there, the compassion, the honor. Know she hadn't been dreaming.

"Looks like the castle is still standing," he drawled, tugging at the knot of his tie. He was a man born to leave buttons unfastened, his throat exposed to the wind and sun.

"Everything is fine. Better than I expected." Eve's voice sounded stilted even to her own ears.

"Sean will be damned glad to hear it."

She could see him honoring her silent plea for distance. He didn't push, instead kept his voice light.

"He's on his way back to the farm. Glad Rory is okay but none too thrilled about our little arrangement to keep the lad out of sight."

"Too bad. Rory's staying here with me."

"So I told him. He's just plain scared the kid is going to explode. And that you don't know what you might be in for. I could hear his jaw drop when I told him you'd seen the worst of it before you volunteered. Pretty plain there could be trouble when you see a kid with a knife in his hand."

"Well, tell him Rory has been no problem at all. He's spent every minute with his horse."

"Don't need you to tell me that." The corner of Halloran's mouth crooked into a knee-melting smile. "Is that where the lad is now?"

"He was just out in the pasture jumping. If you could only have seen him!"

Just a hint of concern creased his brow. "Helmet on?"

"Yes."

"Had a hell of a time getting the kid to wear one."

"Thank God you did. The fence he built is so high, I could hardly believe the horse could get over it."

Halloran's smile deepened with wry humor. "Getting *over* the obstacle has never been Innisfree's problem. Sometimes I think he could jump over the moon if he wanted to. It's the landing that gets rocky—especially for whoever's crazy enough to be on his back."

That was one point in her favor on the "sanity list." She wasn't going to jump over so much as a twig if she ever got up on that monster of a horse. No. Hooves on the ground were a good thing.

"Rory tried to act like it was no big deal that Innisfree got over that fence. But before he could put on his 'Mr. Cool' face again he told me to tell you something about Innisfree kicking arses someplace called Glengarry."

"Glengarry?" Halloran's smile faded. "Sure the boy must know that's impossible now."

"I don't understand."

"Glengarry is a town just over the mountain. Every summer they hold an event to help kids warm up for the riding season. That was Rory's goal, to run Innisfree there. I didn't think he had much of a chance under the best circumstances. Getting Innisfree to perform, period, is a miracle. Getting the horse to do it on a strange course in front of a crowd of people—" Halloran shook his head. "I was willing to let him try it if the horse kept coming along the way he had been, but now, Rory can't ride in a horse show. Someone would be bound to see him. Especially since Moran's posted these around the county."

He dug into his pants pocket, came up with a folded paper. Eve took it, opened it. A grainy image of Rory's face stared out at her—defiant, furious, *scared*, and determined not to let anyone know it. A mug shot taken when he'd had a brush with the law? RUNAWAY! The sign proclaimed in bold red letters. *Potentially dangerous. If you see this boy call . . .*

Eve's spirits sank. They'd labeled Rory "dangerous"

for the whole world to see, as if he were some kind of
mad animal instead of a hurting, confused boy. She
could see mothers dragging their children away from
him, crossing to the other side of the street with dread
and contempt in their eyes. What would it do to Rory
to see that? Feel that kind of censure? He'd felt it all
his life from people who had known him, but to feel it
now from complete strangers. . . . As if that wasn't disturbing enough, the bulletin made it more official that
she was breaking the law in hiding him here. Not that
it mattered, she thought grimly. Even if Moran hadn't
plastered the county with these posters, no court
would ever believe she hadn't known exactly what she
was doing when she'd taken Rory in. Not much had
really changed. Rory wouldn't see the posters because
he had to stay here, hidden away. And she already
knew she could be in deep trouble for the choice she'd
made to protect him. "They didn't waste much time,"
she said after a moment.

Halloran gave a bitter laugh. "Too bad Moran
wasn't this efficient when he was looking into the neglect case against Rory's parents."

"Hey, Michael." A surly voice behind Halloran made
them both straighten. Instinctively Eve thrust the
poster behind her back.

"Figured you'd be talking about me when I saw you
were at the castle," Rory said, sliding past Halloran
through the door. "I hate it when people do—" The
boy stopped. "What's that you're hiding behind you?"

Eve's cheeks burned. She wanted to hide the image
of that angry-looking boy, not let Rory know that
Moran was hunting him, had labeled him "dangerous."
But the boy already knew that, didn't he?

"It's a poster asking people to look for you, report
you to the garda," Halloran said. "Show it to him, Eve."

Reluctantly, she held the paper out to Rory. The boy
took it, his eyes scanning the script. The corner of his
mouth tightened just a whisper, the only sign of emo-

tion. "The least the bloody bastard could have done was find a better picture of me," he said, tossing the poster onto the table as if it didn't matter. "I'm a damned handsome article. You can ask any of the girls back in Dublin."

Eve ached. So much courage in one gangly teenage boy. It made her want to scoop him into her arms, hold him, let him cry out all the anger and frustration and hurt she could see in his face. But Rory would rather die than let her.

"Rory," Halloran said in that soothing voice he used to calm horses and skittish boys, "this is no surprise. We knew Moran would come after you with all guns blazing."

"Sure and we did. He can put up all the posters he wants, but he can't make me go back to my parents."

"Michael and I are going to do everything we can to make sure that doesn't happen," Eve said.

"That we are." Michael shot her a grateful look. "But you're going to have to help us, lad. Do your part."

"I'm here, aren't I?" Rory asked, taking off the edge of his fear at seeing the poster by resorting to his most acid tones.

"Yeah. You're here. And you're going to have to stay here," Michael said carefully. God help him to find the right words. Were there any right words when you were about to break a seventeen-year-old's heart? He glanced at Eve, saw his own dread and helplessness reflected in those wide green eyes.

Rory gave a snort of dismissal. "Whatever. I'll stay as long as I feel like it."

"There's something else you need to understand right up front," Michael insisted. "You can't leave the castle grounds. Not for anything."

"I told you, I'm here, damn it!" Rory threw his hands in the air. "What's the problem?"

Michael sucked in a deep breath, looked straight in

the boy's eyes. "Glengarry. Lad, it's impossible. There's no way you can ride there."

Rory's face paled as if Michael had hit him. Halloran knew he had done far worse.

"But Innisfree's already entered!" Rory sputtered. "I *have* to ride him! Dammit, Michael, you know how hard he's been working."

Not to mention the blood, sweat and love Rory had poured into reaching the first real goal he'd ever dared to have. Michael had always known Glengarry wasn't just a race to the boy or to the horse. It was vindication. Redemption. Damn Moran to hell for taking that away from them!

"Rory, lad, I wish there was some way we could make it happen. But there just isn't. Moran's no fool. Riding events are the first place he'll be looking for you."

"I can't let Innisfree down! I promised him—" Rory's face went brick red with pain, humiliation at the glimpse of vulnerability he'd let slip. "It's my life, Halloran. If I want to dance naked on the boot of Moran's car, I can do it."

"Rory," Eve pleaded. "No one's trying to . . . to control you. Michael's only trying to keep you safe."

"I can take care of myself!"

"But Innisfree can't," Michael said. "Get yourself caught by Moran, and you'll be back in Dublin before you can spit. Sure and the race would have been grand for both you and Innisfree. And, dammit, lad, you almost made me believe you could do it, the two of you. Run without killing yourselves or someone else. But one race isn't worth what it could cost you. You, back with Jamie and Oonagh. Innisfree without you to train him. Eve, at best, thrown out of Ireland. At worst—" He stopped, shook his head. "You know as well as I do that the horse needs you." *Almost as much as you need him*, Michael added to himself. "Tell me, boyo. Is telling the world to stuff it up their arses worth all that?"

Rory swore, the tears threatening in his eyes only

making him all the more furious. "Damn you, Michael, you don't understand!"

He wished he didn't. It wouldn't feel like someone was tearing out his heart. Eve's pale, stark face echoed his own pain. "Maybe I don't understand it all, lad," Michael agreed. "But I know you've worked hard. You deserve better than this. If I could give it to you, I would. But I can't."

"It's not *fair!*" Rory bellowed, and Michael knew it wasn't just the race he was raging over, but seventeen years of hurt, seventeen years of disappointment, people failing him. He reached out to the boy, wanting to comfort him, but Rory would have none of it. He turned and stormed up the castle stairs.

Michael pressed fingers to his forehead and gave a soft groan. "Damn, I wish—" He stopped. He didn't have to explain. Eve looked as devastated as he felt. "Sometimes that's just the way it has to be. Life, I mean."

"Maybe so, but it sucks." Eve's voice wobbled.

"Yeah," Michael said. "It does. I'm, uh, going to visit Bridey. I wondered if you wanted to go with me, stop at the shops on the way back and get some groceries or whatever you need."

The prospect of seeing the old woman again, having a chance to tell her how much she'd come to love Kilrain—to thank her for the gift of time here—was almost more than Eve could resist. Until she glanced up the stairs. The hollow sound of Rory's footsteps fading, then silent. "I think I should stay here, just in case."

"Rory won't want you around, if that's what you're worried about. He's got to sort this out for himself. And when he's hurting, well, he's like a fox with its paw in a trap. Mean as hell, wants to hide away, lick his wounds."

Understanding lit her eyes, so deep Michael was awed by it, intrigued by it. "Maybe that's because no one ever stuck around to talk to him when he's like that," she said softly. "If there's no one else around, you think you *have* to handle things yourself, whether they're too heavy or too hard or hurt too much."

Something in the soft, sad curve of her mouth, the loneliness beneath her thick lashes made Michael wonder who she was talking about—Rory or herself?

"I've got a few boxes of food in the car, things that won't spoil since the refrigerator isn't working. Thought I'd carry them all up after I went to the hospital. I didn't want to muck up my suit. Bridey always gets a kick out of seeing me dressed up. Likes her men tidy, she says." Or in chain mail, Halloran added to himself, trying hard to shake the melancholy that was making it hard for him to smile. He couldn't go to see Bridey looking like he'd just been through hell. The old woman needed all her energy to get well. And Bridey had made it a life's career worrying about people she loved.

His thoughts faded as he felt Eve's gaze on him, heavy, wondering, tender in spite of how badly she was hurting. "Michael, how is Bridey? Really? Do you have any idea when she'll be coming home?"

"Not until she gets her strength back. At least a few more weeks, I'd imagine. Not that the doctors tell me anything except 'we'll see.' When they do release her she'll be coming to the farmhouse, so you'll not have to worry about—"

"It's not that at all. I just—when I visited her, I came to care for her. And being here at the castle, I feel like I know her so well. Silly, isn't it?"

"No. Kilrain is her life. Always has been."

"She's the most remarkable woman. Tell her I love the way you can see the sun come up from that window in the library, the one where her writing desk is. Tell her the heather smells like heaven and sometimes it feels as if I can hear the walls whispering. Tell her . . . tell her I'm happier here than I've ever been anywhere in my life."

"I'll tell her," Michael said, voice gravelly with emotion. Now she was treading on *his* sensitive places. He wondered if she knew how much those words would mean to the old woman. Or how much it meant to him to be able to bring them to Bridey.

"Do you think she'd like it if I sent her a bunch of heather? It smells so sweet." She went to the nearest clump of the purple spikes of blossoms, gathered a handful of them in spite of their tough stems. She put them into Michael's hand.

A gift for Bridey. The fact that Eve had thought to send it would tell the old woman everything she needed to know.

Michael cleared his throat, twirling the blossoms in his hand. He knew that now, every time he saw them, he'd think of Eve.

"Listen," he said, trying to lighten things up, resorting to humor. "You haven't killed the dog, have you, Danaher? I know Bridey's going to want a full report."

"Bonaparte and I are getting along fine," she said, looking astonished as he was at the admission. "He likes to sleep on my old sweater."

Michael stared at her in wonder, remembering her abject terror of the mutt that first morning he'd seen her. What had happened? The dog dragged away her sweater and she was too scared to take it back? "I can get it back for you before I go if you want me to," he offered.

"No." She almost looked, well, sympathetic toward the dog. "I think he misses Bridey. If the sweater makes him feel better, I don't mind."

Halloran tugged at his tie again, trying hard to read her face. He'd seen such a change in her the day she'd watched Joy ride, she'd taken his breath away. And when she'd reached up on tiptoe to kiss his cheek, she'd rocked him to the core.

But she was even more different since he'd last seen her—softer, more open in spite of the pain that lay just beneath the surface. This new Eve was blossoming like the heather, every day unfolding, more beautiful. It was like peering into a rain puddle, and suddenly dis-

covering an enchanted well, full of unexpected depth
and power and beauty. A glimpse of the real Eve who
lay buried beneath all the layers of defenses the world
had made her build.

She made him want to touch her, hold her again.
Kiss away the sadness. She made him want to stay, reassure her that they'd find a way to make things right
for Rory. But he couldn't promise that. He knew all too
well that Rory had to choose to save himself. He
wanted to show her how life could be if she just had
the courage to take his hand, let him into her heart.
The place above anywhere Michael wanted to be.

But he couldn't rush his fences with this woman.
She'd suffered too much. Had already dared more than
she'd probably believed she was capable of risking.
He'd read it in her face that day she'd asked him to
stay away—known what she was asking—time to adjust, to think, to decide whether or not she wanted to
retreat back where it was familiar and safe, or step out
into the sunshine.

"Maybe you should at least take a walk," he said.
"Give the kid time to cool off. I know he's hurting, but
I don't want him taking it out on you."

"We'll be all right."

"Hmm." Michael made a low sound in his throat,
unconvinced. "I'll stop when I get back from Galway
just to make sure."

She stepped out into the sunlight with him, rays
striking her hair through with a gold that shone even
brighter set against the backdrop of the rough, weath-
ered stone of the castle. Dwarfed by the towers, she
looked small and fragile, beautiful. If only she looked
strong. Strong enough to handle Rory now that his
dream had been swept away.

Suddenly he was scared. Damned scared by what
he could see in her eyes. There was a reason she'd in-
vested so much in the boy. A reason she might not
even recognize herself. Atonement. A chance to make

things right. To pay the fates back for what she saw as failing her daughter.

What would happen to that spark of rebirth he'd seen in her eyes if she lost Rory the way she'd lost her daughter? How could she ever survive?

Michael drove back the knot of fear in his chest. He wouldn't let that happen. Not to her. Not to the boy. He'd fight with everything in him. Make them both understand how much they meant to him, how much he . . . loved them.

Love.

It was simple. Natural as breathing to admit it was so. Now if he could only convince Rory that it was true. Convince Eve that she could not only trust him, but her own heart. He looked down at the heather, ready to fight for them both. But right now Rory was the one devastated. In the most immediate danger. He had to give the boy hope.

"When Rory does come down, tell him something for me," Michael said. "Tell him there will be other races. He'll just have more time to practice, get himself ready and Innisfree, too. He'll still get his chance to show everyone how wrong they were. You tell him that for me."

She nodded. But he could see in her eyes that she knew what he knew. Even if Rory rode in a hundred other races, won a hundred other trophies, it wouldn't ever be the same.

Glengarry was his dream. Maybe the first one he'd ever dared, and it had been snatched right out of his hands. How many times could the boy bear such crushing disappointment before he crumbled under the pressure and decided just to quit fighting?

Halloran's hand knotted into a fist around the stems of heather. The stakes were getting far too high. Throat too tight to speak, he raised his other hand in farewell, then turned and walked down the rutted path toward the road. With every step, he could feel Eve's gaze on him, so determined, so wounded. Uncertain and yet digging deep into wells of courage he was sure she hadn't even known existed.

He turned his eyes skyward, peering across the land that had always been more church to him than the three-hundred-year-old building where they held mass in the village. The land that had always been his sanctuary, the only proof he'd ever needed that there was a God.

Please, Halloran prayed, *Rory's come so far. Fought so hard. Don't let Glengarry be the last blow that makes him give up.*

But it wasn't only the boy he worried about now.

It was the woman who was trying to save him.

17

"**I**f I'd died every time the doctors predicted it, I'd have enough grave sites to stretch from Blarney castle to Dingle," Bridey said, burying her face in the bouquet of heather for the dozenth time since he'd arrived a half-hour before. "Chase that gloom off your face, lad, or I'll tell the prettiest nurse I have about the time Assumpta O'Shea stole your knickers while you were swimming naked. Had to walk clear past the village dressed like Adam himself, nothing but a branch of oak leaves t' cover what God gave you. Then what'll you do? Every time you walk through the hospital doors, you'll see it in her eyes. She'll be picturing you in nothing but leaves and wishin' she'd been one of that crowd of young lasses stationed along the way to catch a glimpse of the handsome Michael Halloran, no matter how severe the penance was when they confessed it later to the good father."

Michael laughed, shook his head. "You're a hard woman, Bridey McGarrity."

"That's what the girls said when I ruined their fun. Stumblin' upon you, poor, shamed lad that you were, and giving you the loan of my headscarf. A great sacrifice it was, too. Me hair looked like a haystack by the time we got to the castle."

Michael's smile warmed at the memory. Bridey to the rescue. Unflappable as always. *And if it isn't young Michael himself*, she'd greeted him without batting an eye. *Don't get in a lather, boyo. The lasses wouldn't bother stealing your vitals unless they were plenty interested in what lies beneath 'em. You'll be glad of that one day, so you will. Break every one of their hearts in revenge.* She'd unfastened her scarf and tied it around his waist herself so he could hold the leaves steady until he was decently covered.

Decently, but not much less humiliatingly. The scarf hadn't been much of an improvement—a wad of purple splattered with bright pink roses. But he'd been grateful to have it wrapped tight around his scrawny waist anyway as he plotted his revenge. Bridey had even managed to get his clothes back so he hadn't had to explain to his parents. At least, until word got back from some neighbor that young Michael had been dashing about like a heathen.

In a village where most families had at least a half-dozen children to spread their worry between, there had been distinct disadvantages to being an only child. Ma and Da had fussed over him, worried over him, and prayed over him, their late-life gift, they'd often said. But Michael wondered if sometimes he hadn't seemed more like a curse when he turned their house, so well ordered for twenty-two years, into mayhem with a healthy dose of boyish mischief.

"So, lad," Bridey's voice brought him back to the present—the sharp, antiseptic smell of hospital air, the sterile shine of metal and plastic. The soft whirring of the machine monitoring Bridey's heartbeat. And that lump of fear pushed down deep in his throat. He'd held his mother's hand when she died, and sat by his da's bedside until the end. But hard as that had been, losing Bridey would be worse. She was the mother of his heart—mother to all his boyish adventures, his childhood hurts, his wild-in-the-sky dreams beyond the tiny cottage that had always been his parents' whole world. Dreams that had frightened Ma and Da as much as they'd delighted Bridey.

"Michael-my-heart, are you going to tell me what's troubling you? I promise, I'll not leave you just yet."

He reached up, smoothed a straggling gray hair back from her papery brow. "I'll hold you to that."

"Sure and who are you going to believe? Me or the doctors? I'm living in me own body, aren't I? Should know how I feel then, shouldn't I? Besides, these doctors look like they should still be carting their schoolbooks off to see the good brothers. Get younger an' younger, so they do. Expect to catch one sucking his thumb any minute."

"You know every one of them adores you. His lordship will get jealous."

"Might do him a bit of good after so many years having me all to himself."

She was getting tired. He could see it in her eyes. Reluctantly, Michael stood. "I need to get back to the farm."

"But you've not told me how Bonaparte is doing, wee treasure that he is. It would do my heart good to see him. I miss him almost as much as I miss his lordship, but promise not to tell."

"Bonaparte is fine. He's sleeping on Eve's sweater."

"Ah, and I knew they'd take a liking to each other. I just sensed it," Bridey said with satisfaction. Michael couldn't bear to tell her the animal had almost scared Eve to death.

"And Michael, isn't she the dearest girl? Loving the castle and saying such things to warm my heart. More than I'd even hoped. And sending me heather when I missed it so much. However did she know?"

How had she known? Michael had felt sheepish when he'd seen the delight in Bridey's eyes at the purple blossoms. Heard the old woman croon over them as if they were remarkable as fairies she'd just found under a leaf. He'd berated himself, wondering why he hadn't thought to bring the flowers that could give Bridey so much pleasure. It wasn't like him to be careless about such things. But then, he'd been distracted by the fight for Rory. Even so, it had been no excuse. The only thing that made him feel better was being certain that nothing could ever have reassured the old woman more that she'd done the right thing taking Eve in than those few bright sprays of heather.

"I don't have to tell you a word about Eve. And you know it already. You can stop gloating, old woman," he teased. "You always did love to be right. You picked the right person to take care of Kilrain while you were gone. She . . . she *fits* there." Michael shifted his gaze to Bridey's hands, trying to ignore the warming in his groin. Eve fit other places, too. Walking through the meadows, in the moonlight, lying close to him in the hayloft. In his arms. Against his body. He just wanted to draw her even deeper into his heart, show her that love wasn't anything like what that bastard who'd fathered her daughter had shown her.

"Of course I know Eve is lovely!" Bridey said, more than a little affronted. "And do you think I'd burden his lordship with some . . . some obnoxious, brainless, tiresome houseguest? Or someone loud and cheeky? No, indeed. In spite of what you think, Michael, I'm careful about who I let into Kilrain. You would be, too, if you'd been treated to a few temper tantrums from the Lord of Kilrain. Now, you look at me, my boyo. You should know you can't hide a thing from me by now."

Michael felt color burn into his cheeks, but he did as Bridey ordered. Forty-some years old, and he still obeyed her as if he were eight.

Bridey peered into his face. He squirmed with that familiar feeling that he had a window in his forehead she could see right through to whatever he was thinking.

"Ah, so that's the way of it," Bridey said, her eyes twinkling. "There are other places my poor girl fits, I'm thinking."

He still always felt a jolt when she echoed his feelings so exactly. "One problem at a time, Bridey. Right now, I've my hands full with Rory. He's heartbroken.

Because of Moran, he can't ride in that show he's been preparing so hard for."

Bridey rolled her eyes heavenward and sighed. "Dennis Moran would try an angel's patience, and you, for all I love you, Michael, are no angel. That boy never was happy unless he was putting mud in your chocolate pudding. Probably jealous because he knew no girl would have bothered to steal *his* knickers."

Michael managed a smile. "You know, the first time Eve came to Glenammura she was with Dennis. I think he had the eye for her. When he forced Rory into the car, Eve told him to go to hell."

Bridey chuckled. "The wonder is you managed to keep disliking the girl for so long after that. You always were a stubborn boy, Michael."

"It is a wonder, isn't it? Maybe if I'd just given her a chance in the beginning she would have helped me fight *for* Rory instead of being driven to work against me. Maybe the court's decision would have been different. There's a hell of a lot of fight in that woman. Next time I go into battle over something, you can be sure I want her on my side."

"Ah, well, then, there might be hope for you yet."

"At least as long as you're in charge of me, old woman. I'm scared to death of you." He bent down to kiss her wrinkled cheek. Even the sterile hospital smells couldn't completely obliterate the smell of lavender that had always clung about her.

She caught his face between her hands, just as she had from the time he was a restless, out-of-control boy. First it was her way to make sure he was listening. Later, an excuse to touch him, show tenderness in a way that wouldn't make him bristle with boyish dignity.

"I've been in charge of you a long time, haven't I, Michael-my-heart? Ever since your ma and da went to their rest."

He nodded, pressing her hand tighter against his cheek with his own cupped fingers.

"But even I won't be able to manage you forever." Something in her voice made him wince, something wistful, full of love.

"You'll be ordering people around for another hundred years. Not a person on earth you'd trust to do things the way you would. No, Bridey. You'll never let go of the reins."

"Believe that if it soothes you, my boy. But we, both of us, know different. A body gets tired, Michael, even if the heart is still young as the first breath of spring."

Michael tasted fear in the back of his throat. She'd never talked that way before, always bluff and bluster and claiming she would live forever. The faraway look in her eyes scared him, as if a part of her were already gone.

"Die and I'll run around Kilrain beating pans together, make so much racket his lordship will never get any sleep. I'll open it to the worst kind of tourists and let them whine about everything from the uneven stairs to the dampness of the walls." His eyes narrowed as he latched on to the *coup de gras*. "I'll put a television set in every room and leave them all on at the same time."

No one in Drogheda the day Cromwell sacked the city could have looked more dismayed. "You'll not be tormenting my poor lord like that, Michael! I swear, I'll come haunt you myself."

Michael swallowed hard, a catch in his throat. "I'll be counting on that," he said softly, understanding maybe for the first time how Bridey felt about the Lord of Kilrain. Haunting would be far better than ever having to let go.

"Next time you come, Michael, you'll be bringing my wee American with you, won't you? I'm that eager to see her again."

"She wanted to come today, but she wouldn't leave Rory."

"Ah. Reminds me of someone else I know," she teased, giving him a pointed look. "Taking care of people around them. Maybe by next time the lad will be settled. I pray so."

"Me, too."

"A week should give me plenty of time to think up all the stories about you when you were a boy."

"Maybe I won't bring her after all," he said, but the idea of Bridey and Eve together, sharing old stories, laughing and teasing him, was sweeter than he could have imagined. Seemed so right. Perfect, if he could only brush a little more color into Bridey's pale cheeks, a little more hope into Eve's gray-green eyes.

"Ah, you'll bring her," Bridey said. "You've a soft heart, Michael. You've never been able to tell me no."

I'm telling you no now, he thought. *I'm not letting you go. I don't care how tired your body is. It's your heart I see.*

"Michael?" she called out as he started out the door.

He turned to look at her, so lost in that huge white bed. "What, old woman?"

"Is the fuchsia in full bloom? Out the window it looks as if we've had sun enough."

"They're beautiful. I'll bring you an armful next week."

"Do you know, in eighty-five years I've never missed their blooming. My mother said even as a wee babe I'd crawl over to them, sit beneath the branches as if they were my own little house."

"Next year, Bridey. You'll see them next year."

"Next year," she echoed.

Michael held on to that as he walked away.

Quiet. It was so quiet in Rory's room. Eve expected raging, fury. She would have liked to throw things herself. But she'd heard nothing for so long it was starting to scare her. He was probably just asleep, exhausted from the emotional upheaval of discovering his dream of riding at Glengarry was gone. She had an overactive imagination, and yet . . . she couldn't help but worry that Rory had taken off again—run, the way he had when the world had crashed down on him in that courtroom in Dublin.

"He couldn't possibly have gotten out without me noticing, could he?" she worried aloud to herself. "I've been here the whole time." And castles were designed for defense. One entrance to defend. But there could be others she hadn't even discovered yet.

Panic nudged her hard. If Rory had sneaked out, who knew how far he could have gotten in the time she'd been pacing the floor, trying to give him space to calm down.

No. Rory wouldn't run. Innisfree was still out in the pasture, she'd seen him there just a little while ago, chasing off a flock of birds impertinent enough to land in one of his trees. The big horse didn't know his boy's heart was breaking.

Eve grimaced. She'd be tempted to let the horse out of the pasture and into the castle if she thought Innisfree could find his way upstairs to comfort his boy. But since that was unlikely, she should at least creep up and check on him herself.

She made her way through the library with its tower-high bookcases crammed with books. The leaded glass panes cut twilight into pieces of pink and blue, scattering them across the wooden floor. Like bits of a broken kaleidoscope, Eve thought, or maybe broken dreams. She stepped down two stairs to where the blue and gold study was, a smaller room easily warmed by the fireplace some bookworm must have added in the 1700s. A cozy, drowsy kind of room no one would suspect held a secret.

The few times she'd come upstairs since Rory had been at the castle, the entry to his room had been closed tight against everyone, the door to the priest hole blended in so well Eve almost couldn't find it.

She worried her lower lip, hating the feeling she might be intruding, even a little nervous about Michael's warning that Rory's temper would be hot. She wasn't good at this, she thought uneasily—wasn't good at anger or imposing herself on someone else. Wasn't good at prying into other people's private pain. If Steff were here—

Eve smiled, remembering her friend's technique the night after the disaster of Victoria's graduation. *This knock is a mere formality. I have the key and I'm coming in.* Eve had been furious with her at first. But in the end, she'd been so glad Steff had charged in.

If Rory didn't feel that way, she could always leave once she knew he was all right.

Eve raised her fist to knock on the door. The knock sounded like cannon fire, echoing through the castle. She held her breath. Listened. Silence. Her stomach fluttered with panic. What if Rory *was* gone? What could she possibly do? She didn't have a car and Michael was in Galway. Who knew when he'd even get back?

Bracing herself, she tried to remember how Michael had gotten the damned door open. The trouble with secret panels was that they didn't come with instruction books.

"Rory?" she called out, trying to hide her alarm. "Rory, I just need to talk to you for a second. Then I swear I'll leave you a—*umph!*" She all but crashed into the fireplace as the door gave way.

Rubbing her banged elbow, she straightened and peered into the dark cave that was Rory's room. It took a moment for her eyes to adjust. To her relief, she saw a lanky figure laid out on the cot, arms folded beneath the back of his head. He stared, glaze-eyed at the ceiling.

Good God, Eve thought in sudden panic. He couldn't have done something really crazy? Hurt himself? He couldn't be— She couldn't even think the word. But statistics for desperate teenagers spoke for themselves, every newspaper carrying its occasional article on teen suicide.

She dove for him, grabbing him by the shoulders. He erupted in a tangle of waving arms and indignation.

"Get off!" he roared, shoving her away; with his

heels he jammed himself tighter into the stone corner where the bed was tucked. "Can't you just leave me alone?"

Eve breathed, so glad he was alive she barely even heard what he said. "I can, now. I was just afraid."

"You saw me come up here. Where did you think I was going to go?"

She winced, sheepish. "I don't know. I just knew I didn't want you to."

"To what?"

"Go. Anywhere." Especially six feet under the ground. "I thought you might be hungry. I hoped you might . . . might want to talk."

"Will talking make it so I can ride at Glengarry?" he demanded bitterly.

"No. No, it won't."

"Then what good is it? What good is anything? Michael says—don't ride that horse. The horse is too dangerous. But I do it, and then he says—can't ride him in a show. He's too dangerous. And I work and work and Innisfree tries so damn hard and then—then Michael says—get him trained and you can try him at Glengarry. And I want it so damn bad. I earned the chance to ride there, dammit! So did Innisfree."

"You worked hard, both of you. It must make you so—" *Don't say "hurt,"* Eve thought desperately. *He's not ready to let anyone know he hurts yet. Not even himself.* "Angry," she finished.

"It's not just for me. Innisfree has worked so hard. You should have seen him—how scared he was at first. How mad he was at everyone. I told him he didn't have to be afraid anymore. Nobody was going to hurt him. He'd be able to show them all the kind of horse he is. He deserves the chance to tell all those people who wanted to turn him into glue to bugger off."

"He will do it. I know he'll have that chance. Michael . . . Michael knows how hard you've both worked. He said to tell you there would be other shows."

"But Innisfree is ready now!"

"And so are you," Eve said.

"He didn't do anything wrong. He doesn't deserve to have somebody take things away from him like this."

"You didn't do anything wrong either. The courts were wrong, Rory. Your parents were wrong. I was wrong. This isn't your fault any more than it's Innisfree's. I hate it that you aren't going to be able to ride."

He peered into her face, astonished as though only half believing his own ears. Had anyone besides Michael ever taken this boy's side? The image of Rory facing everything alone wrenched her heart.

"Maybe if I hadn't run away my ma and da would have let me come back for the show, ride him."

Eve closed her eyes. After the court battle waged between Michael and Rory's parents, the bitter things said during that fight, it would take someone incredibly strong to put aside their own feelings and deal with the "enemy" for the good of their child. Power was what Jamie and Oonagh had craved. She'd seen it in their faces, heard it in their voices. That court battle had been a chance to tell someone wealthy and strong and decent like Michael Halloran to go to hell.

They'd enjoyed the sensation of defeating Michael far too much to put their differences on hold long enough to let Rory show Innisfree. The more they could take from Michael the happier they would be. It wouldn't matter a damn to them that they were taking something vital from their son as well. And they'd used Eve as one more weapon to hurt Michael and Rory. The trouble was, she'd put herself in their hands.

"Rory, I don't think your parents would have let you ride, even if you'd done everything exactly the way they wanted you to. But I do know Michael would move heaven and earth to make it happen if he could. He believes in you the way you believe in Innisfree."

Rory's mouth quivered for a moment before he ruthlessly forced it to be still, his face rigid, but his eyes burned with feeling. "Michael . . . Michael said I . . . I saved Innisfree. There wasn't another rider he'd ever met in all his years on the circuit who could have done that."

"He told me that, too. I know you're . . . you're angry. Everything's confused. But it won't always be this way. You're seventeen, Rory. In a year, you will be all grown up, on your own. No one, not the courts, not your father or mother can tell you what to do. You can go anywhere you want. Be anything you want to be."

Eve fought a pang. Hadn't she thought just that a hundred times in the past year, whispered it to her little girl every night? *When you're eighteen you can decide for yourself.* She'd felt the pain of being on the opposite side of that freedom to decide. Knew what it felt like to be left standing, alone, watching your child walk away from you. The difference was that Rory *had* to do it if he was going to save himself the way he had saved Innisfree. Had Victoria felt she had to walk away as well?

"I wish I could say I thought your parents would have let you ride Innisfree no matter how much they hated Michael. That's what real love is. Doing what's right for the person you care about, even when it hurts."

Rory chewed on the inside of one cheek, thinking so loud she could hear the wheels whirring. "Leave me alone for a while, will you?" Rory said, sharp-edged. Then his cheeks colored. "I mean, please. I have some . . . some stuff to think about."

Eve nodded. She couldn't keep from patting one of those restless, gangly legs. "Take as long as you need. I just wanted to make sure you were—well, you know."

Rory grimaced. "Still here."

"Yeah." The last thing the kid needed was to know she'd been afraid of even worse. "If you get hungry—"

"You're always trying to feed me. What is that? Some kind of woman thing? One of the mothers at one of the places I stayed at was like that. She wanted to keep me. Her husband sent me back. I remember she sent me with this package of . . . of biscuits and such, like that could make me feel better. Funny thing was, it did, a little. Usually people were so glad to get rid of me they nearly caught my arse in the door, they slammed it behind me so fast. That lady and Michael are the only two who didn't want me to go."

"I don't want you to go either. That's three. And Innisfree—"

"And Innisfree." Rory echoed, his voice soft, a little bewildered.

Eve went through the door, started to slide the panel closed.

"You don't have to do that," Rory said, surprising her.

She steadied herself, wondering just how much that gesture meant. "Okay."

"And Eve?"

She turned back to him, the faint light glowing deep red in his hair, his face a pale smear in the shadows.

"Thanks for . . ." He couldn't form the words. Didn't know what to say. He didn't have to say anything. There was enough in his eyes to keep her heart warm for a very long time.

Instinctively, she crossed to Rory, took his face in her hands and kissed him on the forehead, the way she'd imagined kissing her own little girl for so long. Her eyes stung at the bewilderment in Rory's eyes, and the frightened, fragile pleasure.

She didn't say anything. She just walked downstairs. Somehow, between them she and Rory had made walls tumble down.

An hour later Michael came to the door, his arms full of groceries, his shoulders bowed. Eve had never seen him look so tired.

"How was Bridey?" she asked, taking one of the bags and holding the door for him to come in.

"Stubborn as usual," Michael said, leading the way to the kitchen. "You'd think the doctors could give her something for that. When I talked to the nurses, they said everyone loves the old woman so much they might never let her go."

Shadows darted into his eyes, and she could sense the buried dread Michael hid even from himself that they were right.

"I wish I'd thought of giving her the heather," he admitted. "It made her light up."

"I'm betting the reason she lit up was seeing you."

"Thank you for that," he said quietly, setting the packages on the counter. "How's the boy?"

"He's—"

"Michael? That you?" Rory's voice. Michael squared his shoulders, and Eve's chest squeezed, knowing he was mustering strength for Rory's sake. The teenager came down the steps, deliberate, not rushed or reckless in usual Rory fashion.

"It's me, lad," Michael called. "Figured you'd need some food to keep up your strength, fighting that horse all the time the way you are."

Rory reached the landing, hesitated there for a moment as if some part of him wanted to turn and beat feet back up the stairs as fast as he could. But he held his ground, looking from Eve to Michael, an unexpected seriousness in his dark-circled eyes. "I wanted to . . . to ask you something."

The boy had rarely asked anything in his life. No point asking when you were damned near certain no one ever cared enough to say yes. Michael stared at him. Stress and disappointment had left lines in his face, pain in his eyes, but there was something unexpected as well, something stronger, quieter. "You know you can ask me anything."

"Eve said . . . she said sometimes when you love someone you . . . you do what's right for them, even if it's not what you want."

Michael's brow furrowed; he looked from Rory to Eve and back. Eve was talking to Rory that much? More amazing, Rory was actually listening? There had been a lot more going on at Kilrain these past few days than just horse training. "I suppose she's right," he allowed.

"Jamie and Oonagh never would have done that. Done something for me even if they didn't want to, I mean."

"I'm sorry about that, boy." Michael sucked in a steadying breath. The boy had never talked once about what he'd suffered at home. Now he was not only probing raw places himself, he was talking about them to someone else. Three months with Rory at Glenammura, and he'd never managed such a breakthrough. Michael felt a twinge of something uncomfortably close to jealousy. He quelled it ruthlessly. *Hell, man, don't be stupid! Isn't this what you wanted? You should be kissing Eve's feet for getting through to him, not feeling hurt. You've watched animals heal kids a hundred times. You never minded that.*

But Rory was different. He'd been different from the moment Michael had first looked into those raging, hurting green eyes. Somewhere, beyond the kid's bluff and bluster, he'd seen something special the two of them could share. The son he'd never had. Why hadn't he realized that until now? Hell, Eve hadn't taken anything away from him. She'd given him a chance to reach the kid after all this time. And given herself a chance to make amends for crimes she'd never committed, mistakes she should have been able to forget long ago.

Rory shrugged. "I don't much care about the way they treated me anymore. The thing is—I was thinking about it and—you would. Do what Eve said."

Michael's throat ached. "I'd try."

"I want to try, too." Rory squared his shoulders, looking eager and afraid and so young it made Michael's chest hurt. "I want you to ride Innisfree at Glengarry."

"What the—?" Michael swore, stricken. "Absolutely not! Under no circumstances! Damned if I'd ever take that away from you! You've worked too hard for it!"

"So has he."

"Rory—"

"I want him to be able to show them all."

"There's time enough for that."

"No! Now. He's ready, Michael. And he deserves the chance to do it. I want him to . . . to have that, even if I can't be the one to give it to him."

Damn, Rory had taken what Eve said and twisted it all around! "The horse doesn't know about Glengarry, lad! It doesn't matter to Innisfree when he gets to race. A few more months—"

"Months! Anything can happen. He could take a fall. Lame himself. You know as well as I do how dangerous jumping can be."

"This isn't about Innisfree!" Michael burst out. "It's about you!"

Michael felt Eve's hand on his arm. He looked down at her, fighting back anger, pain. "You know I'm right, Eve! Tell him!"

"Rory, I think that's the bravest thing I've ever heard," she said softly.

Michael swore, furious. Couldn't she see how much this was costing the boy? Hadn't she seen anything in the days since the boy had come to the castle? How hard Rory had worked? That horse was his whole life! Riding Innisfree in that first event was Rory's dream. Rory's. Damned if he'd take it away from him even if Rory asked him to. Maybe it was brave. Maybe it was a sacrifice that stunned him. But he'd rather cut off his own hand than take that away from a boy who had already lost so much.

"I won't do it." Guilt and anger warred inside him as he saw Rory's face. In all the time Rory had stayed at Glenammura, he'd never asked anyone for anything. Why bother? Nobody would ever have cared enough to help him. Now he was asking Michael—

Michael swore, looking from Eve's pleading face to Rory's wounded one. "No. I won't. I can't."

He turned, stalked out of the castle.

He heard Eve murmur something to Rory, then quick, feminine footsteps following him outside.

"Michael, how could you do that to him?"

Her accusation burned. He spun around, glaring at her. "How could you put something so stupid in his head! My God, Eve, he's beaten himself to a pulp training that horse. It's the first time he's been able to feel proud of what he's done! I want him to show the world—"

"The world doesn't matter half as much as the way he feels about himself." She peered up at him with soft, fairy-green eyes. "Can't you see? Somehow, he's learned something about love."

"I don't want him to sacrifice—"

"It's not about what you want. It's about what he wants. And that he trusts you enough to ask."

"Eve, he's had so little joy in his life. I—"

"You've given him all the joy he's ever had, Michael. All the goodness. You've shown him how to do the right thing. That's what he's trying so hard to do. It's hard enough for him to make the sacrifice. Maybe the bravest thing he's ever done. Don't take *that* away from him—to be better than he's ever had the chance to be. That hurts. I hate that it hurts as much as you do. But it's a good kind of hurt. The kind that will help him grow."

Michael wanted to rage, wanted to bellow at her, wanted to tell her she was wrong. What did she know about troubled kids, anyway? She'd had Rory for a few days, when Michael had built a life around these kids for years! He hadn't even been sure he could trust her with the lad, and now look what she'd done!

Right, Halloran. Look what she's done. Gotten Rory to talk, really talk, to open up, to trust himself and someone else enough to ask for maybe the first favor he'd ever asked for in his hard, bitter life.

And what had Michael Halloran, champion therapist of troubled children, done? Stormed away, refused what Rory asked. He'd listened to Rory, but he hadn't really heard what the boy was saying. Eve had.

"Michael, please. Help him do this. Maybe it won't just open his heart more to Innisfree. Maybe it will bring him closer to trusting you."

"Why should he? Haven't I just blown it? You're doing a hell of a lot better than I am at the moment."

She grabbed both his hands, held them tight. Her eyes shone up at him with so much faith it scared him. So fragile, so strong, so unsure of herself. A woman with so much heart, she humbled him. Eve, wounded as she was, daring to reach out to him. "Rory has never had anyone show him how to be a man. A good man," she said softly. "I don't think he believed someone like you even existed. Any more than I believed—" She stopped, her voice broke. "He needs you more than ever now."

Michael gathered up her fingers, pressed them fiercely to his lips. "Eve—" His eyes burned.

"Go on in. I know he's waiting for you."

He turned and went back toward the castle. Rory was in his room, polishing a bit of bridle.

"Rory," Michael said.

The boy looked up.

"Are you sure this is what you want, boy? Me riding Innisfree at Glengarry?"

"I really want you to do it, Michael."

"All right, then, if you're sure. But if you change your mind—"

"Innisfree deserves this. I know how much he wants it. Nobody's ever cared what he wanted either. But I care."

He cared. Eve was right.

Nothing else mattered.

Rory spit in his hand, held it out earnestly—a gentleman's agreement from the streets. Michael smiled and spit in his own. He shook the boy's hand.

"I'll need your help," Michael said. "That horse won't do half the things for me that he'll do for you."

Rory smiled. Maybe the first *real* smile Michael had ever seen him give. "I'll be there first thing in the morning," Rory said. "And don't be late. You've got yourself a trainer, Halloran."

*E*ve grinned, wondering if it was appropriate to serve horse liniment with sandwiches as she hauled a platter to the pasture where Rory and Michael had been working for the past two weeks. Appropriate or not, she had a feeling Halloran would be happier to get the liniment than anything edible.

He'd thrown himself into training the horse with driving intensity that had left Sean shaking his head and Eve biting her lip until it was chapped. Eve had had the sense to retreat to the castle when things got too bad, but Sean had hovered around like a mother hen until Michael had forbidden his best friend to set foot on Kilrain ground. Michael had his hands full enough without knowing Sean was standing there planning his wake.

If Eve was honest, she had to confess she'd been a little relieved when Sean had left. She had enough insecurities of her own when it came to her dealings with Rory. She didn't need someone constantly hovering over her as if he thought her world would explode at any moment. Especially when she'd wanted to concentrate on other things. Like the magic that was growing between her and Michael Halloran and the things she was slowly beginning to discover about herself. A new freedom just to *be*. A pleasure in simple things. A slow releasing of the feeling that she couldn't be happy and still be loyal to her daughter.

Much as she still missed Victoria, and in spite of her

calls back to the States to Steffie, who was doing what she could to find out where the girl had gone, in spite of letters written where feelings poured out, Eve was learning how to smile. For real. Without constantly looking back with regret at things she could never have.

Michael was teaching her that, and Rory, who had fought his way through so much.

She'd come to look forward to their daily training sessions with Innisfree, the excitement of it, the challenge. Watching Michael with the horse and the boy was a revelation. If Rory was going to trust him to ride, he was going to do the best job possible for the boy. She'd watched the two of them, her heart tender, wondering who was training whom now. Halloran, with years of experience, steady patience? Rory with a boy's enthusiasm, his fierce belief in the horse and the man who rode him? Or Innisfree, who had so completely given his heart to the lad who loved him?

Every moment, they seemed to learn from each other. Tiny miracles, hour by hour, jump by jump. They echoed the miracles unfolding in Eve's heart.

Every minute Halloran could steal away from his work at Glenammura, he was on that horse, while Rory worked with Innisfree the rest of the time.

If Eve wanted company when she brought out the picnic hamper Sean sent from Glenammura every day for dinner, she felt obliged to invite Innisfree, too. God help her if the museum ever found out she'd turned that magnificent urn back into a horse trough, but Innisfree had looked so miserable when she'd tried using a plain stainless steel bowl, she'd felt guilty and relented, filling the urn with water and strewing the floor with oats. It wasn't *her* Saxon urn anyway, she'd reminded herself. It was Bridey's. If Bridey didn't mind horse slobber all over the thing, then why should Eve?

Besides, no gleam of polished metal could match the sparkling of delight in Rory's eyes when he saw his precious horse and Bonaparte sharing their "cuppa." Or when Michael raised tired, tender eyes to hers and gave her that smile she was coming to know belonged to her alone.

If Michael's bond with Rory and the horse had flourished during this time, the bond between Eve and the Irishman had as well, unfolding a petal at a time. Michael so patient, and yet, with an eagerness that made her tingle from head to toe with the promise of pleasure yet to come. And a gift for stealing kisses and giving her long looks as stirring as if he'd touched her.

With each day that passed, Eve was more and more sure that she wanted him to . . . to touch her all over. To kiss her with no barriers between them. To see if he could really love a woman who still had so many places inside herself she was trying to heal. She prayed every night that that would be enough for Michael. That she could bring him even the tiniest measure of the happiness he was bringing to her. But all she could be sure of was the desire that flared between them, something so powerful, so full of wonder, she'd never imagined such a thing existed before she'd found it in Michael's touch.

She shivered, remembering the delicious sensations of Michael's hand on her breast when they'd ducked behind the tumbledown carriage house at the rear of the property, Michael learning her curves under the layers of her shirt, touching skin beneath the cloth. The thick moan that had come from his throat, telling her he needed so much more.

But neither of them wanted a hasty first night together, something secretive and stolen. And for now there was no place they could be together with real privacy, even if they had been able to find the time to steal away. It felt wrong to even consider making love at Kilrain with Rory around, and Bridey's ghost hovering who knows where, watching them.

Eve squinted her eyes against the afternoon sun, saw Michael and Rory working with the skittish horse.

The course the two of them had set up on the castle grounds was enough to turn Eve's hair white—jumps over creek beds, fallen tree trunks, stone walls where erosion had eaten away at the ground on the other side. If it looked like there was a good chance you'd break your neck going over it, Rory and Michael were sure to attempt it. The higher, the harder the obstacle, the greater their delight.

And Innisfree's.

It would have been easier to knock those two stubborn-male heads together if she couldn't see the fierce joy in the horse's brown eyes as well. Magnificent animals, all three of them, full of life and fight and courage. It might even have been fun to watch total strangers race around the way they did, but when you actually *cared* about the necks that might be broken, it changed things entirely.

Michael circled the pasture at a gallop, then leaned over the horse's neck, urging him toward the latest of the terrifying jumps he and Rory had arranged, a tangled brush pile that looked for all the world like thick wood tentacles trying to grab one of Innisfree's legs.

Eve held her breath, letting the tray shift in her hands, a glint of metal shooting off as it caught the sun. She saw Halloran glance over toward her, knew in that heartbeat it was a bad idea. Innisfree gathered himself awkwardly, one back leg hitting a root as he sailed over. A rabbit darted out from the brushpile. Innisfree darted one way. Halloran kept going the other.

Eve screamed, dumping the tray onto the ground with a loud clanging thud as Halloran hit the ground hard.

Rory went after the horse, not even sparing Michael a look.

"Bloody hell!" Rory scolded, gathering the reins of his horse. "Halloran, are you brain dead or just plain stupid!"

Michael dragged himself up stiffly from the ground,

rubbing one grass-stained shoulder sheepishly. "Innis-free lost concentration for a moment. Must've been that rabbit."

Terrific, Eve thought. The horse was distractable in the middle of nowhere with just rabbits around. How was he ever going to be able to perform around a dozen other horses with crowds of people all around?

"Rabbit my arse! Innisfree was steady as a rock. It's *your* concentration that was off. You're s'posed to be concentrating on the jump, not on Eve's legs!"

Halloran's cheeks went red, his eyes flicking to where Eve's legs stretched in slender columns from the cuffs of her blue denim shorts. Heat sluiced up from her toes to pool in her breasts. He'd skimmed his palm over her thigh just last night when she'd walked out with him to say good-bye. The memory made her burn in all the most dangerous places. Shy about showing the fierce attraction she felt toward Michael with Rory looking on, she averted her gaze, looking away from Michael so fast it was a miracle she didn't get whiplash.

"Did he get hurt?" Eve stammered to Rory.

"Just a scrape on his fetlock."

"I meant Michael! He hit pretty hard."

Halloran walked toward them rubbing his shoulder ruefully. "I've hit harder when I've fallen out of bed." Halloran's cheeks reddened, and Eve knew exactly what he was thinking. If only they could both fall *into* one.

Grimacing, Halloran turned to Rory. "Think you'd better walk that horse awhile so he doesn't get stiff."

"I can take a hint if you two want to be alone, Hal-loran." Rory smirked. Eve blushed.

"I just brought out sandwiches," she said hastily. "I didn't want to interrupt your training session, though I'd love to watch you jump."

"Never mind," Rory said in teenage disgust. "Put Halloran back up on that horse with you around and he'll probably run straight into a tree."

"Watch it, you cheeky brat, or next time you get up

on Innisfree's back I'll slip a nettle under the saddle." Halloran flipped off his riding helmet, his handsome features endearingly sheepish.

Rory had no mercy. "Three of the five times you've taken a dive it's been 'cause you saw Eve coming. No place for showing off to the ladies when you're riding cross-country, Halloran. You about took my head off the day Sheila Dare walked past and I was trying to show off. Never heard you yell that loud."

"Just walk the horse, boyo. And take a big stick with you. That rabbit looked real mean. He could strip your carcass to the bone in twenty seconds."

Rory snorted in disgust. Halloran grabbed one of the less grass-stippled sandwiches from the tray and tossed it to the kid. "Eat this. That way your mouth will be too full to smart off."

Rory caught the sandwich in midair despite Innisfree dancing backward. "Maybe I should find a different rider for my horse. Hey, Eve, want to give it a go?"

Eve laughed, making no secret of her relief that she'd won at least a temporary stay of execution. No riding lessons while Innisfree was in training *or* while Michael was anywhere close enough to call a halt to it! "Sorry, kiddo. Don't think there's enough time left in my vacation to teach me to jump on that thing and there are only two days until Glengarry."

He pasted on that too bright smile that made Eve nervous—one filled with yearning and hard lessons learned too young. Disappointments expected, but still hitting hard. "Well, I'll be going up to get some salve for Innisfree's foot. Try and behave yourself, Halloran. You've gotta save your energy for the race."

Eve winced. Rory was still trying to joke, but it wasn't funny. Missing Glengarry still hurt. Bad.

She swallowed hard, watching until the boy and horse walked out of sight. Halloran sighed, sensing, she was certain, the same things she did, feeling the same sting of regret. He stripped off his riding jacket, spread it out on the grass. "Have a seat," he offered. "Can't get the thing any more grass-stained than it is already."

Eve took him up on it, sinking down and folding her legs underneath her.

Halloran went down at the same time, using the opportunity to steal a bone-melting kiss. Eve flushed with pleasure and maybe a twinge of guilt. Halloran groaned as she pulled away and glanced in the direction Rory and the horse had disappeared.

"What's the matter, treasure?" he rasped. "Afraid of that rabbit seeing us?" He shot her a smile that made her breasts tingle. "I promise I'll defend you to the death—besides, the rabbit can't tell anyone anything, not even if I did what I really want to right now, and roll you underneath me until neither one of us can breathe."

He stopped teasing, his eyes soft, warm. "This isn't about the rabbit, is it? What's bothering you?"

Eve shrugged, suddenly shy.

"Maybe we should be more . . . more careful," she said uncertainly. "About the way we're feeling. About each other, I mean. I don't think we're fooling Rory for a minute."

"I don't even try to argue with him anymore." Michael said, holding her hand in a way that made her feel hot all over. "What's the point when the kid knows the truth?"

"And what is that?"

"That I think about you way too much. That even when I'm going over a fence, I'm imagining you in my arms. In my bed. Don't blame me if when I finally do get you in bed I've got bruises over half my body. They're your fault for distracting me."

He kissed her fingers as if she were his Lady Fair, his lips warm, moist, irresistible.

She tingled, still amazed at the notion that she, Eve Danaher, could distract any man that way, let alone a man as beautiful, as fine as Michael Halloran. Surrendering her hand, he stretched out on his unbruised side and reached for a sandwich himself. Brow furrowing, he concentrated on picking bits of grass off the bread.

"Michael, are you sure you're not hurt?" she asked again.

"Only my pride, green eyes. Rory's right. No room for showing off when you're in the saddle. No one should know that better than I do. Haven't even been tempted for years. Not since—"

He stopped, his smile fading just a little. Old pain touched his eyes for a moment. And regret.

"Not since what? From what I saw in those magazines years ago you should be used to women around when you're riding. You usually had half a dozen crowding around you."

"That was easy to ignore. It's harder when there is only one."

Was he remembering something else? Some*one* else? The possibility stung.

"I'll send Bonaparte out with your sandwiches from now on," she said more sharply than she'd intended, wanting to forget about everything that went before, everything and everyone but here and now.

"What's the matter?"

"Nothing. I don't even want to know—" About her. About any other woman who'd pulled his focus, who'd made him smile, who'd brought that hot, bone-melting look of wanting into his eyes. Any woman but Eve herself.

As if he sensed her insecurities, knew just what she needed, his voice warmed, whiskey smooth. "You do play bloody hell with my concentration, lady. I know what you think—you've said it often enough. That I've had women flocking around me. After all, didn't all the magazines show that? Hey, the paparazzi loved *that* Michael Halloran. He doesn't exist anymore."

"No. You're not breaking hearts on the circuit anymore. Just any woman's who happens to stray close to

Glenammura. Even if you haven't noticed a thing, I'd bet you've cut a swath through the women here three counties wide." Maybe the jetsetter Michael Halloran *didn't* exist anymore. But this man—with his love of the land, his steady hand on the reins, his heart wide open to wounded children, wounded animals, wounded souls—was every woman's most cherished dream. Someone to trust. To hold on to in the storm.

Halloran looked out over the meadow, thoughtful, still, in a way he was so rarely. "I want you to know there haven't been any women since I left racing. I just want you to know that you're something special."

Eve dared a glance at him, saw his eyes begging— for what? For her to believe him? It sounded absurd. "Why—?" What was she? Crazy? Asking him about other women? He wanted *her* now. It shouldn't matter what had happened before. "Never mind. So how bad is that scrape on Innisfree? Will it—"

Halloran caught her wrist. "Why, what? Ask me, Eve."

"Just—you know everything about me—my past. I know so little about yours."

He smiled. "You were pretty sure you knew every rotten thing about me when we first met."

"Temporary insanity. Bonaparte scared the brain right out of my head. It's my only excuse."

"No. I reminded you of him—your daughter's father—didn't I? No wonder you hated me."

"I couldn't have been more wrong. You're . . . you're pure gold, Michael."

"You're wrong, I—"

"Listen to me. You are. Everything fine and good. But gold that bright has to be fired in a crucible, all the dirt, the tarnish, the things that dull its shine burned away. I can't help wondering what it was—the test that you came through, that made you you. You help so many people, Michael, understand their hearts. You can't do that unless you've suffered, too."

"You make it sound so noble, so honorable. It was something a hell of a lot less pretty to look at. I got sick with about six months of testosterone overload. Nothing makes a man act more like an idiot. It made me crazy, made me see just how far I would go to get what I wanted—even if it wasn't worth the sacrifice."

She saw the emotions ripple across his face, self-disgust, regret, yet distance, as if he didn't have to relive his mistake over and over again. As if he'd mourned over it, made his apologies for it, and let it go. Eve envied him that.

"Sean and I had been competing against each other since we were in short pants. On horseback, on the football field, wherever and whatever we were doing. Women were no different. It was a race to see who could get to the finish line ahead of the other one. I'm not sure who saw Gail first that summer we were riding in Italy. It didn't matter. We were both off to the races. But somehow, this time it was more serious. I'm still not sure why—maybe we each just kept trying to up the ante, determined to risk the most, give the most, prove ourselves the most. Or maybe it was something about Gail that goaded us on. I thought I was crazy in love. She was gorgeous, funny—"

Two qualities Eve had never possessed.

"Only problem was, Sean was in love with her, too. She couldn't decide between us, she kept saying. But I always thought Sean was in the lead. There was something in the way she looked at him that made me crazy. I know she was playing us against each other. Twenty-some years of friendship wiped away by a pretty smile. Doesn't make me proud to think of it. All I know is I thought I was going to lose my mind. Hell, I'd already lost my best friend."

"You could never lose each other, you and Sean. Even if you were angry for a while."

"I damned near hated him. And he—God, if you could have seen the way we looked at each other.

Everything was a contest. Didn't give a damn who else we beat. We just wanted to drive the other into the ground. Went on about six months. Even the reporters picked up on it. Who would the lovely Gail choose? What if it wasn't me? I couldn't even slink away and be miserable in silence. The whole racing circuit knew the story. Gail had made sure of that. Pretty heady stuff for her, having two of the best riders fighting over her."

Eve had known plenty of women who got off on that sort of thing—two men fighting over her. She'd often wondered if they ever thought about how it felt to be on the other side.

"We were practicing, running a particularly nasty course. Gail had followed to watch us. What fun was it to have men fighting over you where you can't watch the fireworks? We were about to have a go at the course when she came up and gave us each a kiss. Said maybe she'd marry whoever reached the finish line first. We were young and dumb. Had another rider start us off. I still don't remember what happened. Sean was ahead by a length. I was gaining on him. We came to a water jump—creek bed, all rocky on the other side. I could feel that energy a horse gets before it streaks out in front and wins. Sean looked back to see how close I was. Damn, he knew better than that. We both did. We were crowding each other, trying to get the narrowest part of the jump, knew whoever took it would win. Our horses collided as we went over. Sean went down. Hell, Sean had taken plenty of falls. We both had."

His voice dropped low. "I was so hot to win I didn't stop. Didn't even look back. I just rode to the finish line, yelling for joy. I'd beat him. I'd won. The race. Gail. That was all that mattered. Winning."

Eve knew where this was going. Wanted to stop him. But stopping him from saying the words wouldn't erase from his heart the memory of what had happened.

"I turned the horse around, saw the medics running

out onto the field. Sean was lying on the ground. I can still hear him screaming."

"Oh, Michael." Her heart broke for him.

"It wasn't an hour after the doctors told him he'd never walk again that Gail came up to me, told me she'd decided. She'd marry me."

What had that done to a sensitive man like Michael? The accident, the guilt?

"Michael, you didn't mean to hurt him."

"Yeah, Eve. I did. I didn't mean to cripple him, but I wanted to hurt him. I was so damned mad. So desperate. I thought Gail was the only thing that mattered to me. If I lost her, there would be nothing left."

Eve's stomach churned. He must have loved her so much—that wild, passionate, crazy kind of love only gorgeous women could inspire. The kind quiet art restorers only dreamed about. And yet, what had that kind of passion brought Michael but pain and guilt? And the constant reminder of his mistake every time he saw his best friend struggle to take a step?

She reached out, took his hand. "I'm sorry."

"Funny thing—I rarely even remember Gail's face now. But I'll never forget Sean's when the doctor told him . . ." Michael shook his head. "He told me to go to hell. I don't blame him. Believe me, I tried to go to hell as fast as possible. Would have made it, too, if I hadn't gotten a call from Bridey. Sean was staying alone in this stinking little cottage, drinking himself blind. He'd driven off anyone who even tried to help him. Even his sister had finally had to give up, at least for a while. Otherwise, the doctor told her she might lose her baby because of the stress. I told Bridey I was the last person Sean would want to see. There was nothing I could do. Jesus, Mary, and Joseph, Eve, I wish you could have heard her blister my ears. *You've been acting like fools, the both of you! You got yourselves into this, you and Sean, just like you did when you were boys, and that's the only way you're going to get out of it! Together!*"

Michael chuckled. "I spent every waking minute for two weeks telling myself how wrong Bridey was. In the end, I figured if I had to argue that much, maybe she was right. I didn't know if I could do anything to help Sean. But I figured at least I owed him the chance to throw a bottle of whiskey at my head."

"So you took care of him," Eve said softly. "And between you, you made that fall, all that anger and ugliness, turn into something good."

"That's all I wanted to do. Make his pain count for something. That's the only thing that mattered. It's not that I ever made a conscious decision to stay away from women. Glenammura and what Sean and I were trying to build there was just more important."

Eve drowned in the blue of his eyes. He looked up at her, so earnest, so astonished.

"And then there was you," Michael said. He cupped her cheek in his palm, drew her close. His mouth closed over hers, warm, melting warm and full of wonder. She moaned as he pulled away. "Eve, I was . . . was thinking if you came with me when I went to ride at Glengarry, maybe we could be together. Away from everything. Maybe I could finally show you how much I—"

She caught her breath, waiting for the precious words, but instead, Michael jumped to his feet. Then she heard what Halloran must have, the steady clop of hooves as Rory drew near.

And then there was you. Somehow, that said everything.

"Michael, about what you said—about Glengarry. It's what I want, too. I just—I don't want to leave Rory."

Michael nodded. "I understand."

"No, you don't. You can't even begin to imagine how much I want this. Want you." She glanced up, saw Rory closing the gap between them. But nothing in the boy's face showed that he'd heard, guessed what they were talking about, thank God.

"Think you'd better give him another go at that jump," Rory said. "Don't want him to get scared of it."

Halloran nodded, swung into the saddle. Eve tried to remember to breathe as he rode away. She didn't want Rory to see—see that Halloran had tipped her world off its axis. Shattered her. Healed her.

"I wish I could see Innisfree run," Rory said softly. "Michael will be on his back. He'll know how Innisfree jumps and all, but he won't be able to tell me about the look on people's faces when they realize who Innisfree is. When they see how he can fly."

One more rotten piece of injustice, Eve thought, trying to focus on Rory's pain with the power of Michael's kiss still roaring through her and the promise of a night to share. She wanted to run. Wanted to stay forever. Wanted to do something, anything, to catch her balance again.

"I wish I had one of those camera things the tourists are always hauling around," Rory mourned.

Eve's eyes narrowed in relief as Rory gave her something to hold on to. She might not have packed a video camera, but surely she should be able to buy one before the race.

"I could film Innisfree. You could see how he looked going over the fences. I could even take pictures of the crowd so you could see their reaction, too."

Rory's face brightened. "Could you?"

"Hey, they have to have video cameras someplace even in the wilds of Ireland. I'll probably cut off a few people's heads and the film will probably be wobbling all over the place. I'm not the world's greatest photographer. But I'd do my best." She'd be able to spend the night with Michael *and* give this boy something precious. Was it selfish? Or something completely right?

Rory stared at her, stunned, as if she'd turned into a fairy godmother right before his eyes. "You'd really do that for me?"

For the look in the boy's eyes, she'd do it if she had

to walk across the ocean to America to get the damned camera. "I'll do it."

Rory beamed. "Right, then."

She caught her lip between her teeth. "But Rory, I don't want to leave you alone." It was hard to bear the idea of Rory lost in the huge, silent castle while some-one else was riding his horse, winning his dream, even if Rory had asked Michael to do it. "Maybe Sean could make the movie for you."

"He can't even program the VCR at the farmhouse. He'd make a muck of it for sure. I want you to do it, Eve. Please. I'll be fine," Rory assured her. "Just try not to get too close to Halloran. Don't want to scare up any more rabbits on the course."

They'd scared up something far more startling. Hope. A new beginning. A chance. Maybe she could find answers to her questions in that one, promised night of their own. She looked out across the pasture, her breath catching at the beauty, the power, the strength in the man guiding the reckless horse through its paces.

And then there was you . . . Michael's words echoed in her heart.

She watched, breathless, as Innisfree sailed over the obstacle he'd stumbled on before as if his legs were wings and this time nothing on earth could stop him from soaring.

19

There were more buttons on the shiny new video camera than there were on the control panel of the space shuttle, and she'd always been among the technologically impaired, Eve thought wryly as she wound her way through the hustle and bustle of the Glengarry horse show. But at least she knew what button to press to start the film rolling, and could manage the zoom lens on occasion. No great feat since she'd spent a day-and-a-half practicing, filming Rory and Michael riding, Innisfree running free in the pasture, doing his Lord-of-All-He-Surveyed imitations, except, of course, for the brief visits of Bonaparte to the pasture. Somehow the snaggle-toothed pug seemed to be in charge—a fact that caused Eve no end of amusement.

But then, she'd laughed more in the past two days than she had since before Victoria had been taken away from her. And when she and Michael had stolen away to the Glenammura farmhouse to check what she'd filmed on his VCR, she'd blessed Rory a hundred times over for spurring her to get the camera. Maybe you couldn't catch Irish fairies dancing in their fairy rounds, but the tapes she'd made proved that you could capture magic on film.

Not that she needed tapes to remember the past two days. The scenes would play out in her mind even when she was an old woman, Eve knew, each still perfectly tinted, carrying with them the scent of the heather, the salt tang of the wind, the way the light danced on the wild green of the turf. And the glow in Rory's eyes—no camera ever made could do justice to that.

It would have been perfect if Rory's riding silks flashed in the Glengarry sunshine instead of Michael's—the brightly colored clothing Halloran had bought to surprise the boy before his first race. Like a knight's colors from ages ago, so anyone who saw them would know who it was riding into battle.

Michael had chosen bright green and royal blue for Rory, and Eve knew that dressed in them he would have turned the head of every one of the young girls who thronged the area this race day. Girls every bit as horse mad as her Victoria had always been.

She fought back a bittersweet sting as a girl with ginger-colored hair sauntered by, riding crop in hand, her black and red silks gleaming while a woman who must be her mother struggled to keep up in the crowd. Pride and worry and excitement were all marked on the mother's face. Maybe, if Rory had been riding, Eve would have felt the same things—could have tasted what it would have been like to usher Victoria to these kinds of events. A circle of races that cut her summers into slices of wins and losses, of silver trophies and challenges that had made Eve's daughter who she was.

Ever since she and Michael had arrived this morning, Eve had been drinking in the sights and smells and sounds of a horse show, the scene she'd watched a hundred times on television, seen a thousand still shots of in magazines, and visited countless times in her dreams. She'd always known she'd see it for herself someday in person. She'd just been certain when she did it would be at her daughter's side. Victoria showing her all the things she'd done while they were apart, the things she valued most, imagined sharing memories of times Eve had missed. Victoria confiding how much she'd always wanted to look into the crowd to find her mother there.

No, Eve thought, winding her way through the crowd. Maybe this wasn't the way she'd always pictured it. But during the hours of helping Michael prepare while trying her best to be Rory's ears and eyes, she'd come to love the buzz of excitement, the smell of horses and polished leather and adrenaline. The colors of people riding—a crayon box of bright, vivid hues in shimmering silk. Excitement rippled through the crowd of race-goers and she was part of that. One of them, waiting to see the horse she cared about race and the man she cared for too much ride him.

She looked at the cluster of young riders warming up for an upcoming race, helmets tight, horses restive. Had any of them worked as hard as Rory to train the horse they rode? Did any of them care as much as that one redheaded boy?

Was it the pain of that thought, or the yearning she'd always had to watch Victoria race that made her turn back to where Michael's horse trailer was parked? She wasn't certain. Or did she only want an excuse to see Michael's face again? See the promise that glinted in his eyes.

Don't be distracting him!—had been Rory's parting plea. And she had done her best. Michael had his hands full, Innisfree liking crowds and noise about as much as Eve had liked dogs when she'd arrived at Kilrain. Michael needed to give Innisfree his full attention, do the best he could for Rory—but once the race was over . . .

Eve's whole body tingled.

The rest of the night was their own.

He'd parked the trailer as far away from the hubbub as possible, tucked it behind a stand of trees. Eve could see him in his own navy blue and burgundy silks, dulled and softened with age and use. Innisfree shifted restlessly against the lead that tied him to a picket post, the horse's busy brown eyes searching everywhere—looking at all the new sights around him or looking for the boy who had disappeared just after they'd led the horse into the trailer. He'd been so brave up to that moment that it had broken Eve's heart, and she'd wanted to go find him, but Michael had stopped her.

Let the boy go if he needs to. We'll not be making this any harder for him. He'd understood Rory couldn't bear to say good-bye the way he seemed to understand right now just how much the horse missed his boy. Michael stroked Innisfree's nose, big hands so gentle, so powerful, so experienced, his voice a low murmur.

Eve clicked on the camera for a moment, knowing Rory would feel better if he saw these few, centering moments between Michael and the horse as they both prepared to race. Then Michael shifted, and she could see more of his face. Lines carved deep on each side of his mouth, his eyes shadowed. She clicked the camera off, feeling as if she'd been intruding, somehow, spying on something too private to share.

Somber, too quiet, Michael communed with the horse, his eyes distant and troubled. Because Rory wasn't here? That was some of it, Eve sensed. But there was more.

Michael left Innisfree, crossed toward the chair to grab his riding gloves. She knew the moment he realized she was there. Her heart squeezed when he didn't try to hide the emotions she'd seen in his face. He let her see it all—the grief for Rory, the nervousness for Innisfree, and the uncertainty she couldn't quite make sense of.

"I'm glad you came back," he said quietly, and she could see he was. She wished she'd never left him alone with whatever had brought those shadows to his face.

"I wanted to find the perfect place to film—where I could get most of the course and, of course, Innisfree's grand finish. Maybe I got a little distracted."

"I wanted you to wander through the crowd. Get a feel for race day. I just didn't realize I didn't want to be alone until you were gone."

Eve went to him, took his hand, touches that had become so precious in the past few days. She smiled.

"Surely the great Michael Halloran can't be nervous before a little country race like this one!"

"I didn't realize I'd be so damned scared," Michael admitted. "Last time I raced I failed Sean. I don't want to fail Rory."

He hadn't raced since Sean's accident? The colors all around Eve faded. What must it be like for him, stepping back into this world where he'd made such a costly mistake? Hurt so badly someone he loved? The sights and smells and sounds she'd been delighting in were echoes from Michael's worst nightmare. Had Rory guessed how much he was asking when he'd begged Michael to race again? Had Michael even suspected how raw he might feel? No. She'd seen him yesterday, all laughter and skill and drive to make things right. The only demon he'd been wrestling with was his reluctance to leave Rory behind. Or had Michael been hiding from the feelings he'd face here, hiding it even from himself?

Wind ruffled his dark hair against his brow, the mouth that had kissed her suddenly, starkly vulnerable. "It's been a long time since I've raced, Eve. And Innisfree—it's impossible to guess what he'll do here. Especially without his boy around to calm him down."

She wanted so desperately to soothe him. *You can never fail Rory—after everything you've done for him, all the love you've shown him, all the strength you've given him.* But saying that would only make things harder, knowing how much faith the boy put in Michael. Eve winced, remembering the faith that had always shone in Victoria's eyes—absolute trust that her mama would always be there, would keep her dreams safe. She'd never realized what a crushing weight that could be until she was helpless to be everything Victoria had believed of her.

She latched on to something more calming, she hoped, distracting Michael from Rory by turning his attention to the horse.

"It's already going better than you thought it

would." She smiled. "Didn't you say you were surprised at how well Innisfree trailered here?"

"I've had twenty-year-old ponies that have kicked up more of a fuss. Almost got out twice just to make sure the horse was all right, but I was afraid I'd remind him he should be throwing a fit."

"Maybe Innisfree knows somehow—that this is his chance. Rory said he told him." Talking to horses and believing they could understand— Back in New York Eve would have thought anyone who believed that could happen would have been loony-toons. But somehow, here, now, it made perfect sense.

"Rory spent half the night getting the trailer ready, filling it with straw, packing all of Innisfree's things." Michael attempted a smile. "I even found some grapes in there after I took Innisfree out."

"Maybe he could smell Rory in there and it comforted him."

"Maybe."

The buzz of the loudspeaker interrupted, a cultured voice giving the announcements. "Masters class for cross-country, report to the judges."

Michael gave her a brittle smile. "That would be me."

"Good luck. I know you'll both be grand," Eve said, reaching up on tiptoe to kiss him. Michael gathered her against him, crushed her there, hard.

"See you at the finish line." The words were out of his mouth before he could stop them. Oh, God, Michael thought, that's what he and Sean had always said to each other. But Eve was smiling her lost fairy smile.

"Find me when its over," he said.

"You can count on it, Halloran."

He caught her against him another long moment— soft breasts crushed against his chest, thighs brushing his, the crown of her head tucked underneath his chin.

The announcer was speaking again. "Interesting side note for our race-going public. Michael Halloran, the winningest rider in Irish history, will be taking his place at the starting line today. You may remember Halloran left racing after a terrible accident cut short the promising career of one Sean—"

Michael closed out the sound, closed out the memories, held tight to the green of Eve Danaher's eyes.

"For Rory," he said, then, unhitching Innisfree, he swung on board.

Neither he nor Eve saw the figure hiding behind a nearby tree, floppy hat drawn low over his features, bits of hay clinging to clothes that hung three sizes too big on his lanky frame.

"No," Rory whispered, heart bursting. "For Innisfree."

"Daddy, did you hear that?" Victoria asked, tingling with excitement. "Michael Halloran is going to ride!"

"You'd better be concentrating on your own race. Mr. Butler is counting on Puck showing well."

"He will." Little doubt of that, and really little challenge in it. Puck was about as predictable as the fact that it would rain in Ireland, the horse a hard worker, beautiful, but lacking that final spark that would make him into a grand prix–level contender. Victoria looked at the gelding and couldn't keep from feeling a little deflated. She'd had so many hopes for this race, imagined it all so differently. She'd win today, but mostly because Clare was just waiting for her to mess up and Victoria didn't want to give her the satisfaction. But even nasty as Clare had gotten while they trained, there were times Victoria almost felt sorry for her. Clare adored Puck, believed in him, while each day Victoria had worked Puck, she'd grown more certain he wasn't the horse she could go all the way to the winner's circle with. Unfortunately, every time she was up on Puck, her father became more certain he was the greatest horse in Ireland. But then, Daddy didn't understand the magic. The challenge of taking a horse with spirit and drive and independence and forging a connection. He didn't understand that the edge that made a horse a little skittish, unpredictable, was also the edge that made it give its last bit of heart for you to win.

She'd suspected for almost two weeks now that Puck would have performed just as well for Clare or Dara, or even little Katie Butler if her legs could reach the stirrups. But at least the day wouldn't be a total wash if she could see Michael Halloran ride.

"Please, Daddy, I may never get the chance to see someone as good as Halloran ride ever again."

Her father's jaw started to get that stubborn jut, but she begged.

"Please, Daddy. Who knows? I might even see some technique that will make me ride better on my own run."

Her father grimaced. "All right. But then I expect you to concentrate, a hundred percent focus on the task at hand. That's the way you succeed."

"Promise!" Victoria cried. She jumped as the starting gun fired and turned in a whirl of rose and silver riding silks, running toward the finish line as if she were the one racing. She plowed through the crowd—desperate times called for desperate measures—and Halloran was so fast she didn't want to risk the race being over before she'd even caught a glimpse of him.

She dove through an opening at the finish line, all but running over a kid with the baggiest clothes she'd ever seen. She shoved in front of him, breathless as she got the best vantage point to see the riders come over the hill.

"Watch it, you!" a sharp boy voice snapped. A hand closed roughly in the cloth of her jersey, hauling her backward so hard she nearly landed on her bottom.

Victoria jerked away, indignant as she wheeled to glare into hard gray eyes. "Let go! Don't you know Michael Halloran's riding?"

The boy's sharp features pulled into a sneer. "Yeah. I know. And I was here first."

Something about this boy made the hackles stand

straight up on the back of Victoria's neck. But rude as he was, she *had* pushed right in front of him. "I know you probably don't understand since you're not a rider," she started to explain, summoning up all her patience. "But—"

"Who says I'm not a rider?"

"A racer, then. If you were, you'd be in silks." She wanted to watch the race, not argue with some spectator who could never understand the magic of what was happening here.

His eyes sparked, so dangerous she tried to take a step back, but the crowd was too close, and there was no way she was going to miss watching Michael Halloran finish, no matter how mad this kid got. Was he angry? Victoria wondered. Something else was in his eyes.

"I can learn so much from watching a rider like Halloran," she said, straining to see the course. "This means everything to me."

"Yeah, and I'm not in silks so what can it mean to a filthy bugger like—" The boy broke off mid-snarl, then gave a whoop. "Damn his arse, look at him run!"

Victoria spun around to see the racers thundering down the second half of the course, the most difficult, most dangerous. She would have known Michael Halloran just because of the silks he wore and the way he rode, perfection, poetry on horseback. But the moment she saw Halloran's mount clear a fence, Godzilla could have been riding and she wouldn't have noticed.

Victoria froze, gaped as the most beautiful horse she'd ever seen soared two feet above every jump, muscles rippling, heart in his eyes as if he could jump over the moon if he cared enough about the rider on his back.

The boy's hand fell away as if even *he* knew something magic was happening. She could hear his harsh breath, feel him straining almost as if he were the one riding.

A dappled Hanoverian pounded a nose-length

ahead, Halloran's horse skittering sideways just enough
for the most experienced rider to notice. The horse was
afraid, Victoria realized with a start, his eyes white-
ringed, foam flecking the corners of his mouth. But he
ran with so much heart, so much courage, it took her
breath away. The two horses rounded a corner, charging toward the finish line.

"Innisfree!" the boy shouted, piercing through the
noise of the crowd. Victoria gaped. It was as if the horse
heard him. It surged ahead, soaring over the final jump,
charging toward the finish line a full three lengths
ahead of the field.

Halloran fought to rein the horse in, the magnificent animal thrashing around, spooked by the noise
and confusion, but it didn't daunt Victoria at all that
even Ireland's greatest horseman had his hands full
with his mount.

"That's him," Victoria breathed.

"Yeah. That's Halloran," the boy said. "So go tell all
your horsey girlfriends you actually saw him. They'll
probably give you a medal."

"I don't care about Halloran. Not anymore. It's the
horse," Victoria marveled. "That's the horse that's
going to make me a champion."

The boy snorted in shock, disgust. She almost
thought his face paled under the brim of his ridiculous
hat. "That horse isn't for sale."

Patience exhausted, Victoria gave him her very best
glare. "My father says horses are always for sale!"

She winced at the burning scorn that filled the boy's
hard eyes. "I know for a fact Halloran wouldn't sell it.
Especially not to you, little rich girl! Besides, why
would you want Innisfree anyway? That horse has put
more people in the hospital than the rest of the horses
here combined."

"I don't believe you! Did you look in his eyes? He
may be a little edgy yet, but he's got more heart than
any other horse I've ever seen."

The Irish boy looked almost scared. "Michael would never sell him," he said. "You can take that to your da's bank account and cash it."

Michael? This kid called Halloran *Michael?* A sliver of unease slipped under her skin. No, this boy couldn't possibly know anything about that horse. He was just trying to pull her chain.

"Victoria?"

Relief shot through her as she heard her father's voice. She spun to see him making his way toward her—no doubt ready to drag her back to Puck. "Daddy, did you see him? The winner?" she asked, clutching his sleeve. "That's the horse! The one I've been looking for! This *boy* says it's not for sale!"

Her father scowled. "It's not for you to say, is it, kid?"

She'd wanted to wipe the sneer off of the boy's face. She just hadn't expected the sudden, hollow look in his eyes. It made her wince.

"No," the kid admitted. "It's not for me to say."

People were pushing to get closer, congratulations ringing out all around Michael Halloran and his horse.

Her father clapped the kid on the shoulder. "Come with us, Irish, and I'll show you just how quick money can change someone's mind no matter how sure they are they don't want to sell."

Victoria watched as her father started propelling the boy toward the winner's circle, but a stricken look streaked across the kid's face. He yanked away, darted through a break in the crowd. In a heartbeat, he'd vanished. Victoria caught her lip between her teeth, unsettled.

"So, do you even know the name of this horse you're so in love with?" her father asked.

"That boy called him Innisfree."

Michael swung down off Innisfree's back, triumph raging like fire through his veins. "You beautiful, beautiful bastard, you!" he said, wrapping his arms around

Innisfree's sweaty neck. "By God, if Rory could only have seen you! You did it, my beauty."

And Rory was eighty miles away at Kilrain. Regret stabbed Michael's heart. Even though they'd won, they'd lost something as well. There would never be another race like this one. Innisfree, the horse half of Ireland had wanted to shoot, was back with a vengeance. Three people from Innisfree's old stable had already come up to Michael, marveling at the job he'd done gentling the horse. But Michael knew damned well he hadn't done it at all. Innisfree had won for the love of an inexperienced, angry, abused teenaged boy, a boy who had been hurting just as much as this amazing horse.

He strained to look through the crowd, searching for Eve, but she was shorter than most, lost somewhere in the mayhem. He smiled, knowing she'd find him. The knowledge warmed him, unsettled him, made his body hungry for something far different from racing—another kind of triumph he and Eve might share tonight.

He caught a glimpse of a man who looked like one of those *Gentleman's Quarterly* ads for country wear wending his way toward him, a slender girl in riding silks hustling right behind him. Another young rider wanting to shake his hand, Michael guessed—damn, it made him feel like a fool. He'd left all that glory and adoration behind on the course that had shattered Sean's legs. He'd ridden again for Rory's sake, but he didn't want any of that hero-worship he'd been drunk on so many years ago. Now he knew just how much such an inflated ego could cost.

"Halloran, isn't it?" a suave American voice called to him, as the man flashed a toothpaste-ad smile. "I have to tell you, you've impressed the hell out of my daughter."

Michael managed a weak smile and looked over the top of the girl's head trying to catch sight of Eve. "Hope you enjoy your stay in Ireland," he said automatically.

"I think she'd enjoy it a lot more if she spent it riding this horse of yours," the American said smoothly.

Michael's attention whipped back to the two Americans so fast he almost got whiplash. "This—you mean *this* horse? She wants to ride this horse?"

"My daughter thinks he can take her to the championships."

"I wouldn't sell Innisfree to you even if he *was* for sale, which he's not. He'd break her neck in about three minutes. Sorry—uh—"

"Victoria," the girl supplied.

"Victoria." Eve's daughter's name, Michael realized. But then, there must be dozens of girls with that name. He didn't have time to think about it as Innisfree jerked on the reins. The big horse was about a heartbeat away from jerking free entirely. If he ever did, they wouldn't catch him until he was halfway back to Glenammura. "Innisfree's got more than his share of rough edges. You'd get hurt."

Her chin thrust out, something about her face haunting him. "I'm a better rider than you think I am, Mr. Halloran. Let me get up on him and show you."

Teenaged pride. It had gotten plenty of bones broken in riding arenas. Michael maneuvered Innisfree into one of the temporary stalls and shut the gate. The horse might hate being locked away from pastures at Glenammura, but he almost looked relieved to have four sturdy walls between him and the confusion of race day.

"You'll find another horse," Michael assured her. "One that fits you better. Try Trevor Butler. He's a great trainer, terrific at finding the right horses for young riders."

"I want this horse." The girl stepped in front of him so fast he nearly ran into her. She flushed almost as if she realized she sounded like a spoiled brat. Her eyes softened, her lips trembled. "Please, Mr. Halloran, I know this might sound crazy, but I just know this is the right horse for me. I knew it the instant I saw him. I've been looking for him all my life. I'm a better rider than you think I am."

"Besides," Mr. Toothpaste said with a wave of his hand. "Once she has the horse, it's not your responsibility anyway. If she thinks she can handle it—"

The man was jumping up and down on Halloran's last nerve. What kind of an idiot was this guy? Hadn't he just told him the horse was dangerous?

"We came to Ireland to win, Mr. Halloran," the idiot insisted. "If my daughter thinks she can win on this horse, I'll do whatever I have to to buy it for her. Name your price. Three times what it's worth—"

"Michael!"

He caught a flash of blond hair, the glint of sunlight on the video camera, Eve's whole face beaming.

"He's not for sale," Michael said. "I don't care if you own the whole goddamn country! Now excuse me—"

He started to shoulder past the man as Eve burst through the crowd, her face angel bright.

"You did it! Michael, you did it!" she cried, flinging herself toward him, but the instant before she flew into his arms, she slammed to a halt, ashen, so still it scared the hell out of him.

The American man's face crumpled as if he'd just found out his Rolex was a fake. The girl—Victoria, wasn't that her name?—gave a stricken cry.

But Michael could only see Eve, so hurt, so broken.

He grabbed her by the arms, barely keeping her on her feet. "Eve—what is it?"

She gave a tiny sob that cut him to the heart. "Michael," she choked out, "this . . . this is my daughter."

20

*H*er daughter.

The congratulatory crowd that had milled around him because of his win blurred, faded away until it seemed as if the four of them were stranded on an island of Eve's pain, her terrible loss. Michael fought for balance, stomach churning at the agony in Eve's face, fury pulsing through him as he looked from the blond teenager to the man who had stolen Eve's daughter away.

Race adrenaline still raged through his veins, pushing every emotion closer to the ragged edge—joy, triumph, blind, dangerous fury. This was the bastard who had hurt Eve so terribly, put the guilt and grief in her eyes, made her stop believing she deserved love, happiness, a home with someone who loved her. This was the man who had used her innocence, her helplessness, her youth as weapons to take what he wanted.

He'd taken everything that mattered. Her child. Her self-worth. Made her hide her heart away so well she'd almost lived and died alone. Alone, when she had so much love to give. So much courage. In that instant, he knew just how Innisfree felt when he kicked down stable walls, or Rory when he went into blind furies. Michael wished to God he had that luxury.

He closed the space between him and Eve, put his arm tight around her waist. He could feel her trembling with the effort it took not to reach out and touch her little girl.

"So you're Victoria," he said, fighting to gentle his voice. "Your mother has told me so much about you."

The girl's eyes widened with something between shock and panic. He got the feeling she would have bolted if not for the horse. That was how much she wanted Innisfree. Enough to face the mother she'd rejected. But the notion that her mother had been talking about her obviously made the girl uncomfortable as hell. "Talking about me?" Victoria said. "She . . . she doesn't know anything about me."

"I think you're wrong, there," Michael said.

"This might be one instance where your mother can do you some good," Chad said, wiping the shock and distaste from his face in a way that made Michael want to slug him. "Eve, it's obvious you know Mr. Halloran, here. We were discussing the sale of this horse of his."

"Innisfree?" Eve said in a small voice.

"I told you, I'm not selling," Michael started, but Chad cut him off, turning up the pressure on Eve.

"Victoria has fallen in love with this horse. Thinks it can make her a champion. If you hold any influence with Mr. Halloran here, maybe you can convince him to sell. That way you'd be able to contribute at least something worthwhile to Victoria's life."

Michael was far too skilled at reading people and animals to miss the slight curl of contempt in Tolliver's smile, or the smugness that came from thinking he could manipulate anyone.

Eve turned pleading, hungry eyes to her daughter, her voice quavering. "Victoria, this horse belongs to someone else who needs it far more than you do. I'd give you anything in my power, but Innisfree isn't mine to give, and even if I could, I wouldn't. Sometimes, it's wrong to take something away from someone else, no matter how much we want it." Eve looked at Tolliver, but he was too slick to let his daughter see any reaction.

"But I need this horse, too!" Victoria argued. "You just don't understand! But then, how could you? You just disappeared from my life."

"Not by choice. Never by choice."

"This horse is everything I've ever wanted. You say you care about me. Then help me. Please."

Michael could only imagine how much Eve wanted to do just that. She fought to steady herself. "Sometimes we don't get things, no matter how badly we want them. Try to understand. Innisfree belongs to a boy who hasn't got anything else."

"Maybe he's the one I should be talking to," Chad interrupted. "I can make him a wealthy young man."

Eve turned to Chad, actual pity in her face. "He wouldn't sell Innisfree for any price. Not if it was his last hope on earth. I know you can't understand that, Chad, but you can't put a price tag on love. And money can never replace it."

"Let me talk to this boy. See if all your lofty philosophical bullshit is true. Let me have a go at this kid and—"

Michael's hand shot out, grabbing Tolliver by the shirtfront, heard Victoria's scream, Eve's cry. He was too hot to give a damn. "Stay away from him, Tolliver. Legally, the horse is mine, and considering the way you've treated Eve and your daughter, I wouldn't sell you a lame plow horse, let alone a beauty as special as Innisfree." He shoved Tolliver away, wiping his hand on his riding breeches as if to scrub away the taint of something rotten.

"My father treats me wonderful!" Victoria cried, defensive. "He's the best father in the world!"

"He took away your mother," Michael snapped. "Sweetheart, you have no idea just how much you lost when he did."

Eve caught his arm, stricken. "Michael, no."

"Someone should damn well tell her!" Michael cried in frustration. "Rory would kill for a mother like you. So would half the kids I work with. Mr. Bank Account here stole all that away from you, Victoria. Maybe it's time you heard the other side of the story."

Tolliver sneered. "The other side of the story is in all the court records. And in the scar on Victoria's head. I don't suppose Eve told you about that, Halloran."

"You bastard! As if Victoria never got hurt when she was with you! Kids get hurt. It happens all the time! Eve was barely surviving, working rotten jobs just to keep a roof over your daughter's head, food in her mouth. You had buckets of money, but you let them both suffer, do without, until she had no choice but—"

"Michael, no!" Eve cried fiercely, yanking on his arm so hard she spun him around. Anger, desperation, pleading raged in her face. "Not in front of Tori! I won't have it!"

"Don't call me that!" Victoria cried. "Daddy!" Shattered, the girl flung herself into Chad Tolliver's arms. Tolliver gathered her close.

"It's all right, sweetheart. It's all right." He smoothed his hand over her hair, so naturally it turned Michael's stomach.

"Tori, please." Eve tried to touch her. Victoria slammed her hand away, the girl obviously shattered by the truths Michael had let fly. Memories—she had to have some memories of her life with Eve. Michael could almost see the reflection of them in Victoria's eyes—images of the shabby apartment that had once been the girl's home, and the inevitable truth that her father must have known she was living there, her mother struggling. Even Tolliver looked nervous as hell.

"Leave me alone!" Victoria cried. "When I was in school I told everybody you were dead! I wish you were so I never had to see you again!"

Eve crumpled back as if Victoria had struck her.

"We're not finished yet, Halloran, in the matter of this horse," Tolliver said, gathering his bravado. Michael knew he was probably already thinking up lies to tell his daughter to cover his back. "Come on, sweetheart. You still have a race to win."

A race? Michael thought, stunned. How the hell could Tolliver put the girl on a horse when she was like this?

"Damn it, Tolliver, she can't race—"

"Of course she can. And she *will*. She's not like her mother. She's a winner." Chad turned, leading the sobbing girl away.

Eve's whole body was shaking. Michael swore. He had to get her out of here. Innisfree was all right for now. He swooped Eve up into his arms, shielding her from the gaping crowd. She buried her face in the front of his riding silks as he carried her away, back to the trailer, away from prying strangers' eyes that had seen far too much of her private pain.

She was so quiet, so still she scared the hell out of him. He took her to the trailer, the only place he could think of. He was about to set her down in the grass when he saw a long shadow move. He hoped whoever it was would just get the hell away from them.

"Hush, now, hush, angel of my heart," Michael soothed, easing her down, still holding her in his arms.

Suddenly the sobs came. Horrible, body-shaking spasms that seemed like they were tearing her in two.

"My baby—" she choked out. "Oh, Michael, my baby. She . . . she hates me. Did you see the look on her face?"

What the hell could he say? Victoria was terrified, hurting, angry. Scared to face the things Michael had said that had shaken her perfect world. And Tolliver had taken full advantage of all the girl's emotions.

"She'll grow up someday, Eve. Maybe then—"

"Maybe what? He'll never give me a chance to explain to her—and she—Oh, God, Michael, there's not anything on earth that would make her willing to even talk to me."

"Nothing except Innisfree," Michael said bitterly.

"No! I'd never—that horse belongs to Rory—in his

heart. The way money can never buy. The way Victoria should . . . should have belonged to me."

"Ah, God, Eve." Michael's own eyes burned. He kissed her forehead, her cheeks, wishing to hell he could take her pain. "She's the one who loses. If she knew you like I do—"

Damn Tolliver! It was so unfair! To spark that kind of obsession in Victoria's heart for a horse, give Eve a chance, a tool to gain entry into her daughter's life, but only if she were willing to break the heart of a boy who had nothing but the love of that horse.

He cradled her until she'd cried herself out, then tucked her into the truck cab. "I have to go get Innisfree," he said, kissing her tenderly. "Will you be all right alone?"

She curled tight into herself. "I want to go home," she said brokenly.

Raw as he was, Michael smiled. She was talking about Kilrain. Maybe he couldn't give her her daughter back. But maybe Tolliver hadn't taken everything away from her after all. Maybe Michael could still give her a home.

Rory stalked through the crowd, his jaw set, hard. It wasn't fair, someone like Eve crying like that. And over what? That spoiled brat of a girl who thought she could buy Innisfree with her daddy's money.

How could that pain in the arse be Eve's daughter? And she didn't even want to talk to Eve?

Rory's insides curled tight, hard and hurting as he thought of the past two weeks. Eve, daring to come up to his room when he was mad enough to spit, the way she'd listened to him, her eyes all soft, like what he said really mattered. She'd never once acted impatient, like she had better things to do and he was in the way. She'd even offered to let him teach her to ride Innisfree when he knew damned well she was scared to death of all horses, any horses, and she'd seen Innisfree at his bone-crushing worst.

That rich girl was an idiot. She didn't deserve to have a mother like Eve! Eve should be glad she was getting rid of the ungrateful little brat! Rory thought bitterly. Eve had Michael. Anybody would have to be blind not to see that Halloran was crazy about her. *And she has me*, a voice inside Rory cried.

She has you? he scoffed. *It's her daughter she really wants. You saw the way she cried, the way she hurts every time she talks about . . . what was her name? Victoria? Her precious Victoria.*

Rory kicked a can that lay on the ground, lashing out at the only thing he could reach. He felt so damned helpless. Eve had given him a place to stay when no one else would have. She'd talked to him. Laughed with him. He could still remember how she'd touched him even when he'd been so angry, and it hurt so bad he had to fight just to keep breathing. No one had ever touched him like that. Gentle. Like they were hurting, too, just because his life sucked.

Innisfree had kicked arse, and he couldn't even tell anyone he'd seen it happen. Eve was balling her eyes out, sadder than he'd ever seen her. And Michael felt like hell.

That witch of a girl had wrecked things up real good. And he couldn't do a damned thing to change it. Just like he'd never been able to change things in Dublin with his parents or bastards like Dennis Moran.

Rory caught a glimpse of a flyer posted on one of the trees. His own face stared out at him. Or was it? He didn't even know who that boy was anymore with all that anger inside him. Because even when he'd been acting like an idiot, pulling knives, making threats, yelling his head off, Eve had seen someone else deep inside him. The person Innisfree saw when the horse looked at him so trusting, like he wasn't a loser. Like he could move mountains. Like something wonderful was inside him just waiting to come out.

Rory ripped down the flyer, crumpled it into a ball. Maybe it was time to see just what that "something" was. If it was real, or if Eve and Innisfree were wrong about him after all.

What was it Michael had said? The girl wanted Innisfree. That was the only thing that would make her talk to Eve? Maybe it was time to teach the little rich girl a thing or two. Money couldn't buy everything. True. But maybe he and Victoria could work out something different. He'd see just how great a rider she was matched against a nobody like him.

It wasn't hard to track her down. Riders in her division were doing their pre-race stuff, getting ready to run in an hour. The course was quiet, everyone at the arena where dressage was taking place.

Little Miss Rich Girl wasn't even paying attention to the horse she was supposed to ride. She was sitting on a hay bale, sulking, no doubt. Yeah, life was just so tough, Rory thought in disgust.

She looked up. Looked like she'd been crying. Good. Eve sure was, thanks to her. "Go away. Just leave me alone."

"You're a real piece of work, you know that? Fine, if you want to sit and cry I'm sure your daddy will be happy to let you. He's been picking up your messes your whole life, I bet. Probably running after you with a pillow to stick under your arse every time you fall down."

"Shut up! You don't know anything about me!"

"I know you're a spoiled brat. And you're stupid."

Victoria paled, gave a choked sob. "Leave me alone!"

"Wish I could just let you rot here. But I've come to give you your all-American dream, princess. A chance to grab the brass ring. Get what you want. God knows you're used to it."

"What are you talking about?"

"Innisfree."

"You . . . You want to sell Innisfree?"

He wanted to slap her. She swiped away the tears, her eyes hot and sparkling.

"Halloran must have told you how much we would pay. Daddy said—"

"I told you, Innisfree isn't for sale. Not for all the money in Ireland."

"Then why are you bothering me?"

"I'm offering you a bet. A race. You and me, princess. I ride Innisfree. You can ride the Queen Mother for all I care."

"What would we be racing for?"

"If I lose, you get Innisfree."

"Halloran said the horse was his. You can't bet something you don't own."

Unfortunately that was true. Rory would just have to work things out with Michael then. "If Halloran agrees, will you ride?"

Victoria swallowed hard. "Oh, yeah. I'll ride," she said, smiling like she'd already won. "And what if you win?" she asked him, making him feel small, insignificant. Furious. "How much money do you want?"

"Take your bloody money and shove it! I don't want your money!"

"Then what do you want?" she cried in frustration.

"An hour of your time! You race, you agree to give me an hour that you promise to do anything I tell you. Anything."

Victoria's cheeks got all red. "If you think I'd let someone like you touch me—"

"Aw, for God's sake!" Rory swore in utter disgust. "Honey, I wouldn't dirty my hands on a spoiled rotten article like you! Turns my stomach just to think of it!"

"Then . . . then why—"

"That's for me to know! You're so sure you'll win, you won't have to worry about it anyway, will you? Now, will you ride?"

"If Halloran agrees to it, I'd love to give you a lesson on how to win."

"Then come on. I know someplace he'll turn up sooner or later."

She stood up, brushing the hay off her silks. Rory smiled, glad he'd put his own silks on underneath the baggy clothes. Stupid as it seemed, he'd wanted to feel the silk against his skin, imagine what it would be like to wear them racing.

He just hadn't figured he'd have a chance to find out. He strode toward the stall where he saw Michael put Innisfree. Victoria followed right behind.

"Wait around back," Rory said. "I want to talk to Michael alone when he comes."

She nodded, took off. She'd probably spend the time picking out tack to match her colors. Innisfree would puke if he had to wear some stupid-looking pink stable blanket.

Rory slipped into the stall. Innisfree raised his head, recognition and relief flared in the big horse's eyes. "Come here, you beautiful bastard," Rory crooned, holding out his hand. The big horse trotted over like a puppy, leaned his head against Rory's chest. "You've got one more race to win before we go back home."

They settled in, quiet together, like they'd been all those times at the farm. Not doing anything, not saying anything. Just being together. Glad to see each other when no one else wanted to see either one of them. But that had all changed in the past few weeks. Every time Eve saw him, Rory could see the welcome in her eyes. Victoria could have had that all the time, but she didn't want it. Rory wanted it more than he could say.

It didn't take long for Michael to come. He opened the stall door, head down, eyes troubled, not paying attention. Good way to get your head kicked in, Rory thought. But then, he looked like Rory felt. Mad as hell. Helpless. Well, Michael was about to get a lot madder, Rory thought ruefully, once he realized he'd had a stowaway when he'd left Kilrain.

"Hey, Michael." Rory tried to sound cool. Michael's head snapped up. Shock, then fear, raced across his features. He shut the stall door with a bang that made Innisfree snort and skitter backward.

"Rory, for God's sake, boy, what are you doing here?" Michael hissed in a hushed voice. "Damn, when you disappeared at Kilrain I should have guessed—"

Rory shrugged. "Had to make sure you didn't screw up with my horse, boss. You didn't." He couldn't keep the pride out of his voice. "Innisfree ran like hell."

Michael gave him a weary smile. Was it possible that, even scared, Michael was glad to see him? "You did it, boy. You. I wish to hell you had been the one racing him."

"Yeah, well. I've been thinking I might like to try it after all, if . . . if you—" If you'd be willing to risk a horse worth a fortune. Suddenly, the whole scheme sounded ridiculous. Rory had never run a race before. He'd practiced in pastures, only him and Innisfree. No one to run against except opponents in his imagination. Michael would have to be crazy to let him do this.

But Michael loved Eve. Maybe he'd understand.

"No races for you, boy," Michael insisted. "Not until things simmer down with Moran."

"No one's at the cross-country run now. No one would have to see—"

"You're serious, aren't you?" Michael asked, astonished. "Listen, kid. I wish you could take a practice run, just to see what it feels like. But Eve—well, she's had a . . . a tough day—"

"I want to make it a better one." He grabbed Michael by the arm, desperate to make him listen. So used to people *not* listening when he had something important to say, he just had to hold on to make sure. "Michael, I don't want to practice. I want to race. Against Eve's daughter."

Michael's eyes almost popped out of his head. "Eve's daughter? How the hell did you find out about that?"

"I met her while you were riding. I didn't know who she was, but, then, well, I didn't mean to be listening to you and Eve or anything, but I had to hang around the trailer. I didn't want you to leave before I could sneak in and hide myself again. I . . . I heard her crying."

Michael winced, and Rory knew neither of them would ever forget those terrible sobs. Either of them would have given anything to be able to make her smile again. Now they had a chance to do just that if Michael would only listen.

Halloran drove his fingers back through his hair. "Man, what a mess."

"I heard her talk about how she just wanted a chance to talk to Victoria. Trust me, that brat is too spoiled ever to give her the chance."

"Victoria is just too stuffed with her father's bullshit."

"Whatever. I just thought—Eve deserves a chance even if her daughter is a pain, you know? I wanted to give it to her, so I thought—Victoria wants Innisfree."

Michael blanched. "Boy, you can't give her your horse!"

"No way! She'd put him in pink and Innisfree would kick her head off. No, I just made a little bet with her on the side. She wins, she gets Innisfree. I win, she has to give me an hour. Then she'll have to talk to Eve."

"Rory, God, lad, I—"

Were Halloran's eyes shimmering? Hell, he'd almost think the man was ready to cry. Rory squirmed. "It's no big deal—you know I'll win."

"I know how much that horse means to you. That you'd risk Innisfree for Eve's sake—" Michael's voice broke. "You're something special, Rory. I always knew it."

"Then let me do this. I'll win. You know I will. If that horse can win for you, Innisfree will run his heart out for me."

Michael looked like hell, torn inside out, trying to decide. "Rory, Eve wouldn't want you to do this. You know she wouldn't. It's a big risk."

"So what are we gonna do? Just sit on our hands and let Eve be miserable? The girl said she wouldn't do it without your okay. You have to agree. Innisfree doesn't belong to me."

"He's never been my horse. You know that as well as I do."

"If you mean that, let me do this, Michael. I won't let you down."

Michael stared into Rory's earnest face, the boy straining toward him, so sure of himself, so desperate to try. Willing to risk his horse for Eve. God, this was impossible! Michael couldn't let him do it! And yet, hadn't he prayed Rory would be able to transfer his love from horses to people someday? That he cared so much for Eve was a miracle. And now, Eve needed a miracle of her own.

During those magic days at Kilrain, he'd watched Rory ride, thought no one would ever be able to beat the boy when he was up on that horse of his. It was Rory's risk to take. Rory's chance. How could Michael take that away from him?

"All right, boy," Michael said, shaking Rory's hand. No way God would take that horse away from the boy or this chance to heal away from Eve.

Innisfree didn't know how to lose.

How could he when he had a boy like Rory to love him?

"So, where is Victoria?"

"Waiting out there. I don't even want to think about what she's cooking up to do to my horse in that girly little mind of hers."

Michael looped his arm around Rory's shoulders, guided him out of the stall. He would have liked to have had a chance to talk to the girl again. Unfortunately, her father was standing right next to her.

"So, my little girl here says the two of you made some kind of bet? Maybe your boy isn't as impervious to money as you thought, eh, Halloran?"

"The terms of the bet is between the kids," Michael ground out.

"Well, I'm going to make damned sure Victoria doesn't get taken. So what are the stakes? The horse against what?"

"An hour of her time," Rory said. "No touchy feely, nothing illegal. Just talking."

Tolliver smirked as if he understood—Rory was so desperate to put the moves on the guy's daughter he was willing to risk the horse.

But then, how could a man like Tolliver understand the depth in this boy, the selflessness? Tolliver rarely looked past his own reflection in the mirror.

"In a public place? I want my daughter safe."

"Anywhere you want, just as long as you're nowhere around."

Tolliver digested this, glared back at Michael. "What guarantee does Victoria have this kid won't try to pull a fast one? Pull up lame or something if he's losing?"

"Listen, mister," Rory said, showing a hell of a lot more restraint than Michael could have managed. "Unless I cross the finish line first, I lose. Got it? I don't care if the ground splits open and the Tuatha de Danaan start dancing on your arse."

Michael felt a tingle of unease.

Tolliver laughed. "Are you willing to put your money where your mouth is, kid? Sign a contract?"

"I'd bet my life on it."

But it wasn't Rory's life he was betting, Michael knew. It was his heart.

"We don't need a damned contract!" Michael spat in disgust.

"No contract, no race."

"But Daddy!" Victoria started to protest.

"Tomorrow is soon enough to beat him," her father said.

Michael would have liked to beat him. Senseless. But if they met at the grounds early enough, there would be less chance someone might see Rory, recognize him. Even so, it cost Michael to even give Tolliver that much. "All right, Tolliver. Have it your way."

Tolliver chuckled. "Your boy here is pretty confident, Halloran. I'd hate to see him once he loses."

"Not going to happen, Tolliver," Michael said. *Please God, don't let it happen.*

Victoria glared at Rory. Michael knew she was looking forward to stomping the kid into the ground.

"See you at the starting line at six in the morning, Halloran," Tolliver said. "And be sure to bring the horse's papers. You're going to need to sign them over to me when this is done."

Michael fumed as the man strode away.

"Dammit, Rory, now what am I supposed to do? Eve wants to go home!"

"Tell her Innisfree picked up a rock in his hoof, can't be bouncing around in the trailer. Tell her anything you want. Geez, Halloran, do I have to think of everything for you?"

"I'm going to have some fancy explaining to do anyway when she sees you. But hell, we have all night."

"No way, man! I'm not going to spend the night before this race watching the two of you making eyes at each other. I saw enough of that at the castle. No, I'll be perfect right here with Innisfree."

"I can't just leave you—"

"Really, Michael. I'm staying here. There's something about that guy I don't trust. He's the kind that would stick a rock in Innisfree's hoof on purpose, just to make sure his daughter won."

Michael grimaced. He couldn't argue that. "I'll lock you both up in here. That should keep you out of trouble. Come morning—"

"You can't let Eve know about this, Michael. She'll skin us both."

That was nothing compared to what she'd do if Rory lost, a voice inside Michael warned.

But Rory wasn't going to lose. The kid was magic. Sometimes you just had to throw your heart over the fence, no matter what stood in your way.

21

*E*ve hadn't argued when he'd unhitched the truck from the trailer and taken her to the nearby bed and breakfast he'd booked a few days before, his head filled with a hundred dreams of Eve in his arms, in his bed. But any thought of making love would have to be postponed for now. She was limp and exhausted and so sad it tore Michael's heart.

The charming room Michael had chosen for their first night alone could have been a cardboard box for all she noticed. She'd dragged herself to the room Mrs. Cadagon had given them and tried to pull herself together enough to try to get through on the phone to Rory.

Michael had felt a jab of panic. All right, so the chances she could get through were small. But he understood the capriciousness of Bridey's beloved castle well enough not to trust it. It would be just like Kilrain to let Eve's call go through now, since it would get Michael into trouble. Bridey had always said his lordship found it insulting when someone refused to believe in him, and weirdly enough, Michael had always felt he was locked in some sort of surrealistic battle with someone who didn't exist.

So he'd told another lie—stopped her the only way he could think of. Told her *he'd* call the boy. Anyone who cared about her could tell she'd been crying. And they wouldn't want Rory to worry—

He would have felt better if she'd argued with him.

But she'd just gone to the window looking out over the Cadagon sheep pasture, her voice breaking as she said she wouldn't ruin Rory's joy in Innisfree's win for anything. He deserved to be happy.

Michael had left, asked Mrs. Cadagon for use of the phone, and dialed the castle. Damned if that old bastard of a ghost didn't let the phone ring, just as Michael had dreaded. He muttered into the phone just what he thought of six-hundred-year-old dead men who were juvenile enough to still play practical jokes. He lingered as long as he could, hoping to give Eve enough time to do what she needed to get settled—maybe take a hot shower in peace.

After all the hopes they'd both had for tonight, cleaning up in the same room might be painful, awkward, and the last thing Michael wanted was to make things worse for Eve.

Needing a shower badly himself, he'd asked Mrs. Cadagon if he could take a quick one in the shared bath in the hall. Wash the worst of the race-day grime away. The B&B keeper was more than generous, supplying him with towels and soap. After showering and stopping by the kitchen to thank Mrs. Cadagon, he made his way up the wooden stairs.

Hell, how was he going to get through a whole night chafing under lies? Dreading tomorrow, yet anticipating the fierce pleasure it would give him to see Rory wipe that smirk off of Tolliver's face? But it would all be worth it in the end. Tomorrow Eve would have what she'd wanted so desperately. Time to talk to her daughter, to try to make Victoria understand. To tell her child how much she loved her. And Rory, who had never dared to give a damn about anyone else, Rory, the street kid people had believed was nothing but trouble, Rory would be the one to give that chance to Eve.

Bridey was always talking about the power of fate while Michael had preferred to think people made their own destinies through choices they made freely.

But it was harder to refute Bridey's arguments now, considering the strange course that had brought Eve to his valley, into his life and Rory's, the force that had landed her daughter at the horse show where the girl fell in love with Innisfree. Didn't it seem as if some power—be it God or fate or the Irish fairy magic Michael had grown up hearing tales of—was at work here? To heal wounds so deep they once seemed impossible to reach?

You fight life too hard, Michael-my-heart, he could hear Bridey saying. *'Tisn't about slamming your fists into fate, struggling against the current. You have to stop, listen, be still enough to hear God whispering. . . .*

Seemed this time God was shouting at the top of his lungs. Michael prayed he was right with all his heart.

He hesitated outside the bedroom door. He'd imagined this night so differently. A stolen moment, just for the two of them. He and Eve, together. He'd barely managed to sleep the past few nights imagining her eyes as he stripped her clothes away until nothing was between them except the dreams they'd just started to dare. He'd wanted tonight to be perfect. A beginning neither of them had ever expected to find. But there would be other nights. He'd give his sweet, lost fairy forever if she would let him.

Michael knocked softly to warn her, and waited for her soft voice telling him it was okay to come in. The night was going to be long enough without the added misery of stumbling in on her half-dressed, that mist-soft skin bare, glimpses of pink-tipped breasts or long, silky legs, or the sweet golden curls tucked shyly between them would be more than Michael could bear. After all, Bridey was right. He was sure no angel. And he wanted Eve more than he'd ever wanted anything—to ride, to win. Even more than Glenammura.

He heard a muffled voice, shoved open the door, his gaze lighting on the lone double bed in the room. He groaned inwardly. It was going to be a long night.

Eve sat with a bundle of what looked like letters, a blue ribbon discarded, trailing across the pillow. She looked so young, her feet bare, dainty and pale, her hair still tousled from the wind, a cloud of gold framing her heart-shaped face. She'd been crying. The ink was splotched with tears. Any loss he'd felt about the night to come vanished, squeezed out by a wave of compassion.

"What did Rory say about Innisfree's win? He must have been so happy."

Michael's cheeks warmed. "The, uh, phone wasn't working right. His lordship must not like horse racing."

"I wish I could see Rory right now. Tell him how proud I am of him."

If you only knew— Michael thought, heart squeezing. *But tomorrow, please God, you will.*

He crossed to the bed, picked up a few of the scattered pages so he could sit close to her. He glanced down, saw the opening line of the top one. *My dearest angel girl*— Grief knotted hard in Michael's throat. Oh God. Letters. Letters to her daughter.

She looked down at the sheet of paper in her hand, teary-eyed. "You know, it was probably silly to bring these. But I just couldn't leave them behind. I just—it's like keeping a piece of Tori with me, being able to hold her, talk to her. I wanted to write to her about how I felt, seeing a race for the first time, the horse world she loves. I wanted to share that with her."

"Ah, Eve," he murmured.

"I might as well throw these in the fire," she said brokenly. "Victoria will never read them."

"You don't know that, love." Michael gathered up the other pages. Pages and pages and pages as if Eve had tried to capture a lifetime of love with her pen.

"Maybe—"

Maybe by tomorrow you'll get the miracle you've always deserved. Maybe tomorrow you'll have a chance to put these letters into your daughter's hands. Maybe she'll be angry and first, hurt. God knows, she won't like losing. But in the end,

Eve, my precious, precious Eve, your little girl will win. She'll get to know the bravest, most loving woman I've ever known.

But he couldn't say that. Didn't dare. He took the last of the pages Eve held, then set them aside with their ribbon. He cupped Eve's cheek in his hand, hating the dampness on her cheeks, the salty tracks of tears. He feathered his thumb over the fragile skin beneath her eye. "You have to keep believing, Eve. I know it's hard. It's a miracle you've managed to do it this long. You've been so alone. But now . . . now I'm here to help you."

Tears welled up against her dark, curled lashes. She crushed her lips tight together against a sob and shook her head. "I've lost her. Maybe forever."

"Nothing can ever take Victoria's place in your heart. I know that. I don't know for sure if . . . if you've lost her. But no matter what happens, there is so much you've *found.*"

He gathered her into his arms, sliding her onto his lap so he could cradle her against his heart. "Rory loves you, Eve, more than you know. You've changed his life. I wish I could tell you . . . but you have to believe in that."

She tried to smile, nodded just a little.

"Rory loves you. And, Eve, I love you." He kissed her cheek, stroked her hair. "I love you." It sounded so good. So right. He wanted to spend the rest of his life telling this incredible woman just how much.

She tilted her head back, and he fell into the green of her eyes. "Oh, Michael, I wanted tonight to be so different. I know we planned—"

"Hush, now. We'll have other nights. I just don't want you to hurt like this. If I could take the pain away from you, I would."

She smiled, a smile that broke his heart. "But that would mean I never had Victoria in my life. Any pain now is worth that joy."

Michael wanted to rage at God, at Tolliver, at the world, at everyone who had taken Eve's child away from her. Eve with her full heart and her empty,

empty arms. But God willing, he would fill her arms again with babies they'd make together out of this new, unexpected love. If Eve had the courage to risk it, a voice whispered inside him. Motherhood had left her vulnerable, heartbroken, rejected. Hell, if he were Eve he didn't know if he'd have the courage to try it again, no matter how much he loved or trusted his partner. Maybe she would want to just close that painful place out of her life and move on.

Michael felt a wave of disappointment. He'd never realized how he missed having babies of his own until he'd seen their reflections shining out at him from Eve Danaher's eyes. But if Eve would have him as her husband, if she'd risk that much, he'd grab it and be grateful. It was a love he'd never dreamed of. A life with this woman would be enough.

Michael wished to hell he could think of something to do for her. To sooth away the scrapes and burns this day had left on her spirit. He closed his eyes, remembering something his mother had done when he was a lad, constantly neck-deep in trouble and all too often in regret because of the consequences of his mischief.

"You know, when I was a little boy, during the worst times when I'd been called up by the brothers for fighting at school or shocked the whole parish by painting the white spots on Widow O'Flaherty's prize cow, when it seemed like nothing would ever be right again and the whole world despaired of Michael Halloran turning out to be anything but a thief or a brawler, my mother would knock on the door to my room.

"'Michael, Michael,' she'd cluck, shaking her head. 'And to think I was after naming you for an angel. What do you think we should do?'

"I knew my da was downstairs in his big leather chair trying to think of some punishment to make me think next time before I leaped into something over my head. I'm sure he was afraid I'd kill myself some-how. I know, if I ever had a son who did the things I tried, I'd be scared out of my wits. Anyway, Mother's way was gentler. She'd just ruffle my hair with her fingers and say 'And what do you think we should do? Shall we wash this day away?'

"She'd strip away my torn, dirty clothes, hiding them away in a corner where she'd gather them later for washing and mending, then she'd take me to the tub. I'd soak, the hot water easing cuts and bruises from my latest scrape, my mam's soapy washcloth seeming like magic. Because as she scrubbed me from head to toe, it seemed she really *had* washed all the bad and angry right out of me. And when that dirty water swirled down the drain, I always felt like I was clean and new and ready to start again."

"My mother was too busy to care much what I was doing," Eve said. "What with working two jobs, I barely saw her, and when I did she was so tired and stressed, I'd hide up in my room with a book. There was always someone to talk to whenever I wanted as long as I had a book in my hand. I didn't feel so lonely."

So then she had never had anyone to take care of her, watch over her, fuss the way Bridey always had, or even just smile at her the way his parents had, with such adoration he'd known he could never live up to the boy he saw in their eyes.

"My mother died while I was carrying Victoria. The worst thing about it was that when I told her I was pregnant she wasn't surprised. Just tired. Resigned. That's what happened to girls like me. No happy ever after. No great escape. Just drudgery and scrabbling for minimum wage. And if you were lucky, a man to fill your refrigerator with beer and actually bring home his paycheck instead of wasting it on his bookie. My mother always thought I wanted too much, reached too high. I used to think she didn't love me. Maybe she did, so much she was scared I would get hurt. Maybe that was why she shut down around me. Having a daughter was too painful, watching history repeating itself. I wanted things to be different with my baby. Wanted to take care of her, let her know I believed in her. God, Michael, I wish I could wash away this day for Victoria tonight. She must be so . . . so unhappy."

"Upset, maybe. But I imagine her father's ready to rush in with the Band-Aids. I was thinking more about you, Eve. I bet no one ever did that for you in your whole life."

"Did what?"

"Made you feel better. Took care of you. Listened. When I was a lad, I thought it was the soap and the washcloth that were magic, took away the pain. Now I know it was my mother, the way she let me pour out everything that happened, how angry I was at myself for screwing up again, disappointing her and Da. She'd say 'Michael, you could never disappoint us! You were a dream your da and I had never even dared to have. You'll do better next time, won't you? Try again? But even if you fall, paint every cow in the west of Ireland purple, you'll always be our own sweet Michael. Nothing you could do will ever change that.'"

Eve swallowed hard. "She was right. I've never known anyone as special as you are. As strong and kind and good."

"Eve, no, I—"

"And you always do try again when something goes wrong, and you make things better."

"I know I can't heal everything that happened to you today, Eve. I won't even try. But maybe I can wash some of the pain away. Will you let me try?" He ghosted his knuckles across her cheek.

"I'm so . . . so tired, Michael."

"I know. Let me take care of you tonight."

She nodded, and he could feel the complete trust, the utter surrender in her as she melted in his arms. He kissed her, carried her to the bathroom. A small chair was tucked in the corner. He eased her down on it. Reaching over, he turned on the taps, the water spilling into the porcelain claw-footed tub, steaming warm. He tested the temperature with his hand. Satisfied, he turned back to Eve.

"Do you have anything special to use? Soaps? Shampoos?"

"The blue makeup bag in my suitcase."

He went back into the bedroom, opened the case's lid. The contents smelled of lilacs and lilies, Eve's own special scent. Her clothes shifted under his fingers, soft from wear against her skin. Michael's heart squeezed as he found that exquisite old-fashioned nightgown she'd almost given him a heart attack in the first night Rory had stayed at the castle. No comfortable old tee shirt. Eve had packed that gown with dreams of her own, and maybe the memory of the heat it had ignited in his eyes.

We will have other nights . . . he reminded himself again. But this night was Eve's alone. He'd do everything in his power to help her feel loved, cared for, listened to. He'd wash away the pain and hurt and hold her, teach her what it felt like not to be alone.

He caught a glimpse of royal blue bag tucked in a corner of the suitcase. Retrieving it, he unzipped the pouch, saw a clutter of feminine things. The makeup he'd never realized she wore, a bottle of perfume, bubble bath and a tube of shower gel in the same scent. Lilies and lilacs. The scent that would always mean Eve to him.

Gathering up the gel and bubble bath, Michael returned to Eve. She sat on the chair, still as a broken doll, so uncertain his chest ached. She didn't know what to do, this woman who had taken such risks, traveled to a foreign country, tamed the beasts in Castle Kilrain, and faced her own demons with such courage. You didn't have to beat your dragons to be a hero, Michael realized, looking down at her. You just had to be willing to look them in the eye the way she had.

Michael tipped some of the bubble bath under the stream of water, saw creamy white drifts of bubbles foam up, releasing their steamy, flower-drenched scent.

Taking Eve's hand, he drew her to her feet. Her eyes were so wide as she peered into his, so fragile. He knew it would take every scrap of willpower he had not to turn this into foreplay. But this wasn't about what he wanted, what his body needed. This was about soothing and healing and trust.

It was hard to keep his smile steady as he unbuttoned her blue chambray blouse, the tiny crocheted lace edge on the collar tickling his fingers. One by one he moved down past the hollow of her throat to just above her breasts, past the tiny pink rosebud applique on her bra to the dainty arch where her ribs flared to her sides.

Her skin was softer than the lilies she smelled of, the warmth of her stomach as he uncovered its slight swell pushing him closer to the edge than he'd ever been before. Fighting to keep a tight rein on himself, he eased the blouse from her drooping shoulders. He wanted to bury his face in that dusky valley between her breasts, breathe her in, take his first taste of her sweetness. To keep himself from doing so, he fought to detach, folding her blouse as neatly as if the brothers were going to come and inspect the creases.

Putting the blouse on the chair, he turned her around, fingers that had always been deft and supple with the reins feeling clumsy, awkward, as he unhooked her bra. The white scrap of cotton and lace slid down her upper arms, held on only by the white satin ribbon of the straps. His eyes swept in an aching path down the delicate chain of her spine, the hollow of her back, dipping down into the waistband of her coffee-colored slacks. He kneaded the stiff muscles of her neck ever so gently. Then, clenching his jaw, turned her to face him.

Michael's groin tightened like a fist as he saw the pale globes of her breasts, tipped by pink nipples. Tiny white stretch marks trailed along her skin, left there from a time when she'd carried another man's baby.

Had Chad Tolliver ever loved her at all? Michael

wondered. Or had the bastard made her feel as if somehow his loss of interest was her fault? That she hadn't been pretty enough or exciting enough to hold his attention for long?

She'd never doubt just how beautiful Michael Halloran thought she was, he vowed. He'd make damned sure she knew he'd never even dared to dream of a woman so fine and precious. So rare.

"M—Michael. The water—" Eve warned in a hoarse voice. Michael turned, dove for the taps, turning them off. He drained out enough of the water so the tub wouldn't overflow. He doubted Mrs. Cadagon would have appreciated a lake down below in her kitchen, and if Eve hadn't warned him, he might have let the water pour out forever.

He owed Eve better than this. Determined, Michael turned back to Eve, unfastening the waistband of her slacks, sliding them, and a wisp of blue lace panty, down her legs, to pool on the floor.

Light from above painted her skin with cream and roses, her hair shimmering halo-gold. Michael tried to remember to breathe. He gathered her up, naked against the thin fabric of his silks, her skin glowing, luminous against the rich burgundy and midnight blue.

He wanted to hold her that way forever, keep her safe. But ever so gently, he lowered her down into the water. Slowly she sank into the tub, like a shattered goddess, or the runaway fairy he'd imagined her a lifetime ago. Steam rose, water lapped against the skin he was half mad to caress. Her curved little bottom drifted down onto the porcelain bottom of the tub, the downy triangle of curls marking her femininity sinking beneath the surface of rich foam, disappearing from sight. He barely noticed his elbow dip beneath the water's surface until Eve tugged his arm and it came up, dripping.

"I'm getting you all wet," she said. "You'll ruin your silks."

"I don't need them anymore." Her breasts floated in the water, clusters of bubbles clinging to her skin, her nipples an even sweeter shade of pink contrasted against them. Groaning inwardly, Michael dragged his gaze away from them and back up to Eve's face.

"I don't want you to ruin them," she said, a worried crease in her pale brow. "For the rest of my life, whenever I see them I'll remember what you did for Rory today. How you looked when you won. Take your shirt off. It's all right."

Did the woman have any idea how hard she was pushing him? He wished to hell he had a suit of Bridey's damned armor between his body and Eve's, but he doubted even that would keep every nerve in his body from sizzling in response to her. But how could Eve know what he was feeling? How much he wanted her? She was lost in her own pain, grieving for her daughter. She was far too wounded to be imagining how it would feel to slip naked between sheets and find him there, waiting.

"Eve—" He struggled to find the words to explain. "I don't think I can—"

For the first time, she moved without him guiding her, she leaned over the edge of the tub, her nipples dampening the cloth at his belly, and with wet, trembling fingers, unbuttoned his shirt. Three buttons down. Michael knew if she touched just one more, he'd explode. He stood up, turned his back to her, unbuttoning the last of them himself. Stripping off the shirt, he threw it onto the chair. Grabbing the washcloth and his self-control, he returned to the tub, knelt down beside it. White foam piled in soft drifts against her body. Dipping the cloth in the hot water, scooping up bubbles, he concentrated on smoothing them over her skin.

He held up each arm, washing his way down to her fingertips. More warm water, more bubbles. He smoothed them over the stiff muscles in her shoulders. Eve sighed, leaned her head back. Her eyes drifted closed, dark lashes fanned the fragile hollows beneath her eyes as he bathed the slender column of her throat. Water pooled in the hollow shaped by her collarbone, then trickled in rivulets down the slope of her right breast.

He bathed her as if she was the most fragile treasure at Kilrain, knowing that with each tender sweep of the cloth against her skin he was unveiling something precious. A oneness of spirit he hadn't realized he'd craved his whole life. From the time he'd been a wild boy, trying to get attention, loved by his parents but not quite understood. A need he'd tried to fill with the green hills of Glenammura, the heart-stopping flight of horses beneath him, and the children he'd poured his heart into. Something pure. Something he'd stopped believing in after he'd lost his innocence at the foot of the jump that had ended his career.

Something worth waiting for.

His fingers closed around her ankle, and he eased the washcloth in soothing sweeps from toes to thigh.

"Oh, Michael," she breathed as he started on her other leg. "That feels so good. Nobody ever—"

Ever what? Cared enough to comfort her? What kind of a life had she lived before she came to Ireland? She had to have friends, a job. Hell, she might adore New York and never want to leave it, not even for him.

He was in love with a woman he knew almost nothing about. For all he knew, she might have some art restorer boyfriend back home polishing up his— No. She'd been wide-eyed as someone much younger, uncertain in a way that made him sure once Chad Tolliver had burned her, the lady had stayed away from fire. Until now.

"Sit up and lean forward. I want to wash your hair." He started the water running again, used his hands to drizzle water over her hair. Working suds through those sunshine-bright curls. He'd made headlines as a ladies' man during his racing days, been notorious. Hell, he hadn't even guessed some of the things had existed they claimed he'd done during his supposed exploits. But never in his life had Michael Halloran done anything as sensual as washing Eve's hair.

When it was clean, he hooked a finger under her chin, tilted her head back and rinsed her curls. They clung to her throat the way he wished his lips could.

Taking up the washcloth again, he bathed her face, her cheeks, her forehead, her chin. She gleamed with droplets of water, so beautiful, and, thank God, much of the tension that had strained at her muscles had softened under his hands.

He almost dared to hope she'd be able to sleep tonight. "Come on, Sleeping Beauty. Time to get you into bed."

"Bed," she echoed.

Michael helped her stand, tried to ignore the picture she made. The light flashing on drops of water, turning her body sleek and so touchable he knew just how his hands would slide over her skin.

He gathered up a towel from the warming rack and bundled her up in the soft folds, drying her off. Too soon, he slipped her white cotton nightgown over her damp hair, letting the ruffle fall to brush her instep. Bare toes peeked out from under the cotton hem.

Michael kissed her cheek, struggling hard to keep his hands to himself. "Go to bed now, love. Think I'll take a walk." Maybe dive into the stream they'd crossed down the road a bit—hopefully the icy spring water could cool him off.

"No!" Eve cried, the panic in her eyes cutting him deep. "Michael, please don't leave me alone."

Did she have any idea what she was asking?

He forced a smile, then gathered her up again, carrying her to the bed that should have cradled their dreams, their first night. Bracing her against his chest with one arm, he threw back the covers with the other. Ever so carefully, he lowered her down, drew the blankets up over her.

"Hold me?" Such a tentative plea. Michael tugged

off his boots, climbed in. She burrowed against his body like a small sea bird seeking shelter from a storm. Warm, soft, he could feel her against him, her heartbeat throbbing against his naked chest.

Eve. His brave, sweet Eve. She'd flown across the ocean, and landed, a golden-haired miracle, in his arms.

Her damp hair clung to his chest, the crown of her head tucked under his chin. She held him so tight, as if she were certain something would rip him away from her. He'd be lost to her, the way her little girl was.

She lay, holding him forever, her legs twined with his, her arms clutched tight around his waist. Michael knew he'd be happy just holding her like this for the rest of his life. He prayed she'd fall asleep, waited for the rhythmic breathing that would tell him she'd slipped into her dreams.

But suddenly, her breath got quicker, more shallow, tension a low buzz wherever her body touched his. He felt the slightest shift in her, sensed her mind whirling. "What is it, Eve? Do you want to talk about Victoria?"

"No. I want—" she levered herself up on one elbow, peered down into his eyes, her face so earnest, so open, her eyes shimmering green, shy with need. "Michael, I *want*."

She slid her hand across his stomach to the buttons that fastened his riding breeches. Michael couldn't breathe.

"Eve, I don't think—you've been through so much—I want it to be right for you."

"It will be right, as long as it's with you." Her lashes drooped, concealing her eyes. Color stained her cheekbones. "The courts gave Chad my daughter. But after— there was something *I* gave away. Any hope of finding someone who would love me."

"Ah, Eve—"

"I've been lonely for so long, Michael. But now . . . now I'm glad I never—" she faltered. "It was worth those years of waiting. Look what I found. You."

She brought him to his knees, stripped his soul bare, held his heart in her hands. And she was *grateful*—this wonderful, brave, bright, vulnerable woman was grateful she had found him. He wasn't worthy to kiss her feet. A sliver of terror slipped under his skin, cold, steely. What would happen if he failed her—*when* he failed her? He couldn't bear to lose the magic he saw in her eyes. If she ever found out the wager Rory had made or, God forbid, if the boy lost—

She was unfastening the buttons. He could feel them snap free, the material straining over his erection.

She loved him. She wanted him. Maybe he'd been wrong, holding himself away from her tonight, trying to give her space for her sorrow. Maybe she needed him more tonight than she ever would again. Closer than close. Skin to skin. Breath to breath. Inside her. And he wanted it, too.

He groaned, rolled her beneath him, kissing her as all the restraint he'd used during her bath melted away. She tasted of soap and tears and hope. Her lips parted under his, and his tongue swept deep inside her mouth. Michael's hand cupped her breast, tracing it as if learning it by heart, the shape of it, the weight of it, the way her nipple pearled, hard under the brush of his palm.

Tenderness—she needed so much tenderness. A lifetime's worth. He summoned up all the patience he'd learned in years of dealing with damaged horses, damaged children, creatures whose hurts ran so deep they were hard to reach.

Good . . . it felt so good . . . Eve thought dizzily as he caressed her. Too good. Terrifyingly good. His hands were so strong, so gentle, every brush of the callused tips of his fingers against her driving her crazy. For so long she'd been locked up tight inside herself where no one could hurt her, no one could touch the tender part of her soul. If Michael had hammered at it, tried to tear open that gate, she could have resisted, held enough of herself back, aloof from him to feel some measure of being safe.

But he didn't force the lock she'd kept fastened for so long. With murmured praise, sweet kisses, he lured her to that tight-locked door, seduced her into peeking through the keyhole to glimpse the world outside. The world that had seemed too frightening, spaces too open, vulnerabilities too vast for her to venture out.

But Michael was waiting for her, with those wise, loving blue eyes, that healing spirit, solid, dependable, as strong and certain as the green of Glenammura if she just had the courage to trust him.

With everything. Every flaw. Every fear. Every hope. Peering through just a crack in the wall would never be enough for him.

But did she have the courage to risk unlocking that door inside her even for Michael? If something went wrong, how could she survive? Pick herself up again and start over?

Michael's mouth trailed down her throat, his lips skimming her breast. His mouth closed over her nipple and he drew on it so gently it made her moan. She'd imagined what it would feel like to have him touch her, but never had she even guessed at the power of his touch, the magic in it, the promise.

She slid her fingers into his hair to cup his mouth against her, arched against his suckling. She was burningly empty, painfully empty. She spread her legs, letting him settle between them. His erection pressed hard against that sensitive mound, the layers of cloth between them irritating. Michael reached down and grabbed the hem of her nightgown, sliding it up her legs.

He knew just how much it cost her, what she'd surrendered the moment she let him strip the gown away. She shivered, but not because of the sudden chill. Michael stared at her as if he'd found some precious treasure. His eyes glistened, hot embers in their depths. His breath rasped in his throat, lips parted.

"You're beautiful, so beautiful," he breathed.

"Your turn," Eve said with a wobbly smile as she

touched his riding breeches. Michael climbed out of bed and stripped them down his powerful horsemans' legs. Beautiful? *He* was the one who was beautiful. Muscles rippled across a chest dusted with dark hair, his hips narrow, thighs powerful, legs long. It was as if the storms of life had carved away anything false or ordinary about him, left him strong and rare.

Eve swallowed hard, overwhelmed by such raw masculinity. So much of him— Once she let him come inside her there would be no place left for her to hide.

She could see the veins throb at the base of his throat, the straining heat of his erection, the wild need so fiercely controlled in his eyes.

"Eve, don't be afraid. I won't hurt you," he said so soft. "But if you've changed your mind, I can just hold you—"

Hold her. Something she wanted so much. Almost as much as she wanted this over, this decision made, the risk taken—the jump off the cliff finished.

She opened her arms to him, and with a groan Michael covered her naked body with his own. He touched her, stroked her where she was wet and burning, his fingers stirring up sensations that terrified her, that teetering on a cliff on a knife's edge of pleasure— pleasure so intoxicating it was the most dangerous thing Eve had ever known. It had cost her so much, this physical chaos of need raging inside her. She was so scared.

But she couldn't stop him, would have died if he'd stopped. Long, tender fingers dipped inside her, deep, and she thrust her hips against his hand. His thumb circled against her, and she felt something wild, terrifying, soul-shattering threaten to burst free in her body as well as her soul.

She came. Waves of release tearing a scream from low in her throat, her head thrashing against the pillow. Tears streamed from the corners of her eyes as twenty-some years of denial shattered, an Eve she'd never known bursting through. An Eve who might have wandered the garden before the fall, full of need, comfortable in her body, loving its rhythms and secrets and the pleasure it could bring her. That part of being a woman that had terrified her since she was a young girl and discovered she was pregnant.

Michael's touch gentled as the waves of pleasure crashed over her again and again, then, when she sagged against the pillow, he covered her mouth with his own, and, with a raw, masculine growl, drove himself inside her.

Eve cried out as he filled her, his arms shaking as he held his weight off of her, sweat trickling down from his temples. He was trying so hard to hold on to control. She could see it in his face. Wanted to be careful, to be tender. But now that she'd opened the door, stepped beyond the gate, she wanted everything—the rush of color and sensation, the wildness, the recklessness, the feeling of being alive Michael must have felt when he soared over the highest of barriers on horseback.

Eve surrendered herself to the woman emerging inside her, tempting Michael, teasing him, trying to devour all of him, every texture and scent, every movement and ripple of heat.

He thrust into her, telling her how good she felt, how right, how beautiful she was and how brave. How much he wanted her. She felt a stirring in herself where their bodies came together, the friction setting her on fire. She moaned, cried out, clutched at him, her hips rising to meet his thrusts, her heart slamming so hard against his she couldn't tell where she ended and Michael began.

Every muscle in his body went rigid, and she could feel the crest rising in him. Wild excitement rushed through her, and she cupped her hands around the hard curves of his buttocks, pulling him deeper.

Michael cried out, driving so deep it felt as if he touched her soul. She felt him climax, her own body exploding a second time, this time more fiercely than the first.

Michael sagged down on top of her, his whole body trembling, sweat-soaked, as he buried his face in her breasts. She held him until the world stopped its crazy spinning, until he had the strength and will to roll to one side, carrying her with him. Now she sprawled on top of him, looking down into his face.

"I love you, Michael," she said. Saw his eyes glisten with tears. He knew, she thought, marveling. Knew that trusting him with the fact that she loved him was the hardest thing she could do, the biggest risk she could take.

"Ah, Eve!" He cuddled her up close beside him, her head pillowed on his chest. "Everything is going to be grand. Just wait. I promise I'll make it so."

What was it in his voice that unsettled her? Something she couldn't quite put her finger on. Joy, satisfaction, pleasure—she could hear all three. But there was something more.

She was tired, so tired. In the morning they'd go get Innisfree. Tomorrow they'd be back at Kilrain. Rory would be waiting.

Anticipation welled up inside her in spite of the raw place Victoria's rejection had left. Maybe it wouldn't be the family she had hoped for, imagined, what she'd planned. But it would be *hers*. Michael and Rory, Innisfree and Bonaparte and the ghost Michael had griped about, she thought with a smile.

Maybe she could let herself be happy, even if she had this empty hole where Victoria should be in her heart forever.

She closed her eyes, listening to Michael's heartbeat, feeling waves of sleepiness wash over her. You can trust him. He would never hurt you, a voice inside her whispered.

She wanted to go home, she thought, suddenly rejoicing. Home.

She was holding that word tight against her heart when she finally fell asleep.

22

Dawn painted the Irish hills with bright strokes of color, rose and purple, gold and silver. Michael had loved morning from the time he'd been a boy—that sliver of time when the day belonged to him alone. Dew gleamed on every blade of grass, the air washed sweet with it. But somehow, not being able to tell the whole truth about Rory and the race had taken the gloss off the day. But she'd know everything soon.

Once Rory won time for Eve with her daughter, she would understand why they'd kept secrets from her. Even if she got mad, it wouldn't matter. Anger couldn't measure up to the chance she'd been waiting a lifetime for.

He'd left her at the empty trailer to put all the gear away. It had made him feel like hell that she'd been so willing to do that, just stay behind, while images of their lovemaking the night before shone star-bright in her eyes. She'd reached up to kiss him, still shy, so fragile. At least he'd managed to leave some soft sheen of happiness in her eyes.

Michael strode up to the stall where he'd left Rory and Innisfree last night and opened the door. Innisfree stood, saddled and bridled, Rory dressed in his own riding gear as well—the silks Michael had bought him. Michael's throat tightened at the sight the two of them made.

Rory grinned at him. "So, do I look like a rider now?"

"You'll do, boyo. You'll do."

"Even warmed Innisfree up out in the rear arena."

Michael's nerves zinged. "Did anyone see you?"

"What are you worried about? Nobody saw me yesterday."

"*I* hardly recognized you yesterday in that rig you were wearing. It's a whole different matter when you're wearing silks and riding a horse everyone in Ireland knows comes from Glenammura."

"Don't be an old woman."

"Lad, you're an original. You don't exactly blend into the crowd on a good day. On that horse, you might as well strap a flashing red light to that head of yours and yell 'here I am' to Moran. If it wasn't for Eve, I would have nailed you in a tack box and hauled your silks with you in them back to the farm before you could say 'Jesus Mary and Joseph.'"

Rory chuckled. "You'd have to catch us first, Halloran." He turned to the horse watching them with busy, intelligent eyes. "Wouldn't he, you beautiful bastard?"

Innisfree whickered, nudging the lad with his velvety nose. The horse looked for all the world as if he were sharing a secret with Rory.

"Well, let's head out for the starting line. Wouldn't want to keep the princess waiting, would we, boys?" Rory said. "That girl doesn't know it, but I'm about to do her the biggest favor in her life by beating the snot out of her."

"Won't do your ego any harm either, will it? Get a little of your own back from her?"

Rory shrugged. "Maybe. But all I really want is to help Eve. You know, she's been spending all this time writing letters to her—that girl. Sneaked up to read some of 'em just to see what she was doing up there all that time." Rory sobered. "If anyone ever wrote me letters like that, I—" His voice cracked. Michael's heart twisted as the boy threw himself into checking buckles and stirrups, anything to hide the yearning in his eyes. "She loves her daughter a lot, you know?"

"Yeah. I know." Michael thought of the letters scattered across the bed at Cadagon's, the smears where Eve's tears had fallen. How many had she shed over the years? How had she survived Christmases and birthdays? Every holiday, even simple, homey gifts like dinner at the table or popcorn and movies on Friday nights would always have an empty space, a silence where there should have been laughter. Emptiness where there should have been a little girl's face.

"That girl—someone has to show her how lucky she is."

Michael grasped Rory's shoulder—a shoulder still boyishly thin. It had always carried the weight of a man. But then, Rory would be a man before they all knew it. And Michael had hopes he'd be as fine a man as ever walked Ireland, because Eve Danaher had let him into the empty, hurting places in her own battered heart.

"Come on, boyo. You've got a lesson to teach Miss Victoria and her father. Show them what a real rider is. Not someone who can buy a horse someone else has already done all the hard work on. Someone like you who turned something lost into a winner."

Rory turned his face up to Michael's, the hero worship plain in his eyes. "You showed me how. Most trainers wouldn't have let me near a decent horse. If I'd been you, I never would have."

"Not my choice. By the time I could have thrown your arse back to the pony barn, Innisfree had already chosen you. I may risk my neck over jumps no one else will try, but even I'm not stupid enough to argue with that crazy horse."

Michael looped an arm around Rory's shoulder, walking beside him as he led the horse out of the stall and onto the fairgrounds. They were so distracted they didn't even see an old man look from Rory's face to the poster tacked to a hitching post. They didn't know as they passed by that the poster and the old man were gone.

It was too quiet without Michael. The bridles and saddles, brushes and feedbags, lined up like ghosts in the tack boxes. Eve's heart squeezed at one of the tack boxes freshly painted in blue and green. Rory's box, the one Michael had done up for the boy at the same time he'd ordered the riding silks.

What had Victoria's colors been? Silver and rose? Her hair had looked so pretty, curled against the soft colors, her cheeks so bright with enthusiasm until she'd seen Eve's face.

She'd wanted Rory's horse. Wanted Eve to give it to her. And, God in heaven, Eve would have been happy to give Victoria the heart from her chest. Anything she'd asked. Anything except that. Rory's Innisfree . . .

She wondered if she'd ever be able to wipe away the memory of Victoria's face when she'd said no. Even with the memory of Michael's loving to soften the agony of that day.

Michael.

She shivered. This morning her body felt like it belonged to someone else. She was tender, a good kind of tender, between her legs, every step stirring up an awareness of what had happened last night. She could still feel the way he'd touched her, so loving, so hungry, wanting so much to please her, take care of her. Every brush of his fingers, every word he'd murmured against her skin a kind of praise she'd never experienced before.

It had been one of the most precious moments in her life when he had come inside her, so close she knew she could never really be alone again. It would take some getting used to, though, she knew. This not being alone. She'd been that way most of her life.

She stepped out of the trailer, the soft, damp air cooling her cheeks. How long had Michael been gone? Almost an hour? She prayed Innisfree wasn't lamed more badly than Michael had thought. Maybe she should go look for him.

She reached for her jacket inside the truck cab when she caught sight of a red compact car zipping toward the trailer. She shaded her eyes, winced as she recognized the man behind the wheel. Dennis Moran. The last person she felt up to seeing at the moment.

She steadied herself. She couldn't look guilty, let him suspect anything. Thank God Rory was back at Kilrain! They had nothing to hide. At least not here.

Moran pulled to a stop, climbed out of the car. He gave her a look of surprise and censure. "Eve. I didn't expect to find you here, though Michael certainly has a reputation with the ladies. I hoped you had better sense."

"I came to my senses the minute I decided not to ride back to the castle with you." Don't mention the castle, Eve, she thought, unnerved. Don't remind him of anything that might lead him to Rory.

"So you're trailing around horse shows with Halloran now? I didn't know you had any interest in horses."

"Some. My daughter loves them." It was an excuse, though why she felt obligated to give this jerk one was beyond her. She just wanted to distract him, give him anything to think about except one red-haired runaway boy.

"Lots of kids seem to feel that way. In fact, I bet Halloran told you that Rory fancied himself some kind of horseman when he was staying at the farm."

"Did he?" Eve wished she could smack the sneer right off of Moran's face. "Too bad. Not many horses in Dublin."

"Some people don't think Rory is in Dublin. Not anymore. In fact, you're probably wondering why I'm here so early."

"To tack up more posters, I'd imagine."

"They work well enough."

Something about Moran's eyes made Eve edgy as he continued.

"People pay attention to them. Do their civic duty."

"You're wasting your time. Rory wouldn't be stupid enough to come to a place like this when he knows you're looking for him."

"Wouldn't he? And just when did you get to know the lad so well?"

Eve struggled to keep her cheeks from burning. "Michael has told me a lot about Rory. Besides, it didn't take much to see how bright the boy is. After all, he hoodwinked you, didn't he, when he ran away right under your nose." She couldn't help smiling.

Moran's cheeks went red.

"Well, I'm going off to find Michael," she said. "Happy hunting. You won't find Rory here, but maybe you'll enjoy the sights. By the way, you know that horse Rory was training before you jumped in and ruined everything?"

"Should have called the authorities on Halloran then for letting Rory near it! It's a wonder he wasn't killed! That horse should have been shot years ago."

"Innisfree won the cross-country yesterday. I never saw a horse jump that high. It was beautiful. Beautiful."

"You're joking!"

"Michael rode him."

"Halloran? Racing? He turned too much of a coward to ride after the fall Murphy took."

Eve's stomach turned. Was there really some kind of satisfaction in Moran's face? What kind of sick bastard got any pleasure out of someone else's pain? Or wasn't it about Sean at all? More likely, it was pleasure that Michael had carried a shadow of guilt with him from that moment on.

"Why do you hate Michael so much? Because of something that happened when you were kids? Isn't it about time you grew up? Or is it worth being so petty, taking out your frustrations on some innocent boy Michael is only trying to help? A boy you're getting paid to help, I might add."

Moran flushed. "I do my job."

"Too bad Innisfree isn't here right now to do the job he's so good at," she said sweetly. "I'd really love to see him kick you into the next county."

With that she turned and stormed away. Wherever Michael was, she'd find him. Even if she didn't, she needed to walk off some of her rage. Damn that smug, prissy little paper pusher, arranging everyone else's lives! It was his fault Rory wasn't where he belonged, on Innisfree's back, racing like the wind. It was his fault Rory hadn't been the one receiving congratulations after yesterday's race.

His fault . . . a voice whispered inside her. *And yours*. She had opened the door to Rory's parents regaining custody. Moran only walked through it. Her conscience stung. At least Rory was safe at the castle, thank God. Even so, she'd better find Michael and tell him he was right. Moran was poking around. She didn't like the glint in the social worker's eyes. She didn't like it one bit.

Fresh ink shone on the contracts as Tolliver stuck them into his sportcoat pocket, looking as smug as if he'd just struck gold. Michael fought down a jab of panic, an instinct to grab the papers and tear them in two.

The bastard had it all down, every 'i' dotted, every 't' crossed. If Rory won the race, he got to keep his horse; if anything prevented the animal from crossing the finish line, Innisfree was gone. Michael had been racing too many years not to know just how often something unexpected could trip a rider up on a course like this.

He'd almost told Tolliver to go to hell, but Rory had urged him to sign it, so much confidence in his eyes, so much eagerness. The boy was already imagining what it would be like to tell Eve what he'd done, see her eyes when he told her Victoria was hers for at least a little while.

The boy would win. Michael could see the drive in his eyes, the determination, and Innisfree looked as ready as he'd ever been. The horse had raced yesterday for Michael, hanging on by a thread. But with Rory here, the edgy light in the horse's eyes had eased, the trust glowed, fierce, and the loyalty. The horse would do anything Rory asked of him. Even Trevor Butler, for all his skill, couldn't put that kind of heart into a horse. It had to be born there. Innisfree had lost his way for a little while. But Rory had found that incredible spark again, nurtured it, made it glow bright.

Whatever else he thought of Eve's daughter, Michael was starting to think the girl was realizing it, too, dreading it. But she wanted the horse so much she was hoping she was wrong. Wrong or that kismet, that sort of fate she'd been talking about, would jump in and turn things in her favor. Why shouldn't she believe that? He'd bet Tolliver had always given her everything she could ever have wanted. She didn't know what it felt like to want something with all your heart and see it slip away. If she did, she wouldn't have been able to be so hard on her mother. Not with all the pain and longing and loss that always haunted Eve's eyes.

Rory stood face to face with his horse, Innisfree nuzzling his cheek while Rory stroked long sweeps down the horse's silky neck. Innisfree mouthed Rory's hair with his velvety lips. He looked for all the world like he was whispering something in the boy's ear. Rory laughed, then turned to Victoria. "My horse says yours had better get ready to eat his dust."

Victoria scowled. "We'll see who he belongs to after the race."

"Let's get this over with," Michael said. "Mount up, the two of you." He could only thank God the course was laid out in a giant horseshoe shape. He and Tolliver could start the race, then, if they ran like hell, could reach the finish line in time to see the two kids take the last four jumps. No way Michael was going to let Tolliver or his daughter be the judge of who came across the finish line first in case of a close race.

Tolliver crossed over to give his daughter some last words of wisdom, directing her every move.

Rory grinned down at Michael. "Bet that man's never been on a horse in his life. Listen to him talking like he's the world champion or something. Now, you, boss, you're a different matter. Aren't you going to tell me what to do?"

"It's your race, lad. You don't need me to tell you a damned thing about how this horse will run it best."

Rory sobered. "He still doesn't like water jumps much. He's a little edgy because it's a new place. I need to keep talking to him so he knows I'm here with him."

Michael's chest swelled with pride, bittersweet, deep. "That's right."

"Innisfree isn't going to like the princess and her horse anywhere near him, so I need to push hard to get past them as quick as possible. Once he's ahead, he'll relax, just think about running and getting over the jumps."

"That's the secret." Michael could have just clapped Rory on the back, sent him off, but he had to let the boy know how he felt. "Lad, you make me proud. Especially today. The risks you're taking. The work you've done with this horse. The way you've grown."

Michael fought back a hoarse rasp in his voice. "I'm so damned honored to have someone like you in my life."

Rory's face softened. He looked young, vulnerable, *pleased*. "Michael, I—" He stopped, his eyes overbright. "I wished I had known you before. Maybe it wouldn't have been so hard to—I don't know."

"Doesn't matter where you start from, lad. Matters where you end up. And you're going to finish on top of the world. I'm thinking of breeding some racing stock myself to help finance more farms like Glenammura. Need someone to see to it. Not enough time to do it myself. And then, someone will have to train them, ride them in competitions. I was thinking if you felt like it maybe you could be that person."

Rory's eyes nearly popped out of his head. "You . . .

you mean it? But I . . . I don't know anything, really. I mean, I'm just learning—"

"You're the finest natural horseman I've ever seen. And I'll be around to answer questions. But I doubt you'll need much help. Once we get another farm started, I'll need someone to be in charge there."

"But I didn't do good in school."

"That's because you didn't give a damn about it. But when you care about something, boyo, you've got the quickest mind I think I've ever known. When you and Innisfree race, you carry that with you."

Rory glowed.

"We going to race, Halloran, or is your boy there trying to think of a graceful way to back out? Too late. Contract's signed. Only way he can hang on to that horse is to win now."

Rory grinned down at Michael. "I already have."

The lad reined his horse toward the starting line where Victoria already waited, her horse eager to run. Innisfree's eyes widened, nostrils flared as he got close to the other horse. Twice, Innisfree tried to skitter sideways. Twice Rory got him back under control.

Michael stood at the starting line, a handkerchief in his hand. He held it up, both riders' eyes on him, intent, horses restless, ready to bolt. "Go!" he yelled as he let the scrap of fabric go. It swirled in a rush of wind currents stirred up by the horses' feet. An explosion of dust and turf erupted as the two powerful animals thundered away.

Michael's heart stopped as Victoria crowded Rory, Innisfree shying at a run, almost unseating the boy. Rory clung to the saddle with nothing but grit and luck. Michael didn't want to think the girl had done that on purpose. Anyone with as much experience with horses as Tolliver and his daughter had could easily have watched Innisfree race and figured out the other horse's weakness. Used it to gain an advantage. Plenty of riders did it, and Michael had no trouble thinking Tolliver was capable of urging Victoria to do anything to skew the race in his daughter's favor. But she was Eve's daughter, too. The possibility that Eve might be disappointed or disillusioned when she got to really talk to the girl made Halloran's stomach clench.

The girl was a damned fine equestrian, her elite training evident in every move she made, the fluidity of her body on the horse, as if the two melded together, one entity for this ride.

Rory was far more raw—power and recklessness, passion instead of precision. Beautiful in a wild way, something primal, breathtaking. Innisfree soared over the first barrier a mere nose behind Victoria's horse.

Was the girl crowding Rory on purpose? Driving him over toward the higher, harder, more dangerous parts of the jump? It was natural to try to take your own horse over the easiest spot to clear, but the maneuver would have angered or at least unsettled plenty of seasoned riders.

Rory had never been matched against anyone. He'd never heard the sounds of another horse so close, seen it charging, hooves flying. But Rory was a street kid. Michael could see the boy's defiance, grinned as this time Rory was the one who crowded Victoria's horse.

The girl glanced over at him, stunned, dismayed.

Michael swore as they disappeared around a wooded bend. He sprinted across the open field, Tolliver running with one of those 'jog-ten-miles-in-a-color-coordinated-sweat-suit' kinds of gait.

They reached the finish just in time. Michael tensed, hearing the horses before he could see them, the thundering of hooves so close together, it seemed as if they were riding on top of one another.

Rory was ahead, just by a neck, the big horse lathered, nostrils blood red. Rory leaned low over his neck as they raced toward the water jump. Yesterday Innisfree hadn't known what he was sailing over until it was too late to balk. Today, the horse knew what was coming. Michael could see it in the horse's stride, in the tension in his powerful muscles.

Victoria slammed her horse against Innisfree again, hard. The girl looked afraid. Was she losing concentration? Or realizing Rory had a damned good chance of winning?

Innisfree dodged aside, his lead narrowing to a nose. Michael saw Rory lean even more forward in the stirrups, his lips moving, urging the big horse. Innisfree surged forward.

Too fast. A voice inside Michael cried out in panic. *He was going to take the water jump too fast.*

Innisfree was almost a full length ahead of the other horse. He stormed toward the jump, Rory pouring it on, everything he had, risking it, neck or nothing. Michael stifled a cry as Innisfree charged the fence. For an instant, he thought the horse was going to refuse it. Sensed that if he'd been the one on Innisfree's back at that moment, the horse would have sent him flying into the tangled tree stumps that made the obstacle so hard. He would've been seeing stars for a month after he hit the ground.

Did Victoria sense that, too? She let out a whoop to distract him. Innisfree faltered, but it was too late to stop. His haunches bunched, powerful legs thrusting him into the air. Michael's heart stopped. They'd never make it. It was too high. They'd rushed it too fast. Midair the horse thrust himself higher, somehow. Hocks raked the top of the jump, his hooves skimming the fallen tree, bark flying off where Innisfree had struck it.

Michael held his breath, horrified—the damned jump had been designed for nasty falls. But somehow, Innisfree kept his feet under him, and Rory stayed on his back. Pride almost burst Michael's chest as they stayed upright on the other side. The kid streaked out in front, Innisfree running, fire and wind in his feet. No horse could catch him now.

"No! Good God!" Tolliver's strangled cry made the

hairs stand up on Michael's nape. His gaze flashed from
Rory to Victoria. She'd seen the near-crash, her con-
centration shattered. She was barely holding on as
Puck tried to take the fence without her guidance. But
Puck didn't have Innisfree's heart, and Victoria didn't
have Rory's grit.

Horse and rider flew, pell mell over the fence,
crashed on the other side, a tangle of slashing hooves,
rose and silver silks thrashing against the turf. The
horse let out a hideous sound, Victoria screaming as
she tried to roll away from Puck as he struggled.

Sweet God—Michael swore as the horse tried to
scramble to its feet. Victoria's boot was caught through
the stirrup. If the horse bolted she could be dragged to
her death. Reins tangled around Puck, lashing him,
terrifying him even more. Victoria tried to kick free.

Michael ran, Tolliver beside him. They would never
reach her in time.

Rory, victory shining in his face, saw the two men
running, turned his head back to see what had happened. Michael saw a heartbeat of indecision, his memory flashing back to the race with Sean—the prize he'd
wanted to win in that moment more important than
anything else—that wild, drunken feeling of knowing
he was going to win. He could see Rory hesitate, falter.

God knew the way Victoria and her father had
goaded the kid, Michael would never have blamed him
for riding to the finish. How the hell could the kid
guess the cost if he did?

Suddenly, Rory reined Innisfree back. The horse
fought against the command—enough of a cross-country eventer to sense they were going the wrong way,
hungry enough to want to win for the boy he loved.
But Rory wouldn't be shaken. He struggled to turn the
horse around. Even the instinct to win, bred into Innisfree's very bones, couldn't withstand the horse's
need to please Rory. Innisfree surrendered, obeyed,
reached the downed pair in a heartbeat. Rory scram-

bled down off his horse, let Innisfree go. He dove for Puck's reins. The terrified horse spun, kicked at him, dragging Victoria like a rag doll.

Michael heard a terrible thud, hoof connecting with Rory's ribs, but somehow the kid hung on. People were running toward them—stable workers, trainers arriving at the show grounds. Other riders rushing to help. Michael got to the girl, yanked Victoria's boot out of the stirrup. She crumpled to the ground in a heap.

Rory wrestled Puck away from her, fought to calm the fear-crazed animal. Tolliver fell to his knees beside his daughter, started to lift her up.

"Don't move her!" Michael snapped. "Paramedics will be here in a minute. Someone will have called them."

Tolliver shot him a panicked look. "That kid—he made her fall!"

"He probably saved her life!" Michael snarled. He knelt down. "Victoria?" he laid one hand on the girl's cheek, carefully avoiding the scrape on her left cheek-bone. "Honey, open your eyes."

Michael glanced up, looking for the medics, saw Rory still battling with the terrified Puck, other people hurrying to help. Thank God Trevor Butler was among them. The trainer took the horse's reins and Rory moved out of his way, arm curved over the muddy hoofprint where Puck had kicked him in the chest.

Michael should have felt relief things were this much under control, but his gut clenched as his gaze locked on one person not in stable gear. Eve. White-faced, she bolted toward them, her hair wind-tangled, knees muddy where she'd slipped, then clambered up to run again. "Victoria—Rory—what . . . what happened?" she cried as she reached them.

"Racing." Rory choked out, as he unsnapped his chinstrap and ripped off his helmet, letting it fall to the ground. "I wanted to win for you."

"Are you hurt?" She searched his face, desperate. "Rory?"

"No, Eve. I'm okay."

Eve fell to her knees beside her daughter. "Oh, God, Michael, how bad is it?"

He hated to scare her. Still, he couldn't lie. "Can't be sure until she wakes up enough to tell us."

"I don't understand!" Eve cried, taking her daughter's hand. "What happened? This doesn't make any sense! Tori. Tori, open your eyes. Sweetheart, please—" Her voice broke.

Victoria's eyes fluttered open, confused, lost, heartbreakingly like those of her mother. Of the three people bending over her, it was her mother's eyes the girl sought.

"Hurts."

"I know, baby."

Tolliver elbowed Eve out of the way. "Victoria—"

"D–Daddy—lost. S–Sorry I lost—" She tried to sit up.

"Lay back, honey," Michael said, then looked up at Eve in stark relief. "She's moving her arms and legs." Thank God. *Thank God!*

The paramedics on alert for the show swarmed up, shoved them aside.

Color was coming back into the girl's face. "I . . . I'm all right," she said, levering herself upright. "Just knocked the wind out of me."

"We'll let the doctor be the judge of that," Eve said gently, unsnapping the girl's helmet, drawing it off. Sweat-damp bangs clung to Victoria's brow, not quite concealing an old, pale scar. Michael saw anguish fill Eve's eyes at the sight of it, as if the jagged line was alive. The accident—it was from the accident that had shattered Eve's life. He sensed it in his gut. Knew Eve was seeing the old wound open and bleeding, tasting the helplessness, the guilt, as if it were brand new. He would have given ten years of his life to be able to dash those nightmare memories away.

But in spite of the agony Eve was suffering, she only had eyes for her daughter, kept her voice soft, soothing. "We'll get you to the hospital, let them take some X-rays, just to be sure."

Michael knew the moment Victoria really recognized her mother. The girl cringed back, dashed away Eve's hand. "I told you I'm fine! I'm not going to any doctor! Daddy?" That plaintive wail cut right through Michael—Eve's daughter, running for protection to the man who had robbed her of her mother, the ruthless sonofabitch who had destroyed Eve's life. It turned Michael's stomach.

Chad's lips actually curled with something like satisfaction in spite of the worry still in his eyes. "She says she's all right," he snapped. "It's none of your business, anyway! Dammit, can't you just butt out! Go play with your new boyfriend and forget Victoria ever existed! Can't you see it's what she wants?"

Michael started to snap out a reply, but before he could get out a word Rory jumped in, put himself between Eve and Tolliver. "What kind of an arse are you? Eve's only trying to help! Open your fecking eyes, the both of you!"

"Easy, everyone!" A medic with dark hair and eyes warned in a voice that gave no quarter as he checked Victoria over. "I know you've had a scare, but this isn't helping anyone." After a moment, he leaned back on his haunches, satisfied. "Maybe some good news will keep you from tearing each other's heads off. I think the little lady is going to be plenty stiff for a while, but she's going to be fine."

"Thank God," Eve breathed. "But don't you think we should still get some X-rays just to be sure? She was knocked unconscious."

"Just leave me alone!" Victoria begged, tears welling up in her eyes. "I just . . . just want to lie down—"

"Of course you do, poor lamb," a feminine voice with the familiar lilt of Ireland sympathized. Michael watched as a woman in riding breeches and worn boots bustled out of the crowd, her red hair gleaming.

Butler's wife. Michael had met her several times while trading horses at Butler's farm. "And I'll be taking you off to do just that right now."

"Please," Eve begged. "I just—"

"Don't be worrying, now. I've been buried in kids and horses since the day I got married. I've a better record for finding broken bones than half the doctors in the county." Moira Butler leaned toward Eve, her voice hushed so few others could hear. "It's kind of you to worry about our Victoria, poor, motherless lamb that she is."

Eve blanched. "But I am her mother."

Moira paled beneath the freckles sprinkling her nose. "I . . . I'm sorry. I didn't know. She's been staying with us at Butler Farms. If you want to check later to make sure she is all right."

"Please, I just want to get back to Butler Farms!" Victoria was struggling to her feet, tears on her cheeks, desperate to get away.

Moira Butler gathered her into her arms. "And so we will, my sweet angel. Come along with me."

Casting Eve a look of confusion, the woman ushered Victoria away. What must it be like for Eve, seeing her daughter being mothered by someone else? Seeing Victoria cling to Moira when Eve's arms were aching to hold the girl?

"Go with her, Chad," Eve begged him. "She's scared."

But Tolliver shook his head. "You heard what Victoria said. She's all right. Besides, I have to take care of some business for her here."

Tolliver gestured to where Innisfree danced just far enough away from all the chaos that he could feel safe and keep an eye on Rory.

Eve sagged against the jump where Victoria had met with disaster. "I don't understand."

Michael winced when she turned to him. "Michael, what happened here?"

"Why is Rory—" she paled. "Oh, God! Rory! He has to get out of here. I just saw Moran."

"Do what you want with the kid as soon as I get my daughter's new horse taken care of," Chad sneered.

"New horse?" Eve echoed, bewildered. "I saw someone take her horse toward the stable."

"Not that horse. The one that boy was riding," Chad said.

"Innisfree?" Eve asked, confused. "Chad, what are you talking about?"

"Victoria and that boy were racing," Chad said with a shrug. "He bet his horse. He lost."

Panic flashed in Eve's eyes, then fierce denial. "Rory would never risk Innisfree. Besides, he was winning when Victoria fell."

Chad's lips curled the way they had when he'd heard the judgment passed on Victoria's custody. "He had to win to keep the horse. If he didn't finish, he forfeited the animal."

"He stopped to save your daughter's life!" Michael raged. "You were right here watching what happened! You saw it, Tolliver! You can't take his horse for doing that!"

Tolliver shrugged, a hard light in his eyes. "He chose to turn around. He knew the terms of the contract. It'll be a good lesson for him in business. Keep your eye on the prize, not the people you trample on the way to get it."

"Chad, please," Eve begged. "You don't understand. Rory loves that horse."

"Then he shouldn't have risked losing it."

"But—Michael," her eyes sparked with hope. "He can't take the horse! The horse isn't Rory's to lose! Innisfree belongs to you."

Michael's stomach turned. "Eve—I signed the contract Tolliver had drawn up last night. I knew what Rory was going to do."

"But why? Why would he— It doesn't make any

sense! Rory?" She turned to the boy, his silks torn at
the elbow, smudged with dirt and grass-stained from
his battle with Puck. Gray-faced, Rory stood staring
across the space of green that separated him from Innisfree. The horse might as well have been a world
away.

"Rory," Eve said more stridently. "You said something about winning for *me* when I ran up. What did
you mean?"

"I wanted you to get time with your daughter," the
boy said gruffly, trying not to cry. "It wasn't right,
keeping you away from her when you loved her so
much. I read the letters one night when I couldn't
sleep and—if I won, she promised she'd give me an
hour of her time. An hour. I was going to make her
spend it with you. I knew if . . . if she just had a chance
to talk to you, she'd see how special you are and she
wouldn't be able to shut you out of her life anymore."

"No," Eve gasped, stricken. "Oh, Rory, no."

Tears trickled down the boy's cheeks.

"Michael, how could you let him do that?" she
spun on him, furious. "How could you? I never would
have—if I'd known—but you knew, didn't you? Last
night? This morning? You just left me to clean up the
trailer while you came here to meet Rory and let him
lose his horse!"

Michael flinched inwardly. "He should have won.
He would have if Victoria hadn't fallen. If he hadn't
turned back—"

Eve spun back to Tolliver. "Chad, please! I beg you.
Don't do this. He saved Victoria's life."

Tolliver's mouth curved in a hard little smile. "You
tried pleading with me before, Eve. You should know it
doesn't do a damned bit of good. Especially since I always
make sure I've got the law on my side. I won custody of
Victoria, now I've won ownership of that horse. That's
just reality, baby, whether you like it or not. Now, I'm
going to see my daughter and tell her the good news."

Tolliver started to turn around. Michael grabbed his shoulder, spun him back. He would have slammed his fist into Chad's face if Rory hadn't dived between them, the boy's face tight.

"Listen, Michael, you'll not be doin' Eve any good in jail, man," Rory warned. The lad knew far too much about courts and arrests.

"You should listen to the kid," Tolliver said, straightening his jacket. "I would have loved to charge you with assault, hotshot." He turned to Rory. "I guess you're not such a stupid kid after all. Now, get me my daughter's horse."

His heart was being ripped out. Michael watched Rory go to Innisfree, soothe the restive horse. He laid his face against him, cheek to cheek, whispering. But how could Rory ever say good-bye to Innisfree? There weren't enough words.

After a moment, Rory squared his shoulders, led him to Tolliver. The horse glared at the American, and Tolliver signaled for one of the other horsemen to take the reins.

"Tell your daughter he likes grapes," Rory said low, his voice breaking. "It's how I made friends with him. Maybe it will help—"

Help the animal when he realized his boy wasn't coming back? When Innisfree was back in some strange pasture, alone, without Rory to chase away his demons?

"Tolliver—" Michael called out, knowing it was futile. Knowing he had to try. "I'll pay anything. Name your price. Just let the boy keep the horse."

Tolliver smirked. "Weren't you the one who told me money can't buy everything? Seems you were right, after all."

Michael stood, helpless, watching the horse disappear. What would Rory do without Innisfree?

Almost as if he'd heard the thought, Rory turned and fled into Eve's arms. Eve held him, both of them crying, Eve stroking his hair.

"You shouldn't have done it! You shouldn't have done it!"

Michael heard her cry over and over, Rory's answer fierce.

"I'd do it again if I could. I'm sorry I didn't win for you."

"Come on, Rory," Eve said, at last, kissing him on his cheek. "Let's go home."

Rory nodded against her shoulder.

"Not so fast." The cultured tones cut through Eve like a knife. She wheeled, instinctively putting herself between Rory and its source.

Moran. The social worker had been watching everything from the crowd.

"No!" Eve choked out. "Not this. Not this, too."

"Rory, you've caused a lot of people a great deal of trouble. We've been searching all over for you. Now we find it was just as I suspected. Halloran knew where you were the whole time. Unfortunate for the children at Glenammura, but then, Halloran, you always were reckless when it came to other people."

"Michael didn't know I was here until Victoria and I arranged the race," Rory protested. "I knew he'd bring Innisfree here. I wanted to see him run. I never intended for Michael to know. I'll swear it under oath. Take a lie detector's test. Michael never knew."

Moran started to argue, but Rory cut him off.

"You can't prove anything, Moran. And people know all about Glenammura, everything Michael's done there. You think they're going to let you close it down in some kind of a little temper tantrum? Try it and you'll end up looking like an idiot, while Michael will look like a hero."

Moran bristled, flushed. Michael could see the instant the social worker realized Rory was right. Moran swore under his breath, his eyes probing sharply as he faced Rory, the boy so fierce the social worker finally looked away.

"Whatever. I suppose there would be no way to

prove it, anyway. I'll have to be satisfied with taking you back to Dublin, making sure you follow the court order from now on."

Eve clung to Rory, heartsick. "No! I can't let you— It's my fault! This happened because of me!"

Rory turned to her, grabbed her gently by the shoulders. "Because of you I quit hating everybody. Especially myself. I had to . . . to try to do something to help you, the way you helped me. I'm sorry I let you down."

Eve cradled his face in her hands. "You didn't let me down. I'm so proud of you, Rory."

The boy's eyes gleamed through a sheen of tears.

"I can't bear that they're going to take you away."

"Only for a little while. I'll be eighteen in less than a year. Then I can go anywhere I want. Do anything I want and not even Moran can stop me." Rory looked from Eve to Michael. "I think I'll be coming home then, if you'll let me."

Michael's voice broke. "We'll be waiting, lad."

Eve clutched Rory's hands. "Whatever happens in Dublin, you just remember this. You're *my* boy now, Rory."

Rory was the one who stepped away. "I'm ready, Moran," he said. "Jamie and Oonagh can't hurt me now."

Eve watched him stride away, so tall, so changed from the angry troublemaker she'd met her first day at the farm. He'd lost so much today—the race, his horse, his freedom. Why was the boy walking away as if he had won?

The crowd melted away, murmuring, the excitement over. Eve couldn't move.

"Eve," Michael said softly. "I'm sorry. We wanted it too much—for you to have time with Victoria. Rory and I—we wanted you to heal. I should never have let him risk it."

"No, Michael. You shouldn't have," she said stiffly.

"You had no right to break that boy's heart because of me."

"But it didn't break him. Didn't you see? Dammit, Eve, he loves you more than that horse! It's what we've been working for."

"He could have had us both. He deserved us both. Innisfree *and* me. And I deserved the truth from both of you."

"You would have said no."

"It was my right! My choice to make."

"What Rory did wasn't about 'rights.' It was a gift, Eve. One he wanted to give you so much. How could I take that away from him?"

It was true. But Rory had lost so much she couldn't bear it. No one—no one had ever sacrificed anything for her, anything that really mattered to them. Rory had given all he had. Heart breaking, she turned and started across the field. Rory's helmet lay on the ground where he'd flipped it off. She picked it up, hugged it tight against her as she fled back to the empty trailer that wouldn't carry Innisfree or his boy back home.

23

*E*ve lay curled up on a bale of straw in the back of the horse trailer meant to be Innisfree's bed, Rory's riding helmet clutched tight in her arms.

My fault. The words screamed in her head. *My fault. Rory did it for me—raced, risked Innisfree, came out of hiding where Moran could find him.*

And Eve knew she'd be having nightmares forever about Victoria, seeing her daughter as her horse went down, hooves thrashing, Victoria limp, helpless, heart-stoppingly fragile. The way she'd been so many years ago, lost in the pile of wooden crates she'd pulled down on top of herself, blood running down her face.

Eve's whole body shook. She'd wanted more memories of her daughter, new ones. Now she had them. Victoria injured. Victoria demanding Rory's horse. Victoria afraid, hurting, hating her.

For years Eve's single dream had been to heal the wounds that lay between her and her little girl. But in the past months she'd only made things worse. Upset Victoria, true. But more painful than that, Eve had seen things she didn't want to see, come to suspect things about her daughter she didn't want to face.

She didn't know Victoria at all. The truth ground deep. Dear God, was it possible that the baby she'd adored, the toddler she'd cherished, had become so much like her father? A Tolliver, down deep in her bones? Willing to take something she wanted away from someone who needed it far more than she did, break their heart just because she had the power and was selfish enough to do it?

Eve's stomach churned, waves of pain devastating her. Her little girl—her baby—had Chad killed the sweetness in her? The kindness? The spark of compassion that had made Eve's heart glow?

She'd wanted so badly to find her way back into Victoria's life. She'd never guessed that *her* Tori might not even exist anymore.

Disillusionment twisted tight inside her at the memory of the jut of Victoria's chin, that too-familiar stubbornness she'd seen so often in Chad.

But Rory . . . Rory, who had suffered so much, been given so little, Rory had shone through like a vein of pure, unexpected gold.

He'd demanded nothing, worked to heal Innisfree with such patience. He'd had the courage to trust Eve and the generosity of spirit to risk everything for her.

He'd lost. Lost his horse. Had lost his freedom, his home snatched away. Lost everything except his generous heart. That, no one could take away from him.

"Eve?" Michael peered in through the trailer door.

He looked as if he'd been trampled. Eve knew his heart had been. He climbed into the trailer, crossed to where she sat. Hunkering down so he was at eye level, he looked into her face, everything exposed, raw, in his own. "I shouldn't have let him do it," he ground out. "It's just . . . he wanted it so bad, to give something back. If I'd had any idea what would happen— Oh, God, Eve. I'm so sorry."

"*You're* sorry? If I'd never come to Ireland none of this would ever have happened. Rory's parents wouldn't have won custody of him. He'd still be at Glenammura with you and he'd still have Innisfree."

Michael winced. "Eve, you've given that boy so much. Surely you must know that. Maybe things didn't work out the way we wanted them to. But he's

going to come back to us. You heard him. As soon as
he's old enough to be on his own. He's going to make
it. I know that now."

"Maybe he is, but only because he's got more courage
than anyone I've ever known. He shouldn't have to fight
so hard! How does he keep doing it? Keep getting up
every time life runs over him and leaves him broken?"

Michael shook his head. "I don't know how he did
it before. But I know how he's doing it this time. Because of the love you gave him. A place to be safe."

"Safe? I was a disaster for that boy! This was my fault,
Michael! My fault! Oh, God, I wish I'd never come here!"

Michael stood, turned away, but not before she saw
the anguish in his face. "What about us? You and me?
I love you."

"That's a hell of a mistake. Look what happens to
the people I love!"

"Does that mean you love me?" Hope and fear min-
gled in his strong features.

"You have to know I do."

Joy flashed in his eyes, tempered by sorrow.

"But it scares me. Hurts so much. I'm so afraid I'll
fail you."

Michael's expression changed, that wary, careful
look he had when he was dreading that Innisfree was
going to bolt. "Don't be, Eve. I—"

"How can I not be? Look at Victoria. My God,
Michael, she hates me and now I—if she can stoop low
enough to take Rory's horse this way—" she couldn't
finish. It was too terrible, too final. "Maybe I didn't
choose to leave her with Chad, but that doesn't matter.
Chad has turned her into someone as selfish as he is.
How can I live with myself? My God, if you'd have
known her when she was little—she was always so
kind. She was trying to rescue a kitten who'd gotten
stranded on top of a stack of boxes the night of the accident. That's how she got hurt. At the hospital, she
kept asking me if the kitty had to get stitches, too."

Tears burned Eve's eyes, a sob tearing from her throat. "Michael, how can I ever forgive myself?"

He turned, gathered her in his arms, his own cheeks wet with tears. They clung to each other until Eve cried herself to sleep.

Heart heavy, Michael guided the sleepy Eve to the truck and buckled her into the front seat. He wove his way through the maze of horse trailers, trainers, kids and horses, the chaos and excitement he'd loved long ago. The world he'd seen her start to delight in. He'd never forget her face after Innisfree had won his first race, the way she'd run to him, eyes shining, face beaming, arms eager to hold him. And last night, in his arms, she'd been fire and tenderness, magic and yet so real, her lovemaking the purest, most perfect thing Michael had known.

Yes, she was hurting. It tore his heart out to see the shattered places in her soul. But they would get through this, he and Eve. Sometimes love could hurt, but it could also heal. She should know that now, but even after all that had happened, she didn't recognize the miracle she'd worked in Rory's heart. Michael would find a way to show her. It wouldn't be easy to work past the rough edges of everything that had happened. But they'd do it together.

The trailer might be empty, Rory would be gone for a while, but he still had Eve. He held tight to that thought as he guided the truck and trailer through the winding Irish roads. He had to. Every time he glanced at her fragile face, haunted even as she slept, he heard her cry. *I wish I'd never come here—look what happens to everyone I love—*

But what would I be without you? Michael thought, throat tight. *Alone.* Even in the midst of a crowd of kids, a farm full of animals, a lifetime's worth of friends. But this time, he'd have the sense to know it.

Michael pulled to a stop in front of the farmhouse, so weary he could hardly see straight. Sean had taken care of the farm work, but there were still things to check out at the castle—Bridey's dog had supposedly been left in Rory's care. Once he got Eve settled inside, he'd send one of the farmhands from Glenammura over to feed Bonaparte. Thank God the pug had long ago found a way to push open a back window to go outside when nature demanded or there would've been a hell of a mess to clean up. And things were enough of a mess already.

Eve stirred at the sound of the truck door being opened. She straightened, rubbed her eyes. Michael winced as he saw the moment memories flooded back, drowning her in pain and loss.

"Thought I'd carry you up to bed," he said. "Then, once I get the trailer unhitched, fix us something to eat."

"I'm not hungry."

"Eve, starving yourself isn't going to change anything."

Her eyes struggled to focus. "Shouldn't I go to the castle? Bonaparte—"

"I'll send someone over."

"But he doesn't like strangers."

"I'll go myself then. But first let me get you inside. You look like you're ready to drop."

She looked damned stubborn for a moment, then nodded. He helped her out, looping one arm around her waist as they started up to the door—holding her, to steady her? Or because he was suddenly scared to let her go?

He was just reaching for the door knob when it swung open, Sean standing in the doorway. "Hey, Mick! How'd the race g—" His honest, puppy-dog eyes flashed to Eve, curled up in a bundle of misery against Michael. Confusion and concern warred in his features. Sean stepped back to let them inside.

"Mick, what happened? What's wrong?" Sean demanded, looking from one to the other.

"It's a long story and Eve's tired. I'm going to take

her upstairs to rest, then I'll come down and we can talk."

Michael winced as he walked past Sean's room, with its bright windows and pictures of his racing days all over the walls. He passed what had been Rory's room, shades still drawn, closed tight like a secret, cutting off light, locking everyone out. The way the boy had been before Kilrain and Eve had opened doors inside him.

Michael couldn't keep himself from taking Eve past the guest bedrooms where kids stayed on overnights as rewards when they'd done well with therapy or their parents needed a break from the demands of taking care of them. He needed Eve in his bedroom. His bed. The place where he'd dreamed she'd sleep for the rest of their lives.

He pushed open the door, flicked on the light. Prints of horses hung over the big Georgian bed Bridey had given him, a red leather wing chair tucked beside the fireplace. He'd never noticed how lonely it looked there. As soon as he had time, he'd get another chair for Eve. On the opposite walls hung a mishmash of drawings, crayoned or penciled by little hands. Most were barely recognizable, but every one of them was of horses.

"Do you want to lie down? I can turn back the bed."

"No. I just . . . just want to be alone for a little while. I need some time to think." She turned huge green eyes to his, and he could still see the redness from when she'd been crying. "Michael, I don't mean to . . . to hurt you. Please understand."

He didn't want to. He wanted to scoop her in his arms and hold on, tight. But she was here, in his room, on his farm. She didn't have a car, couldn't drive—unless you counted the times Sean had let her tool around the farm roads in his car just for fun.

She wasn't going anywhere for now.

"I . . . I wish you'd go check on Bonaparte now," she said. "I can't help worrying. Take Sean with you. He deserves to know everything that happened."

"I don't want to leave you alone."

"I'm used to it. Need it. I've been by myself for so long I'm still not quite used to having people about all the time. Especially when I'm trying to sort things out. Please try to understand."

Michael hesitated, reluctant. He wanted to stay right there with her, force her to share her pain, her loss, show her shared burdens were lighter. But didn't she deserve time alone if she needed it? Didn't loving someone mean giving them what they needed? It *would* take time to get used to always having people around if you'd spent most of your life alone. Her request was understandable.

"All right," he said.

She smiled, her lips quivering. "Thank you, Michael. For . . . everything. Even after everything that happened, I'll never forget—" she stopped, something that scared him darting into her eyes. But she finished, soothing his nerves. "How wonderful it was to watch you ride."

Michael fought back the knot of panic, struggled to smile himself. She was just hurt, exhausted. It all seemed too much for her. But by tomorrow things would start to look better. He'd let her hold the new baby lamb he'd seen in the pasture on the way in. He'd let her help him with the kids' sessions. And he'd make love to her, show her with every stroke of his hand, every brush of his lips how much he needed her. He'd take her to see Bridey—Bridey, who had seen so much in her life, trouble and joy. Bridey, who had a way of making the world seem brighter, no matter how dark it was before you came to her for solace.

Michael cupped his hand over the softness of Eve's cheek, looked deep into her eyes. "I love you. We'll talk later."

Eve swallowed hard, and it took all her strength to keep her voice from breaking. "I love you, too. Maybe . . . maybe I will sleep for a while. You can wake me up later, when dinner is ready."

"Sleep as long as you want."

Guilt gnawed inside her, but she fought to keep it out of her eyes until Michael slipped out of the door. He shut it behind him, leaving her in the room still filled with him: the scent of him from soaps and clothes. The love in him captured in the drawings by children whose lives he'd touched. The roots Michael had deep down into the Irish soil, captured by furniture loved and worn and aged through generations. Being in this room was like being inside Michael's heart, the place she wanted so much to belong.

But things didn't always turn out the way you wanted them to. She should know that by now.

She watched from the window until Michael and Sean left the house, heard the roar of the motor starting. Michael's car. Sean had left his behind, thank God. If she left a note, hopefully they'd understand. Eve splashed water on her face, dragged Michael's brush through her hair, then made her way down the stairs thanking God Sean Murphy was the most trusting man on earth. She remembered his laughter the first bright, sunny day he'd taken her driving around the farm. "This is the only place I can keep my keys where I won't lose 'em," he'd said as he pointed to the ignition of his car.

She scrawled a quick note, put it on the table. She looked one more time around the farm's bright kitchen with its scarred, much loved table and mismatched chairs, then she slipped out the door.

It was amazing how long a ten-minute car ride could be when you spent the whole time worrying about the person you were leaving behind, Michael thought. Harder than expected to explain what had happened at Glengarry. Finding Rory there and Eve's daughter. The wager the boy had made risking Innisfree. The accident that had all but cost Victoria's life, the boy's decision and all it had cost him. Then Moran showing up, taking the boy away, and Eve's crushing guilt.

"Guilt?" Sean said, amazed. "The woman worked a miracle with that lad. I can hardly believe what you're telling me. That the boy is so changed."

"Eve can only see that he lost the horse because of her. That Moran found him because of her. She's been through hell and there's nothing I can do about it."

"I think you've already done plenty, Mick," Sean said. "I've seen the way she looks at you."

"I love her." Blunt, but honest, the words hung between the two men as Michael piloted the car to the foot of the lane leading up to Kilrain. "I didn't intend to. Didn't want to. Sometimes, I'm not even sure how it happened."

"You pushed her. You made her mad. You wouldn't let her keep up that nice, safe little wall she had built around her. Maybe she only came out of it at first because she wanted to knock you're thick Irish head off. But what matters is that she did come out. And that gave her a chance to . . . to feel."

"She's felt more pain than anything else. She thinks everything that happened was her fault."

"You'll show her it wasn't. Things happen. Sometimes when you jump over a fence, you crash. Looks like disaster, your life over. Then, one day, you wake up and there's a stubborn mick standing over you, dragging you off your arse and out of your self-pity. Making damned sure you try again."

Michael pulled to a stop at the foot of the lane, parked the car, and killed the motor. Still a little bewildered, he turned and looked at his friend. "I never expected this to happen."

"Don't I know it! Been dodging the ladies ever since you bought Glenammura. If you could have seen the wake of broken hearts and sighing women you've left behind. Enough to make a grown man cry at the waste of it."

Sean chuckled, then sobered. "Really, man. I'm damned happy for you. It's time you stopped blaming yourself for what happened with Gail. It was a lifetime ago, and we were different men, the both of us. One of the best things that came out of my accident was that neither one of us married her. But I've been watching you for years, and it seemed damned unfair when I thought you'd miss out on a wife, a family of your own altogether."

Sean's cheeks turned red—too much sentiment for one afternoon. Michael was damned relieved himself when his friend shot him a cocky grin. "Besides, maybe if I can get you married off to Eve, I'll have a chance with the ladies myself. In fact, I've been thinking I might follow your example. You know, I never could stand for you to go over a fence and not go over right after."

"I don't understand."

Sean averted his gaze, a little sheepish. "I've been thinking about asking Majella to go to one of the sessions at the pub with me. I couldn't dance, but maybe she wouldn't mind the limp so much."

"You've had your eye on Joy's mum? Why didn't you ask her before now?"

Sean shrugged. "I thought she was about perfect for you, but if you're with Eve, then maybe there's no harm in my trying."

Michael's throat constricted. He cleared his throat gruffly. "She'd be lucky to have you. You're the best man I know," he said, wishing he could say so much more, knowing Sean would hear it anyway.

"Remind me to thank Eve for putting the idea in my head."

Sean grabbed Michael's hand, his smile warmer, real. "I wish you happiness, Mick. Both of you. And I know you'll take care of her the way she deserves, the way you take care of everyone you care about. You don't know how to do anything different."

They climbed out of the car, started up the rutted path. Michael dragged in a lungful of meadow-sweetened air, feeling better already. Sean was right. He'd cleaned up messes before, worked through hurt and pain. If Michael Halloran was one thing it was stubborn. He'd help Eve see the truth—that she wasn't responsible for what had happened. Sometimes good came, even out of the worst crashes, physical or emotional. And good had come out of her relationship with Rory—more good than anything that boy had ever known.

Michael was whistling by the time they reached Kilrain. Bonaparte objected, gumming his pants leg to death.

"He wants to stand up for you at the wedding," Sean teased.

Michael grabbed the little dog by the scruff of his wrinkly neck, and lifted him into his arms. "Get mad as you want, you little tyrant. That position's already been taken. That is, Sean-o, if you're willing."

Sean's eyes warmed, but his grin was pure hellion. "The things I do to keep you out of trouble. Fine. I'll do it. But I'd rather spend a month in traction again than wear an eejit tie."

The air was cleared by the time they got back to the farmhouse, and Michael knew Sean was as grateful for that as he was. Now, if he could just find a way to ease Eve's pain, help her start to heal. Maybe the little stowaway he had hooked under his arm would help. Bonaparte snorted in disdain at the undignified way he was being carried. Somehow, Michael suspected, the ungrateful little dictator had wriggled his ugly way into Eve's heart.

She hadn't turned on the lights, Michael noticed, in spite of the coming of twilight. Maybe she'd slept after all. He'd take the dog up to see her.

"I'm going upstairs," Michael called over his shoulder to Sean, who'd crossed to the table.

"Michael—I think you'd better wait." Something about Sean's voice made him edgy. He turned. Nervousness took a leap into something tighter, like dread. Sean's face paled. "She's not upstairs. She left a note."

"She has to be somewhere close," he said, trying to soothe himself. "Can't get far without a car."

Sean winced. "She took mine."

Numb, Michael set Bonaparte down on the floor, made his way to the table, his legs feeling wooden, his chest cold.

Dear Michael,

   Please forgive me for leaving like this. I've been so hurt, so confused. I've felt so helpless. But not anymore. Try to understand this is something I have to do. I would have waited, told you face to face, but I knew you'd try to stop me. I have to do this alone. Whatever else happens, you've given me the strength to do what I have to. I'll always be grateful for that.

                                                            Love,
                                                            Eve

   P.S. Sean, I'm sorry about the car. I promise you'll get it back in one piece.

Michael could feel Sean watching him, heard him shifting back and forth uneasily on his feet.

"Mick, what does it say?"

Michael tried to close out the sound of Eve's voice in his head. *I should never have come here . . . my fault . . . my fault . . .*

"She's gone."

"Yeah, but gone where? She must have said—"

"No. But she . . . was afraid I'd stop her." Michael looked down at the little pug scrabbling at his boot. "That must mean . . ." he could hardly bring himself to say it. ". . . she must have gone back to America."

"That doesn't make any sense! All her stuff is still at the castle. She probably doesn't even have her passport."

"Plenty of people keep it with them. She may have

had it in her purse. As for the rest of the stuff—maybe she was in such a hurry to get away she just didn't care she was leaving it behind."

What about you, Halloran? Didn't she care she was leaving you behind? A voice mocked him. *And leaving Rory, too . . .*

No. She wouldn't do that, he told himself. But he couldn't forget the desolation in her eyes, the guilt, the slow shattering of the confidence she'd worked so hard to earn these past weeks. She'd run away before. Who was to say she wouldn't try to outrun this pain the way she had the pain of Victoria's rejection?

"Go after her, man!" Sean said, grabbing his arm. "For God's sake—"

The buzz of the phone made both men jump. Sean spun, dove for it. "That has to be Eve. Please let it be—Hello?"

Michael watched him, frozen, saw the color wash from his friend's face.

"When? How long? I understand. We'll be there right away."

Michael gripped the edge of a chair, holding on, sensing, somehow, his whole world was about to be swept away. "What is it?" he demanded when Sean hung up the phone.

"Bridey. She—they say she's dying."

Michael choked back a cry. "I don't believe—she wouldn't—"

He crumpled the letter. Wherever Eve was, he'd find her, dammit, but for now he had no choice. He had to go to the hospital. He couldn't let Bridey die.

24

*E*ve white-knuckled the steering wheel, glancing down at the crumpled map she'd bought at a gas station three hours before after nearly taking out one of the pumps by zigging when she should have zagged. It was harder than it looked, driving on the wrong side of the road—maybe it would have been better if she was good at driving, period. But except for Sean's allowing her the use of his car, it had been years since she'd been behind the wheel. And the narrow Irish roads had made this trip a test of Eve's resolve, with hairpin turns bordered by roof-high hedges that kept a driver from seeing another car practically until she felt the wind as it zipped by.

Twice she'd been hopelessly lost. Might have ended up back in Dublin if it hadn't been for an old man with an apple-cheeked face and a roguish twinkle in his eyes that must have made him a lady-killer in his day. Tipping his tweed cap gallantly, he'd been happy to point her in the direction of Trevor Butler's place, "the finest trainer you'll find in Ireland since Mick Halloran broke our hearts and vanished into the mist."

She'd winced at the mention of Michael. He'd have found her note by now. God knew what he was thinking. She'd hated to leave it, knew it would worry him, probably hurt him. But she hadn't dared be more specific. If he'd figured out what she was about to do he would have come after her. If there was one thing she'd learned about the man she'd fallen in love with it was that Michael Halloran couldn't bear to let people he loved face their dragons alone. And she had to do this alone, Eve thought grimly.

Her gaze caught a white sign lettered in red—BUTLER FARMS, TREVOR BUTLER, HORSE TRAINER. Eve's heart thudded in her chest, a bubble of panic pushing hard. She'd been desperate to find this place, but now that she'd identified the rolling hills to her right as the farm she'd been seeking, she had to pull over, stop for a moment. Remember how to breathe and try to make her hands quit shaking.

Oh, God, what was she doing? Charging in like this, demanding to talk to her daughter. Chad would never let her within a hundred yards of Victoria. And even if she managed to talk to the girl, there was no way Victoria would listen to what Eve said. Victoria hated her.

Old pain flared, but it was tempered with something harder, something new. As it happened, Eve was none too pleased with Victoria either at the moment. Her lips firmed. Maybe it was time she gave her daughter something real to hate her for, so Victoria didn't have to rely on the lies Chad had filled her head with. Whatever happened in the future, Eve resolved this was one time her daughter would hear what her mother had to say.

She'd rehearsed it a dozen times during the long drive, said it a dozen different ways. She'd felt sick in the pit of her stomach, dreading what she might discover about the daughter she'd loved from a distance for so long. But she could stall on this stretch of road forever and it wouldn't make it any easier to say the things she needed to say. Better to get it over with, worry about picking up the pieces afterward.

Squaring her shoulders, Eve put the car into gear and maneuvered her way down the long snaking drive toward the cluster of bright white buildings that comprised the stables. So this was where Victoria was staying. A tidy Elizabethan manor house, tended lovingly through the years, sat like a queen on the highest point, much newer barns sprawling every which way like ladies of honor in the house's wake. Horses of every size and color dotted the pastures while equestrians of every age buzzed around like swarms of bees in riding boots.

It was too busy, too crowded, Eve thought, remembering the sweet sense of serenity that blanketed Glenammura. But then, Michael's was a special farm. This was a training ground for competitors, filled with horses and kids being taught to ride. And to win at any cost the way her daughter was willing to.

Eve winced. Was Innisfree racing around one of these unfamiliar fields? Scared? Alone in spite of the confusion all around him? Waiting for Rory to come?

And where was Rory? Back with his parents in Dublin by now? Probably. But he'd promised to come back to Glenammura the minute he turned eighteen. And as he'd walked away with Moran he'd looked stronger than Jamie and Oonagh, stronger than poverty or the streets that had almost claimed him. More sure of himself, more confident than Eve had ever been. Even without his horse, the boy shone, rare, unique, the brightest treasure she'd found in Kilrain.

Her daughter needed to realize just how special he was.

Eve pulled to a stop among a scattering of cars in a parking area. Brushing her bangs back from her forehead, she climbed out of the car. It would be plenty difficult to walk up to the house and demand to see her daughter. Chad had probably told Moira Butler the whole terrible story about how she'd lost custody because she'd neglected her child. The entire Butler family would probably run away as if she were the Wicked Witch of the West. But nobody—not Chad, not an army of Butlers—could keep her away from Victoria. Not today. No matter what.

A pair of girls were strolling past, giggling, the two looking as if they were about Victoria's age. Eve called out, "Excuse me, may I ask you a question?"

The taller girl smiled. "Sure. I'm Dara Butler. This is my da's farm. I should be able to point you in the right direction."

"I'm looking for Victoria Tolliver. She trains here. Do you know where I might find her?"

Something unreadable flashed across Dara's face. "Saw her just a few minutes ago. Out by the back pasture."

She hardly believed her luck in finding Victoria so easily.

Dara Butler's friend, a ginger-haired girl with eyes like a cat's, made a face. "She's out there moping. Found the perfect horse, but all her da's money can't tame the thing. No one can even get in the same pasture with it. Tries to kill you every time you cross the fence."

Eve's heart squeezed. Snippy though the girl might be, she was also right. All that Tolliver money would be worthless in this case. There had been plenty of money and skill spent trying to straighten the horse out in the years before Innisfree came to Glenammura. The horse had told the best trainers in Ireland to go to hell, from what Michael had said. Only Rory had been able to reach him. Innisfree wouldn't forget Rory for any price. Loyalty like that ran bone-deep.

Eve forced a smile. "Which way is the pasture?"

The ginger-haired girl pointed. "Be careful. Trevor's ready to shoot someone. Just can't decide who to shoot first—the horse or Victoria. She racked up Trevor's best jumper to win some stupid bet and then she came home with that worthless piece of dog meat that practically kicked in the side of his trailer. He's not too happy. And neither is she." She smirked with that snide satisfaction teenage girls are masters at.

Whoever the girl was, she didn't like Victoria. Perhaps it was jealousy, for whatever reason. Eve hurried down the path the girl had indicated, winding down toward the barns. She kept her head down, praying her luck would hold. From what the girls said, Tori was alone. Hopefully Chad would stay wherever he was—as long as it was far away from the pasture.

Her quick step faltered when she rounded a corner and caught her first glimpse of the lone girl sitting on top of the fence. Shoulders slumped, head down, Tori was a picture of misery, while in the pasture beyond, Innisfree dashed madly from fence-edge to fence-edge, as if the place were closing in on him, as if he couldn't breathe. A cluster of grapes lay crushed into the dust just inside the paddock where the horse had obviously taken his frustrations out on them. Angry as she was with Victoria, she felt a squeeze of sympathy for the girl. Eve knew just how deeply it cut to be rejected when you wanted something so badly.

Part of her wished she could comfort her daughter, that instinct she'd always had to ease Tori's pain. A chance she'd been waiting for ever since her baby had been taken from her arms. But this time she couldn't tell her everything was going to turn out fine. And she couldn't pretend she didn't know how much what she had to say was going to hurt.

Eve sucked a deep breath into lungs white-hot with tension. "Victoria?"

The girl turned around. She should have looked much better than when Eve had last seen her, crumpled on the ground after being thrown by her horse. But somehow, she seemed worse. The scrape on her cheekbone slashed bright red against a face still too pale. Swollen, red eyes looked as if she'd been crying there, all alone. Eve hurt so much for her—a girl so woebegone, terribly young and vulnerable. As if the defiant, self-centered girl Eve had seen at the horse show earlier or the hurting, desperate girl clinging to Moira Butler, so anxious to escape from Eve, had never existed.

Eve had felt lucky that Chad wasn't around, but now she was irritated instead. How could he just leave Victoria alone out here, so sad?

Victoria's eyes widened in surprise and Eve could sense her struggle to hide her emotions—the wistful confusion, disappointment, and burning humiliation there a moment before. She slid down off the fence. The easier to make a run for it if she needed to? Eve wondered.

"How did you find me here?" Victoria demanded, acting as if she were brushing her bangs out of her eyes. Eve knew she was really checking to make sure she'd wiped away any traces of tears she might have missed.

"At Glengarry Mrs. Butler said I could check on you here. How—" Eve hesitated. It was absurd to ask how Victoria was. She looked like she'd just lost a war. Eve shifted what she was going to say. "Are you getting stiff yet? You hit the ground pretty hard."

"Well, I'm fine, as you can see. No broken bones."

Only a broken heart, Eve could see all too well. "When I saw you there, on the ground—I was so—" She couldn't finish, gasped, as Innisfree charged at the fence.

"No!" Victoria whimpered as he aimed straight for the boards. He stopped at the last moment, kicked, opening up a gash on one leg where he'd scraped the wood. He wasn't even trying to jump, Eve knew instinctively. He was just trying to get away. Away from whatever demons still haunted his memory.

White circles ringed his eyes, his nostrils flared red, lather bubbled at the corners of his mouth. While his coat—brushed to a sheen by Rory every day—was roughed up in spots where he'd crashed into trees, fences, trailers, whatever he saw as keeping him away from his boy.

Eve had been scared to death of the horse when she'd seen him in the stall at Glenammura, pacing, kicking out, that wild look in his eyes. But if this is how Innisfree behaved before Rory came into his life, Eve could understand why the other trainers had wanted to give up on the horse. She'd known from the beginning that what Rory had done was remarkable, but now, looking at the horse, who seemed to be shattering before her eyes, she realized just how much courage it must have taken to take that first step into Innisfree's pasture.

"How long has he been like this?" she asked.

"From the moment Mr. Butler tried to get him in the trailer. But he . . . he just needs time. He'll get used to it here. Mr. Butler's not so sure, but Daddy says if that kid can ride him, I'll be able to do it, too."

Eve thought for a moment, looking at the miserable horse. "And what do you think?"

"He's my horse. And I'm good. You don't know how much I want this. I'm going to make it happen. Daddy says I can't let anything stop me."

"From having what you want? But what if it isn't right for Innisfree?"

"I won him. Fair and square."

"Not fair, Tori. You know that as well as I do."

Victoria's chin stuck out, defensive in spite of her pain. "That boy signed the contract. He knew what would happen if he didn't finish the race."

She was changing again, getting that look that reminded Eve of Chad. Stubborn. Blocking out any perspective but his own. It was legal. Binding. He'd gotten what he'd wanted, so then it must be right no matter who he trampled over to get his way. Did Tori really believe that, too? Or was she trying desperately to justify keeping Innisfree?

"I saw what happened on that course," Eve said. "You could have been killed if Rory hadn't turned back. He saved your life."

"My boot could've pulled free any time all by itself."

"Do you have any idea what that cost him? Trying to help you?"

"A horse that didn't even belong to him anyway."

"You know better. Look at Innisfree! My God, Tori, you've always had the best of everything, anything you wanted. Horses, school, riding lessons, trips all over the world. Parents who love you."

"Oh, please!"

"All right, then. A . . . a father who has always been there for you. Rory grew up in the worst part of Dublin. His parents neglected him."

"You neglected me. Isn't that what the courts said?"

"God knows, I've wanted to tell you what happened for so long. What really happened. My side of the story."

"It wasn't your fault. There was nothing you could do," Victoria said as if reciting by rote. "What mother wouldn't let a four-year-old climb around on wooden boxes stacked halfway to the ceiling in a storeroom? Especially at one o'clock in the morning?"

"I had to take you to work with me. The baby-sitter was sick. We had to eat." Eve saw Victoria flinch, sensed she was remembering what Michael had said at Glengarry. Her brow creased, troubled. Was it possible she'd remembered at least a little? How shabby the apartment had been? The games they'd played when the room got too cold? Making "igloos" out of frayed blankets and saying they belonged to the Polar Bear Club?

"I'm sure Daddy wouldn't have let me starve!" Victoria exclaimed. Was she defending Chad to Eve or trying to reassure herself?

Eve ground her teeth, biting back words that could only devastate her daughter. Starve? Maybe Chad wouldn't have let Victoria starve, but the harder things got for Eve the better he'd liked it. The more pressure Eve was under the closer he figured he got to what he wanted—her surrendering Victoria. He'd probably seen the accident as a godsend. Wait and watch for your opportunity, then go for the jugular. That was the Tolliver way.

Eve struggled to find the right words, stay focused. "This isn't about me, Tori. It isn't about what happened years ago. It's about what happened at Glengarry. Didn't you wonder why Rory would risk a horse he loved in exchange for just an hour of your time? Don't you still wonder?"

"He wasn't going to touch me." She gave a little shudder. "I made sure he knew that."

"Rory would never do such a thing!" Eve said in a flash of defensiveness. "He knew about the daughter I'd lost touch with, about how much I wanted a chance just to talk to you. I'd been writing letters, saving them in case you ever were willing to read them. He found them. When he realized that you were my daughter he hoped he could give me the chance I'd been wanting for so long. He risked Innisfree to win me an hour with you."

Victoria stared, taken aback.

"He didn't race for money, or glory. He didn't even race for himself. He raced for me and—I know you'll have a hard time believing it—but he raced for you, too. He couldn't stand to see either of us throw away a chance for something he would have given anything to have. A chance to love each other, be there for each other, be the other half of the family neither of us ever had. The bottom line is this, Tori: A boy probably saved your life and in return you've taken away everything he has in the world. I know you want the horse. I *know* that. But it isn't right for you to take him."

Victoria's face crumpled. "You only care about this because of that other kid. I've got the scar to prove just how much you cared about me. Weren't you the one who let me knock that whole stack of boxes down on my head?"

Eve's heart ached for Victoria. She was groping to hold on to everything Chad had taught her to believe. She was fighting and scared because all those lies were crumbling around her.

Eve didn't want to hurt her. Had no choice. She curled her fingers tight into her palms, her eyes burning. "I remember every detail about that night you got hurt. Do you?"

"The only thing that matters is that I've got a five-inch scar across my forehead because of you!"

"I've blamed myself forever, but the truth is there was nothing I could have done to stop it."

"The judge didn't think so. He wouldn't even let you near me again. And it seemed like that was okay with you! I didn't hear a word from you for fourteen years—not a birthday card, not a Christmas present."

"I sent things every birthday, every Christmas. I tried to see you, fight for custody, but you were in Europe. I couldn't reach you. I didn't even know where you were half the time. I have books and books filled with pictures, things I wanted to give you, dresses I wanted to buy. Even Ireland—the only reason I thought to come here was that I had dreamed of coming with you."

"Oh, spare me!"

The expression on her face was so much like Chad's Eve wanted to retch. It hurt. Hurt so bad she could barely talk.

"What kind of person are you, Tori? What kind of person takes advantage of someone who has suffered as much as Rory? Someone trying so hard to do what's right? Look at that horse! He's beating himself to a pulp! He's tearing his heart out because he loves that boy so much. You say you care about Innisfree? How are you going to feel when he breaks a leg thrashing around trying to get away from you?"

As if he heard, Innisfree kicked out at something not even there, then stood, exhausted, chest heaving, coat sweat-soaked.

"Will you have the courage to put him down yourself when that happens? No. You'll be off somewhere with your father while somebody else does the ugly stuff for you. But Rory—Rory would be right there, holding on to Innisfree, talking to him, crying with him until it was over."

Victoria cried out, a ragged sob. "Leave me alone!"

"Oh, Tori," Eve whispered. "All those years I dreamed of finding you again. I never expected this. The little girl who climbed up on those boxes that night—she was the most loving, brave, bright little girl who'd ever been. You'd been curled up, sleeping on the blankets I'd brought, the horse I made you for Christmas tucked under your arm. Fly—that's what you named her. Do you remember?"

"Why would I care about one stupid toy?" Victoria scoffed, but something in her eyes made Eve suspect—suspect what? That Victoria *did* remember the little stuffed animal? It was ridiculous to think that was possible. Fly was probably the first thing Chad had thrown out, along with the secondhand clothes Eve had picked out at thrift shops and worked so hard to keep spotless. He'd probably brought Tori home to a room stuffed with shiny new plastic toys, silken-haired dolls and stuffed animals fat and plush and perfect with the price tags still on them.

"I went into another room to check on something," Eve continued. "But you had such a big heart. You heard something crying. You didn't even look for me. You just went off to find it. A kitten . . . this tiny gray and white kitten stuck up on top of the boxes." She fought to put distance between this angry girl and that pain, but it was no use. Eve's voice broke on the memory of her intrepid little one. "Tori, don't you remember? You didn't even call me. You just climbed up, trying to reach it. But you wouldn't put your stuffed horse down. You said you were afraid she would fly away. When the boxes fell—oh, God, even in the emergency room all you kept asking was whether or not the kitty was okay."

Memories haunted Victoria's eyes in spite of how hard she tried to hide them. "That was a long time ago."

"Not so long ago, sweetheart. All this time I've wanted to find my Tori again," Eve said. "But if you keep Innisfree—if you can keep Rory's horse knowing what he tried to do for you, seeing how desperate, how miserable Innisfree is without him—then my Tori doesn't exist anymore."

She braced one hand against the fence, fighting to steady herself. "Other people have decided a lot of things for you, Victoria. I'm sure your father picked out what schools you went to, what trainers you learned to ride under. The best money could buy. The courts decided to take me out of your life and not let me see you until now. It's up to you whether or not you'll ever decide to let me back in your life again, find out who I am, see whether or not you'd like a mother." Eve struggled to keep the tears from starting, feared if she did she'd never be able to finish what she needed to say. "Whatever you decide is up to you, Tori. I have so much I want to tell you, so many memories of you when you were tiny and we loved each other. When you were all I had in the world and all I ever wanted."

Eve had struck a nerve. Victoria bit down hard on her lower lip.

"But whatever happens between us, you have other decisions to make. Big ones about who you want to be when you grow up. The kind of person who takes what isn't yours no matter what it costs someone else or the kind who climbs up on boxes to save stray kittens. No matter which you choose, it changes you."

Tears welled up in Victoria's eyes. She turned, looked at Innisfree, so miserable in the pasture. "I forgot—forgot about the kitten. You went back and found it, made sure they didn't just throw it out in the snow. You promised we could go see it, but you never took me."

"Before I could, social services placed you with your father. But I went and made sure the kitten had a good home. Whenever I saw you, you'd ask—"

"You promised you'd come get me, too. That I was only staying with Daddy for a little while."

"I couldn't believe they'd really take you away from me. I shouldn't have promised, but I kept hoping, even to the last moment—"

"You didn't cry—when you gave me to Daddy. I wanted you. I cried and cried but you didn't."

"How could I make it any harder for you? Tori, I was screaming inside. For weeks, all I could do was cry. I'd hold your little clothes to my face, smell your smell, imagined you holding on to Fly and thinking of me, remembering me. I didn't think anyone could take those memories away from us, those four precious years. You were so little, but so . . . so smart. I was sure you wouldn't forget me. But now, I don't care if you do forget me as long as you remember yourself. Who you are. Who you want to be."

"What the hell?" Chad's voice made Victoria jump. Eve's heart slammed to her toes. "What are you doing here, Eve? How the hell did you track us down here?"

"She came to tell me what a terrible person I'll be if I keep Innisfree," Victoria said, but her voice was strained, fragile.

"For God's sake! The horse is ours! Get over it!"

"I wanted him to be mine." Victoria's voice quavered. "I wanted it so much. But he's not. He . . . he never will be."

Eve watched in wonder, hardly daring to hope. "Tori, do you mean—"

"Innisfree loves Rory. And when somebody loves somebody else like that it's wrong to . . . to take them away."

"Victoria, that horse is worth a fortune! You don't want it?—fine, we'll sell it at a profit and buy you a horse you *do* want! Don't knuckle under just because your bleeding heart mother comes around whining!"

"She's right, Daddy. I could have gotten hurt, but Rory turned back to help me. How could I ever really be happy taking his horse? Even if I *could* ride it?"

"Victoria, it's not for you to say."

"I'm giving the horse back. Sending Innisfree where he belongs. Or I swear, I'll never ride again."

Chad wheeled on Eve, furious. "Dammit, this is your fault!"

"I hope so," she breathed.

Defeated, enraged, Chad sneered. "Fine. You want that horse so much, you go out and get him! A one-time offer! You always were scared to death of animals."

Eve looked from Chad's mocking eyes to her daughter's wary ones.

"No," Victoria warned. "No, don't. It's too dangerous. You saw how Innisfree kicks—"

Eve slipped a lead rope from the fence post, fought down the lump of fear in her throat. Gingerly, she climbed over the fence. It would serve her right if the horse put her in the hospital. What did she know about him? Except that he was lost and Rory had found him. And somehow, maybe, please God, maybe Innisfree had helped her find her daughter once again.

Innisfree eyed her warily, pawed at the ground, and gave a defiant snort.

Eve held her breath and scooped up some of the crushed grapes. "It's time to go home, Innisfree," she murmured in the tone she'd heard Rory use so many times. "Home, you beautiful bastard."

Did the horse recognize the endearment? Smell something familiar about her? The scent of Glenammura's hills? Or did he remember that the boy had loved her, too?

Eve wasn't sure. It didn't matter. Innisfree danced back for just a moment as she got close. She extended her hand, the grapes balanced on her flattened palm. "We have to go home, Innisfree, so when Rory comes back, you'll be waiting."

She steeled herself not to move as Innisfree stretched out his neck, sniffed the grapes. He delicately took one between velvety lips, his bristly whiskers tickling Eve's palm. Slowly, carefully, she snapped the lead rope onto the ring in his halter.

She turned to where Victoria and Chad stood: Chad astounded, Victoria looking fragile, sad, and yet . . . dared Eve hope—*proud*? At least intrigued, as if wondering what kind of woman her mother really was.

Maybe the time would come when she'd want to find out for herself.

Somebody near the barn saw what was going on, called inside. Moira Butler came bustling out, brushing straw from her hands.

"What in the world?" she gasped.

"She's taking Innisfree back where he belongs," Victoria said.

"Is she now?" Moira smiled so wide, so warm. "We'll see if your mother can load this pretty devil into the trailer without caving it in. Victoria, run off and get Trevor."

Tori nodded, dashed off, Moira following close behind.

Chad glared at Eve, but she could see the fear in his eyes. "Will you just stay away from her now?"

"She may not want me to anymore." Eve clung to the possibility, the miracle she'd been praying for for so long.

"Don't even think of trying to tell her lies about me! I'll sue you for libel so fast it'll make the last lawsuit look like a picnic."

"Lies are your style, Chad, not mine. Besides, I want to give Tori a mother, not take away her father. Unlike you, I always knew she needed us both. If I hadn't believed that, I never would have let you back into her life when you came looking for her."

"She was my child! When my parents said I had a duty— I thought I'd just get it over with. I never knew how much I'd love her."

"That's the one good thing you've done as far as I'm concerned. You did love her. I'd love to scare the hell out of you, make you pay for all those years I lost with her— all the pain of not tucking her in at night, watching her school plays, seeing her with her teeth in braces. But that wouldn't give me those moments back. It would only take something away from Victoria, something . . . precious. So you're safe. Not because you deserve it. But because I love Tori more than I hate you. I just wish you could have done the same fourteen years ago."

Chad pulled at the collar of his shirt, clearly uncomfortable. Chad Tolliver was used to wielding power over other people, not having it wielded against him. He couldn't fathom that anyone could have it and choose not to use it.

"In exchange for my silence, you just have to answer one question," Eve said.

Chad glared at her, defiant, trapped.

"Why? Why did you have to take her away from me completely? You knew how much I loved her. Knew I would have given my life for her. That what happened when she cut herself was an accident. So why?"

"Because I could."

Because he could. That's was why he'd taken Tori. Left Eve in hell for fourteen years. It had cost her so much, his selfishness. Cost Tori so much. But he hadn't taken everything. Underneath it all, Tori was still the little girl who saved kittens. In the end, she hadn't taken Innisfree just because she could.

Eve blinked back tears, leaned her face against Innisfree's neck, the warm, silky coat soothing beneath her cheek.

"Now haven't I seen everything?" Trevor Butler said low as he walked toward them. "You can be loading him in the trailer right now if you will, miss."

"I hate to put you to any trouble. I'm staying with Michael Halloran. I'm sure he can pick the horse up himself later."

"Just as soon get him off the property as quick as possible. You lead the way and I'll haul him myself. Follow you to Glenammura. And when you see that boy who was riding him, tell him he can have a job training horses with me any time."

"He's already taken," Eve said. "Isn't he, Innisfree?"

She looked at Victoria, standing a little ways apart, sad but strangely at peace. "Do you want to say goodbye to him? I think he'll let you now."

"Maybe . . . maybe I'll come see him at Halloran's

farm once he gets settled. If you think that would be okay. Rory probably never wants to see me again and Halloran must hate me."

"You'll be welcome at Glenammura any time, Victoria. I . . . I'll be so glad to see you when you come."

"You can call me Tori if you want."

Eve looked into her daughter's eyes, seeing the little girl she had been. She couldn't wait to discover the young woman Victoria was going to be.

"Tori," she whispered softly. "I'll be waiting."

Trevor Butler unhooked the gate, everyone standing at a healthy distance. Eve led Innisfree through the astonished cluster of people to the trailer with its kicked-in side. She couldn't wait to see Michael's face when they pulled in at Glenammura.

"Sometimes you do get what you wish for," she said to Innisfree as she led him into the metal stall and tied his lead rope firm. "Let's fly away home."

25

$\mathcal{S}$he was dying.

Grief squeezed Michael so tight he couldn't breathe as he looked down at Bridey's face, skin almost transparent, blue veins running in rivers over her hands and face. The eyes that had always been so clear now misted as a young nurse bent over to tuck more blankets around Bridey's frail body.

"So you are Bridey's son, Michael. I've heard so much about you."

"No. No, I'm not her son. We're not related," Michael said automatically, a voice inside him whispering "unless you can be joined at the heart." "How long has she been like this?"

"Since after the solicitor came yesterday. She seemed well enough until then. The doctor said that once she started to fade she shouldn't have lasted this long, but he doesn't know how determined Bridey can be. I think her mind was wandering—in different centuries. She said to tell his lordship to hold his horses. She was waiting for you."

Michael's throat felt on fire. He blinked hard. Dammit, he wasn't going to break down. He was going to rage at Bridey, argue with her, annoy her so much she'd come back from the edge of the grave just to put him in his place.

"A man should be coming in pretty quick, reddish-blond hair, a limp. Name's Sean. He's here for Bridey, too. He's signing some paperwork." Avoiding hospital rooms as much as he can. After Sean's accident the man had been almost phobic about hospitals. Hospital smells, the chrome and shiny lino, the echo of nurses' heels in the hallways, had been shadows from his nightmares.

It was a weakness Bridey had understood. A testimony of Sean's love for her that he managed to come at all. But then, truth was that Michael was glad of time alone with Bridey. From the time they were lads, Sean had always had his big, loving family surrounding him. He'd loved Bridey, but he'd never needed her, been close to her in the same way as Michael had.

He sounded ridiculous. What did it matter to this nurse where Sean was? This was work to her. She saw people die every day, saw people grieve, giant holes torn in their lives where someone they'd loved used to be. No matter how compassionate or caring or skilled this woman was, tonight she would go home to her little house, her own kitchen table where every plate would be set and every face there to smile at.

"I'll watch for him, send him in."

Bridey's eyelids fluttered, and Michael could tell just how hard it was for her to open her eyes. He took her hand in his as if it were made of ash that could crumble away in an instant. Her fingers felt ice cold, a little stiff.

"Bridey?" Michael choked out her name.

She managed to pry her lids open a little farther, her dry lips curving in a smile. "Ah, it's my boy. My boy. I told them you would come. Were after burying me a bit early, they were, but I told them I wouldn't go. Not without saying good-bye to my sweet Michael."

Michael's jaw clenched, tears threatening. He tried to hold them back for her. "It's too soon. I've got so much to tell you. About Eve—how much I love her and how scared I am that she's—" No. He couldn't tell

Bridey Eve was missing. Not now. He groped for something else to say, something that would make Bridey want to hold on, get well. "And what if I do get married?" he asked, suddenly, painfully aware of how sweet that suddenly seemed. Eve in his arms every night while he slept, her face the first thing he'd see every morning. "What do I know about marriage?"

"You're asking a woman who's spent a lifetime in love with a ghost?" Bridey chuckled.

"I need you here," he said, "so I can talk to you. So you can straighten me out when I'm making a mess of things. So you can hold my babies when they come. I'm not ready, Bridey. I'm not ready to let you go."

"It's time, Michael. I'm tired. So tired. And I've kept his lordship waiting long enough." She sighed, seemed to fade before his very eyes. "I'll have to peek at your wee ones from the shadows of Kilrain. You know I'll never be leaving it. The castle will just have to make room for another ghost. You'll not mind, though, will you? A little chain rattling now and then?"

"Not if it's you."

"It will be. So you and Eve love each other. I knew it would be so from the first time I heard her voice. She needed healing, Michael-treasure, and no one in Ireland has a more healing heart than you do. Remember how you'd cart every stray animal you came across up to the castle door? Your mammy and da couldn't let you keep them, what with your da being so weak in the lungs he coughed his head off whenever he got near anything with fur. But you'd bring them to me. I never knew what creature you'd show up with next— a fox with a broken leg, a duckling who'd had one of its wee feet nipped off by a turtle. But the best thing you ever brought me besides the love in your heart was my wee darling Bonaparte. A man grown, you were, but you still showed up on my doorstep, Bonaparte soaked to the skin and shivering, only his wee sweet head peeping out of the burlap bag someone had tried to drown him in."

"I remember." Michael squeezed the words through a raw throat. He'd had a whole farm by then, could have kept an army of pugs if he'd wanted to. But Bridey's age had started to show. She couldn't wander the hills as easily as she once had, chatting up anyone she happened to meet on her way. He didn't want her to be lonely.

"You were always a man made for loving a wife and a brood of babies, Michael. I was so worried you'd miss it all because you still blamed yourself for making one mistake. I'm that glad you've found happiness."

Please, God, he had. Unless Eve had run away . . . But he hadn't been mistaken when he'd seen floodgates break inside her, felt her letting herself love him the night they'd made love in the big bed at Mrs. Cadagon's. He looked down, staring hard at Bridey's hand, trying to keep her from seeing the fears and doubts he knew must be haunting his eyes. She'd always seen straight through him, the good, the bad, everything he was. The miracle of Bridey was that she had loved him—not in *spite* of his flaws, but *because* of them.

Bridey gave a ragged sigh and patted Michael's hand. He could feel every birdlike bone. "Always wondered what it must be like to be able to touch the person you love, feel their skin, the warmth of their breath, to be able to kiss them whenever you chose."

Michael swallowed hard, his heart hurting for this kind, generous, loving woman who had never known the kind of miracle he and Eve had shared last night. What was it like? *It's magic. And you know you'll never forget the way she tasted, like honey and heather, the way she smelled, like soap and flower-scented shampoo, the way her breath caught in her throat just before you kissed her . . .*

"Michael," Bridey asked wistfully, "do you suppose it will be possible for me to touch his lordhip once I reach the other side?"

"I don't know." Michael shook his head. She was

talking about a ghost, something he didn't even believe existed, and his Bridey was almost eager, as if part of her had been waiting for this chance to go to the other side for a long time. Michael winced at a sharp stab of jealousy, felt rotten because of it. Who was he to take away whatever comfort Bridey could find when she was so sick?

"I wonder if heather will still smell as sweet in the spirit world? I'd hate to miss the scent of it or the feel of wind on my face when I stand on the roof of Kilrain's tower. Philosophers chatter on about the afterlife like they know what they're talking about. Is there a heaven? Is there a hell? How many prayers does it take to get a soul out of purgatory? But they never talk about what really matters. Things like Will I smell heather and Will I ever get to hold my wee little Bonaparte again? He'll not understand, my poor babe, why I've gone. It hurts my heart to think about him, Michael, always looking for me, waiting for me, thinking I forgot about him. I'd not cause him that pain."

Michael raised her hand to his lips, kissed her fingers. "He'll always have a home with me. You know that."

Bridey nodded and gave him a shadow of her old smile. "That's what a good brother is for, then, isn't it?" she teased. "My two boys together."

A chuckle rose in Michael's throat, sounding half like a sob. "Bridey, I just want you to know how much you've meant—"

"Don't be wasting what time I have left telling me what I already know. About what we've meant to each other. I've not much time and so much to say. The castle— My solicitor's suspected for years I was crazy. Now he's sure of it. But you don't let him tamper with things." Her fingers tightened on his. "You fight if you have to, Michael. I've got things the way I want them."

"Whatever you want, Bridey." *Just promise not to leave me.*

"I didn't leave Kilrain to you. Plenty of people will

say I was daft. Others will say we must have had a
falling out. It will give the gossips something to talk
about, trying to figure out what you did that got my
feathers so ruffled I took you out of my will. But
you'll always know the real reason. You've got a
home. Always had one. Roots so deep in Irish ground
I don't think you could take a step anywhere on this
island and not feel home welcome you. But Eve—
she's never had anywhere she felt safe. Any place of
her own. You can hear it in her voice, see it in her
eyes."

Michael's eyes widened, incredulous. "You've left
the castle to Eve?" It seemed so right. Most people
would call Bridey crazy, but this made perfect sense—
Bridey with her eccentric blend of daring and common
sense, cutting to the chase, doing what was needed no
matter what anyone else thought about it. Even if it
meant being faithful to a ghost for eighty-five years.

Bridey smiled. "She's been a wanderer her whole
life long, has Eve, and she never wanted to be. Now
she'll have somewhere all her own."

Michael couldn't even imagine the red tape Bridey
must have made her solicitor cut through.

"Simms wanted to put things off—let me think
about it until he could get hold of you so you could
talk me out of it. But I wouldn't have it. I knew he was
hoping I might slip off before I could cause him so
much trouble. But I can be a determined woman,
Michael, when I know what needs to be done."

Michael hated himself for the spark of happiness he
felt. No matter where Eve had gone, she'd have to
come back if she'd inherited Kilrain. She wouldn't be
able to keep running. And when she did come back, he
would make sure she knew that this was where she
belonged, that it didn't matter how rough things got,
they could get through any storm as long as they were
together.

"Michael . . . I'm tired."

"No!" He fought back panic. "Not yet. Just . . . just give me a little while more."

"And if I promise not to leave before I say good-bye? Will you give me a bit of peace then, boyo?"

Michael's eyes narrowed, wary.

"Come, lad, have I ever broken a promise to you?"

"No," he admitted grudgingly. He felt like he was eight years old again, fascinated by Bridey, her delight in him when he was being his most mischievous and her stories of ghosts that gave him such delicious shivers. But not made him afraid, never afraid. The only thing he'd feared was that she'd disappear into the shadows of the castle and never come back to him again. When he'd grown up he'd chuckled over that boyhood dread, ridiculous as monsters in closets and witches on All Hallow's Eve. He'd never realized until now that his worst fear would happen someday. Bridey would slip away from him and even promises couldn't hold her.

"Come now, my sweet lad." The corners of her lips wobbled as she struggled to smile. "I'll not be breaking this promise either." She groped for an extra pillow, cuddled it close in the crook of her body, right against her stomach.

"Are you hurting?" Michael asked, unable to bear the thought of Bridey in pain. "I can call the nurse, get some medicine—"

"There's no pain, my darlin'. I'm telling you true."

"But the pillow—"

"I pretend it's my Bonaparte," she said, stroking the cotton pillowcase. "Comforts me. Been just the two of us night after night for so many years. My poor wee one."

Michael shook her gently, insistently, until her eyes fluttered open. "You promise you won't . . . won't go anywhere? You promise?"

"I've been waiting for his lordship forever, Michael-my-heart. I suppose I can wait with you a wee bit longer. Until your Eve comes."

Michael winced, saw Sean hovering in the doorway, face stricken. *I know*, Michael wanted to say. *How can I tell Bridey she might have to wait a long time? Eve doesn't even know Bridey is so sick, doesn't know how much I need her right now to hold on to.*

Michael squeezed Bridey's hand, grateful as Sean walked into the room. "Look, Bridey. Sean is here."

"Sean? Poor lad. Just let me look at you a moment. You're a good boy to come here. I promise you won't have to stay too long."

Michael's hands trembled, his chest feeling like it was about to crack. He'd always been the one other people clung to when things got too painful, too frightening, too bad. Michael Halloran, steady and strong as the cliffs that fell down to the ocean. But now, he was falling apart, here in this tiny hospital room, holding on to Bridey's hand.

"I need you, Eve," he whispered. But he might as well be talking to Bridey's Knight of Kilrain. Wherever she was, Eve couldn't hear him.

Eve reached the house a few minutes before Trevor and the trailer. She burst through the door, her heart full as she called Michael's name. The first time in so long she'd felt the sensation of someone eager, waiting to see her. So much she had to tell him, she thought with a skip in her step. She couldn't wait to see his face!

She flicked on the lights, Bonaparte scrabbling at her feet. She bent down to pat his wrinkly forehead for an instant, looking around the kitchen. The house was too quiet, dishes still clean on the table as if in all this time no one had eaten from them. Place settings for three. Her note had been disturbed, crumpled along the edges as if Michael's hand had clenched on the page as he'd read it. She felt a pang, knowing how worried he must have been. But as soon as she found him everything would be all right. Everything would be wonderful. Wait until he saw Innisfree back where he belonged.

She ran up the stairs, wondering if Michael had gone to sleep. He must have been exhausted after everything he'd been through the past two days. But the second floor was as empty as the first.

Unease prickled the back of her neck. What if Michael had gone looking for her? He could never have guessed where she'd gone, but it would be so like him to try to find her anyway. She winced with regret, hating to think of him driving around, searching for her, getting more and more distraught until he was so tired he had to surrender. Bad as she felt about it, she could take comfort in the fact that when he reached the end of his endurance, he'd come back here, and she would be waiting. But even if Michael was out looking for her, wouldn't Sean have stayed here? The empty house didn't make any sense.

By the time she got back to the kitchen Trevor came in, tweed cap swept off his head, ruddy cheeks glowing. "I'm thinking Innisfree smells his stall. He's getting that restless, he is. Where does Mick want to put him?"

"Michael isn't here right now. I don't know where to find him."

"Mick's probably got plenty of work to do after being gone at the show, but it's late even for him," Trevor observed.

Eve stopped, glimpsed something she hadn't noticed on the table before, a white sheet of paper covered with Sean's handwriting. "Maybe this will tell us where they've gone."

Distracted, Eve skimmed the note. Nervousness tightened into dread. She stumbled back, feeling as if she'd been kicked in the chest. "Bridey—a friend of Michael's—she's dying."

"Bridey McGarrity? The mistress of the castle? A crying shame it will be to lose her. Never be another like her."

"I have to go. To the hospital," Eve said, her heart pounding. "Michael—I need to be with Michael."

"Go on with you, then. I'll set Innisfree loose. He'll show me to his pasture himself. I'll make sure he's good and settled before I leave."

Eve grabbed up the keys, started for the door, but Bonaparte curled up in a miserable ball right in front of it. He whined so pitifully she thought her heart would break. Eve hesitated, couldn't keep herself from gathering the shivering little dog in her arms. Round black eyes looked up at her as if he somehow knew . . .

Her own eyes burned as she laid her cheek against the pug's raggedy coat. Bridey had adored the dog, Michael had said. Like the child she'd never had.

If Bridey was dying, didn't she have the right to tell him good-bye?

Eve cuddled Bonaparte close, his whimpering quieted, and he nuzzled, forlorn, against her breast.

"We're going to see your mammy, Bonaparte," Eve said to the little dog. Not long ago she'd been so afraid of him. Now it was as if she could feel his heart breaking.

She thanked Trevor as she ran out the door. At the car, she stripped off her own sweater, made a bed for the dog on the seat beside her. "I'm hurrying, Bonaparte. I'm hurrying," she said, whether to comfort the dog or herself she wasn't sure. She put the car into gear and stepped on the gas. They had to get to Bridey—to Michael, before it was too late.

It seemed to take forever to reach the hospital, a miracle she didn't get lost on the dark night roads. But she felt as if Bridey herself were showing her the way. She could feel it in her gut, a pulsing, insistent whisper telling her to hurry. Hurry.

When at last she pulled into the parking lot, she gave a heartfelt thanks to whoever or whatever had guided her. Gathering Bonaparte and wrapping him in her sweater against the night chill, she hurried up the stairs and into the building.

The entryway was almost deserted, it was so late. Anyone visiting at this hour would know their way to whatever room they were keeping vigil in. Eve tried to remember which elevator would take her to Bridey's floor.

She picked the second one, pressed the button, praying she was right. The doors opened and she sighed in relief, recognizing the painting by Matisse over the nurse's station.

"Almost there, Bonaparte," she whispered to the little dog, his face so worried, his eyes pleading.

Bridey was only a few doors down if Eve remembered right. She'd almost reached the room when a strident voice barked out. "Stop right there, whoever you are, and don't be taking another step!"

Eve spun around, saw a nurse the size of a small tank and just as menacing barreling down on her.

"I have to see Bridey McGarrity," Eve protested. "There's no time—"

"With that bundle of germs in your arms? Not on my shift. Fine way to start it, too, coming on the floor to find you here! What kind of an eejit are you bringing such a mangy thing onto a hospital floor? And who are you anyway? An American I'm thinking, from that accent of yours! Only immediate family is to be here! We've rules, we have and—"

"Only the immediate family, you say?"

"That's the way of it."

"Then get out of my way. Bridey is dying and this dog is the only family she has." Eve's jaw set hard. She'd already faced down Chad. There was no way this nurse was going to make her turn back. She didn't have any idea how she was going to get past the nurse, but dammit, nothing was going to keep her out of Bridey's room.

The nurse puffed up with indignation and Eve braced herself, ready to make a dash around her if she had to. But at that instant a man stuck his head out of Bridey's room.

Michael.

Huge, dark circles ringed his eyes, deep lines carved along either side of his mouth. His breath was shallow, sharp, as if he'd been marking Bridey's breathing for too long, matching his rhythm to hers. Those blue eyes Eve loved so much were haunted, desperate, so very sad. But the instant he saw her, need flashed into them.

"Eve." Her name. Just her name. But it said everything.

He needed her.

Her.

This was what she'd been terrified of for so long. Now, with Bonaparte snuggled against her and Michael devouring her with his eyes, reaching for her—being needed seemed like the sweetest thing she'd ever known. And to think she'd almost missed it.

Michael's arms opened and she stepped into them, Bonaparte and all.

"God, where did you go? I was so damned scared you'd left me. Run away for good. And Bridey—"

"Mr. Halloran?" The nurse's sharp voice cut in. "Will you tell your friend here that we don't allow dogs in Irish hospitals, whatever outlandish things they might do in America!"

Eve started to turn to reply, felt Michael glaring at the nurse over her head. "Didn't you hear Miss Danaher? She said this is the only family Bridey has. We can go around you or we can go through you but Bridey is going to have the comfort of this dog with her if she—" He couldn't say it. Eve felt the yanking back inside of him, the thought of Bridey dying so painful he kept denying what was right there in front of his eyes.

Eve had faced down her share of those famous Halloran glares. She couldn't blame the nurse for backing down.

"It's on your head then if she gets an infection because of this!" the nurse sniffed.

"I take full responsibility," Michael said. Arm

around Eve's waist, tight, he guided her toward Bridey's room.

Full responsibility. He'd had that for so long, Eve thought. She'd marveled at it, the way he kept taking more and more people into the circle of his strength. She was thirty-six years old and she knew so little about the human heart. It had taken a man like Michael to teach her that it could open wider and wider to bring people into its warmth, that the farther it reached the stronger it got, the more beautiful it became. Eve knew she'd never keep her heart so small again. *That* was what had hurt her—that hard little knot she'd kept locked so tight in her chest for so long where her heart should have been.

But what if you fail him? Make a mistake? her old doubts whispered.

Michael's love is big enough to forgive them. Maybe in time he'll even help me learn to forgive myself.

"How did you know where to come?" Michael asked.

"Sean left me a note."

"Thank God. I didn't think—couldn't think—"

"I know," she said gently. "Is Sean here?"

"Went for a walk outside to get some air. The hospital—he's got bad memories here. I know how hard it is for him."

It was harder for Michael, Eve knew. She loved him all the more for staying.

Eve squeezed Michael's hand, then stepped through the door, the hospital room just as she'd remembered it. Stark and sterile, warmed only by the face of the old woman who lay inside it.

"I think she looks a little better," Michael said hopefully, and she knew how much he wanted her to tell him he was right. "Maybe it's just another scare."

Eve wished she could say what he wanted to hear, but it was as if Bridey was already gone. The energy, the life in her, the restless enthusiasm that had made her seem young in spite of her years and the ravages of her illness had faded until it flickered like the flame of a candle in the wind.

"Michael, I'm sorry," she said softly. She felt his shoulders sag. Bonaparte whined, scratching at Eve's arm with his paw as he caught sight of his mistress.

Eve leaned down, putting the little pug on the bed. Bonaparte scrambled past a mound of pillow to reach Bridey's face, licking it with his little pink tongue, his corkscrew tail wagging. But Eve could tell even Bonaparte knew what Michael couldn't face.

Bridey's eyes opened. A tiny sob tore from her throat. "Bonaparte?" she quavered, incredulous. "No! Oh, no! I promised Michael I wouldn't die yet!"

"You didn't break your promise, Bridey," Eve soothed, laying a comforting hand on the old woman's shoulder. "Michael is right here and so am I."

Bridey struggled to lever herself up on one elbow, Bonaparte squeezing his small body as close against her as he could. "Eve? Eve, and is it you? I've been holding on. Couldn't leave Michael alone without you and Sean. I love the boy dearly, but he's worthless as most men are at a time like this." She groped for Eve's hand, squeezed it. "You'll take care of Michael for me? My sweet, sweet boy. Look after him the way I did all these years? He takes care of so many—people, animals, the land—whoever needs him. He's just no good at taking care of himself."

Eve's throat ached, tears burning her eyes. "I'll take care of him. I promise."

'The castle—it's to be yours now. Michael will tell you—"

"Mine? You can't—I couldn't—"

"Argue with a dying woman, will you? Don't they teach you manners in America?" Bridey asked so tenderly Eve's tears spilled free. "You've spent your life flying about, too hurt to ever make yourself a nest. Now you'll have a place all your own, Eve. A home."

Had anyone else ever known how desperately she'd

wanted one? As a little girl being dragged from shabby apartment to shabby apartment as her mother found new jobs? As a woman trying to escape rooms that should have been filled with her child's laughter, rooms too perfect, too clean, too quiet? "Bridey, how can I ever thank you?"

"It's me who should be thanking you. I'm an old woman and I've seen life kind and cruel. But I never was afraid of anything except this—leaving Michael alone and leaving the castle without someone who understood it, someone who would love them both as much as I did."

"Oh, Bridey!" Eve clung to her hand, tears streaming down her cheeks, feeling a loss she'd never felt even when she'd said good-bye to her mother. Strength flowed into her hand where Bridey touched it. This frail old woman—giving her everything she'd cherished most in the world, trusting her to keep them safe. "I love Michael so much. But I'm so scared."

"You're a blessing, child. And haven't I known it from the first time I heard your voice on the telephone? It was as if I could feel the hurt in you, the empty place and knew I could fill it. Fill it with loving and laughing and show you that you can hold on to the good things forever, even when the bad times come. Michael?" she called out, ever so faint.

"I'm here."

Eve could hear the grief in his voice, the denial. Knew that this time it was Michael who wanted so desperately to run away.

"Eve will be taking care of you now. I've kept his lordship waiting long enough. Don't want our first meeting face to face to be lost in one of his temper tantrums. A most impatient man he can be."

Eve's heart ached at the sound of Michael trying to crush a sob.

"Bridey, I love you. You know—"

"I know. Now, Michael-my-heart, won't you be letting me go?"

Eve felt Michael's whole body stiffen, felt the wildness in him, like Innisfree in the paddock at Butler's farm, racing at fences he couldn't clear, trapped someplace he couldn't bear to be. Helpless. Hurting.

Eve turned to him, took his hand, held it tightly in her own. She looked deep into his eyes. Gently she nodded, whispered. "It's time."

Michael knelt down by the bed, laid his head against Bridey's narrow chest, Bonaparte licking his face. "Tell his lordship he'd better take good care of you. If he doesn't I'll raze that castle until he's haunting nothing but rubble."

Eve heard a sound, glanced up to see Sean in the door, hovering there, unable to make himself come in. His cheeks were wet with tears.

"Ah, Michael," Bridey breathed. "Michael, open the window, lad. Bonaparte and I, we love to smell the heather."

Michael climbed up, stumbled over to the window, tugging it open. Bridey cradled Bonaparte close, kissed his wrinkled little head. She smiled as the night wind blew in, cool, fresh with that hint of rain and sea and magic only Ireland could call its own.

Bridey's eyes fluttered closed, a smile crossing her face as the wind tugged at strands of her hair. She lay her cheek against Bonaparte's little coat and then she was gone.

Michael reached for Eve, an anguished sound, both pain and denial rising in his throat. She rushed into his arms, giving him something he'd never asked for, something he needed so badly. Someone to hold on to.

26

~

*M*ichael woke, eyes gritty and sore, his chest still aching, the knowledge that Bridey was gone pressing down like a rock on his chest. He shoved the blankets Eve had covered him with aside, and climbed stiffly out of bed.

How long had he been sleeping? The first hint of twilight was staining the square of green framed by his bedroom window. It was open, the breeze Bridey had loved threading past the edges of the curtains.

It had almost been noon when they got to Glenammura. A quiet drive, little said except a few plans for Bridey's wake. She'd always wanted a hell of a party, Michael remembered. A celebration of her life. He'd make damned sure she got it.

Somehow he'd tell stories with all the glen folk who would flock to pay their respects to the mistress of the castle, as if they were still her serfs and she was their queen. Michael would laugh with them, drink with them, listen to them say that there would never be another woman like her. And he'd know they were right. A world without Bridey was a much darker place.

He never could have borne the drive at all if it hadn't been for the warm hand that had held his the whole way back to the farm. He'd clung to Eve while she cradled Bridey's pug on her lap.

She'd held him together. She'd taken over, firmly but gently sheperding them along, getting them home.

He'd told her there were chores to do. A farm didn't stand still even for death. Animals had to be fed, cows milked. But when they'd pulled into the drive, Michael had been touched to see neighbors just getting ready to leave—parents of kids he'd taught to ride, forty-year-olds with eyes that said they had loved Bridey, too. Somehow, through that inexplicable mental telegraph unique to the west of Ireland, the word of tragedy had gone out. The farm work was done in no time by the crowd.

Eve had taken him upstairs, made him eat a bit of brown bread and jam. It had tasted like dust in his mouth. Then she'd helped him undress and put him to bed, held him until he'd gone to sleep.

Michael winced. It had taken a long time for sleep to come. His grief, his anger, his pain, had poured out like poison. She had taken all of it, let it beat against her, and stroked his hair until the storm had passed.

She'd kissed his brow, his cheeks, his eyelids. She'd cried her own tears.

He'd thought she'd stay with him until he woke up, but she was gone. He shoved into his clothes and pulled on his boots, then went downstairs, raking his fingers through his hair.

Sean was at the table, a book of phone numbers in front of him. He looked up, bleary-eyed, but smiled. "Do you know how many friends that old woman had? I'm going to be too hoarse to say anything at the wake by the time I let everyone know she's gone." Sean's eyes filled. He looked down.

"Have you seen Eve?"

"She went out to Innisfree's pasture. She said—well, said to have you come there when you woke up."

Michael grimaced. Weren't things bad enough without her pouring acid on that wound? What was she doing? Grinding blame into herself by staring at the empty field? Thinking about Rory and the horse he'd never ride again?

She blamed herself too harshly. This time he'd put an end to it. He walked outside, threading his way along the path between stables and barns and sheds until he reached the pasture farthest from the house, the only one he dared put Innisfree in.

As he rounded the corner of the last outbuilding, he froze, staring. Eve was in the paddock, her outstretched hand filled with grapes as Innisfree nibbled them delicately.

Innisfree?

Michael rubbed his eyes, thinking exhaustion and grief must be making them play tricks on him. Eve wouldn't get near that killer of a horse even if Innisfree *had* been in the pasture, which he couldn't be. Tolliver had taken him. There was no power on earth that could change the bastard's mind. He heard a soft laugh, opened his eyes.

Innisfree was still there, the last rays of sun turning his coat to silk as he neglected the grapes and lipped at a wisp of Eve's hair. Michael's heart thudded against his chest in dread. Eve should know better—the horse was unpredictable at best. But she looked almost comfortable, only the tiniest hint of shyness about her as she dropped one of the grapes into a more appreciative mouth. Bonaparte's.

Ever so carefully, so as not to spook the horse, Michael climbed over the fence. He might as well have lit off Roman candles. Bonaparte barked as if they were being invaded by the fairy king's army.

Innisfree danced back a few steps, raised his regal head to see the intruder. Michael could almost see the horse shrug him off as if to say "It's only you."

Eve looked up at him, and the smile that crossed her face was unbearably sweet, full of love and empathy, questions and answers, comfort and strength. Dropping the rest of the grapes for the animals, she brushed her hands off on her jeans and came toward him, a fresh-faced angel in a rose-colored tee shirt.

"Michael. It's been so hard not to wake you up. I decided I'd better get out of the house before I did it. Besides, the neighbors were so kind to help with the animals, I didn't want Innisfree to make them sorry they'd bothered. You know how he is about letting anyone he doesn't know in his pasture."

"I know," Michael said numbly. "But what is he doing here? In his pasture?"

"That's where I went—to get Innisfree back if I could. Victoria and I came to an understanding—"

"But Tolliver—he'd never give this horse up. I know it."

"He couldn't stand up to our daughter. She's strong. With a little guidance, she'll use it for good instead of the way Chad does, just to get what he wants. Best of all, I think she might let me—" Eve hesitated, the possibility too precious to jinx by saying it aloud. "She asked if she could come back here, visit Innisfree. I told her she'd be welcome any time. It was too scary to say she wanted to see me, but I could tell. I don't know how long it will take, but when we talked she remembered, Michael. Remembered how much I loved her."

Michael's heart burst for her. Eve, facing down her demons—not for herself, never for herself—but for a boy who'd known so little love in his life, and for the horse that had shown him the way.

His gut knotted at the thought of Tolliver anywhere near her. He could imagine what the bastard had said to her. "Why didn't you tell me what you wanted to do? I would have gone with you."

"Don't you see? That's exactly why I couldn't tell you. It was something I had to do alone. I had to know if I could. I just wish I'd known Bridey would get so sick. I never would have left you if I'd had any idea."

He gathered her in his arms, held her.

"I couldn't let Rory lose his horse. And I couldn't let Victoria keep it. After what happened. In time, she would have known how wrong it was. It would have bothered her. Either eaten her alive with guilt or made her hard inside. I had to try to stop that from happening."

"And you did. No wonder Bridey left you the castle. She knew you could slay dragons."

Eve laughed, grew pensive. "I wish I could have known her longer. Better."

"Everything there is to know about Bridey is in that castle. Do you feel like running over there? We need to get your things, move you into the farmhouse. That is . . ." he hesitated, ". . . unless you need some time alone."

"After you and Sean left, it was too quiet. I guess I got used to having you and Rory and Bonaparte underfoot all the time. Having someone to talk to whenever I needed to. I found out I liked it."

"I'd like to be underfoot even more. Every morning when you first wake up. Every night when you go to sleep. Even when you dream, I want to be holding you in my arms. I never thought much about 'forever.' I know you didn't either. But now, I think about it all the time— what it would be like to smile at you in the kitchen every day. To hear you laugh. To grow old together, knowing you'll always be perfect, beautiful to me, just the way you are now. Marry me, Eve. Give me forever."

"I never even knew how much I wanted it until you. I'd quit dreaming of a home, a family. Anything except getting through the day, trying not to stumble into the empty hole losing Tori left inside me. I feel like I've been wandering forever, Michael. But somehow . . . somehow, when I stepped into Kilrain I found a home. Then you came into my life and taught me how to fly. I never would have dared to learn without you."

"I wish I could promise you everything will be perfect. You deserve perfect, Eve Danaher. But troubles will come. Sometimes we'll both make mistakes. When that happens, we'll face it together. I promise, I won't let you fall."

"I know. That's the miracle, Michael. I'm sure of it in my heart. I will marry you."

"As soon as possible, Eve. I don't want to waste another day." Michael's brow furrowed. "What is it? What's wrong?"

"I just wish . . . wish Rory . . ."

Michael shook his head. "I wish he could be there, too, but Jamie and Oonagh would never let him come. We'll just have to be happy with the chance to surprise him when he comes home. Maybe he'll forgive us if we make him godfather to our first baby."

"Babies? You want—"

"Only if you do," Michael said hastily, realizing in that instant how the thought might scare her, making herself vulnerable to another child—even his—no matter how much she loved him.

Eve thought for a moment, and he saw the last vestige of fear slip from her face. "Bonaparte shouldn't be an only child. He'll need to learn how to share. And not to gum unsuspecting visitors' ankles."

Michael laughed, held her close. "I was the devil of a boy. No telling what babies with my blood in 'em might do."

"We'll have two ghosts to help keep them in line, that is, unless you want to stay at the farmhouse."

"Sean can take the house. He may be building a family of his own if he has anything to say about it. It seems he's been trying to work up the courage to ask Majella out. I think they could be almost as happy as we are."

"It would be wonderful, Michael. For both of them. And for Joy. But the farmhouse is your home. I know how precious that is. I wouldn't want you to lose it."

"I want to raise our babies in the castle that helped us find each other. Remember what Bridey said? It was a place you could sink down roots. I think you have already."

"I love it. Love it all. The clutter, the history, besides, with the stove not working, you'll never have to find out what a terrible cook I am."

Michael laughed.

"Please, Michael, can we go there now? I want to make sure Bridey knows—"

"That her plotting all worked out? That she's got everything just the way she wanted it? You know, I think Bridey planned this from the beginning. It almost makes me believe in all that magic and fate stuff of hers."

"I know I do. I love you as much as she's loved her lordship. I just hope she'll be able to look down and see all the gifts she's given us. Second chances. A place to heal. Each other."

"We'd better get to the castle before dark," Michael said. "We can take the car if you want. Of course, it would be faster if we could ride double on my gelding. He's gentle as a—"

"I trust you, Michael. I'd like to see what all this fuss about riding on animals tall as skyscrapers is all about. You see, I need to get some practice. I have one last plan to surprise Rory when he gets home." She gave Michael a mysterious smile, wouldn't say another word.

He got the gelding ready in a matter of minutes, lifted her up into the saddle. Eve bit her lip, and he could see nervousness and excitement in her eyes.

She thought this was dangerous—his Eve. But she was still willing to try. Michael swung up behind her, guided the big horse across the fields where Glenammura spilled into the lands of Kilrain. First, Eve clung to him, fingers digging deep, fighting the rhythm of Tristan's stride.

He could feel her start to relax, sensed when she actually started to enjoy it, the wind blowing back her hair, the horse's strides eating up the ground beneath them.

"It *is* like flying!" she breathed, leaning her cheek against him.

She was unsteady when he lifted her down in the castle yard. He knew tomorrow she was going to be stiff. Muscles she didn't even know she had would be aching. But she'd get used to it. He'd even buy her a horse of her own. A pretty little mare Trevor Butler had been raising said to be the great-, great-, who knew how many greats, granddaughter of the Knight of Kilrain's destrier. It was impossible to prove, but the mare had the famous marking, a streak of black lightning down her left haunch. Bridey would approve.

Eve unlocked the castle door with the big key Sean had convinced her to hide in a holly bush. She stepped inside, feeling a welcome that left small room for grief. She felt Bridey here, surely as if her arms were surrounding them.

She looked up at Michael, saw he felt it, too.

"Let's go to Bridey's room first," he said. "Get something fine for her to wear for her wake. She'd want to be in her best finery when she meets his lordship."

They wound up the tower stairs past Eve's room, past the library with it's priest hole hidden in the drawing room just beyond. Eve felt like they must be climbing to the moon.

"How did she ever climb all these stairs at her age? Why didn't she move into one of the rooms farther down?" she asked, a little breathless.

"Can't you guess?" Michael asked as they reached a heavy wood door. "This was his lordship's room."

"You can't be serious. When I was exploring I tried to enter this room, see what was there. I couldn't budge the door. There's no way little Bridey could."

Michael braced himself, shoved on the door hard. It swung open so easily he almost landed face-first on the old Oriental carpets. He arched one eyebrow at Eve.

"Rory must have put oil on the hinges," she said. "It wouldn't open, I swear—"

Michael flicked on the light. Eve gasped as her gaze locked on the huge portrait over the ornate medieval bed.

"What is it?" Michael demanded. "What's wrong?"

She stared at that familiar face, dark beard, arrogant eyes, the distinctive hawklike nose. She'd seen them all before under the frayed edge of Fingall's tweed cap. She could almost hear that deep voice sneering *"and do ye believe in ghosts?"*

"Michael . . . Michael this is crazy but—I've met this man before."

Michael chuckled. "What the—don't tell me you've been seeing ghosts around here, too? Just make sure you don't go falling in love with him like Bridey did."

"No danger of that. We didn't like each other very much. He told me I had no business at Kilrain, just like you did. Tried to scare me away."

"Eve, I don't understand—"

"The night I first came here Bridey had a man pick me up."

Michael looked confused. "Bridey said not to worry about how you were going to get to the castle. I assumed you'd take a taxi."

"Believe me, I wished I had. He made the ride hell. He dropped me off at the bottom of the lane in the dark, made me walk alone all the way up to the castle carrying my suitcases. It rained, and—"

"Ah, someone who looked a little like him, then. It was dark."

"No, Michael. It was this man! I know it was! Tell me, what was his lordhip's name?"

"I think Bridey said it was Fingall."

"He had the same name. Michael, I swear it."

Michael stared at her. She wasn't sure if even he could believe her. Then a strange expression crossed his face. "Bridey said—I remember she said his lordship wasn't any happier than I was about your coming. She hoped he wouldn't be up to any of his tricks. But she knew you were strong enough to stand up to him. Maybe she was right."

Eve crossed to the bed, touching an exquisite length of cloth laid out on it. Pale, beautiful, it could have adorned his lordship's bride three hundred years ago. A note lay beside it, scribed in Bridey's hand.

> *Michael, bury me in this. Let the whole glen talk about how strange it is, a daft old woman being buried in such a thing. I always dreamed of wearing this for my wedding day. Imagined myself young and beautiful when I did. But his lordship always sees me that way, no matter how many wrinkles I've got. That can happen when you've got love in your eyes.*
>
>   *Bridey*

> *P.S. Tell Eve I hope his lordship wasn't too much trouble when he came to pick her up. He was determined to have a look at the woman I was moving into his house.*

She handed Michael the note, heard him choke as he read it. He turned it over in his hand. A few lines, scribed on that side of the page, stared back at them.

> *It's time this castle was filled with real loving. Bodies that can touch instead of just hearts.*

"I can't believe—I—" Michael stammered.

"I can." Eve smiled, looking around her, feeling love and welcome. Belonging. "Be happy, Bridey."

"And you?" Michael said. "Be happy, Eve-of-my-heart."

"Completely," she promised.

27

*E*ve laughed as Joy stomped back and forth between barn and gate, her little face eager, her steps far steadier than they had been when Eve first saw her eight months before. A miracle that had made Eve's first months as Michael's wife unbearably precious, made her dare to dream of another little girl of her own.

But from the day of their simple wedding in the tower room of Kilrain, her life had grown full of dreams, as if Bridey had scattered blessings from wherever she and her lordship were looking down. In fact, Eve had been the one who'd insisted on the tiny wedding in the castle, since the two guests of honor were unable to make it out to the church.

No longer alone, Eve had learned to revel in laughter and learning and surprises. It was impossible to imagine how she'd endured her life before Ireland—a prison of sameness and drudgery and playing it safe she'd inflicted on herself.

Not that change was always *easy.* She'd been on her own so long it had taken adjustments to learn to be a wife. Not to mention adopting a new country and overseeing a haunted castle stuffed with so many treasures it would take a lifetime to catalogue and restore them all. Kilrain. Home. A place where she was blessed to feel Bridey's presence every day, her wisdom, her strength, her whispers of encouragement to let herself fly no matter how far down she might fall or how many people might laugh if she did.

It was astonishing how quickly Eve had settled into the glen, how warm people were. It seemed that if Michael and Sean and Bridey accepted her, that was enough for them.

But no one's approval had been more deafening than Steff's the day Eve called to tell her the news and ask her to send her clothes and give most of the rest of her stuff to Goodwill. She was getting married to the most amazing man who'd ever lived.

A castle and *a prince charming?* Eve's ears were still ringing from Steff's whoop of triumph. *You go girl!*

Though hospital responsibilities had kept Steff from the wedding, she was already planning her next vacation at Kilrain, and Eve couldn't wait to see her, show her, tell her everything.

"It's taking too long!" Joy wailed, yanking Eve back to the present. "Eve, are you sure Michael said he'd be here by noon?"

Sean chuckled. "This girl's got no patience. Since the moment she found out Majella and I are getting married, she's not given us a moment of peace."

Eve tugged the little girl's braid. She couldn't get enough of it—touching, teasing, loving. "Michael said noon. I'm sure of it."

"I'm so hungry I could eat the whole cake!" Joy exclaimed, then sobered. "But I won't touch it without Rory."

"Maybe if I cut a little piece off the back he'd never notice."

Eve's heart skipped a beat at the sound of Victoria's voice, earnest, still a little shy as she walked into the barn after looking over a promising foal with Sean. But she was growing less uncertain with every visit, Eve thought gratefully. She'd even asked for the letters Eve had written her. Eve didn't know if Victoria had read them yet, but someday she would. It would take time to heal old wounds, begin to trust, but they had the rest of their lives. And they'd made a beginning. One that surprised Eve, made her hope. Nothing had stunned her more than the night Tori asked to be here when Rory came home.

It was almost too much to hold—that much happiness, that much hope. Eve wasn't used to dreams being realized. But after today, she'd have nothing in the world left to wish for.

Victoria busied herself cutting Joy a bit of cake, but the little girl could have cared less the instant she heard the sound of a car engine. She rushed out by the fence, shrieking. "A car! A car is coming! It's Michael and Rory!"

Eve grinned, as Sean and Tori hurried out of the barn with its opened doors and its waiting secret. It hadn't been easy letting Michael get Rory alone when she'd wanted to see her boy so badly, but someone had to stay behind—someone who could handle Innisfree.

Eve had volunteered, saying she didn't want to see Rory's parents, she was afraid what she might do—and it would be bad form for her to spend his first night home in jail.

She could still remember Michael's laughter.

She hung back, afraid to get too far from the stable in case Innisfree got spooked by the commotion. But she didn't have to worry about Rory getting a great welcome. Joy tried to climb into his arms, braces and all, jabbering about how well she was walking. Sean almost knocked Rory into the next county, he slapped his back with such hearty welcome. Even Victoria gave a stiff smile, her piece of cake in her hands.

Rory emerged from the rain of hugs and saw Tori. His brow wrinkled in confusion as he set little Joy down. Eve could see a hard spark of hurt, dislike in his eyes, then saw it soften and knew Rory was remembering that this girl was her daughter. He struggled for a heartbeat, got that cocky street-kid look on his face. "So, what are you doing here, princess? Don't they feed you over at Butler's? You have to start on my cake without me?"

Victoria flushed, almost threw the cake at Joy. "It's for her! She was hungry. Tired of waiting."

Rory grinned, drew in a lungful of air, closed his eyes in bliss. "I've been waiting, too. A long time. But it's over now, isn't it?"

His gaze flicked to the sliver of green visible past all the barns, the pasture where he'd tamed Innisfree. Eve saw a twinge of loss, sadness, saw him push it away. He looked past everyone, eager, his face so young and seeking it squeezed at her heart.

"Eve?" he said. "It's past time I got to kiss the bride."

He put Joy down, came to Eve. She reached out, held him tight. "I've missed you so much, Rory. I've thought about you every day, but there's someone else even more impatient than I was."

Joy giggled. Eve could see Michael beaming.

Rory stared, bemused. "But everybody's here. Who—?"

A whicker echoed inside the barn, a snort, and pawing of hoof. Rory froze. His eyes widened in disbelief as he glanced from Eve to Michael to Victoria, then back to Eve.

Victoria shrugged. "My mom came to Butler's farm, said Innisfree belonged to you—in his heart. Like he could never belong to me. She told my dad—well, it doesn't matter. I guess I just knew she was right."

Rory gaped at her. "You mean that's—Innisfree?"

Tori nodded.

He walked into the barn, so slowly, afraid if he moved too quickly everything would disappear. But it was all there—a cake with Happy Birthday written on it in squiggly blue icing, the first birthday cake he'd ever had, balloons on strings and presents wrapped up with ribbons. But he barely saw anything except the horse tied up to the picket fence, just out of reach of the birthday table.

Innisfree perked up his ears, his head so beautiful, regal as a king's. Dark, liquid eyes welled up with such joy Rory choked on a sob.

"You bastard!" Rory breathed. "You beautiful bastard!" He flung his arms around Innisfree's neck.

"Eve worked real hard on another surprise for you today," Michael said. "She's learned how to ride. She's been keeping Innisfree in shape for you. But the doctor said it would be a bad idea for now."

"Eve? Riding Innisfree? You've got to be kidding!" Rory exclaimed in disbelief, then his face tightened with worry. "But you said something about a doctor. Did she get hurt?"

"Not hurt, boyo. Pregnant. And in bad need of a godfather if you're available."

"A baby . . . and you want me to—" Rory stammered, bewildered. "But I'm not—I'm the last person you should—"

"It's the one way we could think of to make you officially part of the family," Michael said.

Rory felt Eve touch him, gently, like she was trying to make sure he was real. "We missed you so much at the wedding we wanted to do something special."

Rory's throat itched. He wasn't about to cry in front of all these people. He forced himself to grin. "Thank God you didn't wait until I got back here to make it legal, Mick. No, wouldn't have wanted the old biddies to be counting between your wedding day and my godson's birthday and coming up short. Everything's going to be perfect for him. I'm going to see to that. I'm going to teach him how to ride and how to fight and make sure he always knows he can come to me if he needs to."

This *was* home, Rory thought in wonder. Eve and Michael and Innisfree, these barns and the green pastures and kids like Joy who would love him no matter what he'd done before.

He held on tight. He was never letting go.

Eve smiled, finding it so easy to see what was on

Rory's face, sense what was in the boy's heart. She put her arms around Michael and whispered. "Remember when you asked me to marry you? You told me we'd have troubles? Make mistakes?"

"Why think about that today?"

"Because today is perfect. And I just realized something strange. It was all the mistakes that led us here. Your mistakes that made you start Glenammura. Rory's mistakes that sent him charging into our lives. Innisfree's mistakes that put him in that pasture so that he could heal our boy. And Victoria's mistake—that's what gave me the courage to go face her after I'd all but given up."

"I hadn't thought of it that way."

"I spent all my life terrified of making another mistake, Michael. If I'd known they'd lead me here, to you, maybe I would have seen them differently. I can never be grateful for losing so much time with Victoria. But all the rest of those mistakes—I thank God every night for them. Without them, how would I ever have found you?"

"I just wish it hadn't been such a hard journey. You've flown a long way, Eve, to land safe in my arms. Whatever comes, this much I promise you. I'll never let you fall."